KILL SIX BILLION DEMONS was first published as a webcomic.
It can be found at: http://killsixbilliondemons.com

Both the webcomic and this print edition were created by:

TOM PARKINSON-MORGAN

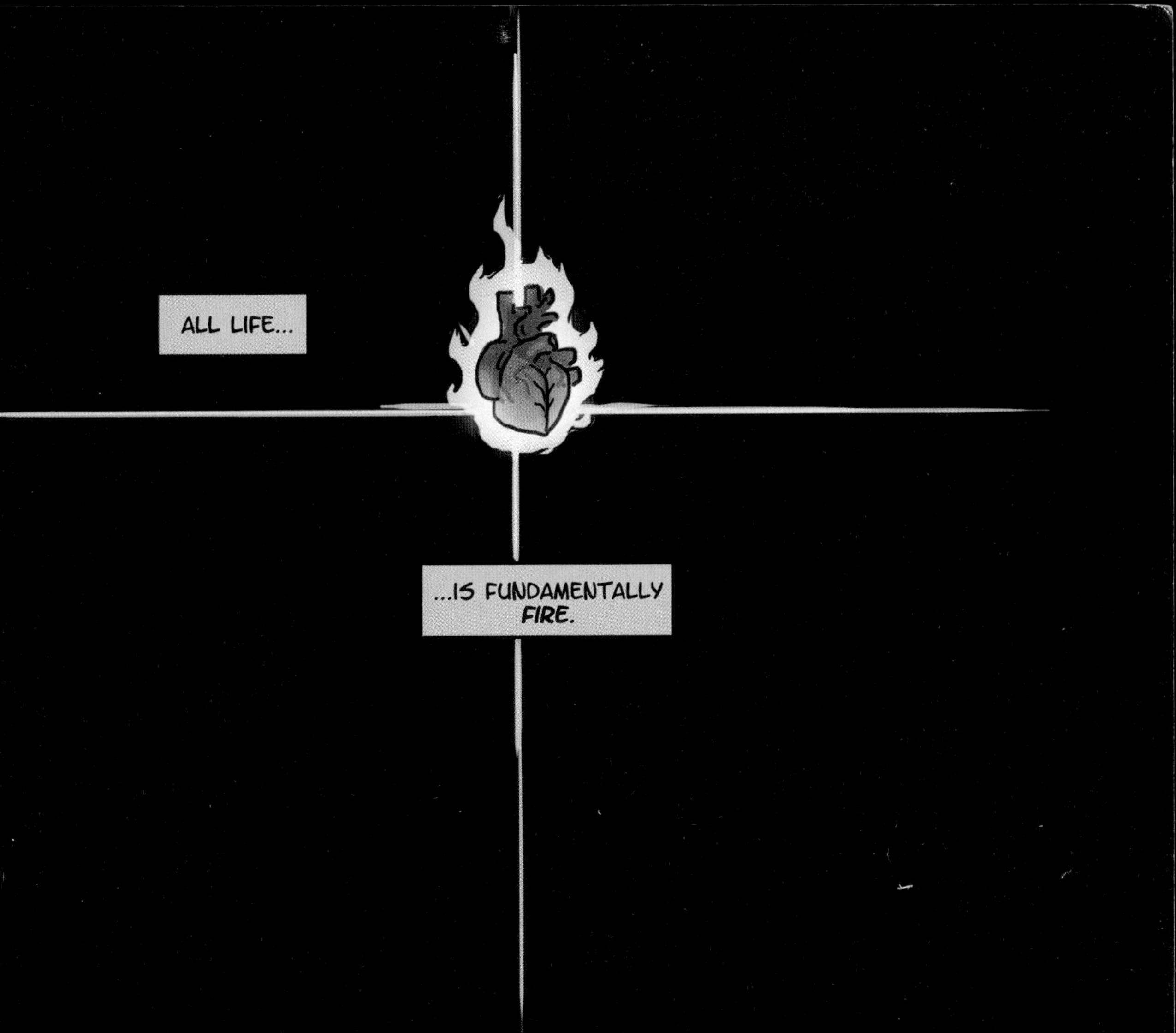
ALL LIFE...
...IS FUNDAMENTALLY FIRE.

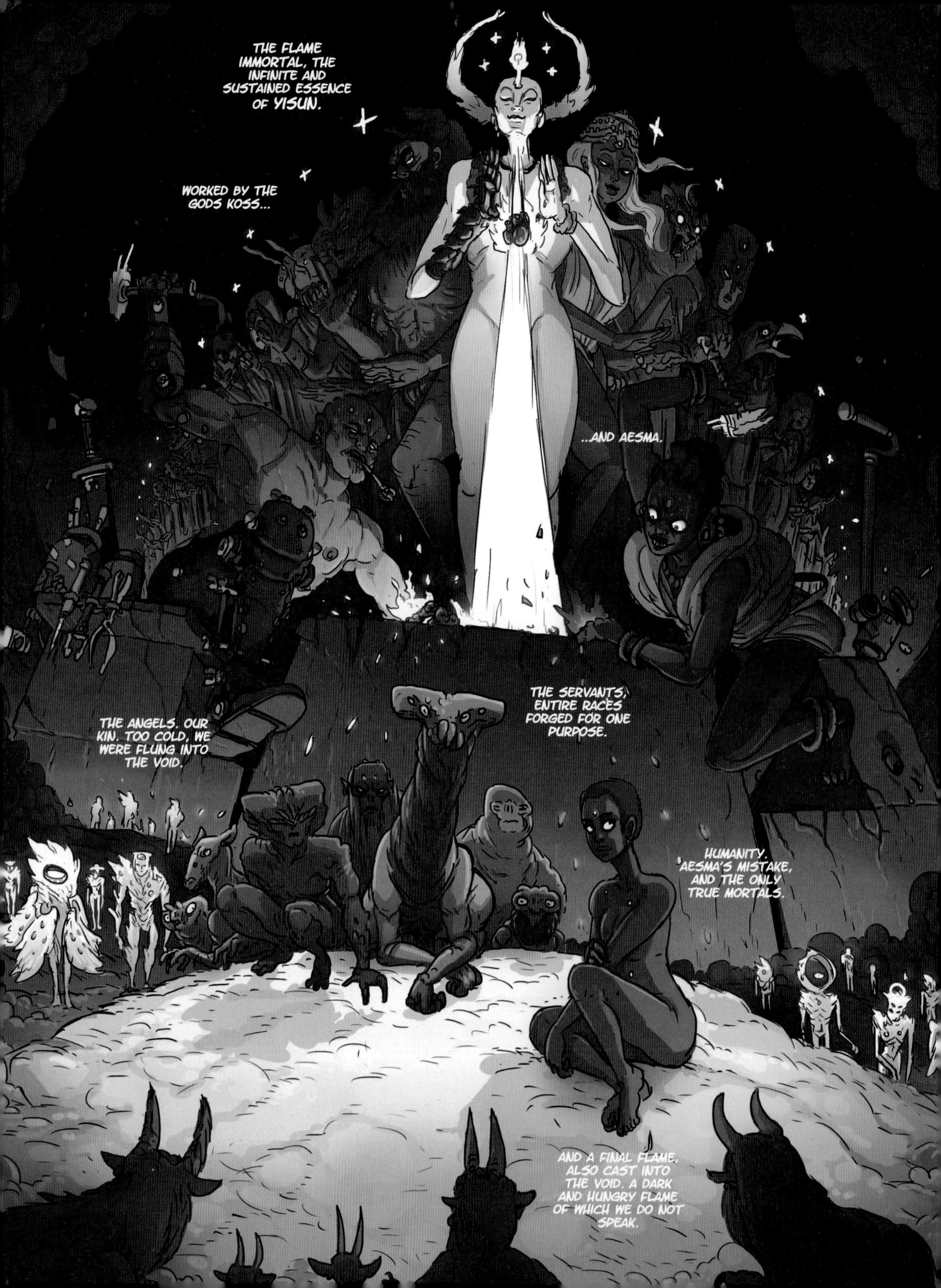
THE FLAME IMMORTAL, THE INFINITE AND SUSTAINED ESSENCE OF YISUN.
WORKED BY THE GODS KOSS...
...AND AESMA.
THE ANGELS. OUR KIN. TOO COLD, WE WERE FLUNG INTO THE VOID.
THE SERVANTS, ENTIRE RACES FORGED FOR ONE PURPOSE.
HUMANITY. AESMA'S MISTAKE, AND THE ONLY TRUE MORTALS.
AND A FINAL FLAME, ALSO CAST INTO THE VOID. A DARK AND HUNGRY FLAME OF WHICH WE DO NOT SPEAK.

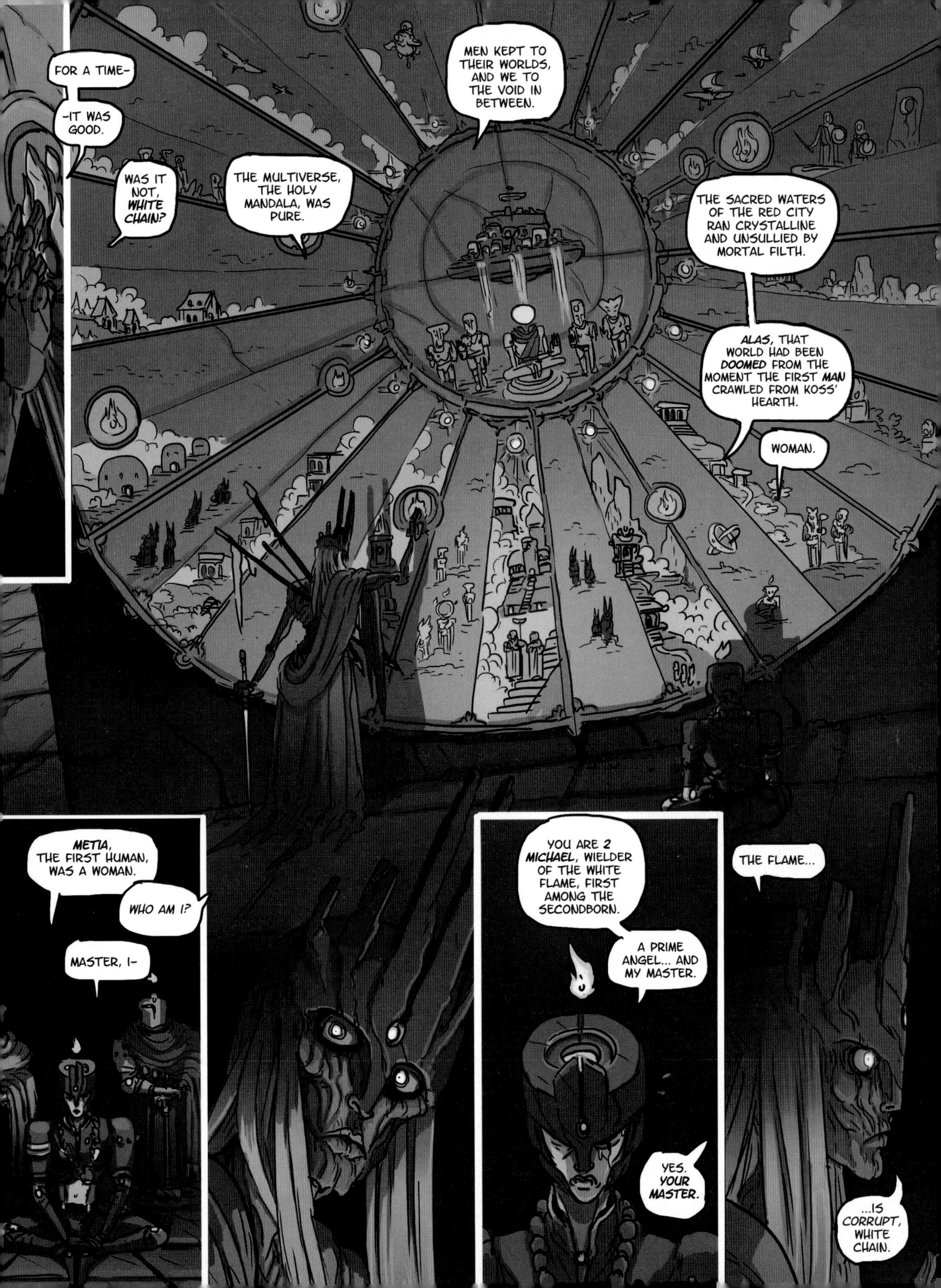

FOR A TIME-
-IT WAS GOOD.
WAS IT NOT, WHITE CHAIN?
THE MULTIVERSE, THE HOLY MANDALA, WAS PURE.
MEN KEPT TO THEIR WORLDS, AND WE TO THE VOID IN BETWEEN.
THE SACRED WATERS OF THE RED CITY RAN CRYSTALLINE AND UNSULLIED BY MORTAL FILTH.
ALAS, THAT WORLD HAD BEEN DOOMED FROM THE MOMENT THE FIRST MAN CRAWLED FROM KOSS' HEARTH.
WOMAN.
METIA, THE FIRST HUMAN, WAS A WOMAN.
WHO AM I?
MASTER, I-
YOU ARE 2 MICHAEL, WIELDER OF THE WHITE FLAME, FIRST AMONG THE SECONDBORN.
A PRIME ANGEL... AND MY MASTER.
YES. YOUR MASTER.
THE FLAME...
...IS CORRUPT, WHITE CHAIN.

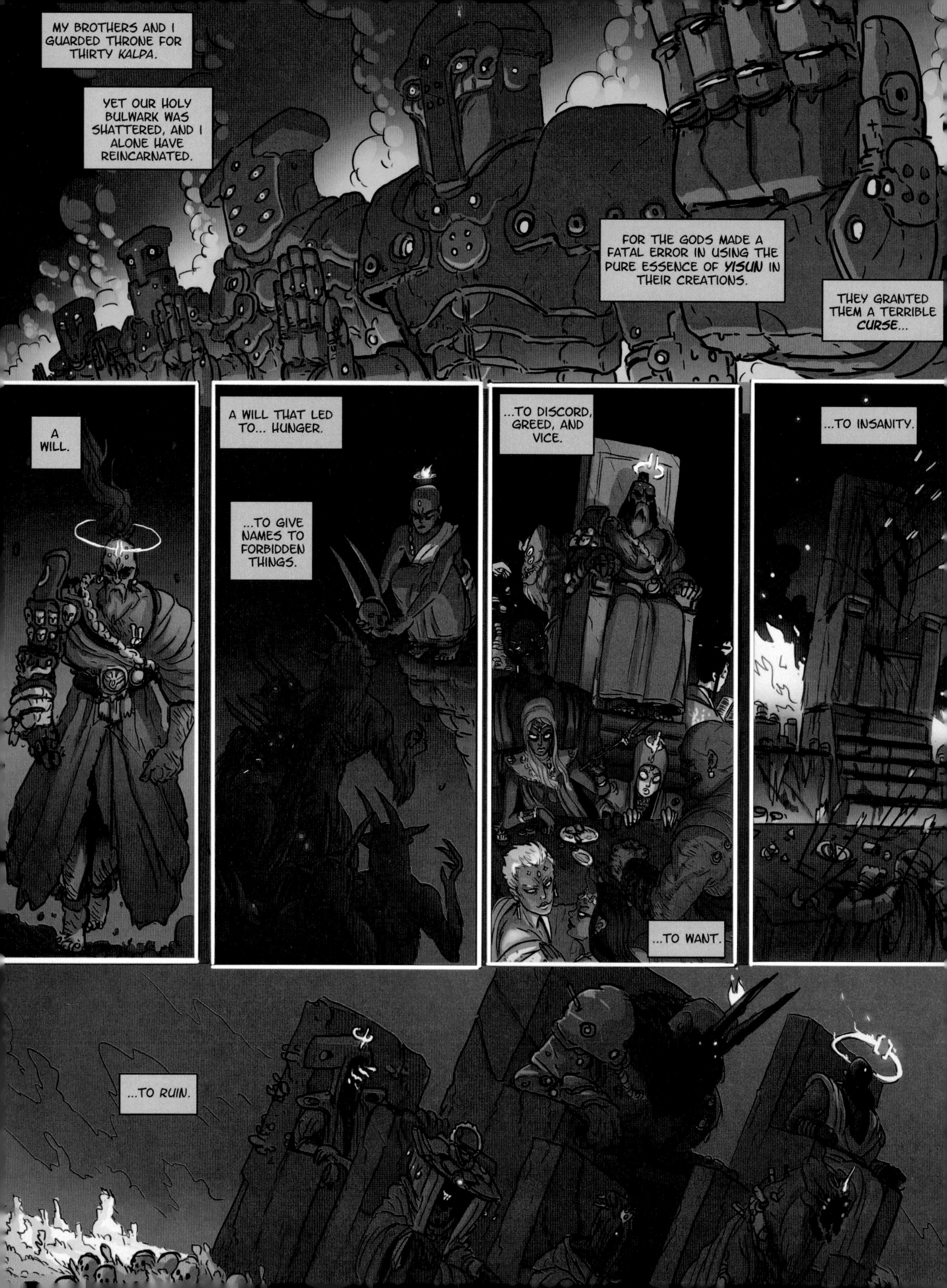
MY BROTHERS AND I GUARDED THRONE FOR THIRTY *KALPA*.
YET OUR HOLY BULWARK WAS SHATTERED, AND I ALONE HAVE REINCARNATED.
FOR THE GODS MADE A FATAL ERROR IN USING THE PURE ESSENCE OF ***YISUN*** IN THEIR CREATIONS.
THEY GRANTED THEM A TERRIBLE ***CURSE***...
A WILL.
A WILL THAT LED TO... HUNGER.
...TO GIVE NAMES TO FORBIDDEN THINGS.
...TO DISCORD, GREED, AND VICE.
...TO WANT.
...TO INSANITY.
...TO RUIN.

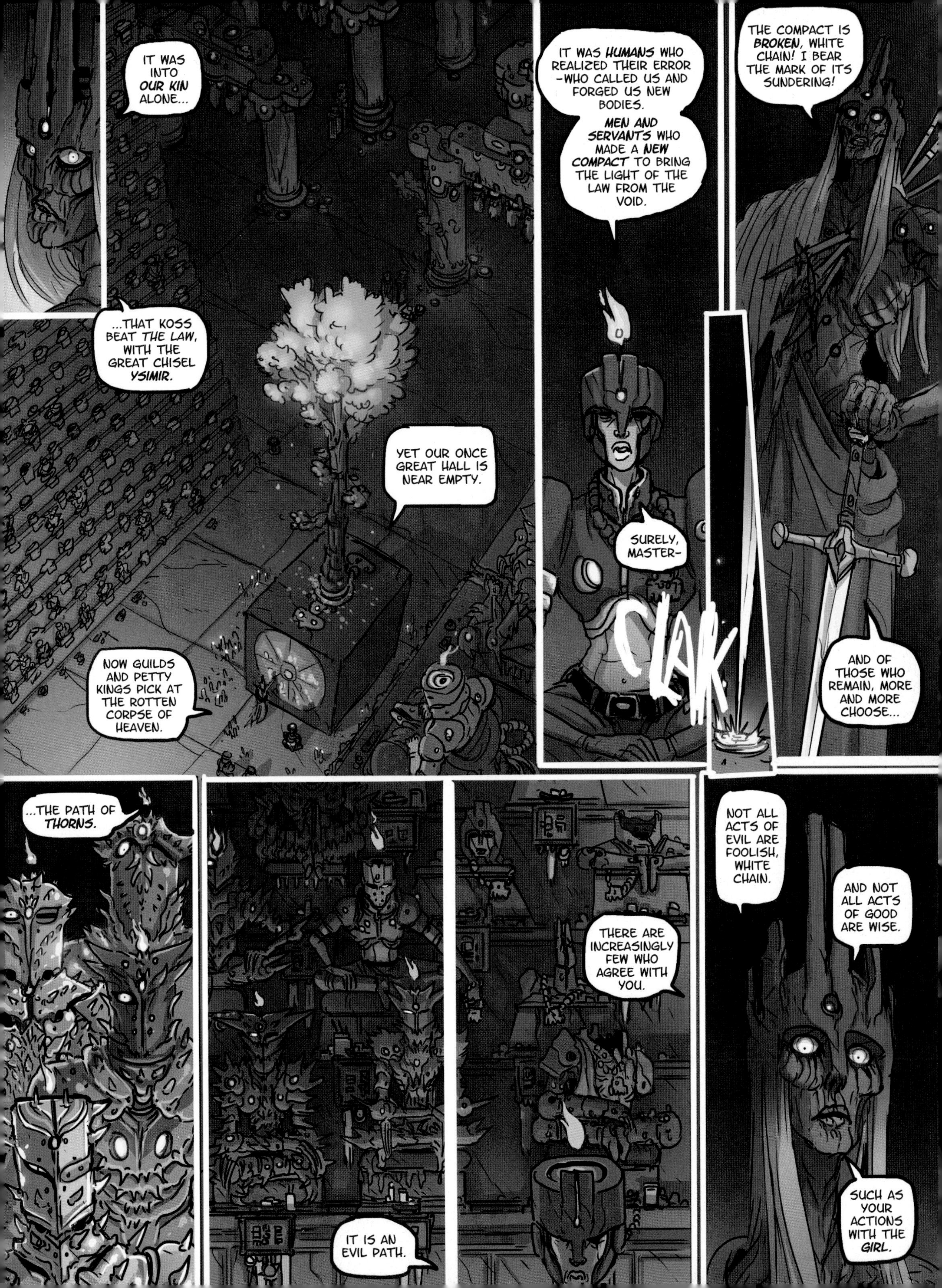
IT WAS INTO OUR KIN ALONE...
...THAT KOSS BEAT THE LAW, WITH THE GREAT CHISEL YSIMIR.
YET OUR ONCE GREAT HALL IS NEAR EMPTY.
NOW GUILDS AND PETTY KINGS PICK AT THE ROTTEN CORPSE OF HEAVEN.
IT WAS HUMANS WHO REALIZED THEIR ERROR -WHO CALLED US AND FORGED US NEW BODIES.
MEN AND SERVANTS WHO MADE A NEW COMPACT TO BRING THE LIGHT OF THE LAW FROM THE VOID.
SURELY, MASTER-
CLAK
THE COMPACT IS BROKEN, WHITE CHAIN! I BEAR THE MARK OF ITS SUNDERING!
AND OF THOSE WHO REMAIN, MORE AND MORE CHOOSE...
...THE PATH OF THORNS.
IT IS AN EVIL PATH.
THERE ARE INCREASINGLY FEW WHO AGREE WITH YOU.
NOT ALL ACTS OF EVIL ARE FOOLISH, WHITE CHAIN.
AND NOT ALL ACTS OF GOOD ARE WISE.
SUCH AS YOUR ACTIONS WITH THE GIRL.

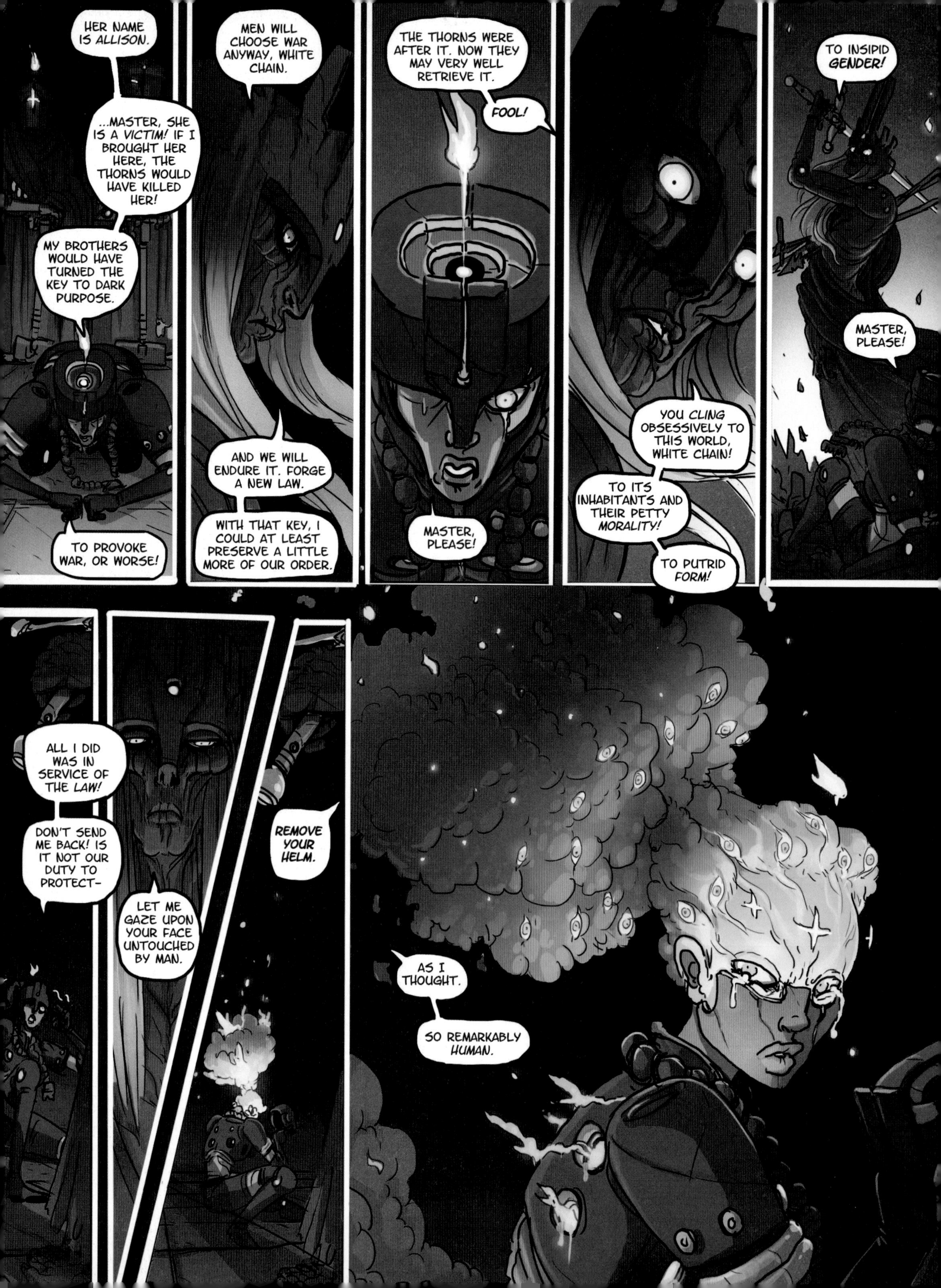
HER NAME IS *ALLISON*.
...MASTER, SHE IS A *VICTIM!* IF I BROUGHT HER HERE, THE THORNS WOULD HAVE KILLED HER!
MY BROTHERS WOULD HAVE TURNED THE KEY TO DARK PURPOSE.
TO PROVOKE WAR, OR WORSE!
MEN WILL CHOOSE WAR ANYWAY, WHITE CHAIN.
AND WE WILL ENDURE IT. FORGE A NEW LAW.
WITH THAT KEY, I COULD AT LEAST PRESERVE A LITTLE MORE OF OUR ORDER.
THE THORNS WERE AFTER IT. NOW THEY MAY VERY WELL RETRIEVE IT.
FOOL!
MASTER, PLEASE!
YOU *CLING* OBSESSIVELY TO THIS WORLD, WHITE CHAIN!
TO ITS INHABITANTS AND THEIR PETTY *MORALITY!*
TO PUTRID *FORM!*
TO INSIPID ***GENDER!***
MASTER, PLEASE!
ALL I DID WAS IN SERVICE OF THE *LAW!*
DON'T SEND ME BACK! IS IT NOT OUR DUTY TO PROTECT-
LET ME GAZE UPON YOUR FACE UNTOUCHED BY MAN.
REMOVE YOUR HELM.
AS I THOUGHT.
SO REMARKABLY *HUMAN*.

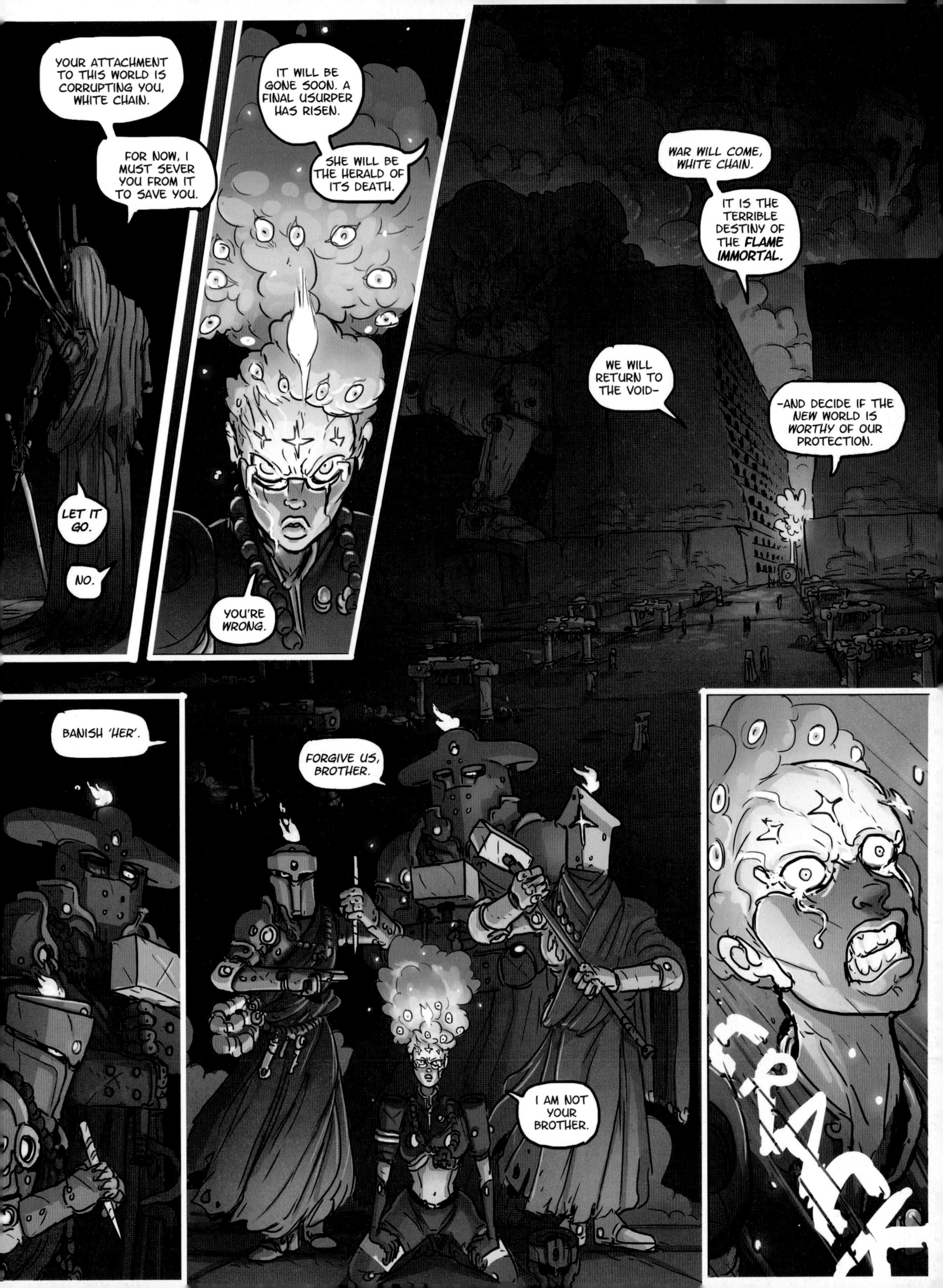
YOUR ATTACHMENT TO THIS WORLD IS CORRUPTING YOU, WHITE CHAIN.
FOR NOW, I MUST SEVER YOU FROM IT TO SAVE YOU.
LET IT GO.
NO.
IT WILL BE GONE SOON. A FINAL USURPER HAS RISEN.
SHE WILL BE THE HERALD OF ITS DEATH.
YOU'RE WRONG.
WAR WILL COME, WHITE CHAIN.
IT IS THE TERRIBLE DESTINY OF THE FLAME IMMORTAL.
WE WILL RETURN TO THE VOID-
-AND DECIDE IF THE NEW WORLD IS WORTHY OF OUR PROTECTION.
BANISH 'HER'.
FORGIVE US, BROTHER.
I AM NOT YOUR BROTHER.
CRACK

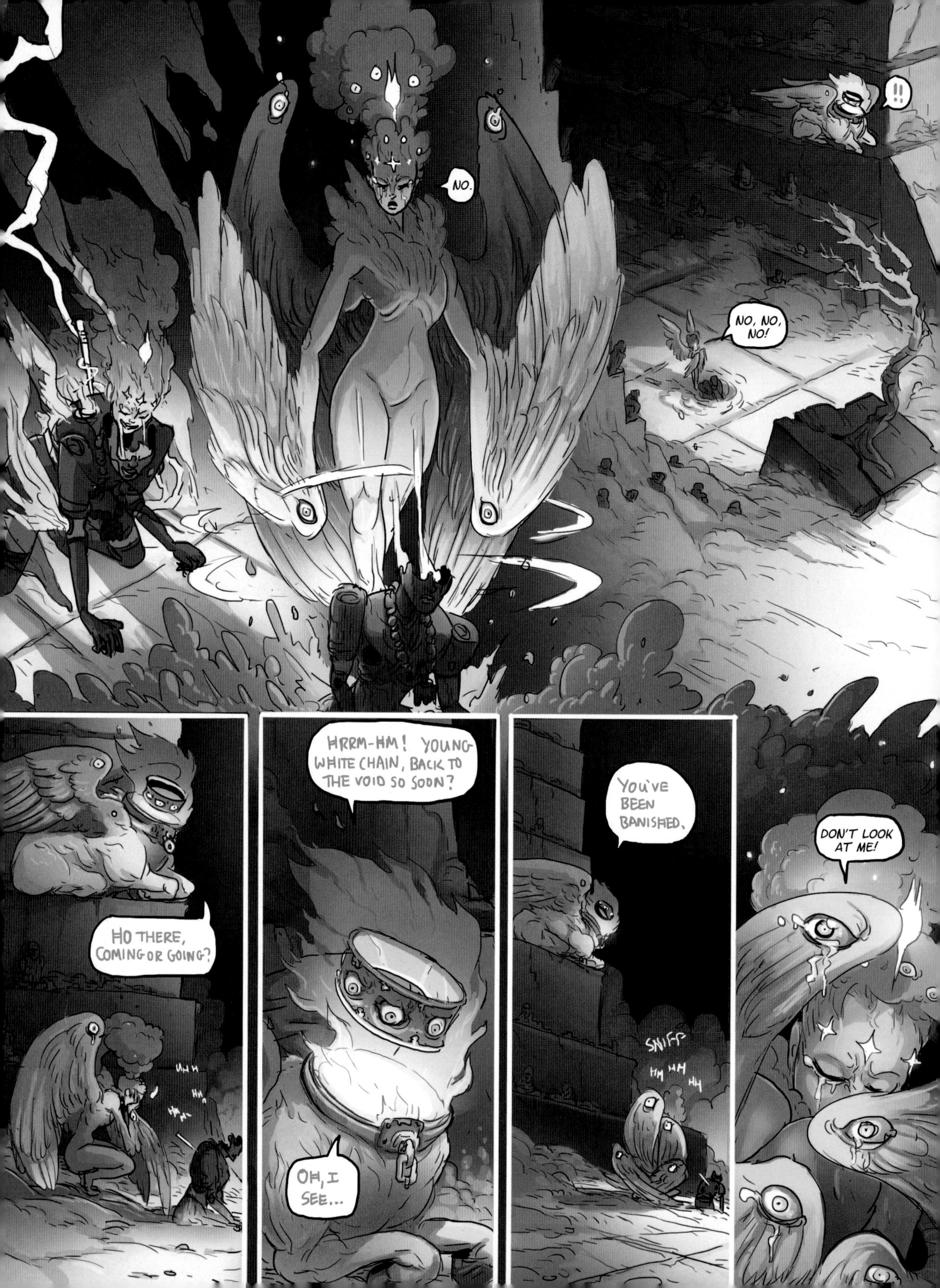
NO.
!!
NO, NO, NO!
HO THERE, COMING OR GOING?
UHH
HH
HRRM-HM! YOUNG WHITE CHAIN, BACK TO THE VOID SO SOON?
OH, I SEE...
YOU'VE BEEN BANISHED.
SNIFF
HM HM HH
DON'T LOOK AT ME!

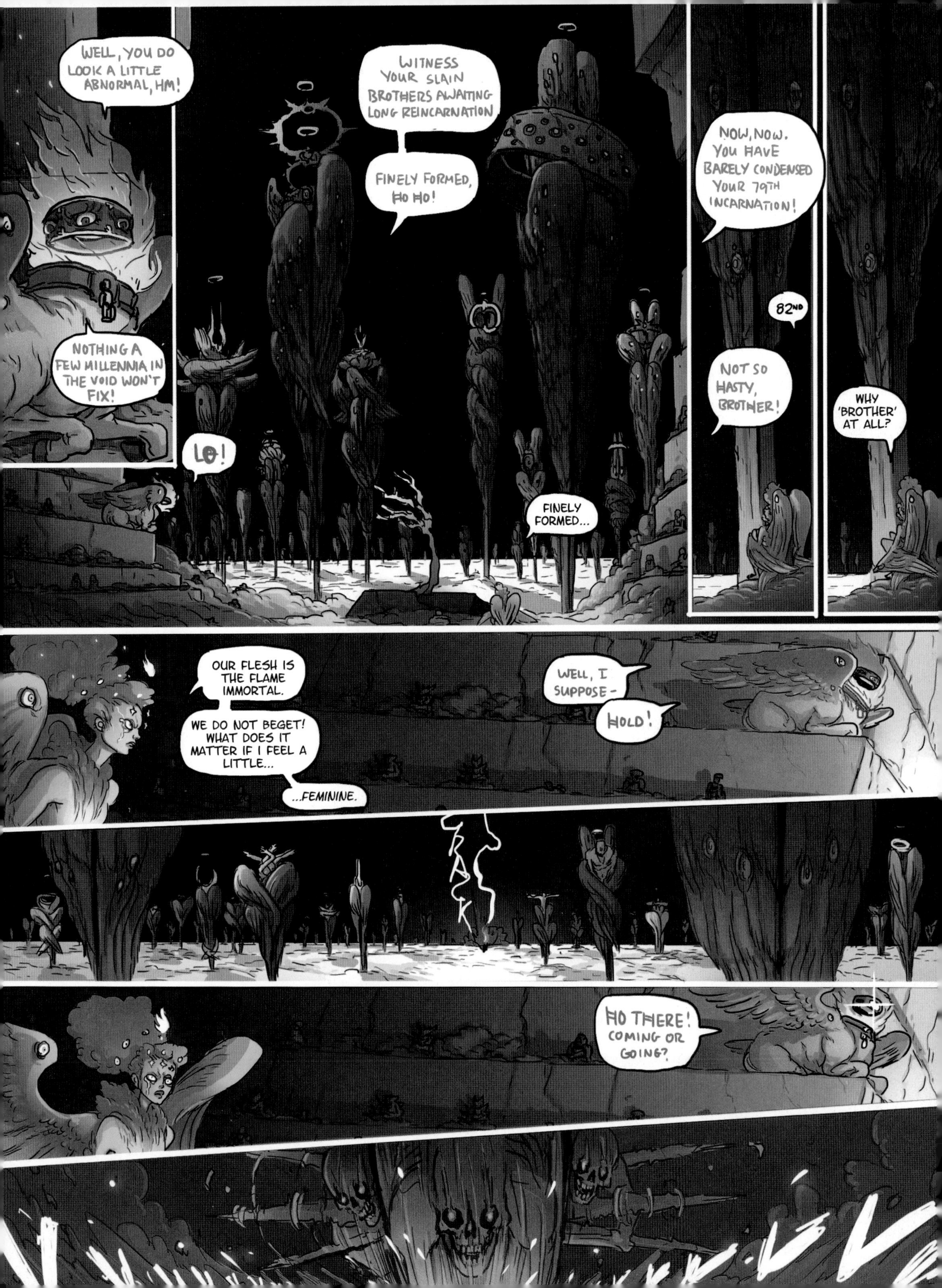
WELL, YOU DO LOOK A LITTLE ABNORMAL, HM!
NOTHING A FEW MILLENNIA IN THE VOID WON'T FIX!
LO!
WITNESS YOUR SLAIN BROTHERS AWAITING LONG REINCARNATION
FINELY FORMED, HO HO!
FINELY FORMED...
NOW, NOW. YOU HAVE BARELY CONDENSED YOUR 79TH INCARNATION!
82ND
NOT SO HASTY, BROTHER!
WHY 'BROTHER' AT ALL?
OUR FLESH IS THE FLAME IMMORTAL.
WE DO NOT BEGET! WHAT DOES IT MATTER IF I FEEL A LITTLE...
...FEMININE.
WELL, I SUPPOSE-
HOLD!
KRAK
HO THERE! COMING OR GOING?

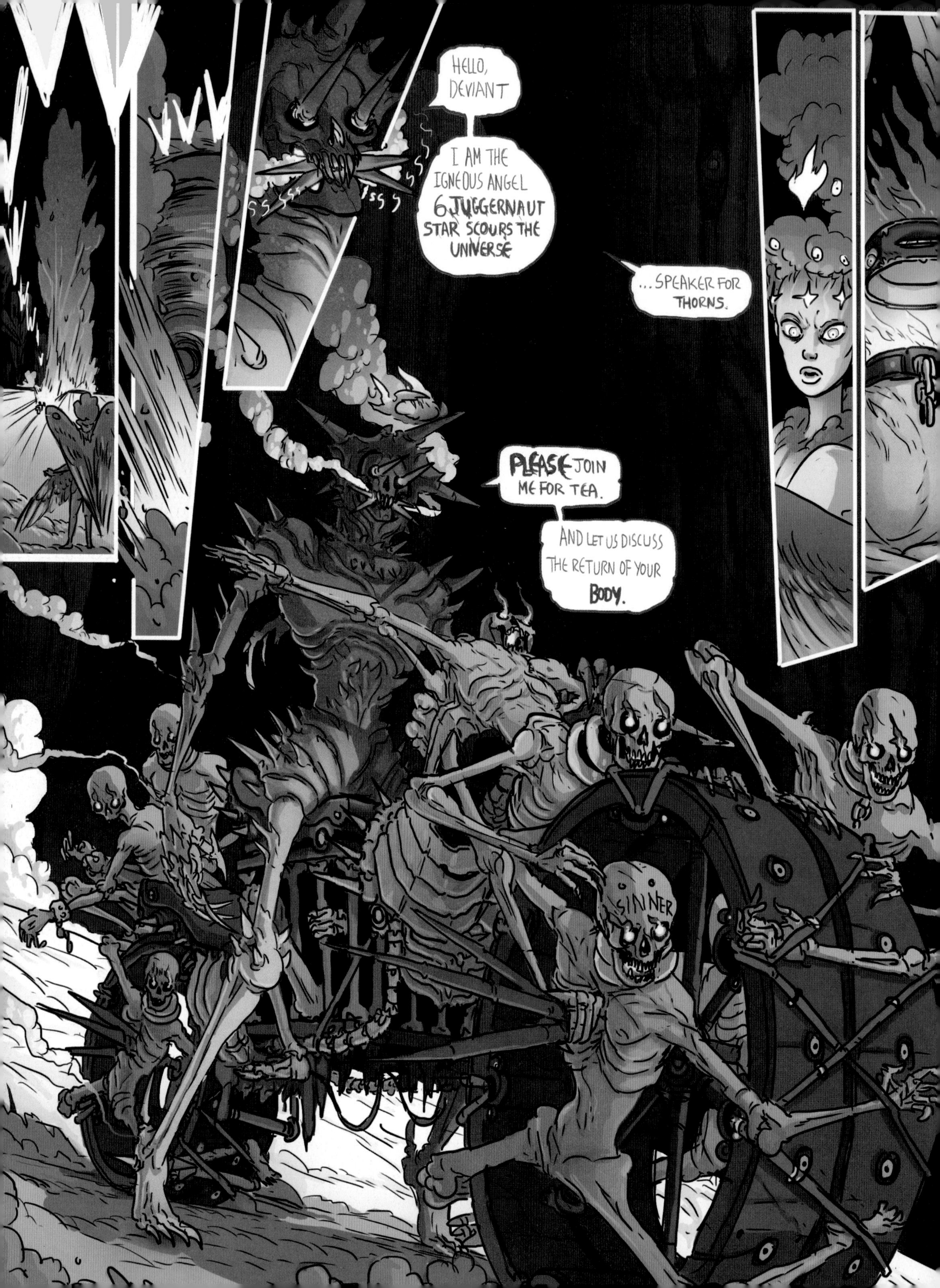
HELLO, DEVIANT
I AM THE IGNEOUS ANGEL 6 JUGGERNAUT STAR SCOURS THE UNIVERSE
...SPEAKER FOR THORNS.
PLEASE JOIN ME FOR TEA.
AND LET US DISCUSS THE RETURN OF YOUR BODY.
SINNER

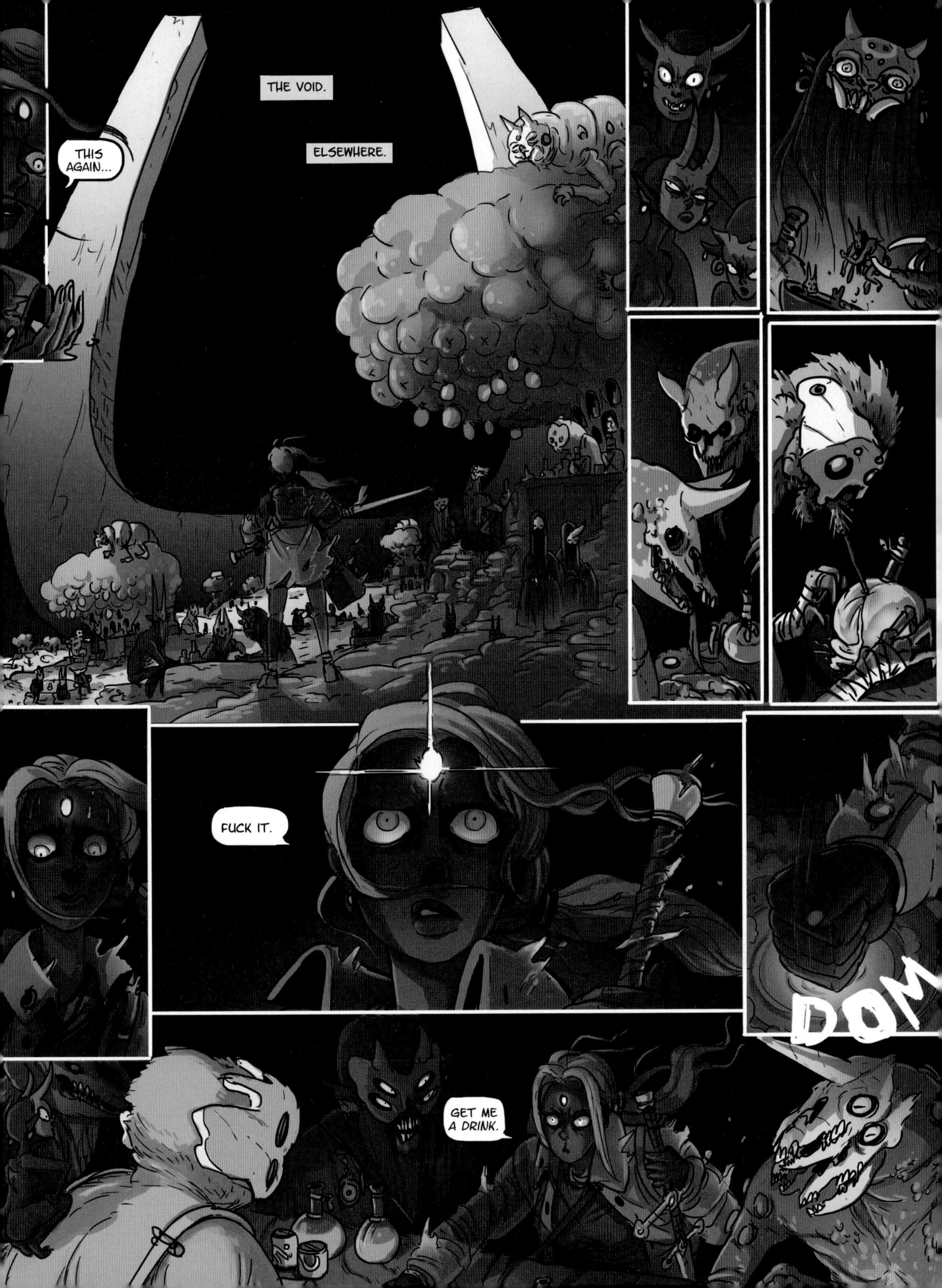
THIS AGAIN...
THE VOID.
ELSEWHERE.
FUCK IT.
DOM
GET ME A DRINK.

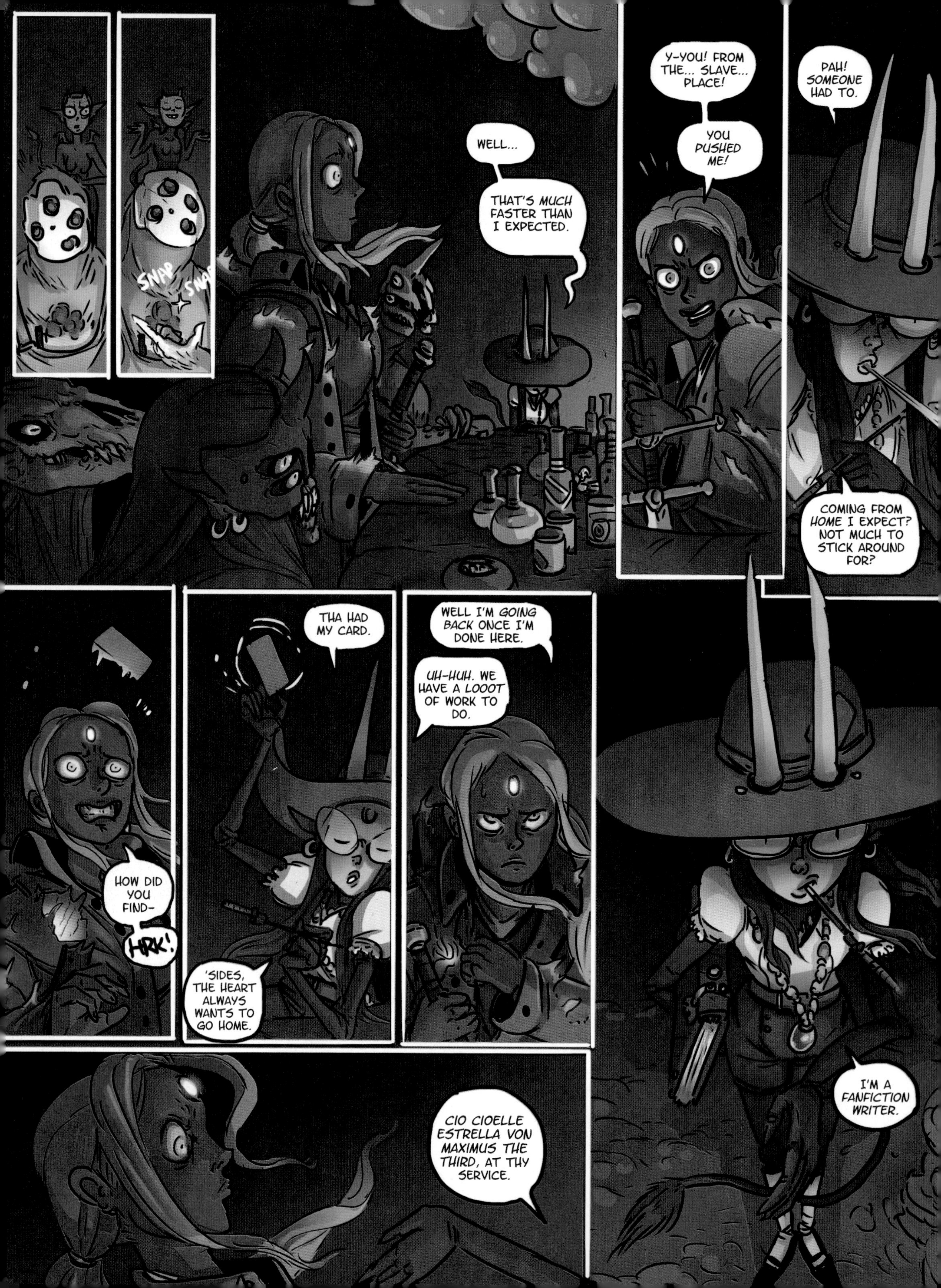
SNAP
SNAP
WELL...
THAT'S MUCH FASTER THAN I EXPECTED.
Y-YOU! FROM THE... SLAVE... PLACE!
YOU PUSHED ME!
PAH! SOMEONE HAD TO.
COMING FROM HOME I EXPECT? NOT MUCH TO STICK AROUND FOR?
HOW DID YOU FIND-
HRK!
THA HAD MY CARD.
'SIDES, THE HEART ALWAYS WANTS TO GO HOME.
WELL I'M GOING BACK ONCE I'M DONE HERE.
UH-HUH. WE HAVE A LOOOT OF WORK TO DO.
I'M A FANFICTION WRITER.
CIO CIOELLE ESTRELLA VON MAXIMUS THE THIRD, AT THY SERVICE.

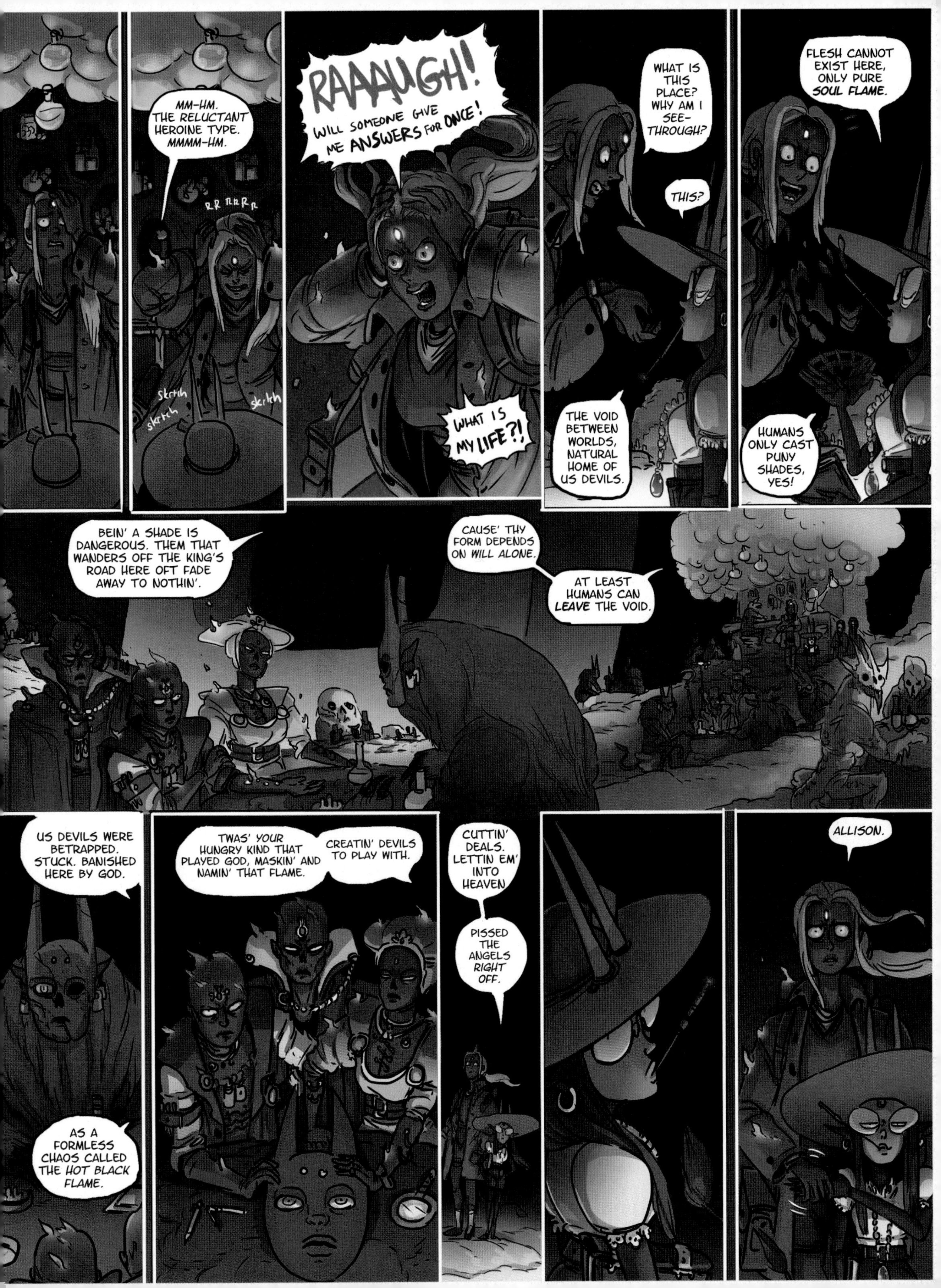
MM-HM. THE RELUCTANT HEROINE TYPE. MMMM-HM.
RR RRRR
skrtch skrtch skrtch
RAAAUGH!
WILL SOMEONE GIVE ME ANSWERS FOR ONCE!
WHAT IS MY LIFE?!
WHAT IS THIS PLACE? WHY AM I SEE-THROUGH?
THIS?
THE VOID BETWEEN WORLDS, NATURAL HOME OF US DEVILS.
FLESH CANNOT EXIST HERE, ONLY PURE SOUL FLAME.
HUMANS ONLY CAST PUNY SHADES, YES!
BEIN' A SHADE IS DANGEROUS. THEM THAT WANDERS OFF THE KING'S ROAD HERE OFT FADE AWAY TO NOTHIN'.
CAUSE' THY FORM DEPENDS ON WILL ALONE.
AT LEAST HUMANS CAN LEAVE THE VOID.
US DEVILS WERE BETRAPPED. STUCK. BANISHED HERE BY GOD.
AS A FORMLESS CHAOS CALLED THE HOT BLACK FLAME.
TWAS' YOUR HUNGRY KIND THAT PLAYED GOD, MASKIN' AND NAMIN' THAT FLAME.
CREATIN' DEVILS TO PLAY WITH.
CUTTIN' DEALS. LETTIN EM' INTO HEAVEN
PISSED THE ANGELS RIGHT OFF.
ALLISON.

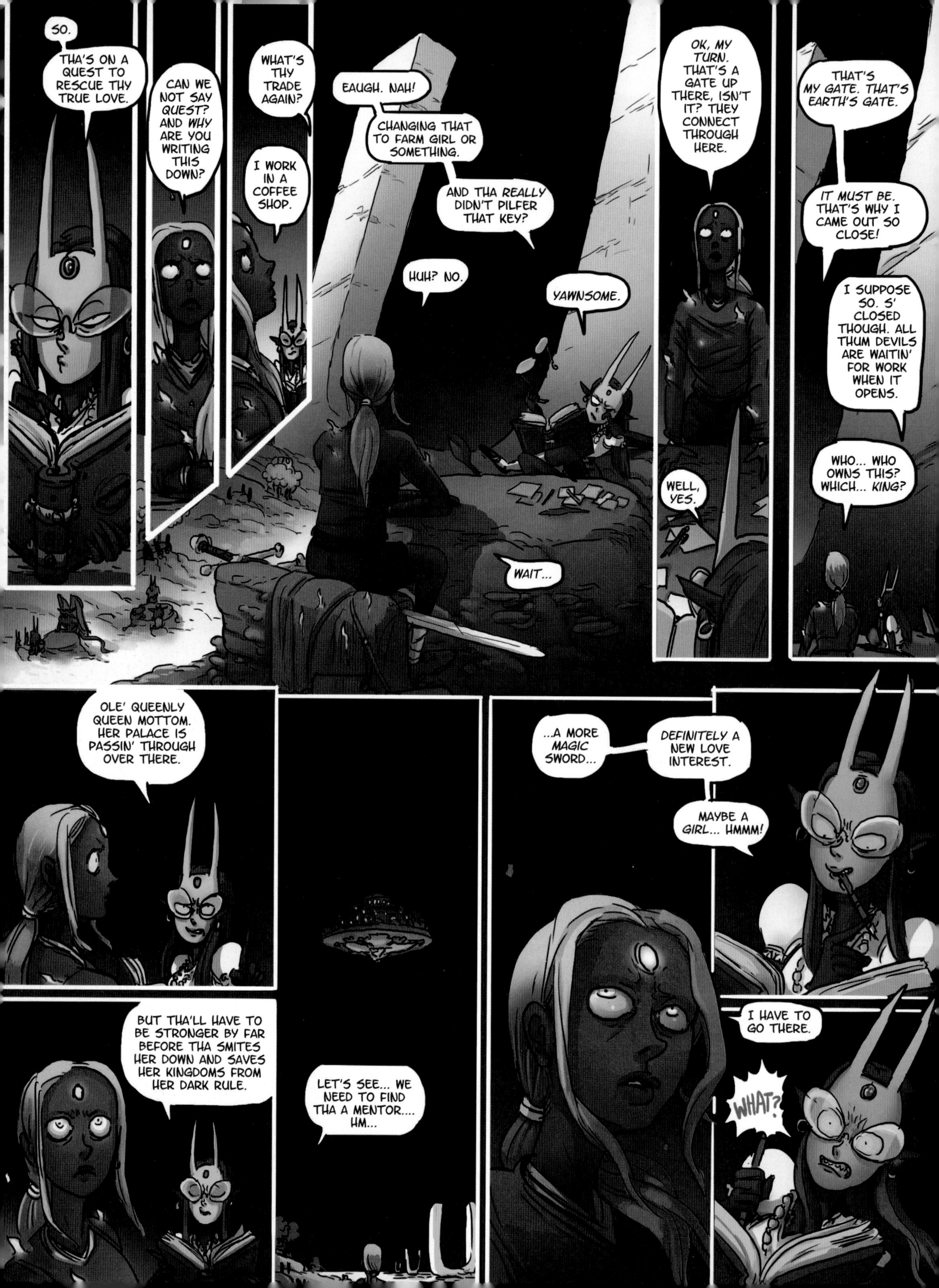
SO.
THA'S ON A QUEST TO RESCUE THY TRUE LOVE.
CAN WE NOT SAY QUEST? AND WHY ARE YOU WRITING THIS DOWN?
WHAT'S THY TRADE AGAIN?
I WORK IN A COFFEE SHOP.
EAUGH. NAH!
CHANGING THAT TO FARM GIRL OR SOMETHING.
AND THA REALLY DIDN'T PILFER THAT KEY?
HUH? NO.
YAWNSOME.
WAIT...
OK, MY TURN. THAT'S A GATE UP THERE, ISN'T IT? THEY CONNECT THROUGH HERE.
WELL, YES.
THAT'S MY GATE. THAT'S EARTH'S GATE.
IT MUST BE. THAT'S WHY I CAME OUT SO CLOSE!
I SUPPOSE SO. S' CLOSED THOUGH. ALL THUM DEVILS ARE WAITIN' FOR WORK WHEN IT OPENS.
WHO... WHO OWNS THIS? WHICH... KING?
OLE' QUEENLY QUEEN MOTTOM. HER PALACE IS PASSIN' THROUGH OVER THERE.
BUT THA'LL HAVE TO BE STRONGER BY FAR BEFORE THA SMITES HER DOWN AND SAVES HER KINGDOMS FROM HER DARK RULE.
LET'S SEE... WE NEED TO FIND THA A MENTOR.... HM...
...A MORE MAGIC SWORD...
DEFINITELY A NEW LOVE INTEREST.
MAYBE A GIRL... HMMM!
I HAVE TO GO THERE.
WHAT?

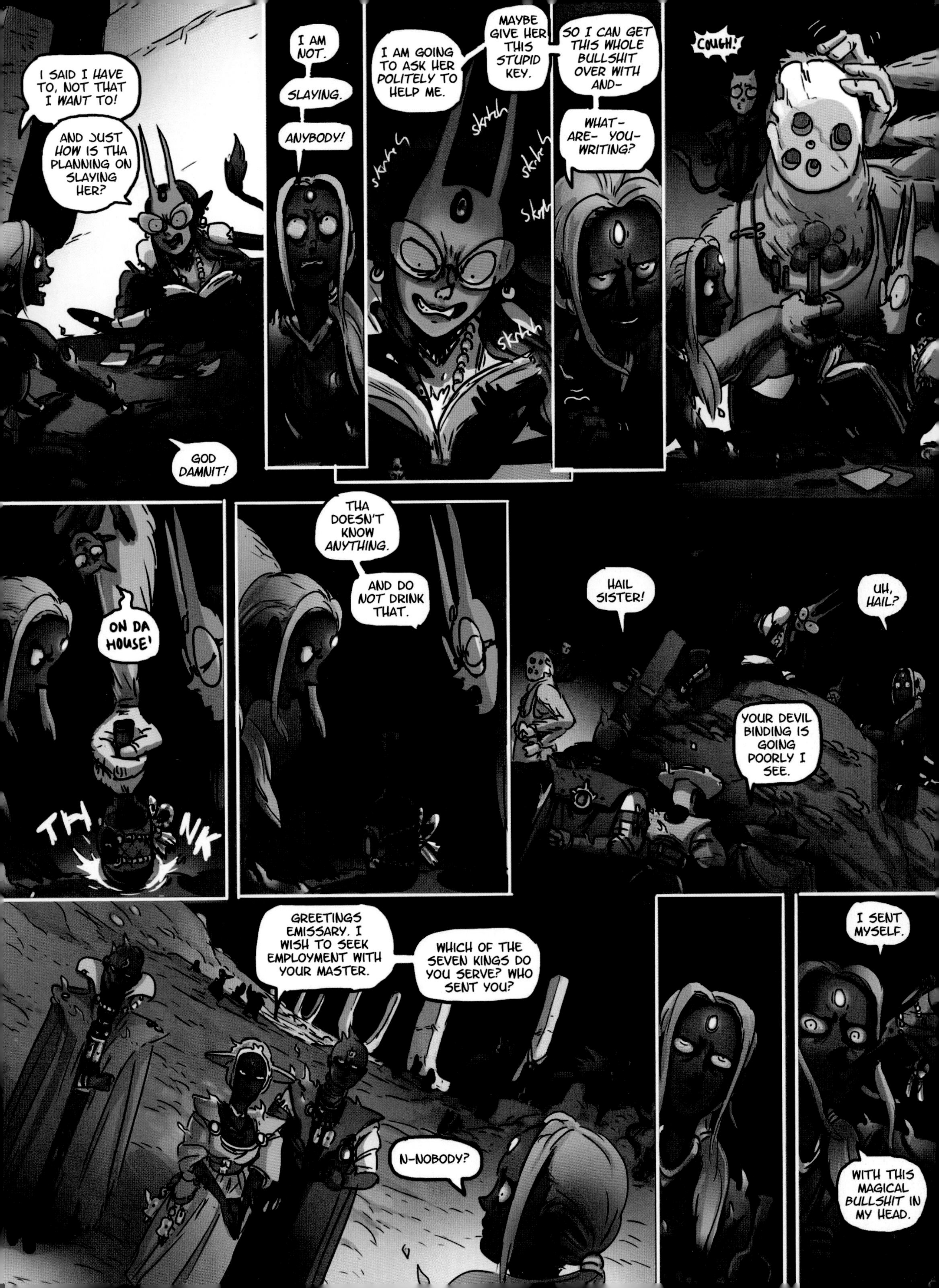
I SAID I HAVE TO, NOT THAT I WANT TO!
AND JUST HOW IS THA PLANNING ON SLAYING HER?
GOD DAMNIT!
I AM NOT.
SLAYING.
ANYBODY!
I AM GOING TO ASK HER POLITELY TO HELP ME.
MAYBE GIVE HER THIS STUPID KEY.
SO I CAN GET THIS WHOLE BULLSHIT OVER WITH AND-
WHAT- ARE- YOU- WRITING?
COUGH!
ON DA HOUSE!
THUNK
THA DOESN'T KNOW ANYTHING.
AND DO NOT DRINK THAT.
HAIL SISTER!
UH, HAIL?
YOUR DEVIL BINDING IS GOING POORLY I SEE.
GREETINGS EMISSARY. I WISH TO SEEK EMPLOYMENT WITH YOUR MASTER.
WHICH OF THE SEVEN KINGS DO YOU SERVE? WHO SENT YOU?
N-NOBODY?
I SENT MYSELF.
WITH THIS MAGICAL BULLSHIT IN MY HEAD.

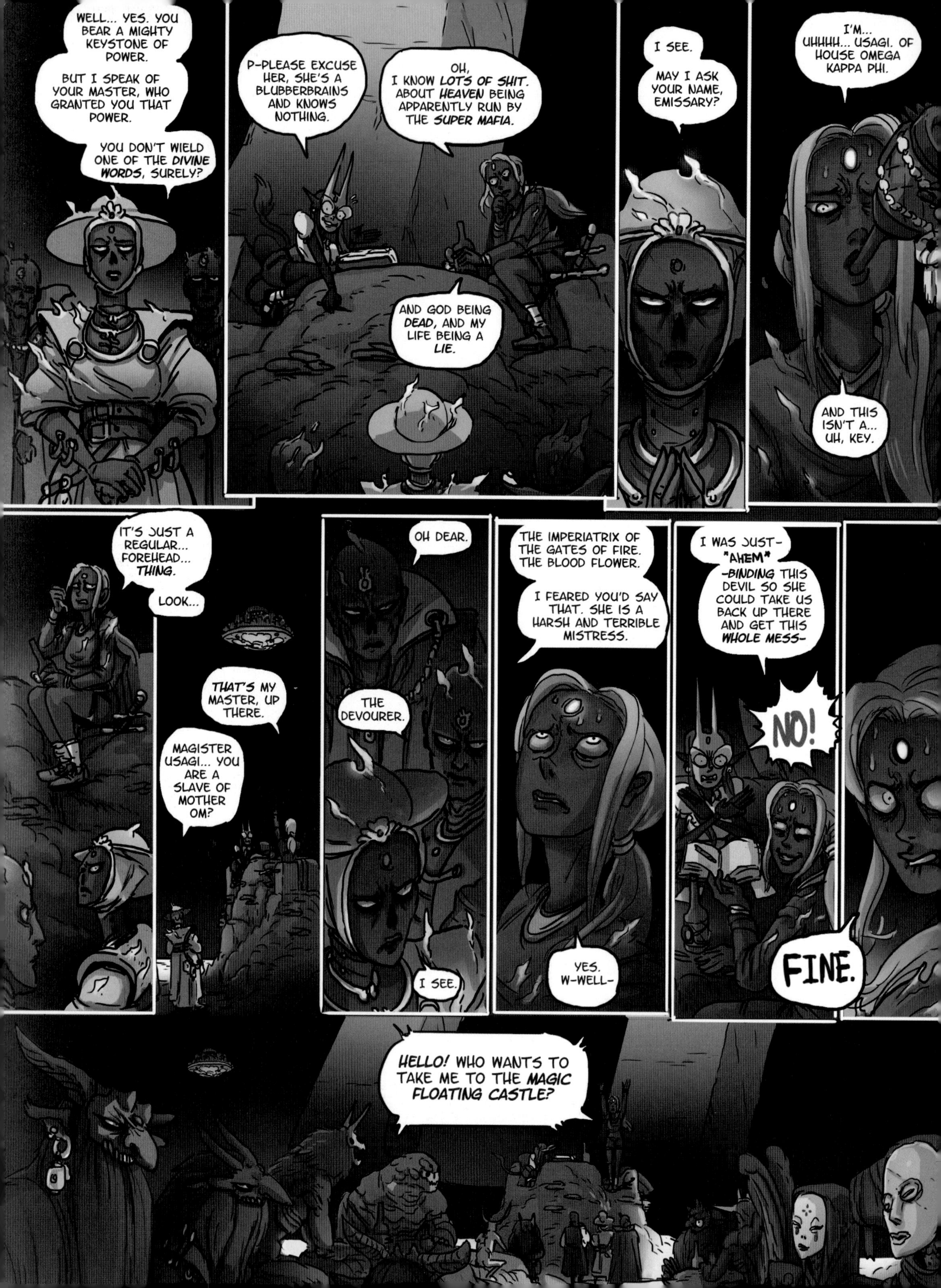
WELL... YES. YOU BEAR A MIGHTY KEYSTONE OF POWER.
BUT I SPEAK OF YOUR MASTER, WHO GRANTED YOU THAT POWER.
YOU DON'T WIELD ONE OF THE DIVINE WORDS, SURELY?
P-PLEASE EXCUSE HER, SHE'S A BLUBBERBRAINS AND KNOWS NOTHING.
OH, I KNOW LOTS OF SHIT. ABOUT HEAVEN BEING APPARENTLY RUN BY THE SUPER MAFIA.
AND GOD BEING DEAD, AND MY LIFE BEING A LIE.
I SEE.
MAY I ASK YOUR NAME, EMISSARY?
I'M... UHHHH... USAGI. OF HOUSE OMEGA KAPPA PHI.
AND THIS ISN'T A... UH, KEY.
IT'S JUST A REGULAR... FOREHEAD... THING.
LOOK...
THAT'S MY MASTER, UP THERE.
MAGISTER USAGI... YOU ARE A SLAVE OF MOTHER OM?
OH DEAR.
THE DEVOURER.
I SEE.
THE IMPERIATRIX OF THE GATES OF FIRE. THE BLOOD FLOWER.
I FEARED YOU'D SAY THAT. SHE IS A HARSH AND TERRIBLE MISTRESS.
YES. W-WELL-
I WAS JUST- "AHEM" -BINDING THIS DEVIL SO SHE COULD TAKE US BACK UP THERE AND GET THIS WHOLE MESS-
NO!
FINE.
HELLO! WHO WANTS TO TAKE ME TO THE MAGIC FLOATING CASTLE?

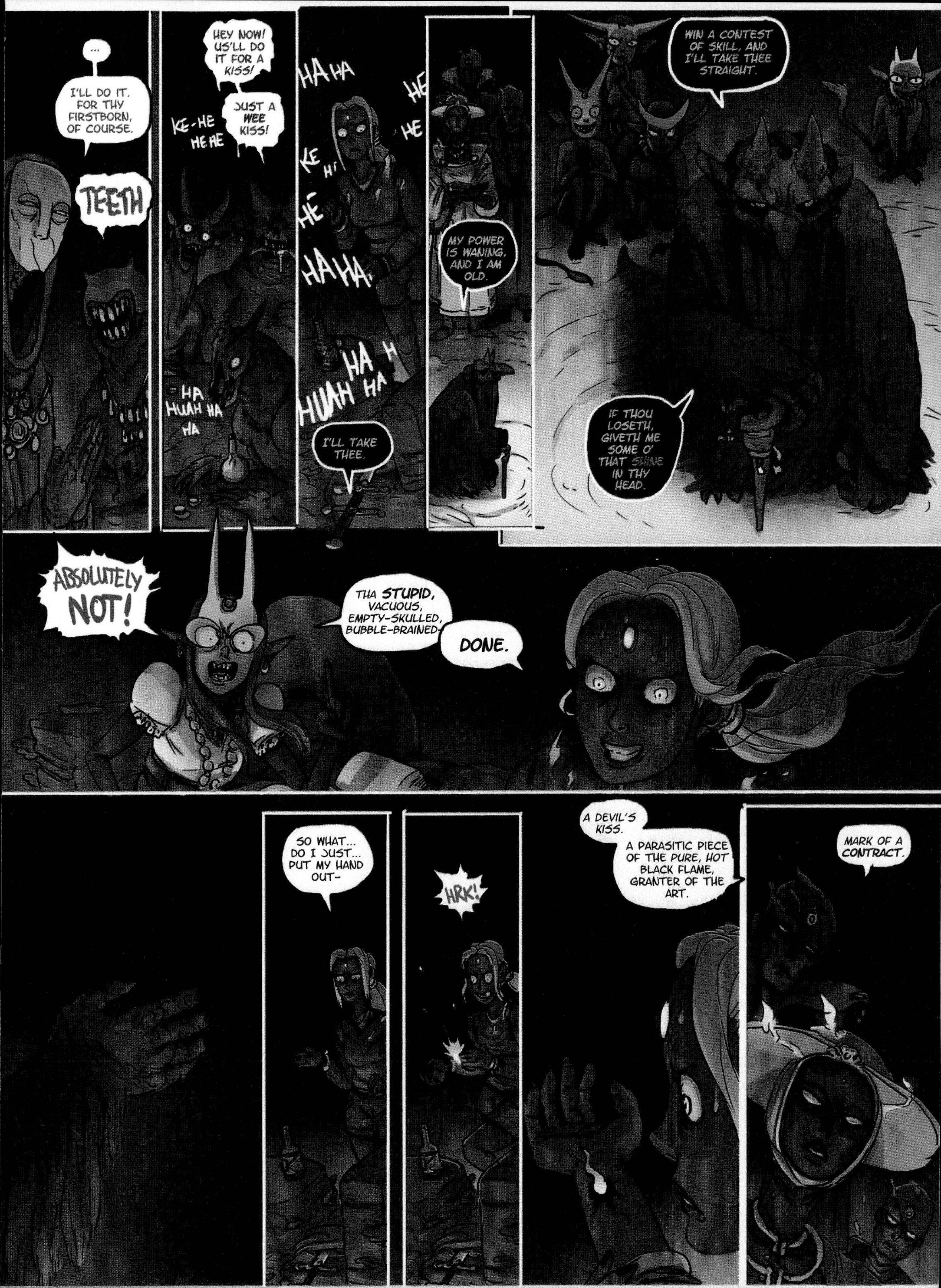
...
I'LL DO IT. FOR THY FIRSTBORN, OF COURSE.
TEETH
HEY NOW! US'LL DO IT FOR A KISS!
JUST A WEE KISS!
KE-HE HE HE
HA HUAH HA HA
HA HA
KE HI
HE
HAHA
HA HA H
HUAH HA
HE HE
I'LL TAKE THEE.
MY POWER IS WANING, AND I AM OLD.
WIN A CONTEST OF SKILL, AND I'LL TAKE THEE STRAIGHT.
IF THOU LOSETH, GIVETH ME SOME O' THAT SHINE IN THY HEAD.
ABSOLUTELY NOT!
THA STUPID, VACUOUS, EMPTY-SKULLED, BUBBLE-BRAINED-
DONE.
SO WHAT... DO I JUST... PUT MY HAND OUT-
HRK!
A DEVIL'S KISS.
A PARASITIC PIECE OF THE PURE, HOT BLACK FLAME, GRANTER OF THE ART.
MARK OF A CONTRACT.

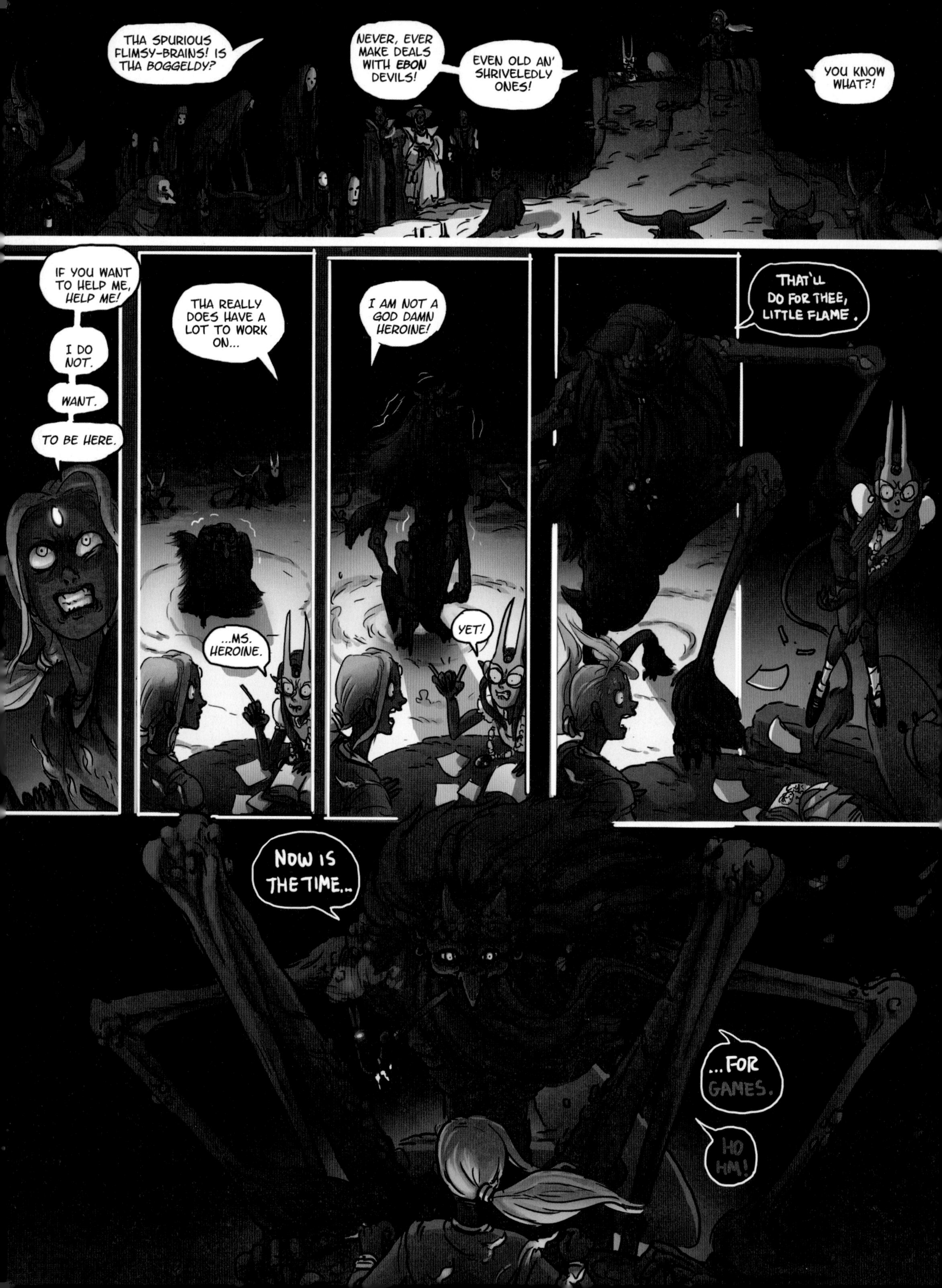
THA SPURIOUS FLIMSY-BRAINS! IS THA BOGGELDY?
NEVER, EVER MAKE DEALS WITH EBON DEVILS!
EVEN OLD AN' SHRIVELEDLY ONES!
YOU KNOW WHAT?!
IF YOU WANT TO HELP ME, HELP ME!
I DO NOT.
WANT.
TO BE HERE.
THA REALLY DOES HAVE A LOT TO WORK ON...
...MS. HEROINE.
I AM NOT A GOD DAMN HEROINE!
YET!
THAT'LL DO FOR THEE, LITTLE FLAME.
NOW IS THE TIME...
...FOR GAMES.
HO HM!

"Here is my sword," said Intra. "Your semiotics cannot contain it. It's blade is made from gloaming steel. Look how it whispers!"
"But Lord Intra," cried the assembled, "You have no sword!"
"So it is," said Intra.

-Psalms

Lord Intra gathered his retainers, who were hungry for tutelage.
"Lord Intra!" said his sandal bearer, "What is the first step on the path to Royalty?"
"There are no steps," replied Intra,
"It is zero-sum with your reality. It is not measured in finger-lengths."
"Lord Intra," said his bodyguard, "Is the path to Royalty the path of struggle, then?"
"No," said Intra, "One may attain it without any effort at all. It is the antithesis of struggle."

Intra's steward was very discontent with his master's evasiveness. "Lord," he said, "Allow us lowly men some small measure of understanding. For sympathy's sake, and the sake of we good and loyal servants, please tell us in plain language the nature of Royalty."

"I will tell you precisely what Royalty is," said Intra, "It is a continuous cutting motion."

-The Song of Maybe

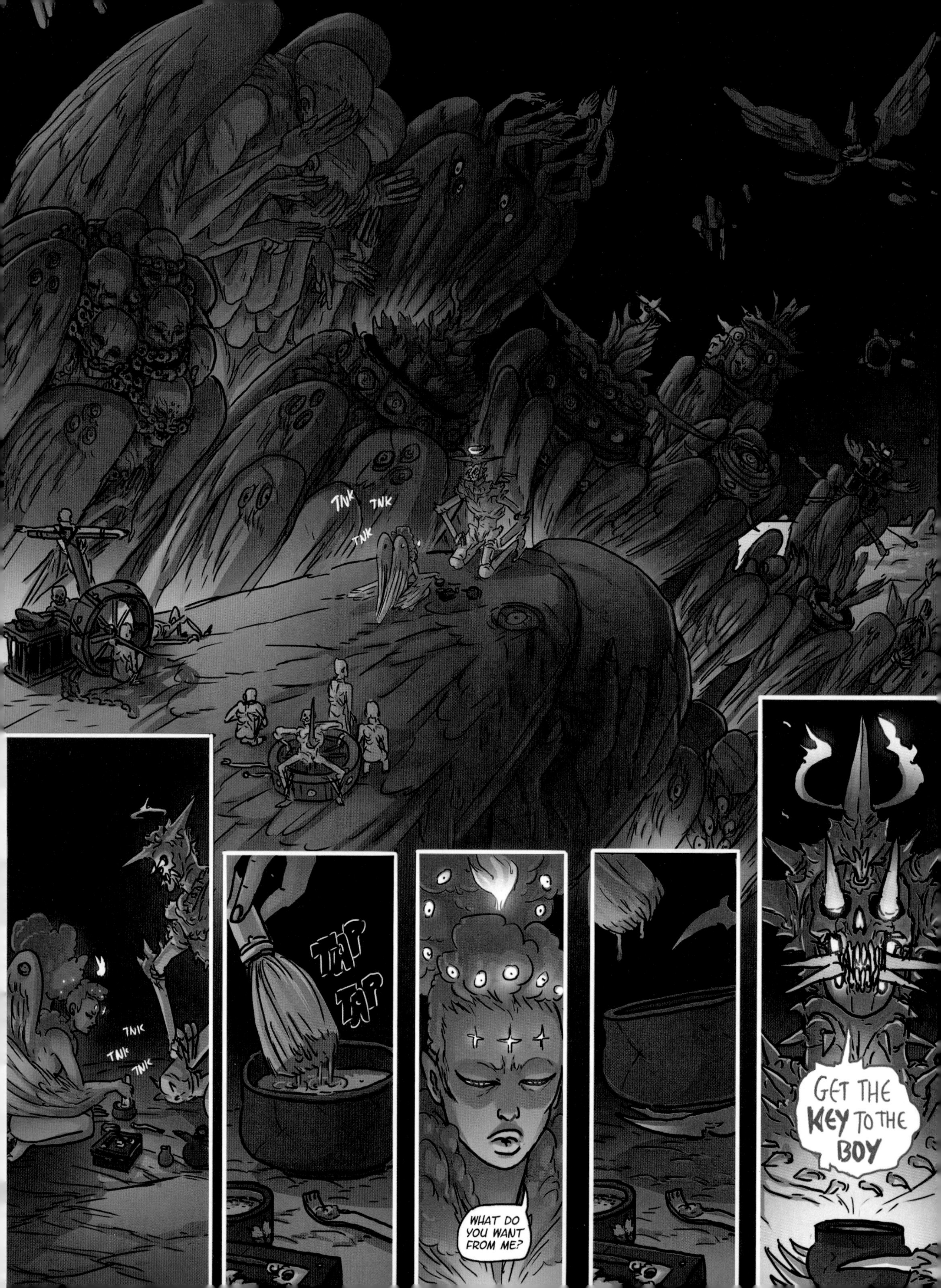
TNK TNK
TNK
TNK
TNK
TNK
TAP
TAP
WHAT DO YOU WANT FROM ME?
GET THE KEY TO THE BOY

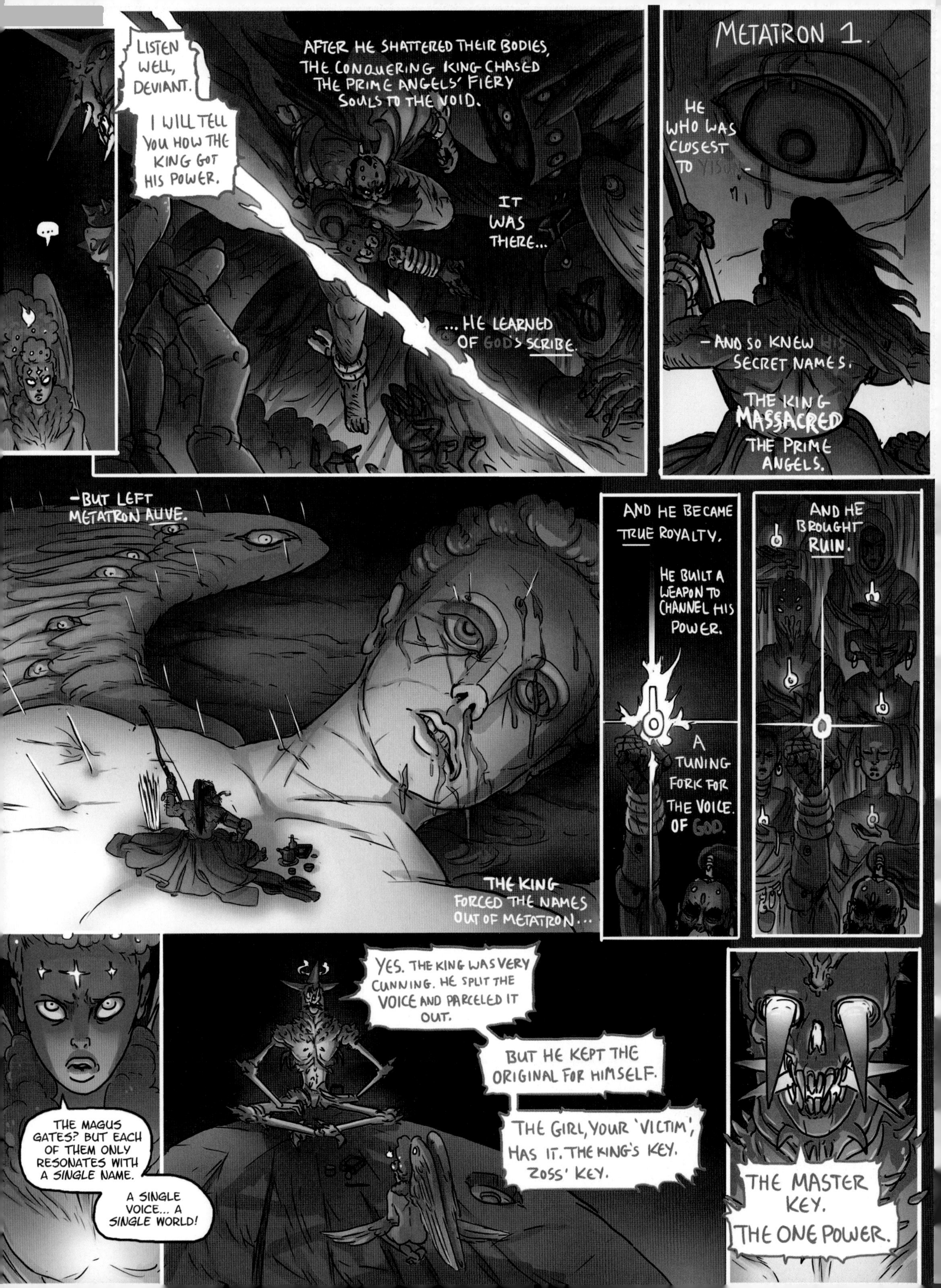
LISTEN WELL, DEVIANT.
I WILL TELL YOU HOW THE KING GOT HIS POWER.
AFTER HE SHATTERED THEIR BODIES, THE CONQUERING KING CHASED THE PRIME ANGELS' FIERY SOULS TO THE VOID.
IT WAS THERE...
...HE LEARNED OF GOD'S SCRIBE.
METATRON 1.
HE WHO WAS CLOSEST TO YISUN-
-AND SO KNEW HIS SECRET NAMES.
THE KING MASSACRED THE PRIME ANGELS.
-BUT LEFT METATRON ALIVE.
THE KING FORCED THE NAMES OUT OF METATRON...
AND HE BECAME TRUE ROYALTY.
HE BUILT A WEAPON TO CHANNEL HIS POWER.
A TUNING FORK FOR THE VOICE OF GOD.
AND HE BROUGHT RUIN.
YES. THE KING WAS VERY CUNNING. HE SPLIT THE VOICE AND PARCELED IT OUT.
BUT HE KEPT THE ORIGINAL FOR HIMSELF.
THE GIRL, YOUR 'VICTIM', HAS IT. THE KING'S KEY. ZOSS' KEY.
THE MAGUS GATES? BUT EACH OF THEM ONLY RESONATES WITH A SINGLE NAME.
A SINGLE VOICE... A SINGLE WORLD!
THE MASTER KEY.
THE ONE POWER.

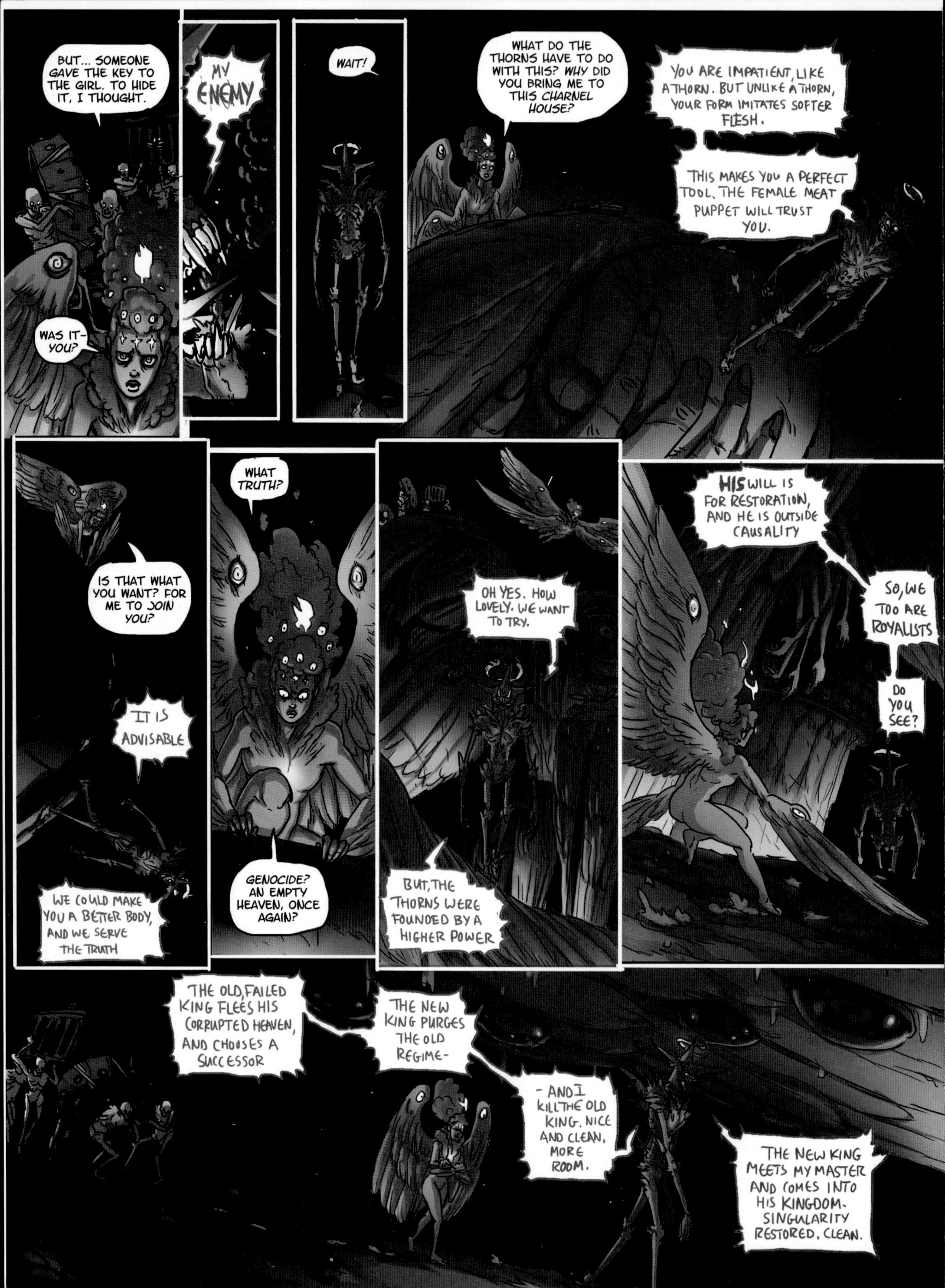
BUT... SOMEONE GAVE THE KEY TO THE GIRL. TO HIDE IT, I THOUGHT.
WAS IT- YOU?
MY ENEMY
WAIT!
WHAT DO THE THORNS HAVE TO DO WITH THIS? WHY DID YOU BRING ME TO THIS CHARNEL HOUSE?
YOU ARE IMPATIENT, LIKE A THORN. BUT UNLIKE A THORN, YOUR FORM IMITATES SOFTER FLESH.
THIS MAKES YOU A PERFECT TOOL. THE FEMALE MEAT PUPPET WILL TRUST YOU.
IS THAT WHAT YOU WANT? FOR ME TO JOIN YOU?
IT IS ADVISABLE
WE COULD MAKE YOU A BETTER BODY, AND WE SERVE THE TRUTH
WHAT TRUTH?
GENOCIDE? AN EMPTY HEAVEN, ONCE AGAIN?
OH YES. HOW LOVELY. WE WANT TO TRY.
BUT, THE THORNS WERE FOUNDED BY A HIGHER POWER
HIS WILL IS FOR RESTORATION, AND HE IS OUTSIDE CAUSALITY
SO, WE TOO ARE ROYALISTS
DO YOU SEE?
THE OLD, FAILED KING FLEES HIS CORRUPTED HEAVEN, AND CHOOSES A SUCCESSOR
THE NEW KING PURGES THE OLD REGIME-
- AND I KILL THE OLD KING. NICE AND CLEAN. MORE ROOM.
THE NEW KING MEETS MY MASTER AND COMES INTO HIS KINGDOM. SINGULARITY RESTORED. CLEAN.

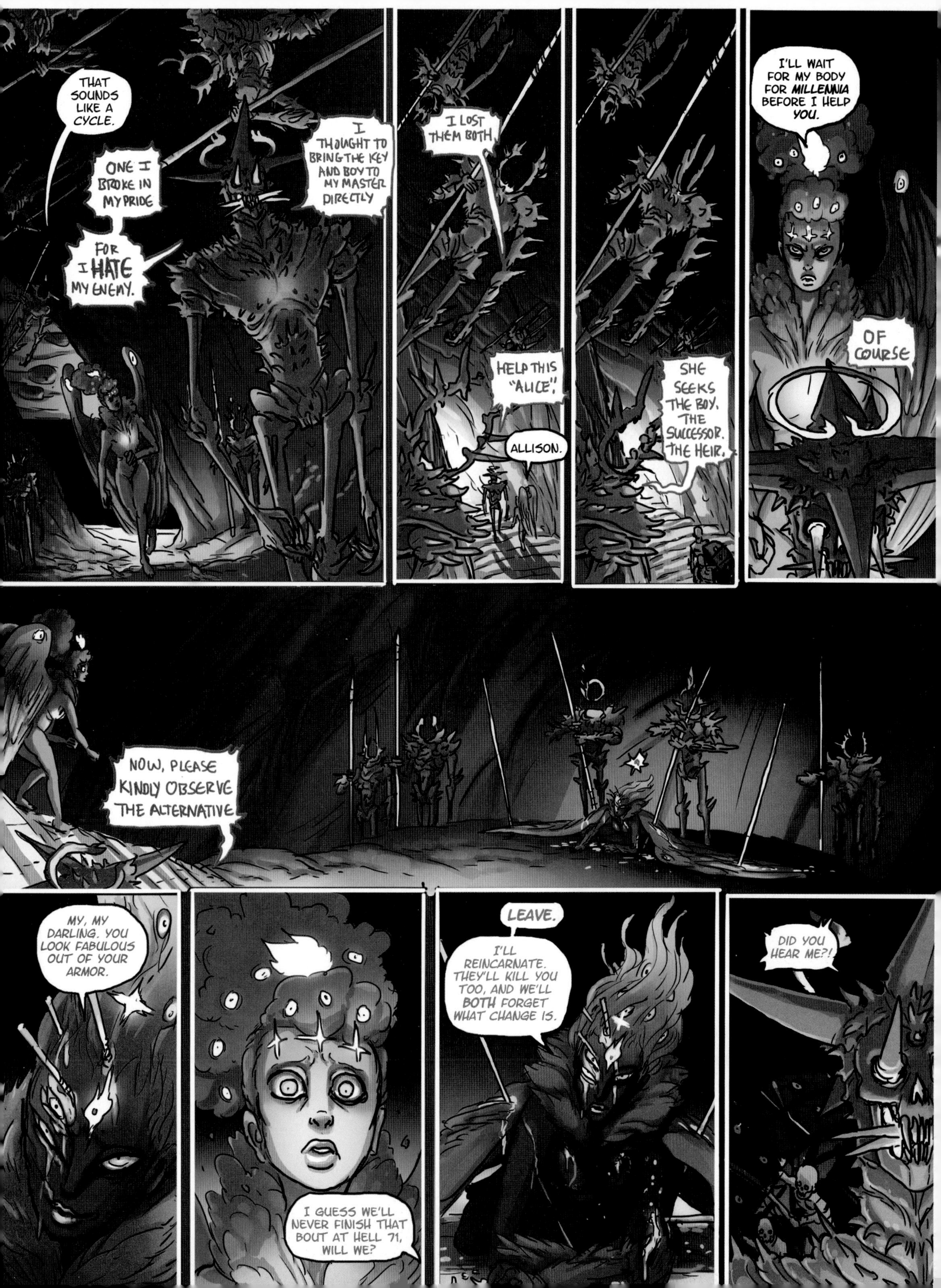
THAT SOUNDS LIKE A CYCLE.
ONE I BROKE IN MY PRIDE
FOR I HATE MY ENEMY.
I THOUGHT TO BRING THE KEY AND BOY TO MY MASTER DIRECTLY
I LOST THEM BOTH
HELP THIS "ALICE".
ALLISON.
SHE SEEKS THE BOY. THE SUCCESSOR. THE HEIR.
I'LL WAIT FOR MY BODY FOR MILLENNIA BEFORE I HELP YOU.
OF COURSE
NOW, PLEASE KINDLY OBSERVE THE ALTERNATIVE
MY, MY DARLING. YOU LOOK FABULOUS OUT OF YOUR ARMOR.
I GUESS WE'LL NEVER FINISH THAT BOUT AT HELL 71, WILL WE?
LEAVE.
I'LL REINCARNATE. THEY'LL KILL YOU TOO, AND WE'LL BOTH FORGET WHAT CHANGE IS.
DID YOU HEAR ME?!

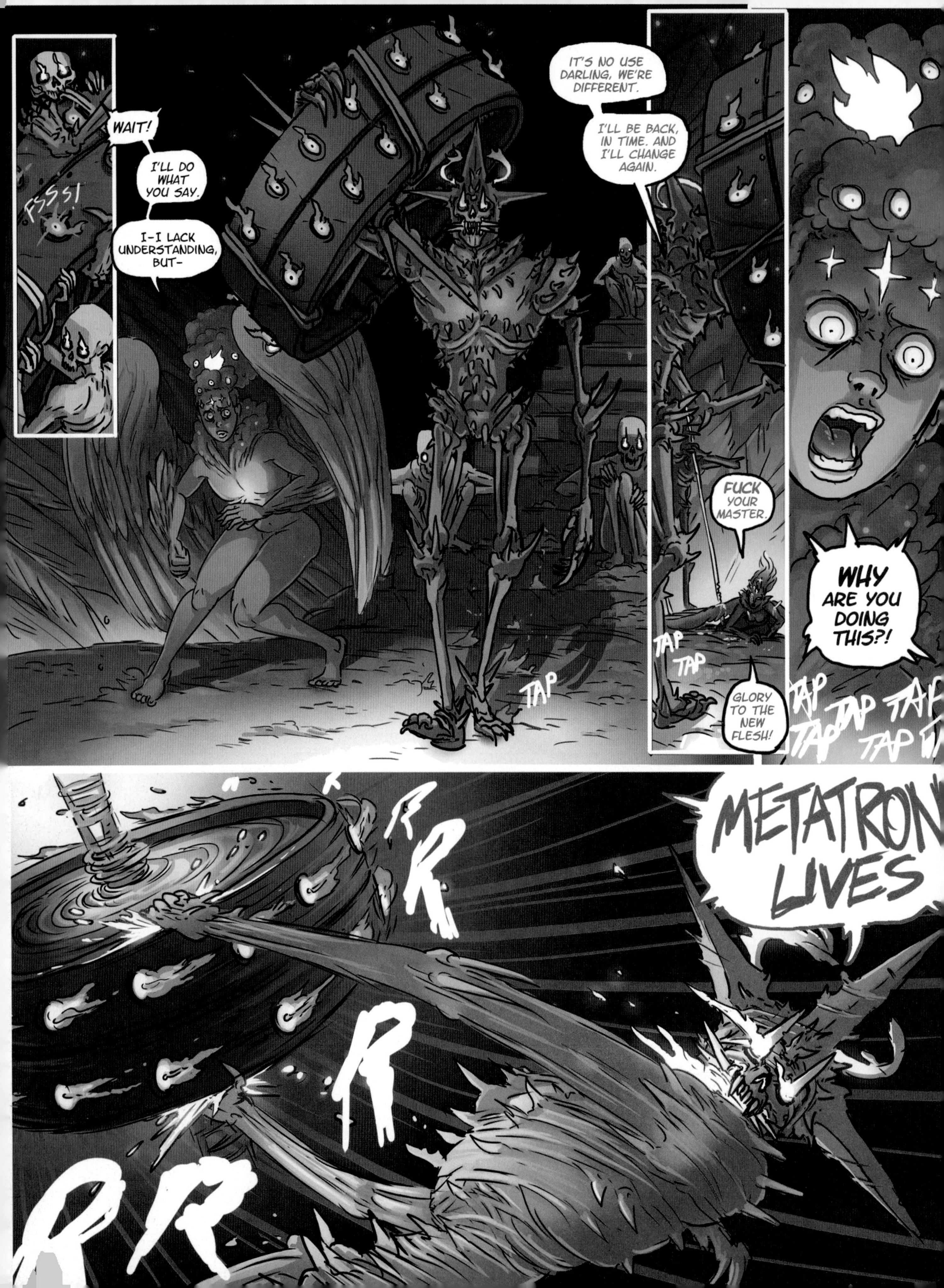
WAIT!
I'LL DO WHAT YOU SAY.
I-I LACK UNDERSTANDING, BUT-
FSSS!
IT'S NO USE DARLING, WE'RE DIFFERENT.
I'LL BE BACK, IN TIME. AND I'LL CHANGE AGAIN.
TAP
FUCK YOUR MASTER.
TAP TAP
GLORY TO THE NEW FLESH!
WHY ARE YOU DOING THIS?!
TAP TAP TAP TAP TAP
METATRON LIVES
R R R R R R

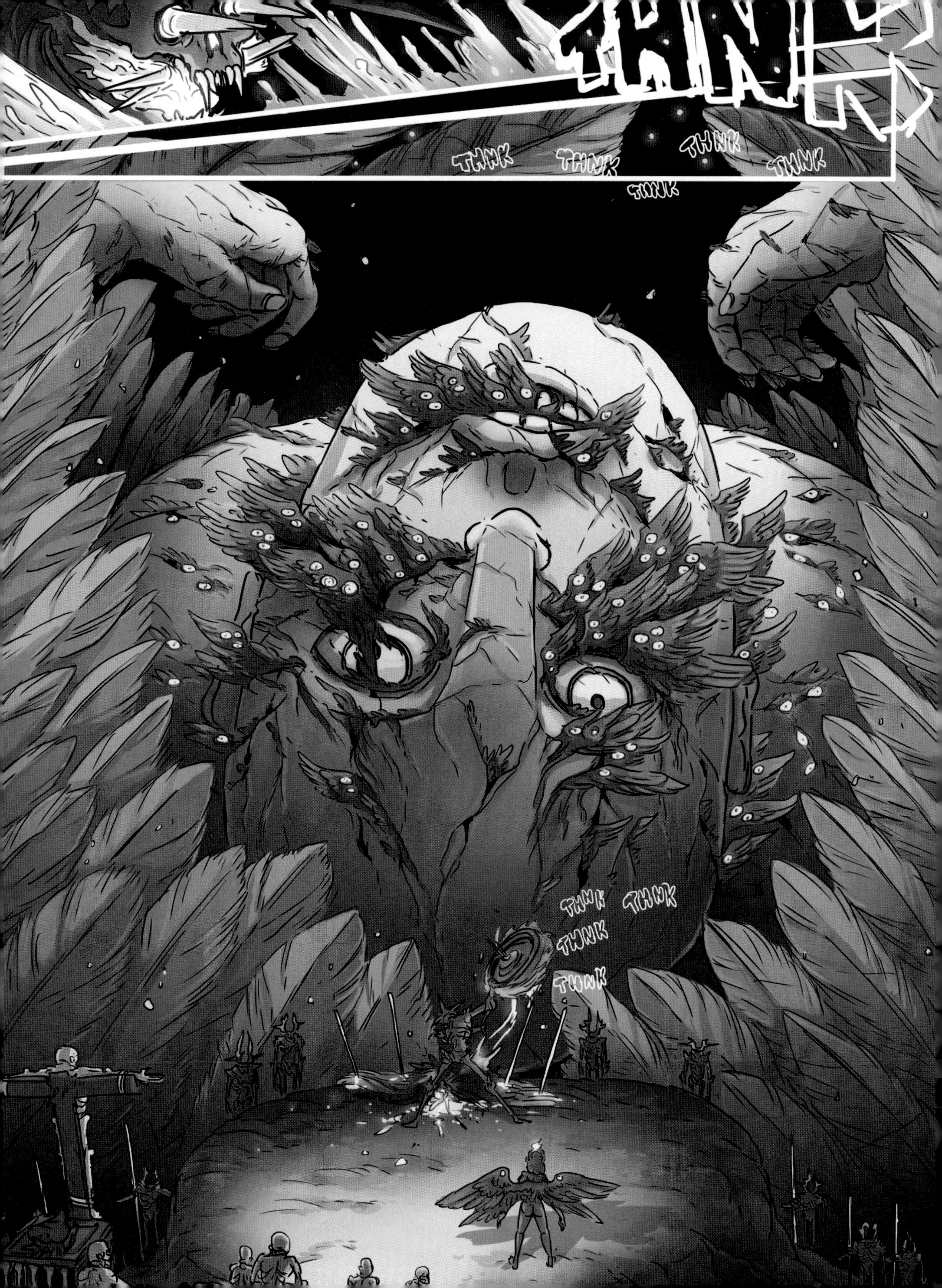
THNK
THNK
THNK
THNK
THNK
THNK
THNK
THNK
THNK
THNK
THNK

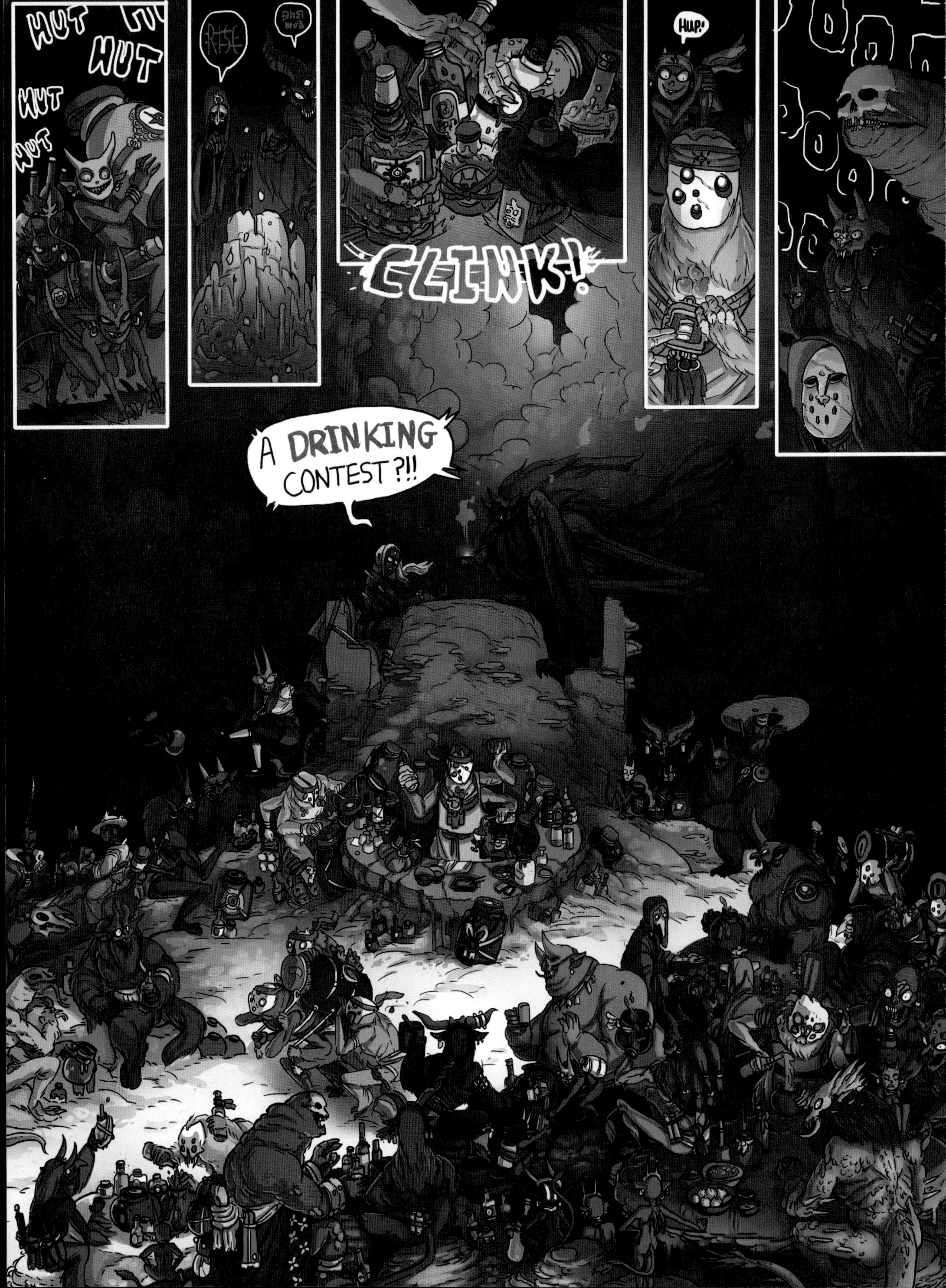

HUT
HUT
HUT
HUT
RISE
HUP!
CLINK!
A DRINKING CONTEST?!!

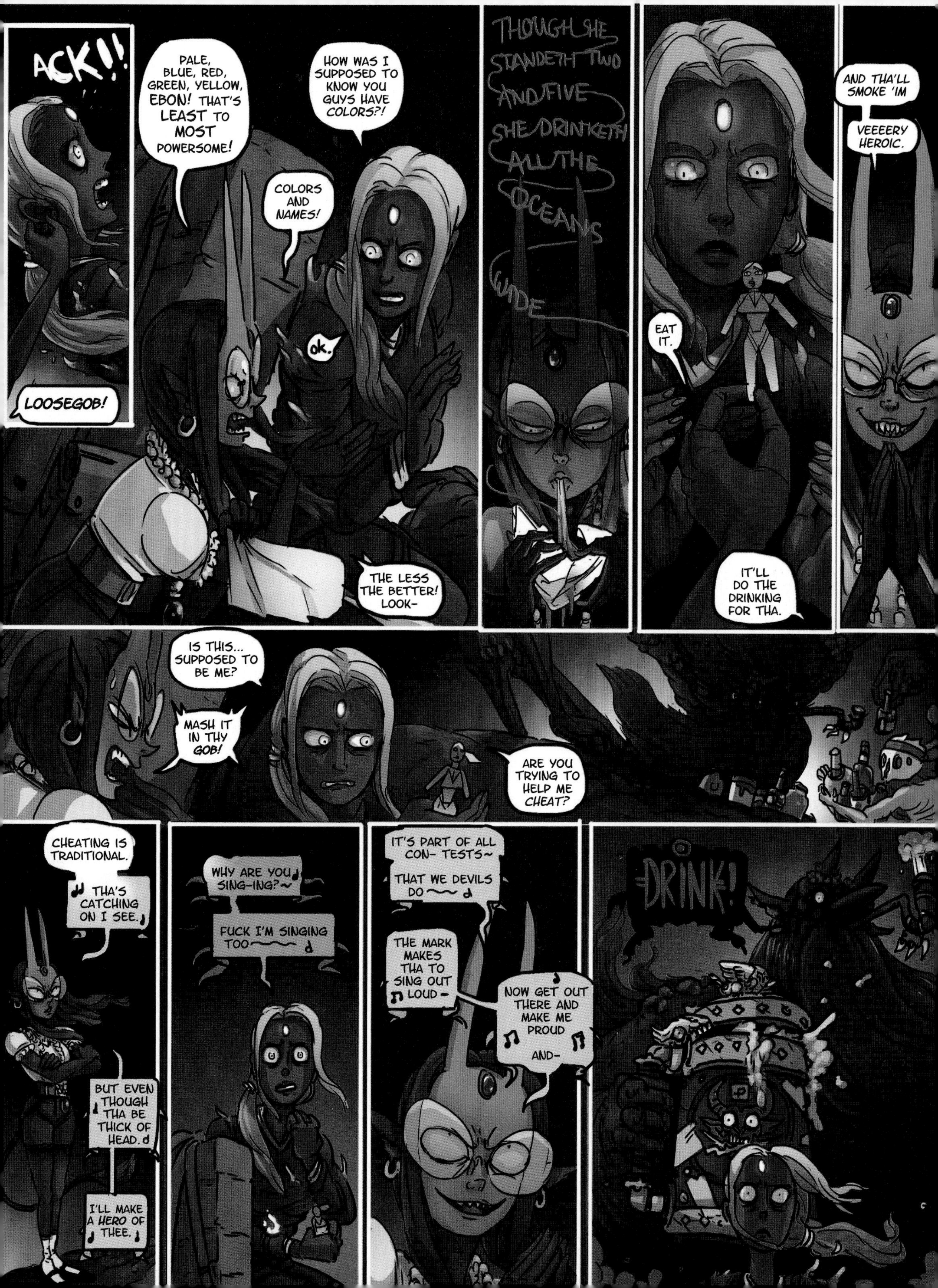
ACK!!
LOOSEGOB!
PALE, BLUE, RED, GREEN, YELLOW, EBON! THAT'S LEAST TO MOST POWERSOME!
HOW WAS I SUPPOSED TO KNOW YOU GUYS HAVE COLORS?!
COLORS AND NAMES!
ok.
THE LESS THE BETTER! LOOK-
THOUGH SHE STANDETH TWO AND FIVE SHE DRINKETH ALL THE OCEANS WIDE
EAT IT.
IT'LL DO THE DRINKING FOR THA.
AND THA'LL SMOKE 'IM
VEEEERY HEROIC.
IS THIS... SUPPOSED TO BE ME?
MASH IT IN THY GOB!
ARE YOU TRYING TO HELP ME CHEAT?
CHEATING IS TRADITIONAL.
THA'S CATCHING ON I SEE.
BUT EVEN THOUGH THA BE THICK OF HEAD.
I'LL MAKE A HERO OF THEE.
WHY ARE YOU SING-ING?~
FUCK I'M SINGING TOO~~~
IT'S PART OF ALL CON- TESTS~
THAT WE DEVILS DO~~~
THE MARK MAKES THA TO SING OUT LOUD-
NOW GET OUT THERE AND MAKE ME PROUD
AND-
DRINK!

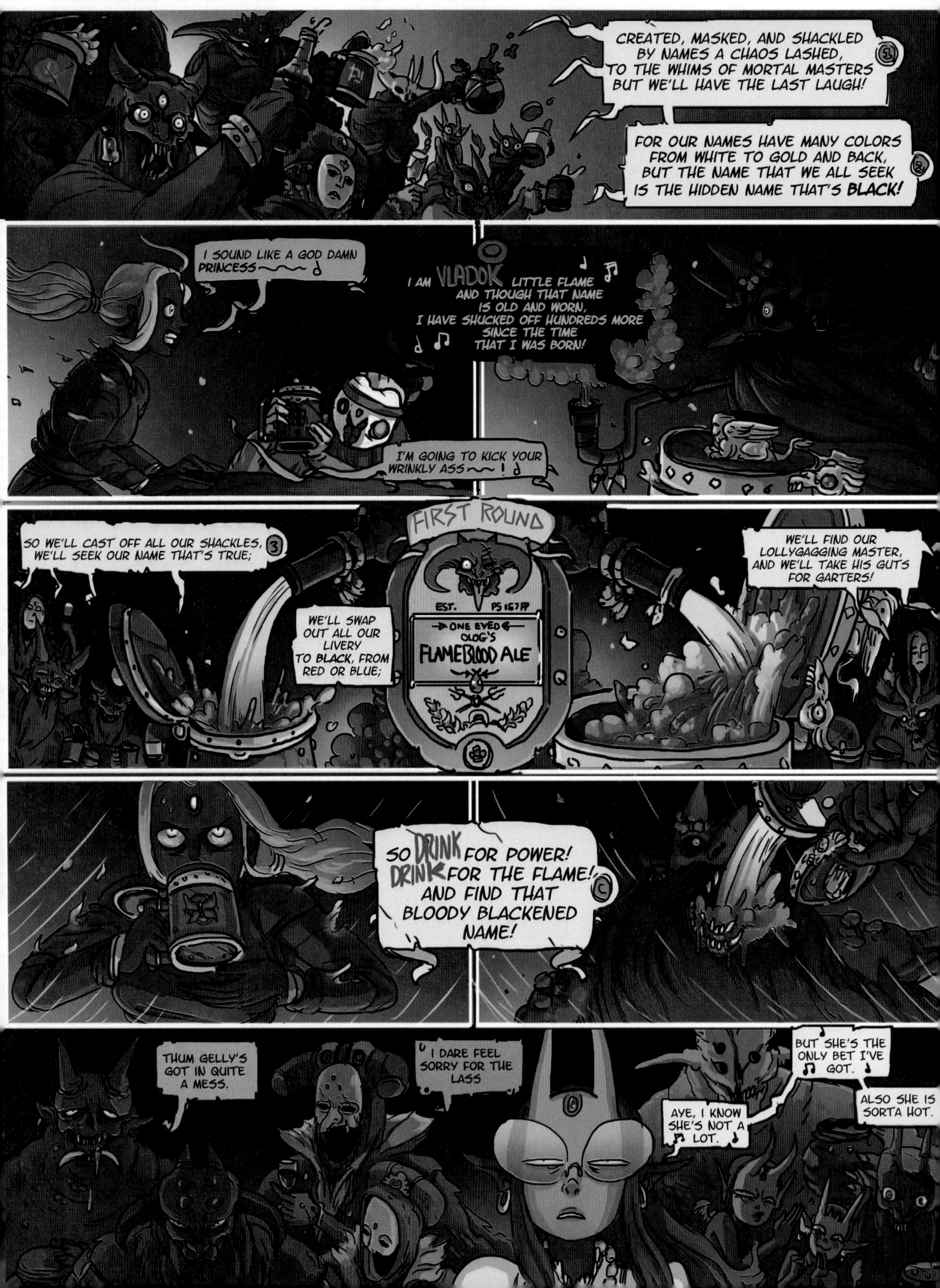

CREATED, MASKED, AND SHACKLED BY NAMES A CHAOS LASHED, TO THE WHIMS OF MORTAL MASTERS BUT WE'LL HAVE THE LAST LAUGH!
FOR OUR NAMES HAVE MANY COLORS FROM WHITE TO GOLD AND BACK, BUT THE NAME THAT WE ALL SEEK IS THE HIDDEN NAME THAT'S BLACK!
I SOUND LIKE A GOD DAMN PRINCESS~~~
I AM VLADOK LITTLE FLAME AND THOUGH THAT NAME IS OLD AND WORN, I HAVE SHUCKED OFF HUNDREDS MORE SINCE THE TIME THAT I WAS BORN!
I'M GOING TO KICK YOUR WRINKLY ASS~~~!
FIRST ROUND
SO WE'LL CAST OFF ALL OUR SHACKLES, WE'LL SEEK OUR NAME THAT'S TRUE;
WE'LL SWAP OUT ALL OUR LIVERY TO BLACK, FROM RED OR BLUE;
EST. PS 167 FP
ONE EYED OLOG'S
FLAMEBLOOD ALE
WE'LL FIND OUR LOLLYGAGGING MASTER, AND WE'LL TAKE HIS GUTS FOR GARTERS!
SO DRINK FOR POWER! DRINK FOR THE FLAME! AND FIND THAT BLOODY BLACKENED NAME!
THUM GELLY'S GOT IN QUITE A MESS.
I DARE FEEL SORRY FOR THE LASS
AYE, I KNOW SHE'S NOT A LOT.
BUT SHE'S THE ONLY BET I'VE GOT.
ALSO SHE IS SORTA HOT.

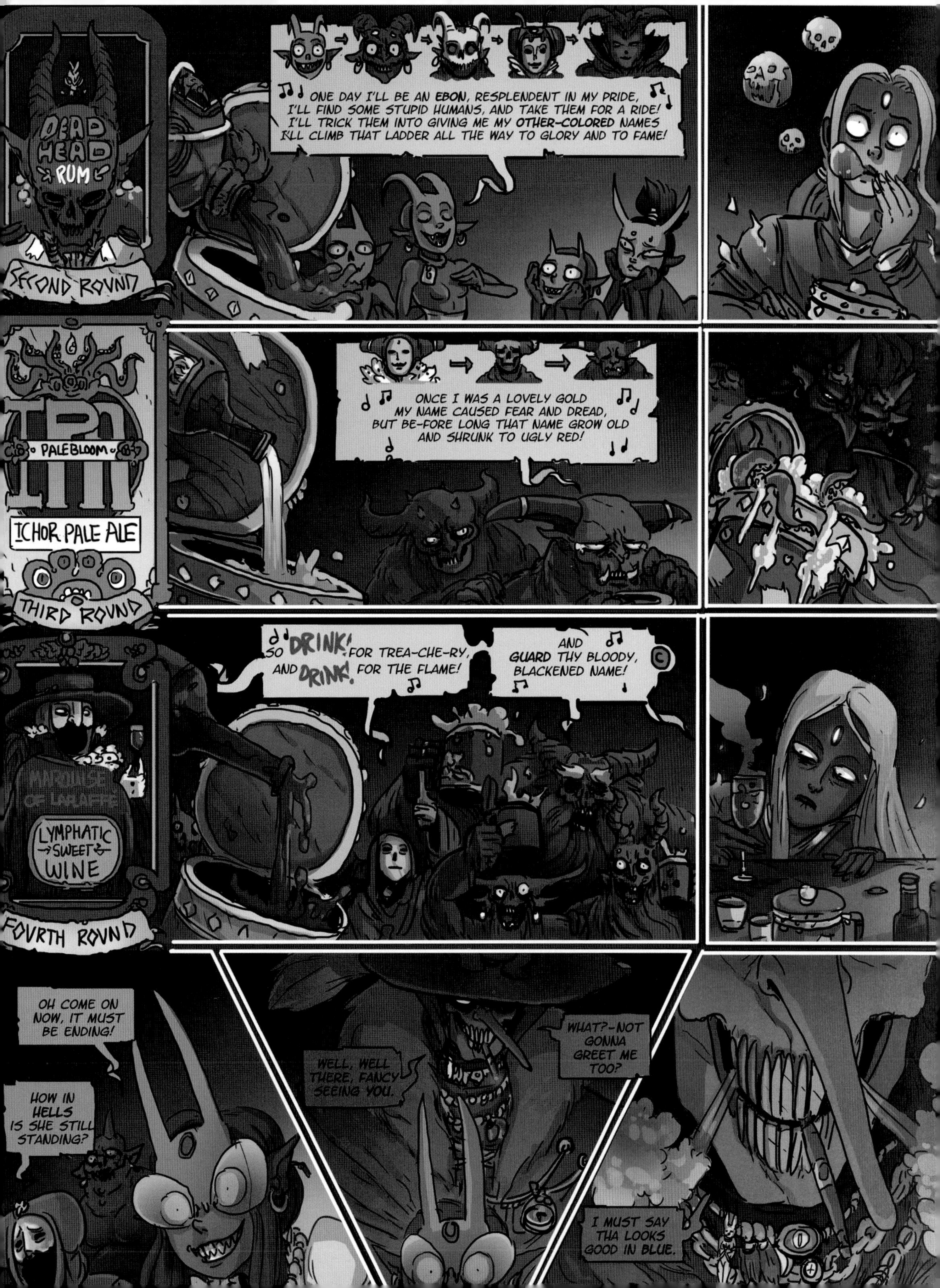
DEAD HEAD RUM
SECOND ROUND
ONE DAY I'LL BE AN EBON, RESPLENDENT IN MY PRIDE, I'LL FIND SOME STUPID HUMANS, AND TAKE THEM FOR A RIDE! I'LL TRICK THEM INTO GIVING ME MY OTHER-COLORED NAMES I'LL CLIMB THAT LADDER ALL THE WAY TO GLORY AND TO FAME!
PALEBLOOM
ICHOR PALE ALE
THIRD ROUND
ONCE I WAS A LOVELY GOLD MY NAME CAUSED FEAR AND DREAD, BUT BE-FORE LONG THAT NAME GROW OLD AND SHRUNK TO UGLY RED!
MARQUISE OF LARAFFE
LYMPHATIC SWEET WINE
FOURTH ROUND
SO DRINK! FOR TREA-CHE-RY, AND DRINK! FOR THE FLAME!
AND GUARD THY BLOODY, BLACKENED NAME!
OH COME ON NOW, IT MUST BE ENDING!
HOW IN HELLS IS SHE STILL STANDING?
WELL, WELL THERE, FANCY SEEING YOU.
WHAT?-NOT GONNA GREET ME TOO?
I MUST SAY THA LOOKS GOOD IN BLUE.

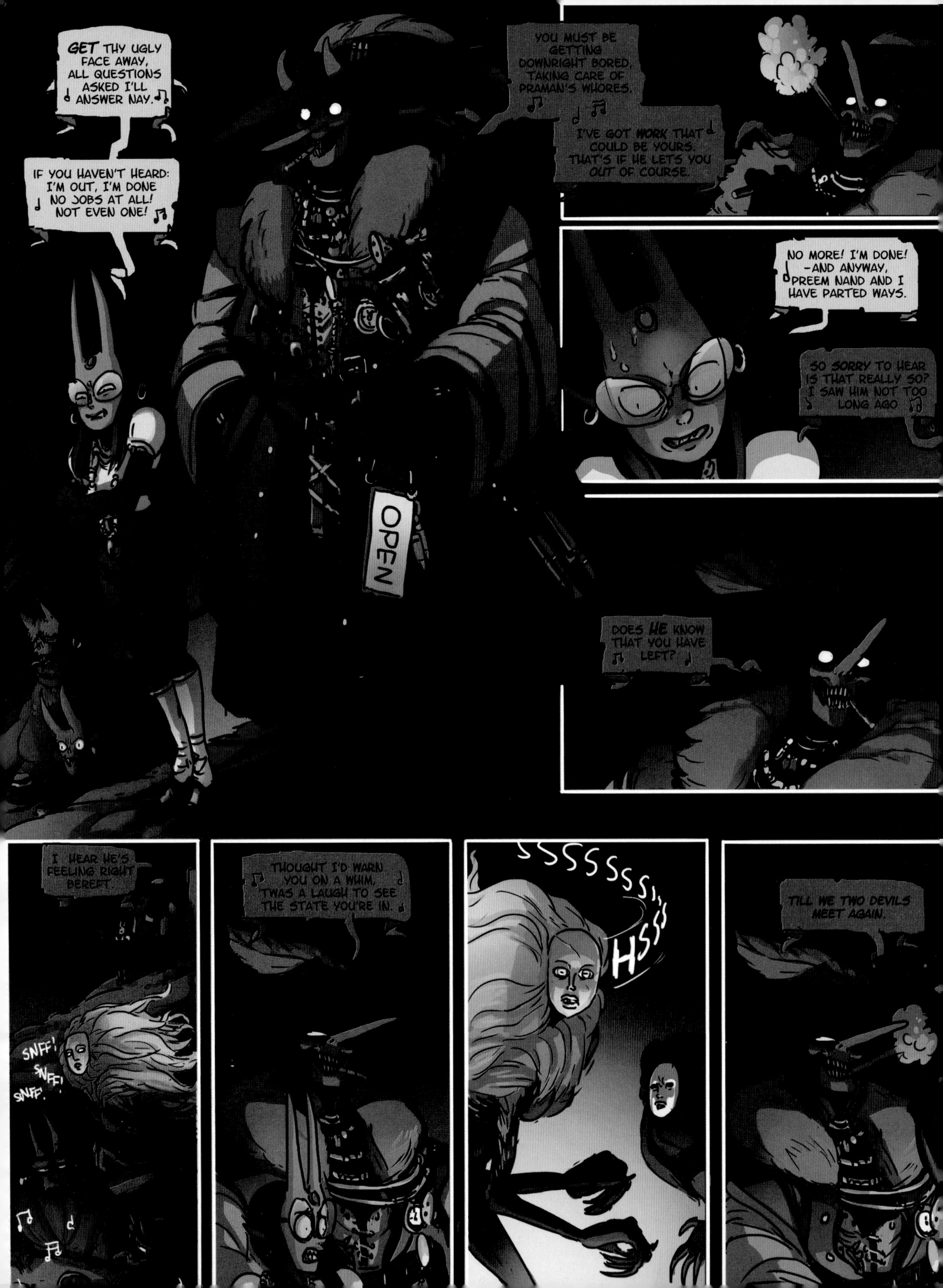
GET THY UGLY FACE AWAY, ALL QUESTIONS ASKED I'LL ANSWER NAY.
IF YOU HAVEN'T HEARD: I'M OUT, I'M DONE NO JOBS AT ALL! NOT EVEN ONE!
YOU MUST BE GETTING DOWNRIGHT BORED, TAKING CARE OF PRAMAN'S WHORES.
I'VE GOT WORK THAT COULD BE YOURS. THAT'S IF HE LETS YOU OUT OF COURSE.
OPEN
NO MORE! I'M DONE! -AND ANYWAY, PREEM NAND AND I HAVE PARTED WAYS.
SO SORRY TO HEAR IS THAT REALLY SO? I SAW HIM NOT TOO LONG AGO
DOES HE KNOW THAT YOU HAVE LEFT?
I HEAR HE'S FEELING RIGHT BEREFT
SNFF! SNFF! SNFF.
THOUGHT I'D WARN YOU ON A WHIM, TWAS A LAUGH TO SEE THE STATE YOU'RE IN.
SSSSSSSS HSSS
TILL WE TWO DEVILS MEET AGAIN.

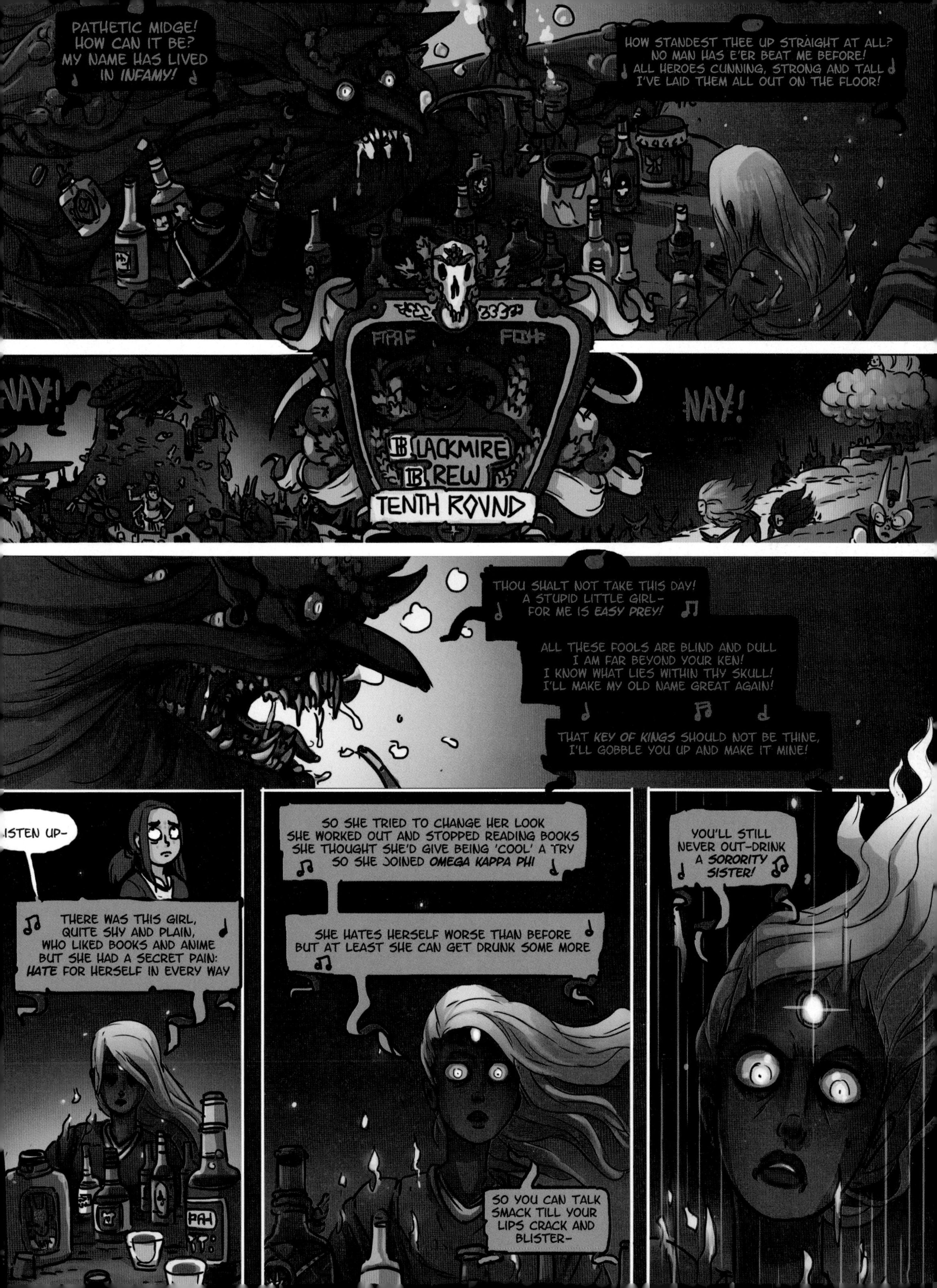

PATHETIC MIDGE! HOW CAN IT BE? MY NAME HAS LIVED IN INFAMY!
HOW STANDEST THEE UP STRAIGHT AT ALL? NO MAN HAS E'ER BEAT ME BEFORE! ALL HEROES CUNNING, STRONG AND TALL I'VE LAID THEM ALL OUT ON THE FLOOR!
BLACKMIRE BREW
TENTH ROVND
NAY!
NAY!
THOU SHALT NOT TAKE THIS DAY! A STUPID LITTLE GIRL– FOR ME IS EASY PREY!
ALL THESE FOOLS ARE BLIND AND DULL I AM FAR BEYOND YOUR KEN! I KNOW WHAT LIES WITHIN THY SKULL! I'LL MAKE MY OLD NAME GREAT AGAIN!
THAT KEY OF KINGS SHOULD NOT BE THINE, I'LL GOBBLE YOU UP AND MAKE IT MINE!
ISTEN UP–
THERE WAS THIS GIRL, QUITE SHY AND PLAIN, WHO LIKED BOOKS AND ANIME BUT SHE HAD A SECRET PAIN: HATE FOR HERSELF IN EVERY WAY
SO SHE TRIED TO CHANGE HER LOOK SHE WORKED OUT AND STOPPED READING BOOKS SHE THOUGHT SHE'D GIVE BEING 'COOL' A TRY SO SHE JOINED OMEGA KAPPA PHI
SHE HATES HERSELF WORSE THAN BEFORE BUT AT LEAST SHE CAN GET DRUNK SOME MORE
SO YOU CAN TALK SMACK TILL YOUR LIPS CRACK AND BLISTER–
YOU'LL STILL NEVER OUT-DRINK A SORORITY SISTER!

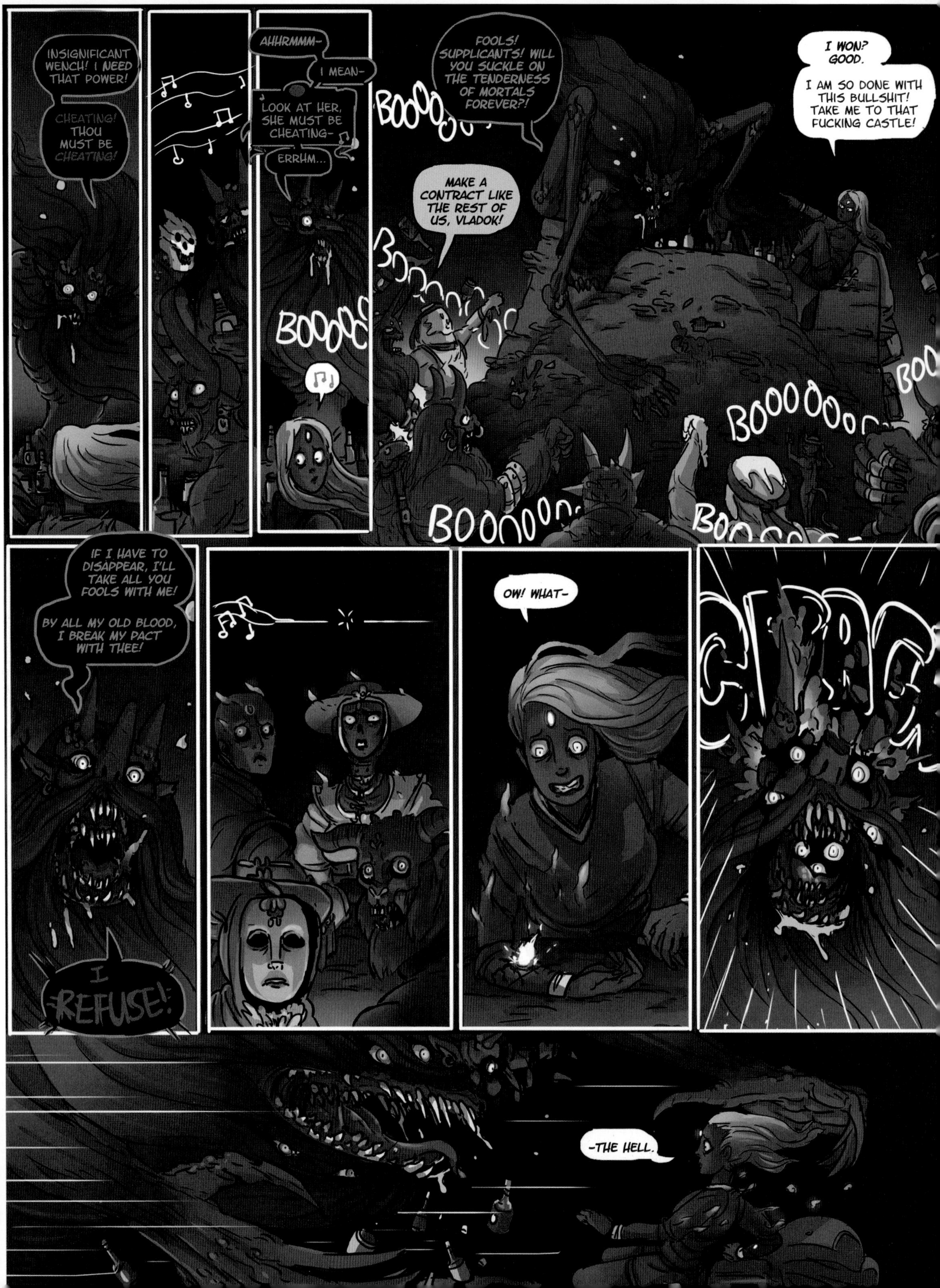
INSIGNIFICANT WENCH! I NEED THAT POWER!
CHEATING! THOU MUST BE CHEATING!
AHHRMMM-
I MEAN-
LOOK AT HER, SHE MUST BE CHEATING-
ERRHM...
BOOOOO
FOOLS! SUPPLICANTS! WILL YOU SUCKLE ON THE TENDERNESS OF MORTALS FOREVER?!
BOOOOO
MAKE A CONTRACT LIKE THE REST OF US, VLADOK!
BOOOOO
I WON? GOOD.
I AM SO DONE WITH THIS BULLSHIT! TAKE ME TO THAT FUCKING CASTLE!
BOOOOO
BOOOOO
BOOOOO
IF I HAVE TO DISAPPEAR, I'LL TAKE ALL YOU FOOLS WITH ME!
BY ALL MY OLD BLOOD, I BREAK MY PACT WITH THEE!
I REFUSE!
OW! WHAT-
-THE HELL.

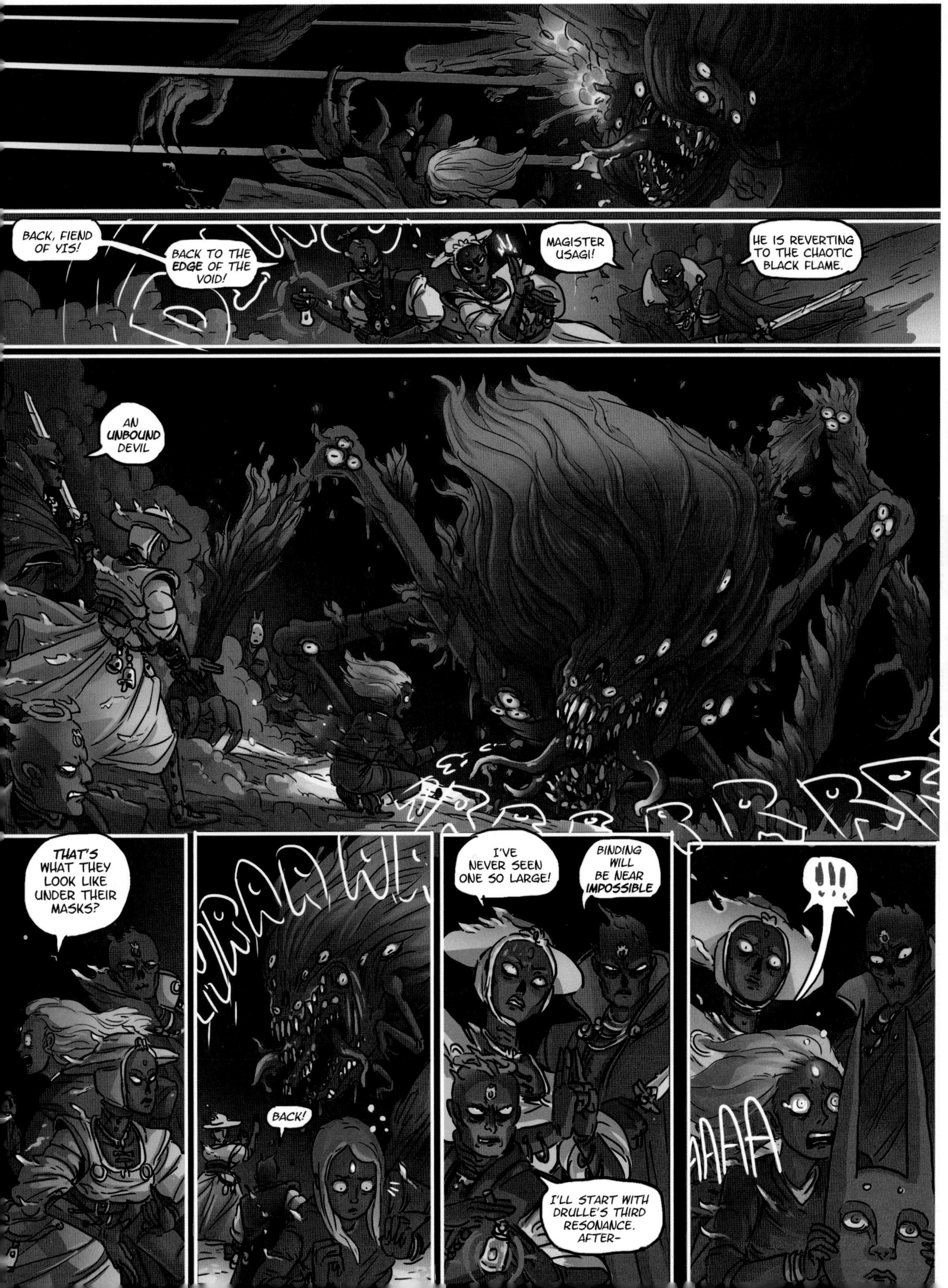
BACK, FIEND OF YIS!
BACK TO THE EDGE OF THE VOID!
MAGISTER USAGI!
HE IS REVERTING TO THE CHAOTIC BLACK FLAME.
AN UNBOUND DEVIL
RRRRR
THAT'S WHAT THEY LOOK LIKE UNDER THEIR MASKS?
RAAAWL
BACK!
I'VE NEVER SEEN ONE SO LARGE!
BINDING WILL BE NEAR IMPOSSIBLE
I'LL START WITH DRULLE'S THIRD RESONANCE. AFTER-
!!!
AAAA

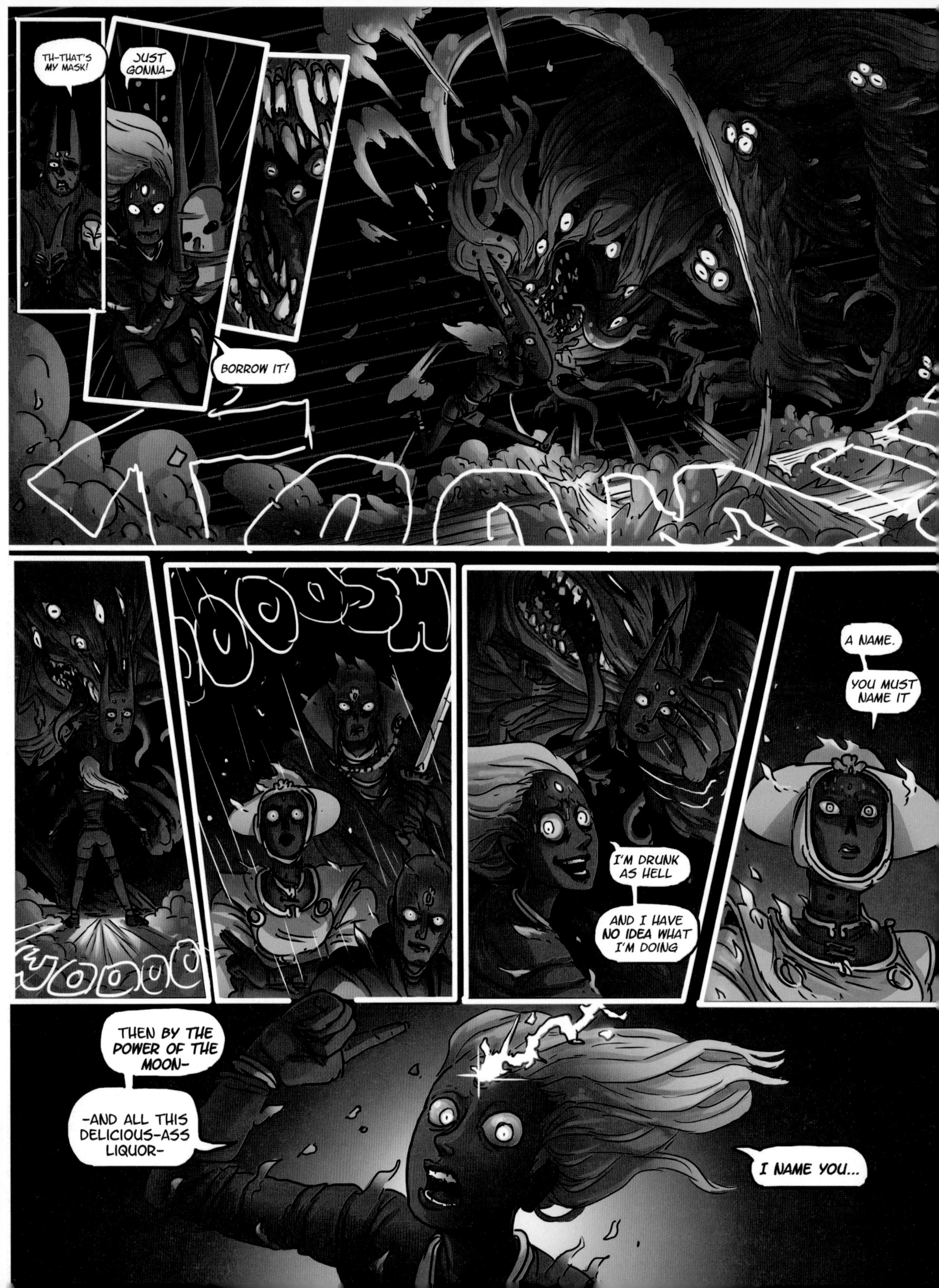
TH-THAT'S MY MASK!
JUST GONNA-
BORROW IT!
I'M DRUNK AS HELL
AND I HAVE NO IDEA WHAT I'M DOING
A NAME.
YOU MUST NAME IT
THEN BY THE POWER OF THE MOON-
-AND ALL THIS DELICIOUS-ASS LIQUOR-
I NAME YOU...

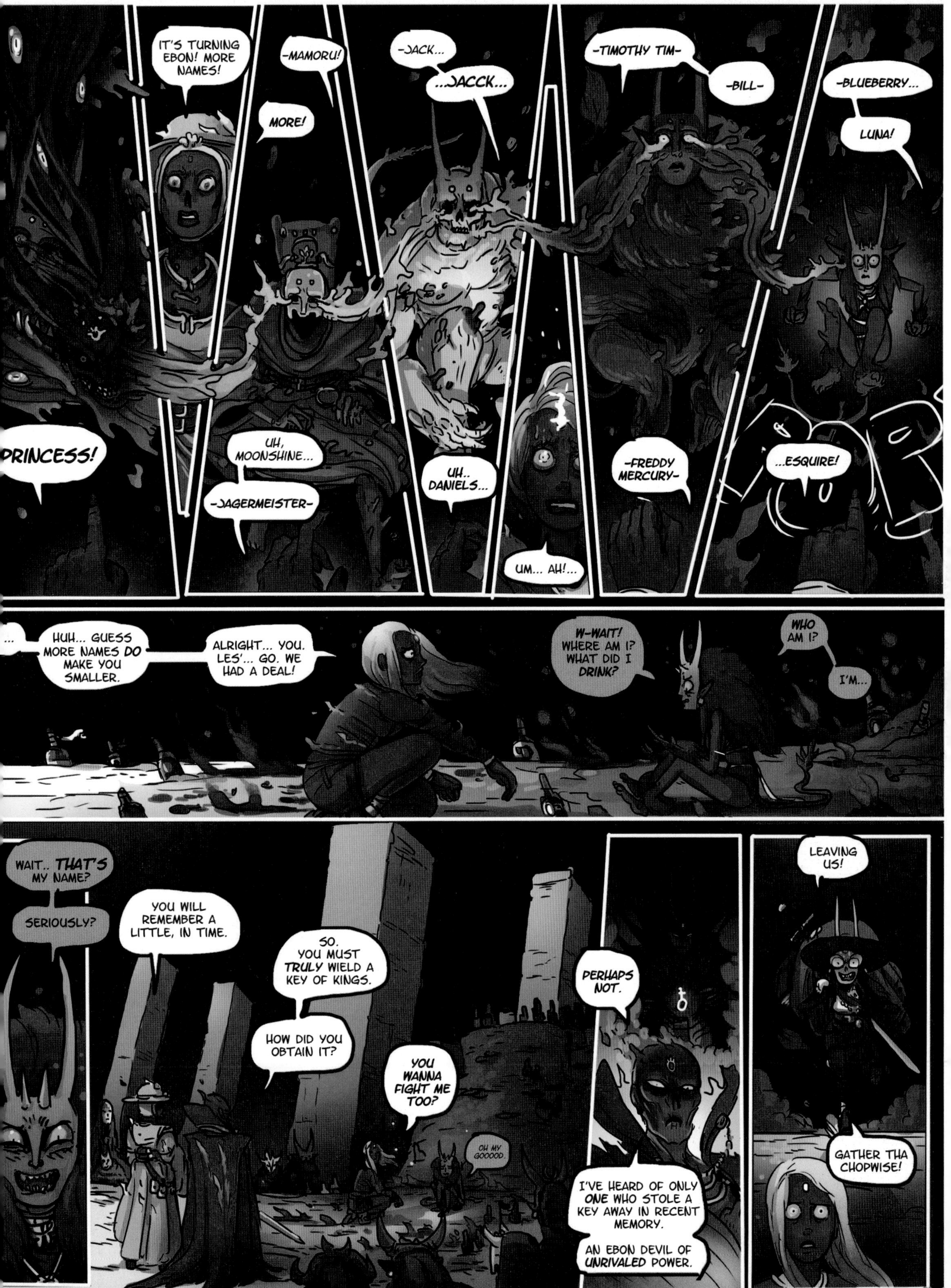
PRINCESS!
IT'S TURNING EBON! MORE NAMES!
-MAMORU!
MORE!
UH, MOONSHINE...
-JAGERMEISTER-
-JACK...
...JACCK...
UH.. DANIELS...
UM... AH!...
-TIMOTHY TIM-
-BILL-
-FREDDY MERCURY-
-BLUEBERRY...
LUNA!
...ESQUIRE!
...
HUH... GUESS MORE NAMES DO MAKE YOU SMALLER.
ALRIGHT... YOU. LES'... GO. WE HAD A DEAL!
W-WAIT! WHERE AM I? WHAT DID I DRINK?
WHO AM I?
I'M...
WAIT.. THAT'S MY NAME?
SERIOUSLY?
YOU WILL REMEMBER A LITTLE, IN TIME.
SO. YOU MUST TRULY WIELD A KEY OF KINGS.
HOW DID YOU OBTAIN IT?
YOU WANNA FIGHT ME TOO?
OH MY GOOOOD.
PERHAPS NOT.
I'VE HEARD OF ONLY ONE WHO STOLE A KEY AWAY IN RECENT MEMORY.
AN EBON DEVIL OF UNRIVALED POWER.
LEAVING US!
GATHER THA CHOPWISE!

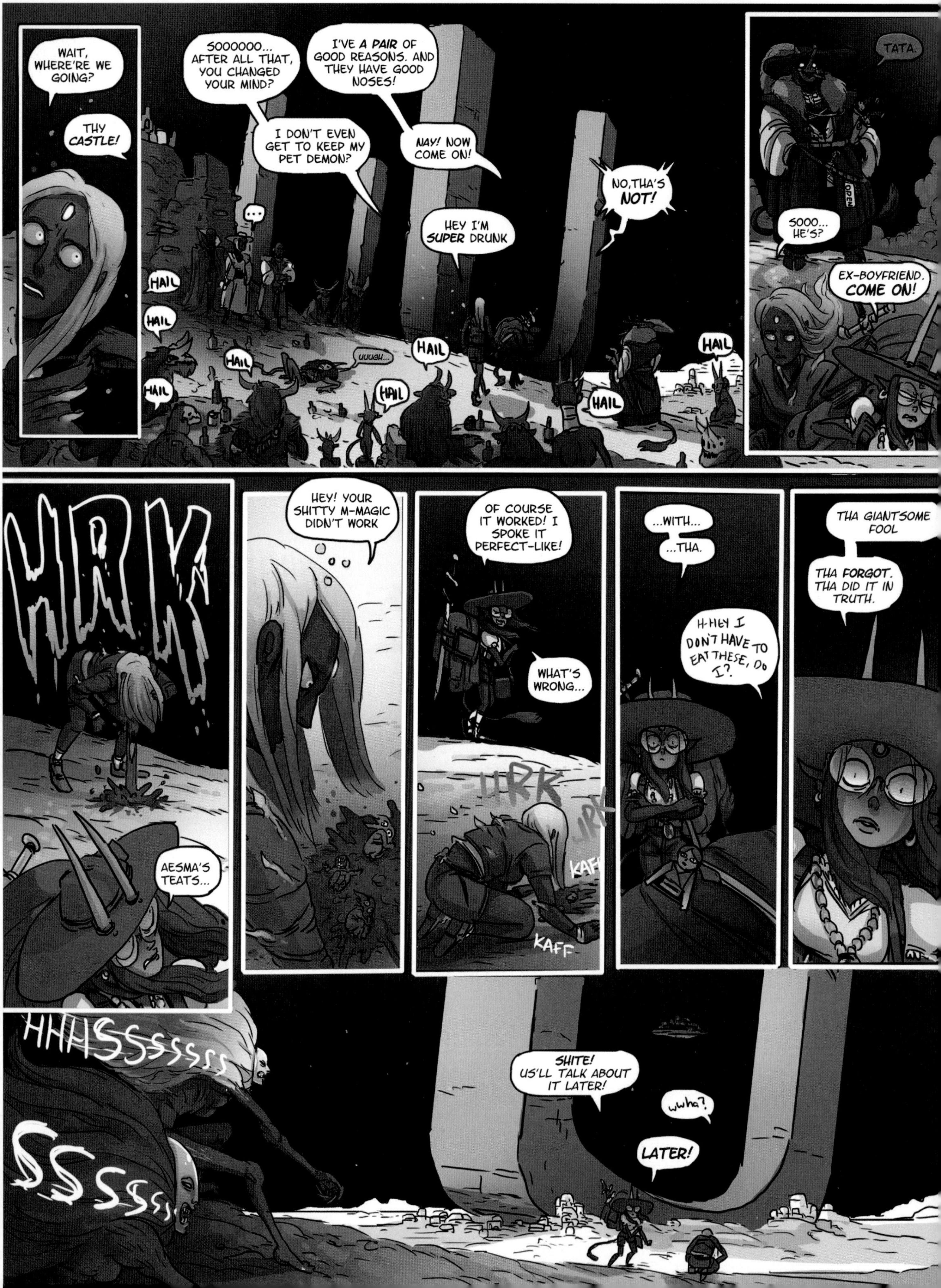
WAIT, WHERE'RE WE GOING?
THY CASTLE!
SOOOOOO... AFTER ALL THAT, YOU CHANGED YOUR MIND?
I DON'T EVEN GET TO KEEP MY PET DEMON?
I'VE A PAIR OF GOOD REASONS. AND THEY HAVE GOOD NOSES!
NAY! NOW COME ON!
...
HEY I'M SUPER DRUNK
NO, THA'S NOT!
HAIL
HAIL
HAIL
HAIL
uuugh...
HAIL
HAIL
HAIL
HAIL
TATA.
SOOO... HE'S?
EX-BOYFRIEND. COME ON!
HRK
AESMA'S TEATS...
HEY! YOUR SHITTY M-MAGIC DIDN'T WORK
OF COURSE IT WORKED! I SPOKE IT PERFECT-LIKE!
WHAT'S WRONG...
HRK
KAFF
KAFF
...WITH...
...THA.
H-HEY I DON'T HAVE TO EAT THESE, DO I?
THA GIANTSOME FOOL
THA FORGOT. THA DID IT IN TRUTH.
HHHSSSSSSSS
SSSSsss
SHITE! US'LL TALK ABOUT IT LATER!
wwha?
LATER!

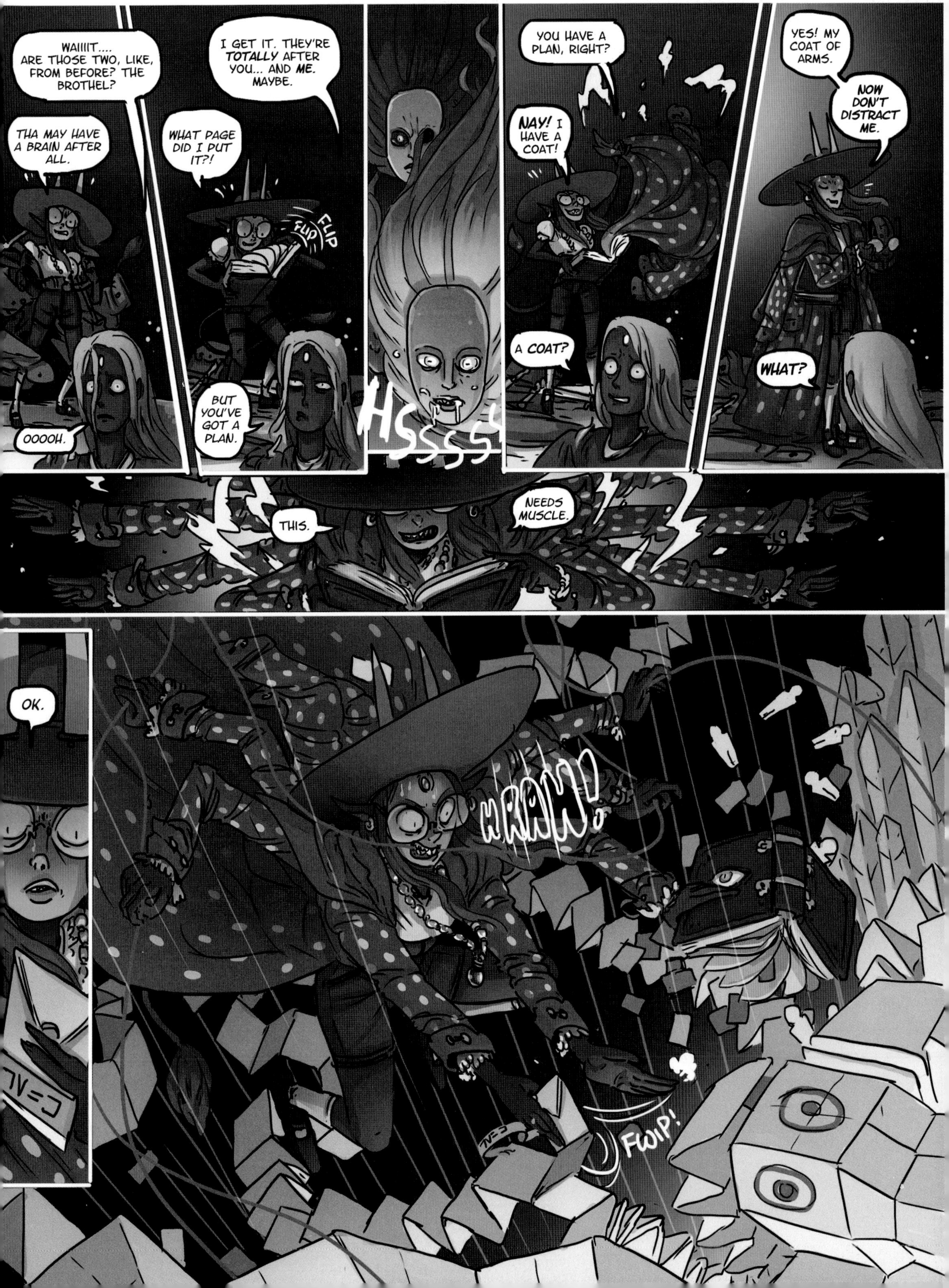
WAIIIIT.... ARE THOSE TWO, LIKE, FROM BEFORE? THE BROTHEL?
THA MAY HAVE A BRAIN AFTER ALL.
OOOOH.
I GET IT. THEY'RE TOTALLY AFTER YOU... AND ME. MAYBE.
WHAT PAGE DID I PUT IT?!
FLIP FLIP
BUT YOU'VE GOT A PLAN.
HSSSSS
YOU HAVE A PLAN, RIGHT?
NAY! I HAVE A COAT!
A COAT?
YES! MY COAT OF ARMS.
NOW DON'T DISTRACT ME.
WHAT?
THIS.
NEEDS MUSCLE.
OK.
HRAAH!
FWIP!

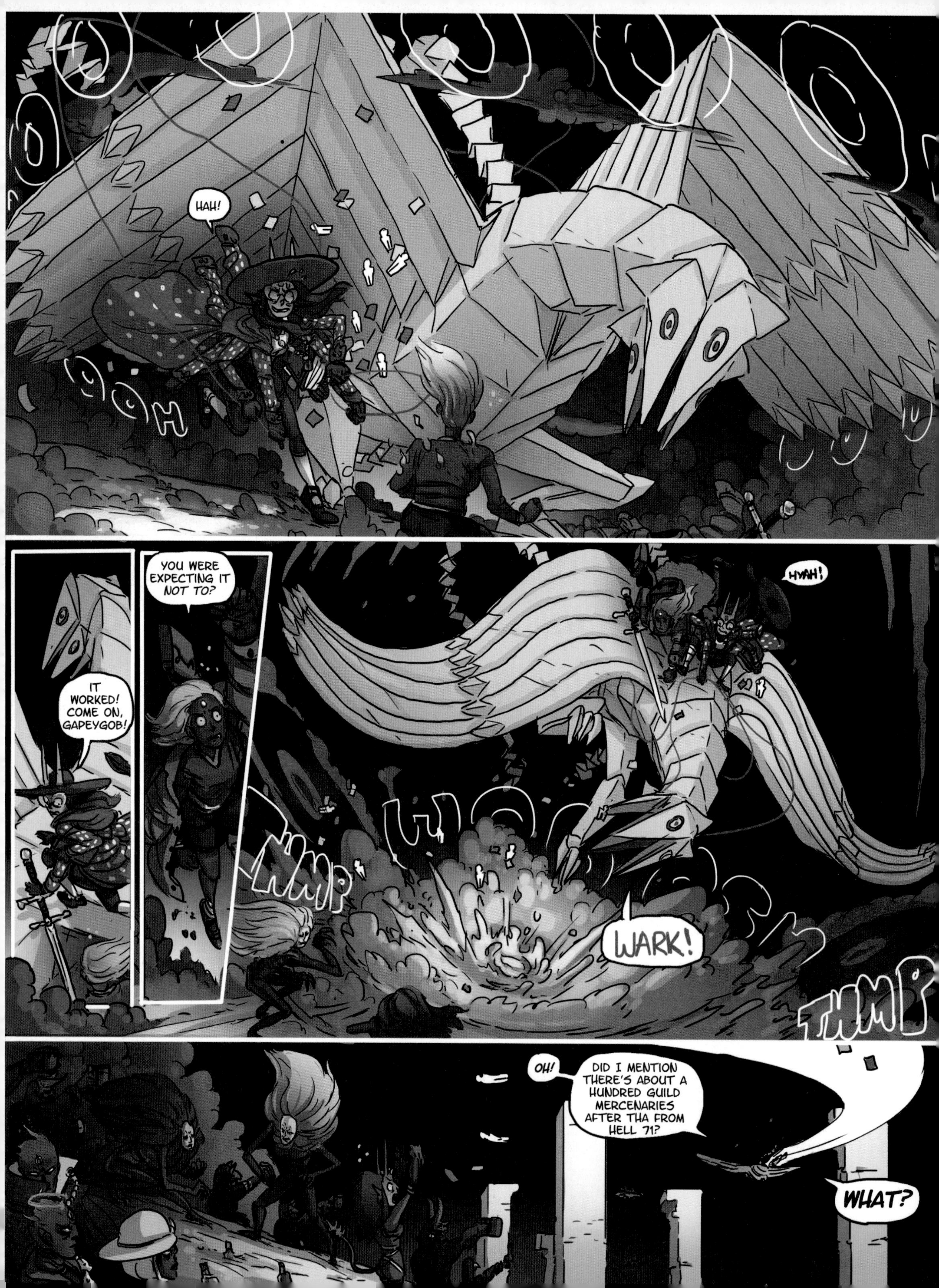
HAH!
HOOH
HYAH!
IT WORKED! COME ON, GAPEYGOB!
YOU WERE EXPECTING IT NOT TO?
THMP
WARK!
THMP
OH!
DID I MENTION THERE'S ABOUT A HUNDRED GUILD MERCENARIES AFTER THA FROM HELL 71?
WHAT?

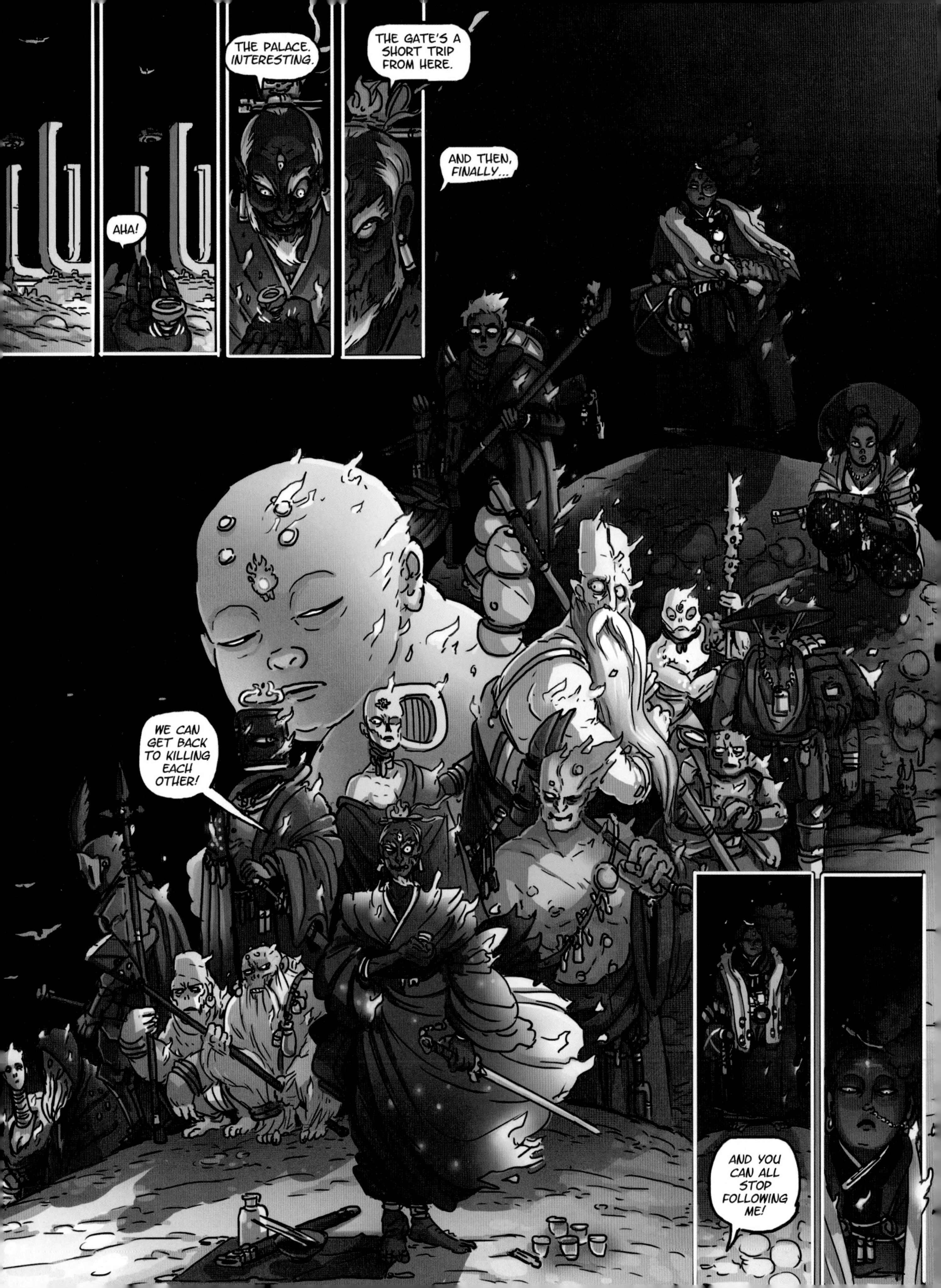
AHA!
THE PALACE. INTERESTING.
THE GATE'S A SHORT TRIP FROM HERE.
AND THEN, FINALLY...
WE CAN GET BACK TO KILLING EACH OTHER!
AND YOU CAN ALL STOP FOLLOWING ME!

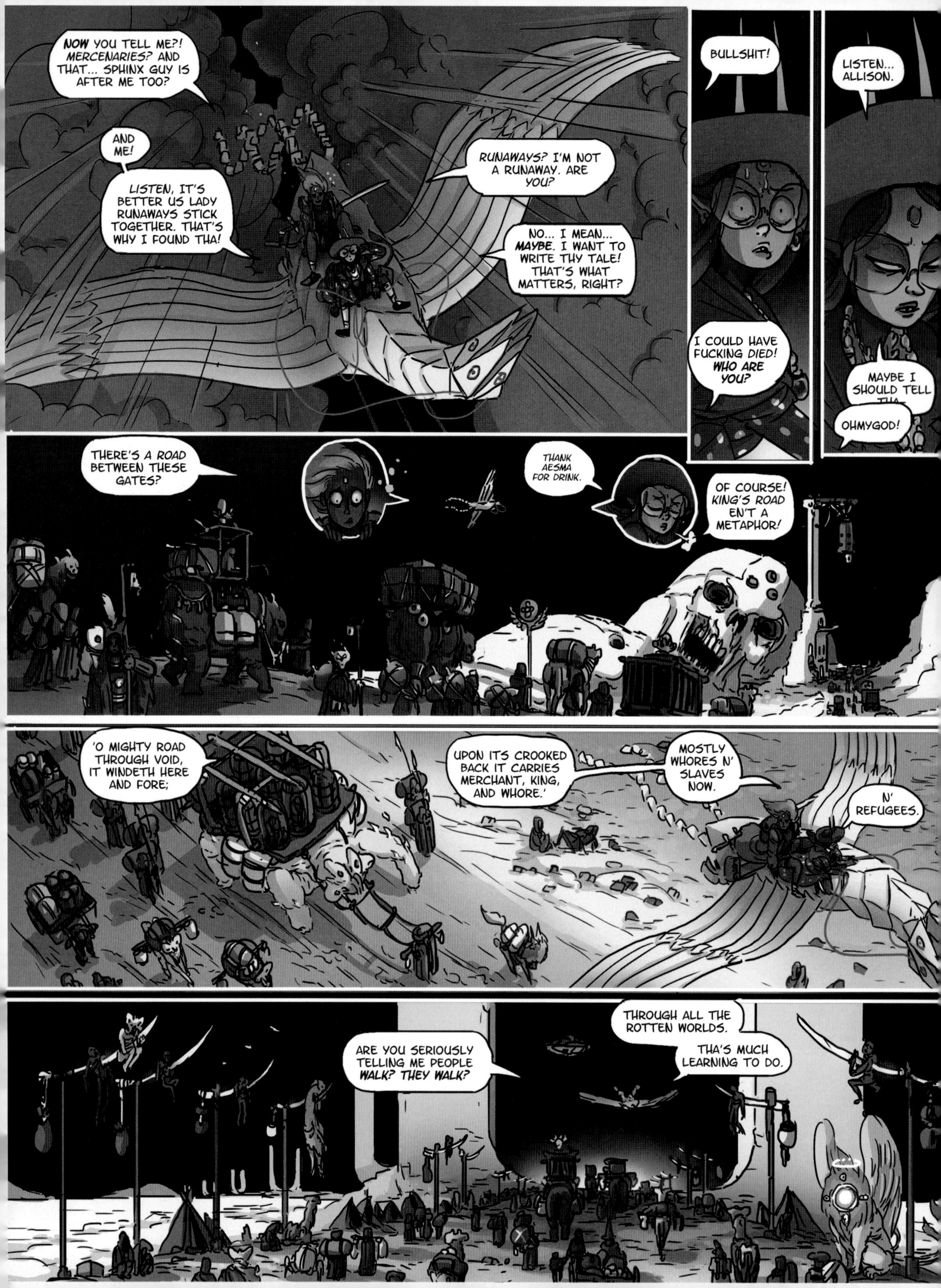
NOW YOU TELL ME?! MERCENARIES? AND THAT... SPHINX GUY IS AFTER ME TOO?
AND ME!
LISTEN, IT'S BETTER US LADY RUNAWAYS STICK TOGETHER. THAT'S WHY I FOUND THA!
RUNAWAYS? I'M NOT A RUNAWAY. ARE YOU?
NO... I MEAN... MAYBE. I WANT TO WRITE THY TALE! THAT'S WHAT MATTERS, RIGHT?
BULLSHIT!
I COULD HAVE FUCKING DIED! WHO ARE YOU?
LISTEN... ALLISON.
MAYBE I SHOULD TELL THA-
OHMYGOD!
THERE'S A ROAD BETWEEN THESE GATES?
THANK AESMA FOR DRINK.
OF COURSE! KING'S ROAD EN'T A METAPHOR!
'O MIGHTY ROAD THROUGH VOID, IT WINDETH HERE AND FORE;
UPON ITS CROOKED BACK IT CARRIES MERCHANT, KING, AND WHORE.'
MOSTLY WHORES N' SLAVES NOW.
N' REFUGEES.
ARE YOU SERIOUSLY TELLING ME PEOPLE WALK? THEY WALK?
THROUGH ALL THE ROTTEN WORLDS.
THA'S MUCH LEARNING TO DO.

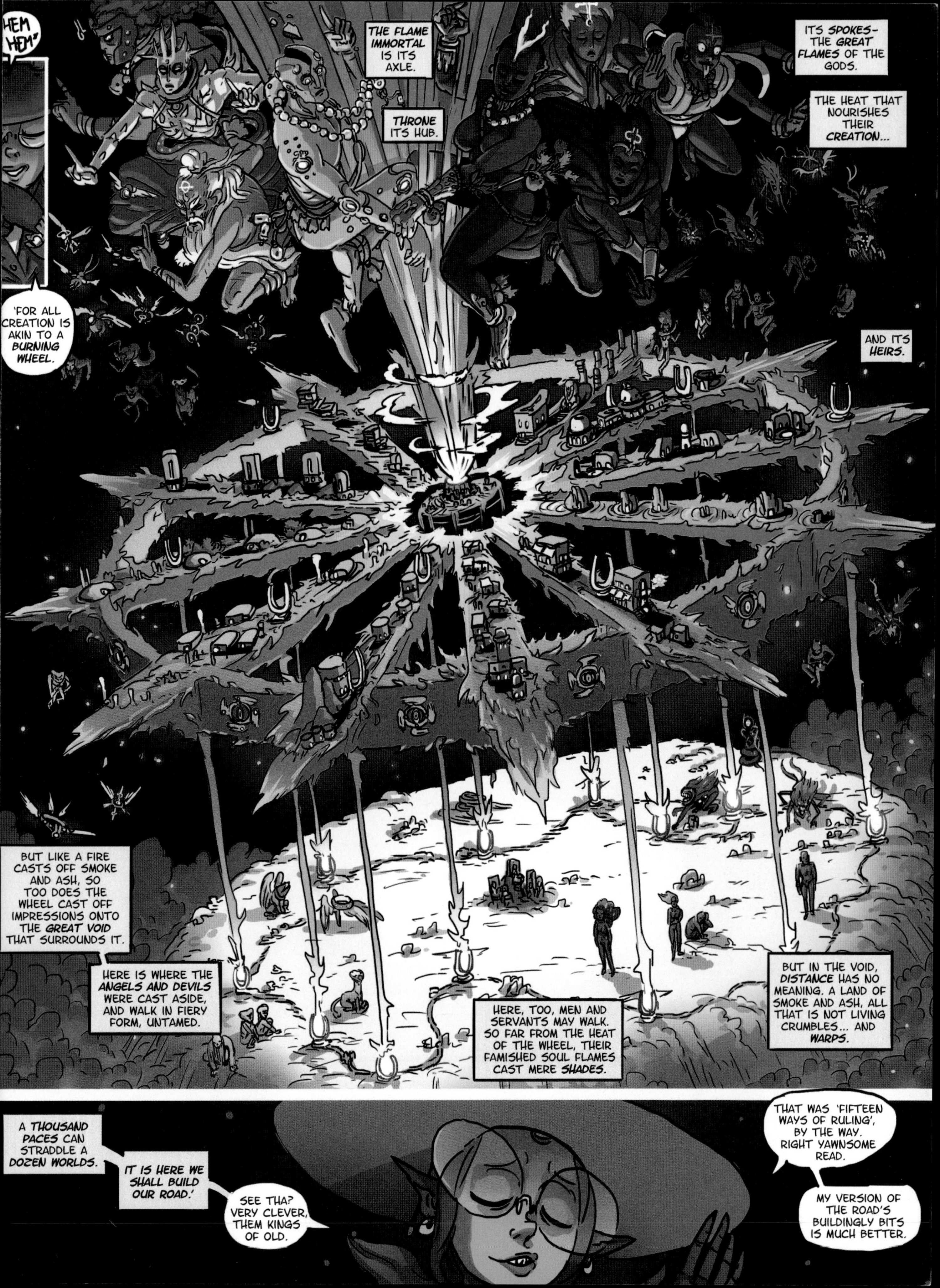
HEM HEM
'FOR ALL CREATION IS AKIN TO A BURNING WHEEL.
THE FLAME IMMORTAL IS ITS AXLE.
THRONE ITS HUB.
ITS SPOKES– THE GREAT FLAMES OF THE GODS.
THE HEAT THAT NOURISHES THEIR CREATION...
AND ITS HEIRS.
BUT LIKE A FIRE CASTS OFF SMOKE AND ASH, SO TOO DOES THE WHEEL CAST OFF IMPRESSIONS ONTO THE GREAT VOID THAT SURROUNDS IT.
HERE IS WHERE THE ANGELS AND DEVILS WERE CAST ASIDE, AND WALK IN FIERY FORM, UNTAMED.
HERE, TOO, MEN AND SERVANTS MAY WALK. SO FAR FROM THE HEAT OF THE WHEEL, THEIR FAMISHED SOUL FLAMES CAST MERE SHADES.
BUT IN THE VOID, DISTANCE HAS NO MEANING. A LAND OF SMOKE AND ASH, ALL THAT IS NOT LIVING CRUMBLES... AND WARPS.
A THOUSAND PACES CAN STRADDLE A DOZEN WORLDS.
IT IS HERE WE SHALL BUILD OUR ROAD.'
SEE THA? VERY CLEVER, THEM KINGS OF OLD.
THAT WAS 'FIFTEEN WAYS OF RULING', BY THE WAY. RIGHT YAWNSOME READ.
MY VERSION OF THE ROAD'S BUILDINGLY BITS IS MUCH BETTER.

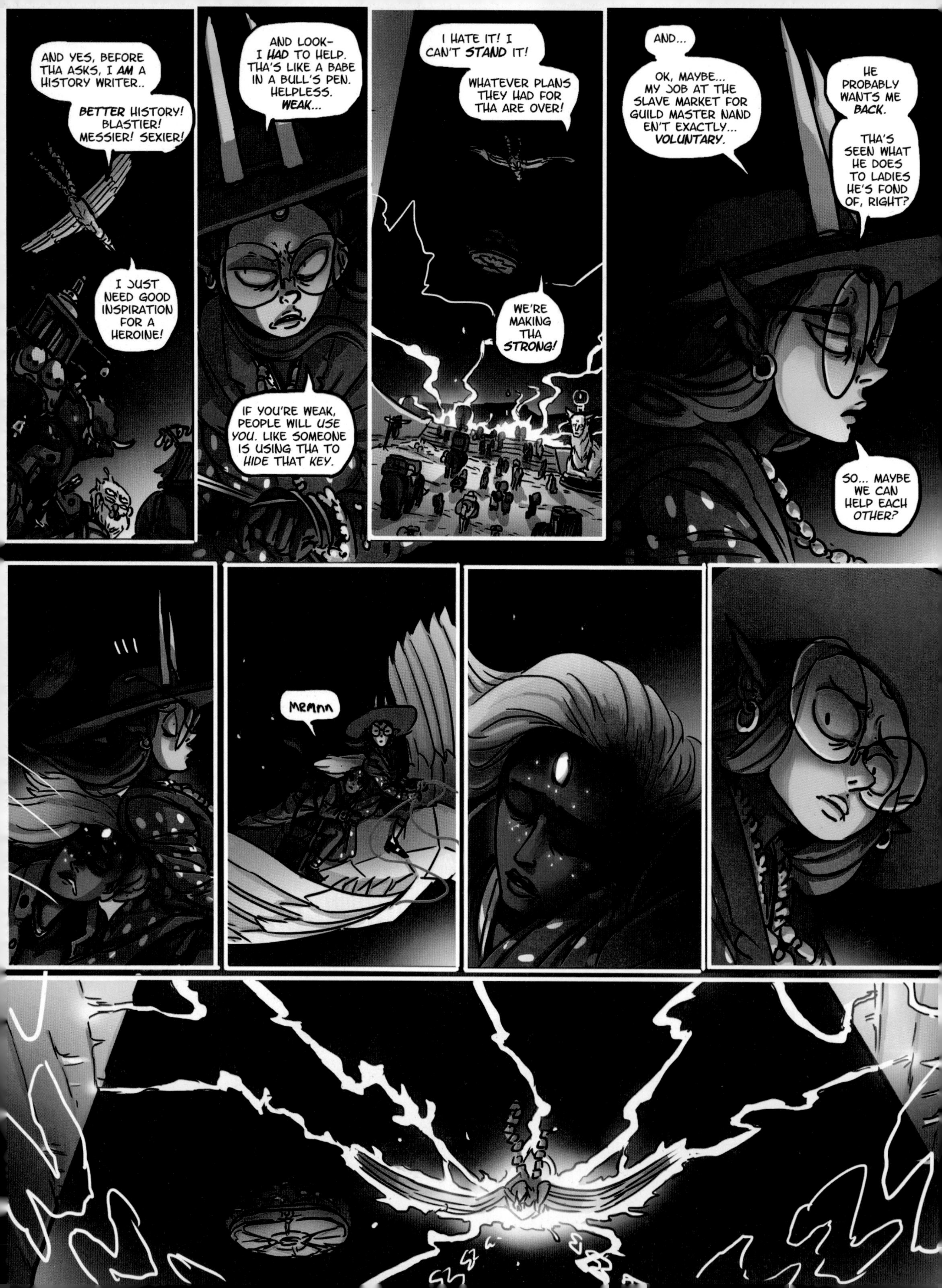
AND YES, BEFORE THA ASKS, I AM A HISTORY WRITER..
BETTER HISTORY! BLASTIER! MESSIER! SEXIER!
I JUST NEED GOOD INSPIRATION FOR A HEROINE!
AND LOOK– I HAD TO HELP. THA'S LIKE A BABE IN A BULL'S PEN. HELPLESS. WEAK...
IF YOU'RE WEAK, PEOPLE WILL USE YOU. LIKE SOMEONE IS USING THA TO HIDE THAT KEY.
I HATE IT! I CAN'T STAND IT!
WHATEVER PLANS THEY HAD FOR THA ARE OVER!
WE'RE MAKING THA STRONG!
AND...
OK, MAYBE... MY JOB AT THE SLAVE MARKET FOR GUILD MASTER NAND EN'T EXACTLY... VOLUNTARY.
HE PROBABLY WANTS ME BACK.
THA'S SEEN WHAT HE DOES TO LADIES HE'S FOND OF, RIGHT?
SO... MAYBE WE CAN HELP EACH OTHER?
...
MRMNN

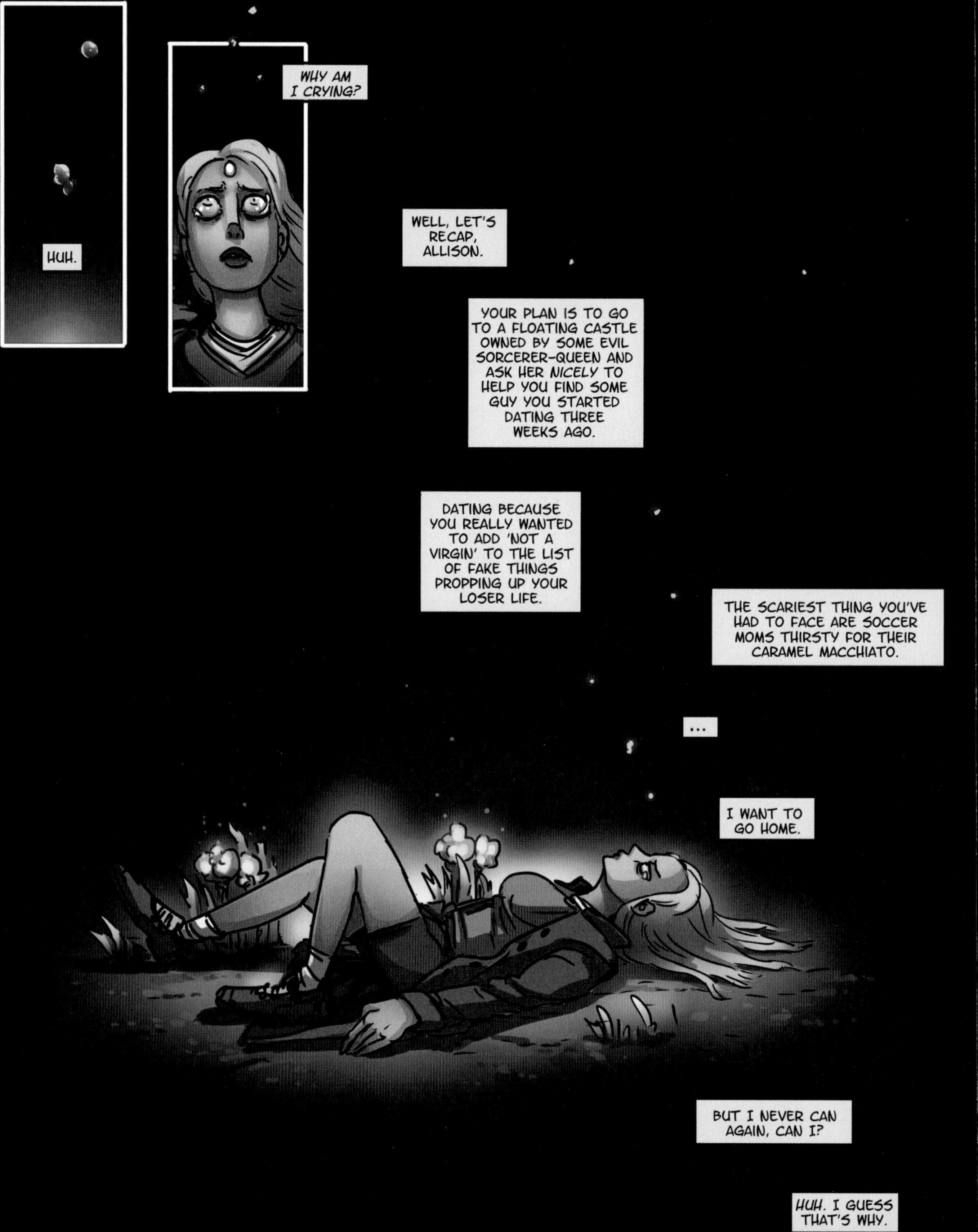
HUH.
WHY AM I CRYING?
WELL, LET'S RECAP, ALLISON.
YOUR PLAN IS TO GO TO A FLOATING CASTLE OWNED BY SOME EVIL SORCERER-QUEEN AND ASK HER NICELY TO HELP YOU FIND SOME GUY YOU STARTED DATING THREE WEEKS AGO.
DATING BECAUSE YOU REALLY WANTED TO ADD 'NOT A VIRGIN' TO THE LIST OF FAKE THINGS PROPPING UP YOUR LOSER LIFE.
THE SCARIEST THING YOU'VE HAD TO FACE ARE SOCCER MOMS THIRSTY FOR THEIR CARAMEL MACCHIATO.
...
I WANT TO GO HOME.
BUT I NEVER CAN AGAIN, CAN I?
HUH. I GUESS THAT'S WHY.

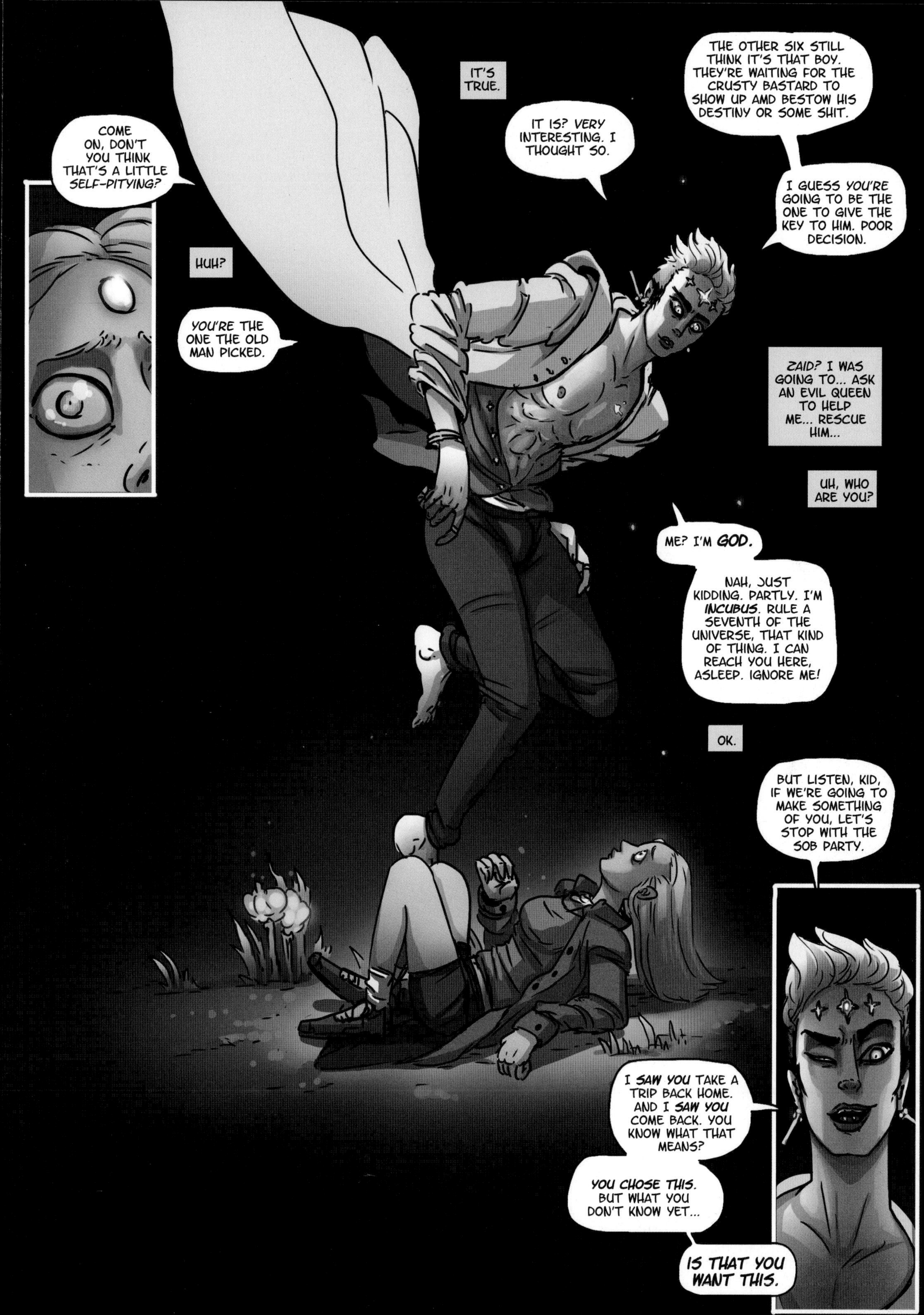

COME ON, DON'T YOU THINK THAT'S A LITTLE SELF-PITYING?
IT'S TRUE.
IT IS? VERY INTERESTING. I THOUGHT SO.
THE OTHER SIX STILL THINK IT'S THAT BOY. THEY'RE WAITING FOR THE CRUSTY BASTARD TO SHOW UP AMD BESTOW HIS DESTINY OR SOME SHIT.
I GUESS YOU'RE GOING TO BE THE ONE TO GIVE THE KEY TO HIM. POOR DECISION.
HUH?
YOU'RE THE ONE THE OLD MAN PICKED.
ZAID? I WAS GOING TO... ASK AN EVIL QUEEN TO HELP ME... RESCUE HIM...
UH, WHO ARE YOU?
ME? I'M GOD.
NAH, JUST KIDDING. PARTLY. I'M INCUBUS. RULE A SEVENTH OF THE UNIVERSE, THAT KIND OF THING. I CAN REACH YOU HERE, ASLEEP. IGNORE ME!
OK.
BUT LISTEN, KID, IF WE'RE GOING TO MAKE SOMETHING OF YOU, LET'S STOP WITH THE SOB PARTY.
I SAW YOU TAKE A TRIP BACK HOME. AND I SAW YOU COME BACK. YOU KNOW WHAT THAT MEANS?
YOU CHOSE THIS. BUT WHAT YOU DON'T KNOW YET...
IS THAT YOU WANT THIS.

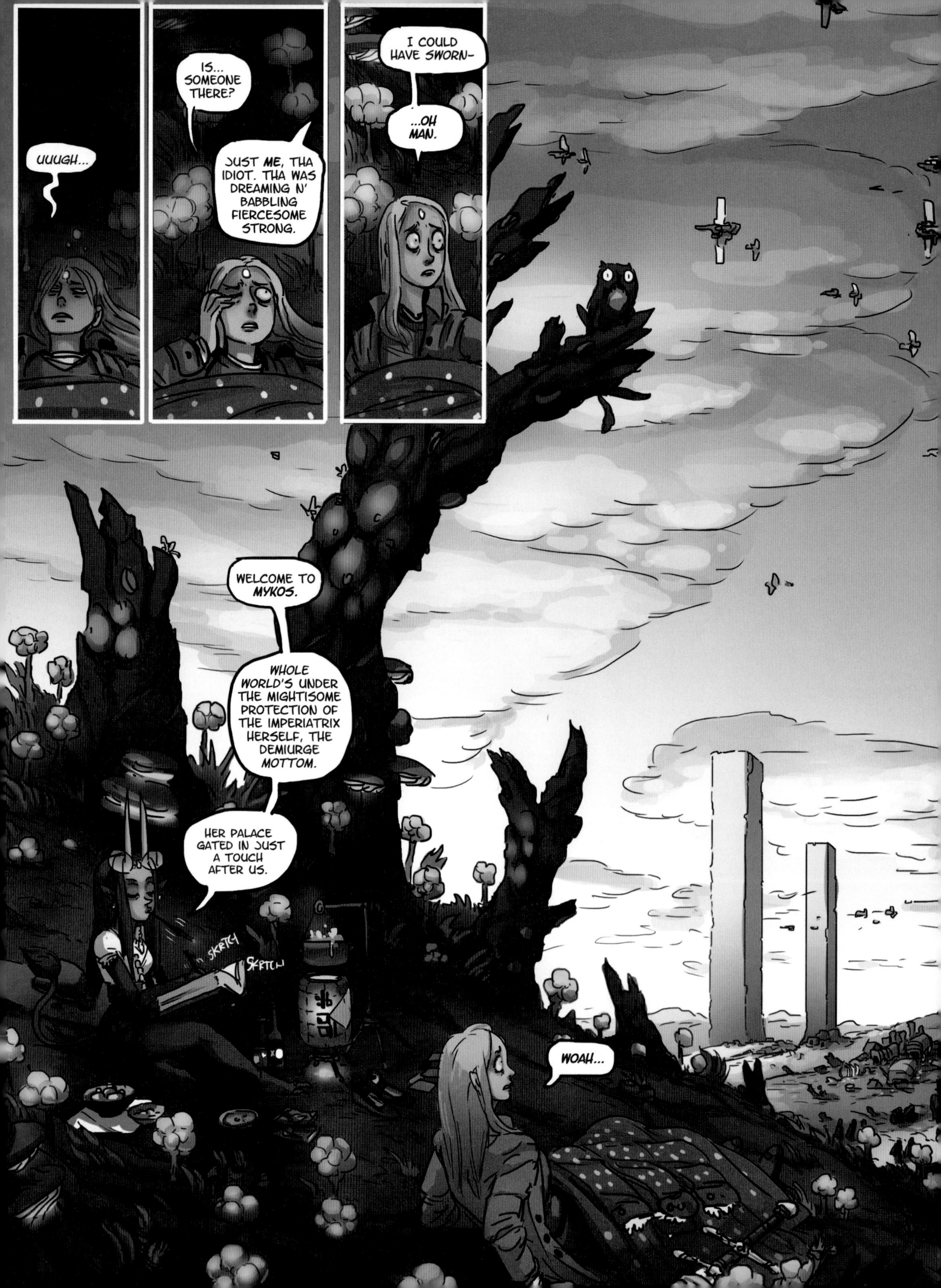
UUUGH...
IS... SOMEONE THERE?
JUST ME, THA IDIOT. THA WAS DREAMING N' BABBLING FIERCESOME STRONG.
I COULD HAVE SWORN-
...OH MAN.
WELCOME TO MYKOS.
WHOLE WORLD'S UNDER THE MIGHTISOME PROTECTION OF THE IMPERIATRIX HERSELF, THE DEMIURGE MOTTOM.
HER PALACE GATED IN JUST A TOUCH AFTER US.
SKRTCH
SKRTCH
WOAH...

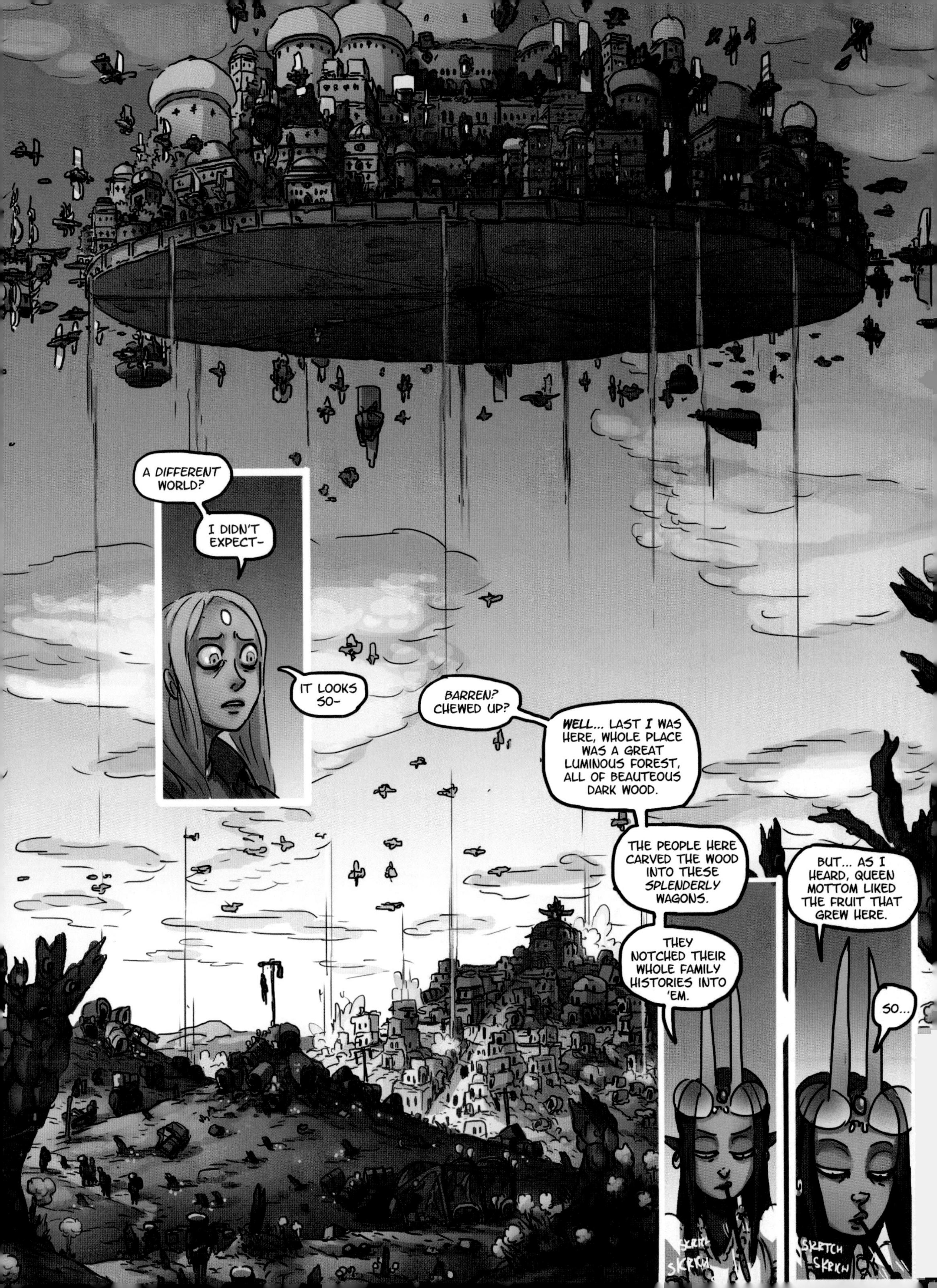
A DIFFERENT WORLD?
I DIDN'T EXPECT-
IT LOOKS SO-
BARREN? CHEWED UP?
WELL... LAST I WAS HERE, WHOLE PLACE WAS A GREAT LUMINOUS FOREST, ALL OF BEAUTEOUS DARK WOOD.
THE PEOPLE HERE CARVED THE WOOD INTO THESE SPLENDERLY WAGONS.
THEY NOTCHED THEIR WHOLE FAMILY HISTORIES INTO 'EM.
BUT... AS I HEARD, QUEEN MOTTOM LIKED THE FRUIT THAT GREW HERE.
SO...
SKRTCH SKRTCH
SKRTCH SKRTCH

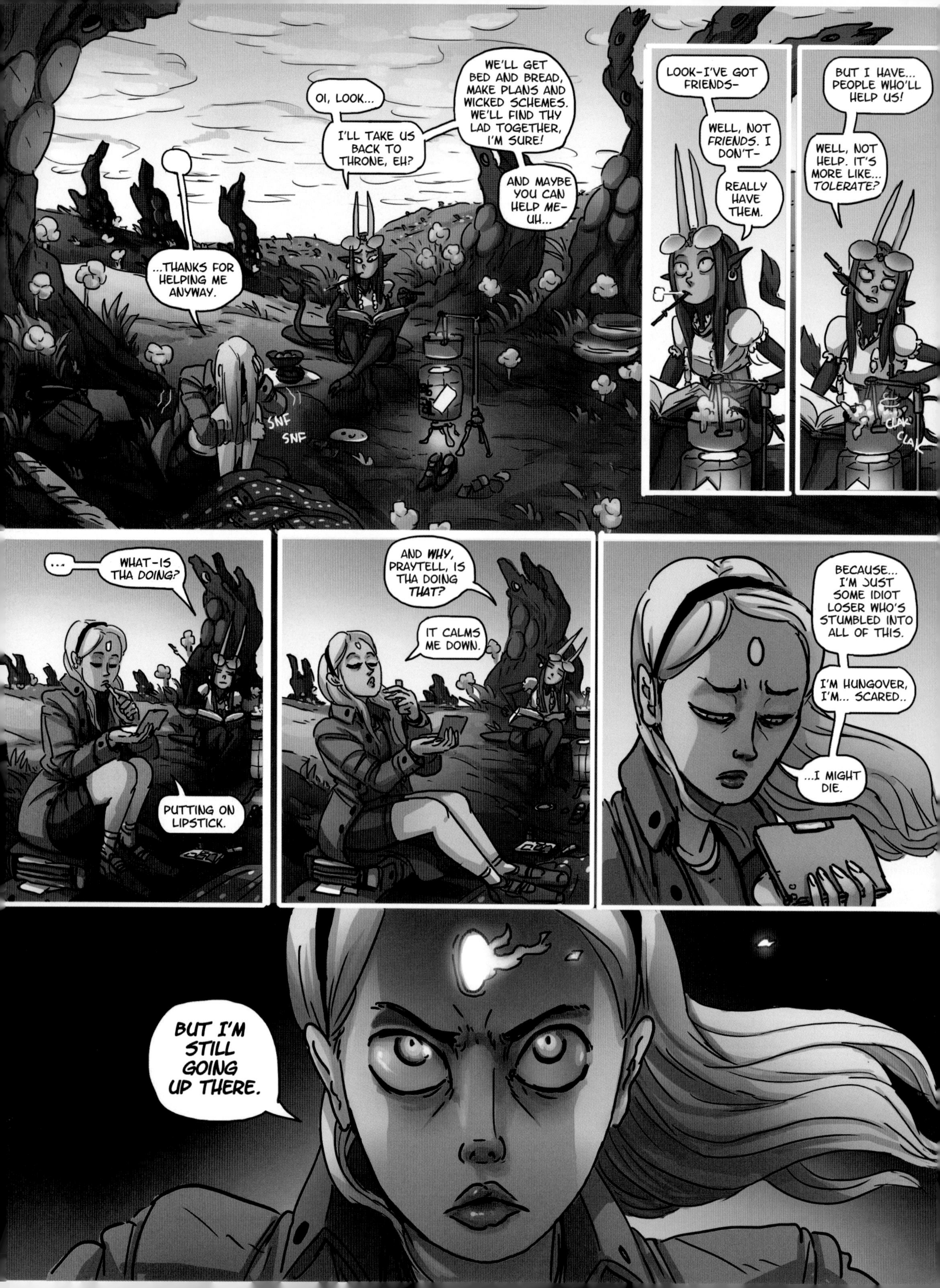

...THANKS FOR HELPING ME ANYWAY.
SNF SNF
OI, LOOK...
I'LL TAKE US BACK TO THRONE, EH?
WE'LL GET BED AND BREAD, MAKE PLANS AND WICKED SCHEMES. WE'LL FIND THY LAD TOGETHER, I'M SURE!
AND MAYBE YOU CAN HELP ME— UH...
LOOK—I'VE GOT FRIENDS—
WELL, NOT FRIENDS. I DON'T—
REALLY HAVE THEM.
BUT I HAVE... PEOPLE WHO'LL HELP US!
WELL, NOT HELP. IT'S MORE LIKE... TOLERATE?
CLAK CLAK
...
WHAT—IS THA DOING?
PUTTING ON LIPSTICK.
AND WHY, PRAYTELL, IS THA DOING THAT?
IT CALMS ME DOWN.
BECAUSE... I'M JUST SOME IDIOT LOSER WHO'S STUMBLED INTO ALL OF THIS.
I'M HUNGOVER, I'M... SCARED..
...I MIGHT DIE.
BUT I'M STILL GOING UP THERE.

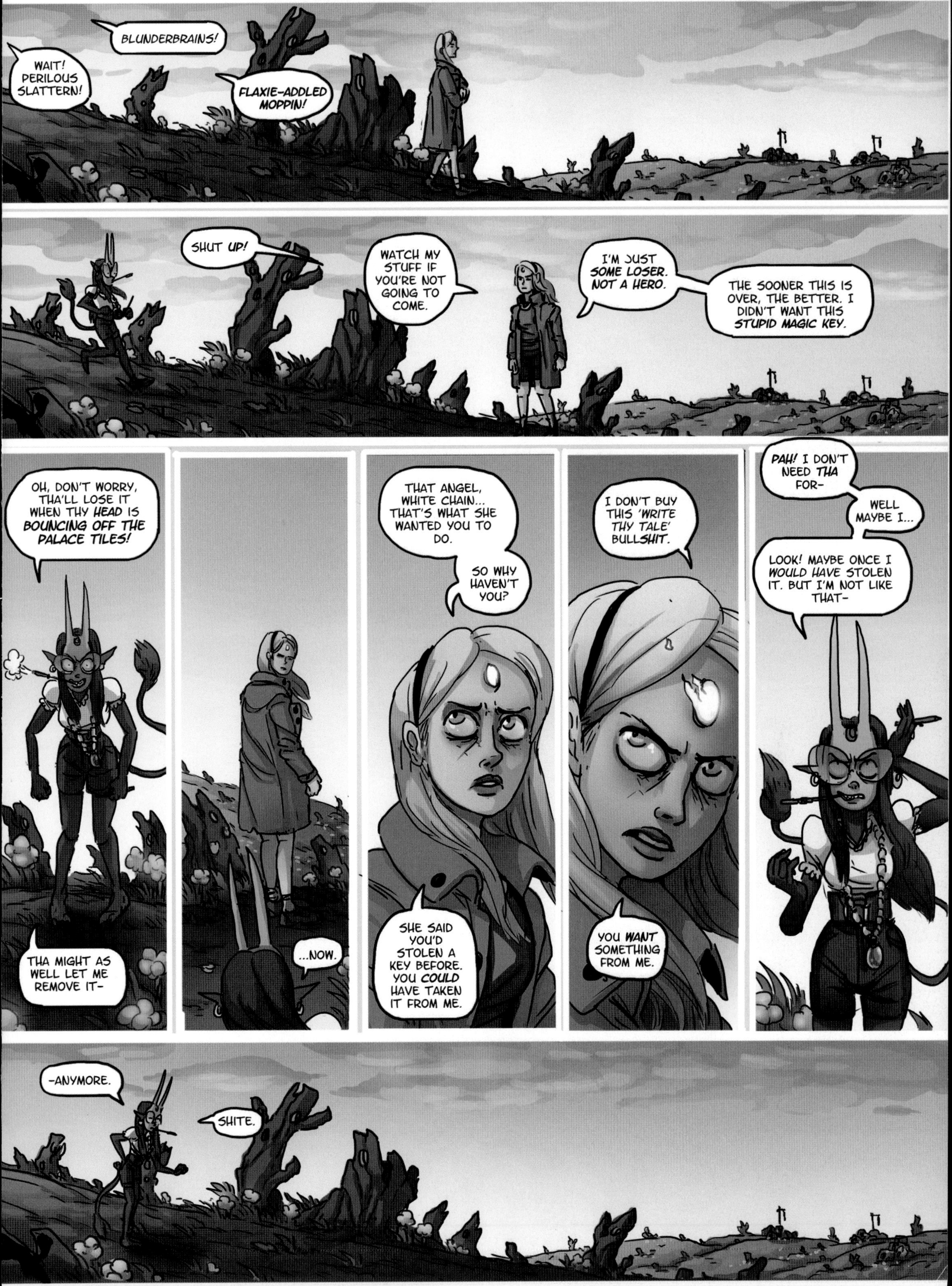

BLUNDERBRAINS!
WAIT! PERILOUS SLATTERN!
FLAXIE-ADDLED MOPPIN!
SHUT UP!
WATCH MY STUFF IF YOU'RE NOT GOING TO COME.
I'M JUST SOME LOSER. NOT A HERO.
THE SOONER THIS IS OVER, THE BETTER. I DIDN'T WANT THIS STUPID MAGIC KEY.
OH, DON'T WORRY, THA'LL LOSE IT WHEN THY HEAD IS BOUNCING OFF THE PALACE TILES!
THA MIGHT AS WELL LET ME REMOVE IT-
...NOW.
THAT ANGEL, WHITE CHAIN... THAT'S WHAT SHE WANTED YOU TO DO.
SO WHY HAVEN'T YOU?
SHE SAID YOU'D STOLEN A KEY BEFORE. YOU COULD HAVE TAKEN IT FROM ME.
I DON'T BUY THIS 'WRITE THY TALE' BULLSHIT.
YOU WANT SOMETHING FROM ME.
PAH! I DON'T NEED THA FOR-
WELL MAYBE I...
LOOK! MAYBE ONCE I WOULD HAVE STOLEN IT. BUT I'M NOT LIKE THAT-
-ANYMORE.
SHITE.

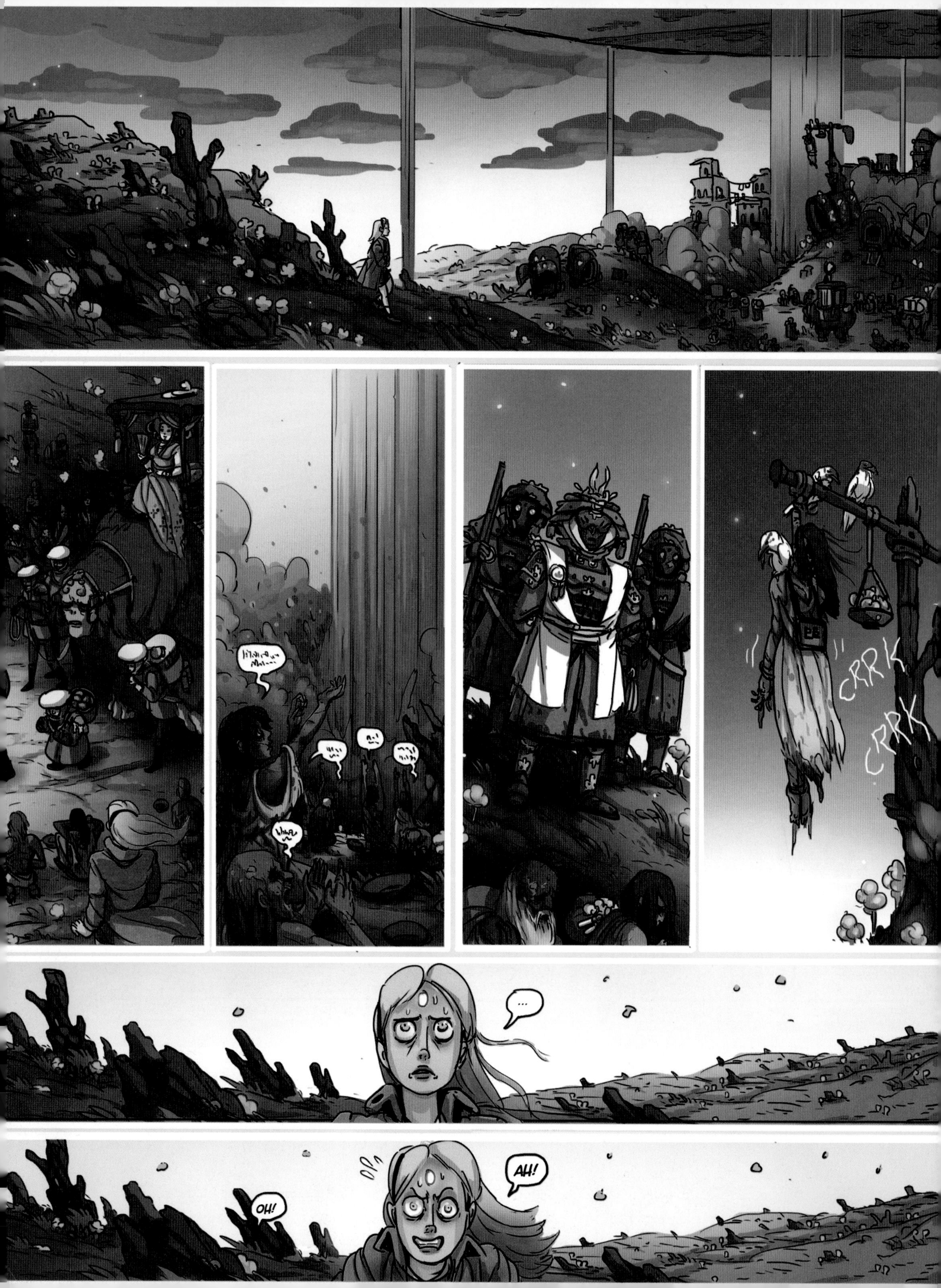
CRRK
CRRK
...
AH!
OH!

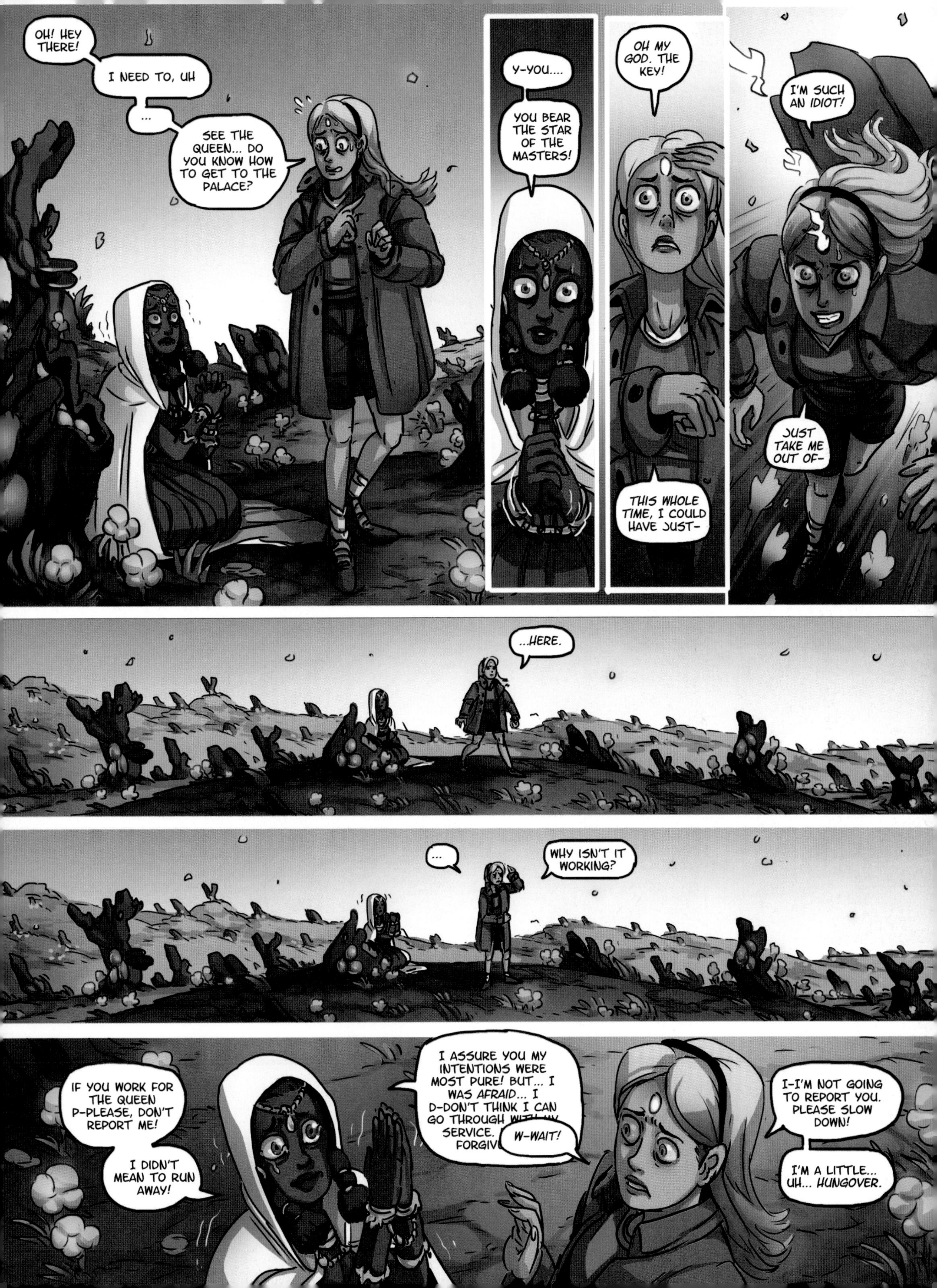
OH! HEY THERE!
I NEED TO, UH
...
SEE THE QUEEN... DO YOU KNOW HOW TO GET TO THE PALACE?
Y-YOU....
YOU BEAR THE STAR OF THE MASTERS!
OH MY GOD. THE KEY!
THIS WHOLE TIME, I COULD HAVE JUST-
I'M SUCH AN IDIOT!
JUST TAKE ME OUT OF-
...HERE.
...
WHY ISN'T IT WORKING?
IF YOU WORK FOR THE QUEEN P-PLEASE, DON'T REPORT ME!
I DIDN'T MEAN TO RUN AWAY!
I ASSURE YOU MY INTENTIONS WERE MOST PURE! BUT... I WAS AFRAID... I D-DON'T THINK I CAN GO THROUGH WITH MY SERVICE. FORGIV
W-WAIT!
I-I'M NOT GOING TO REPORT YOU. PLEASE SLOW DOWN!
I'M A LITTLE... UH... HUNGOVER.

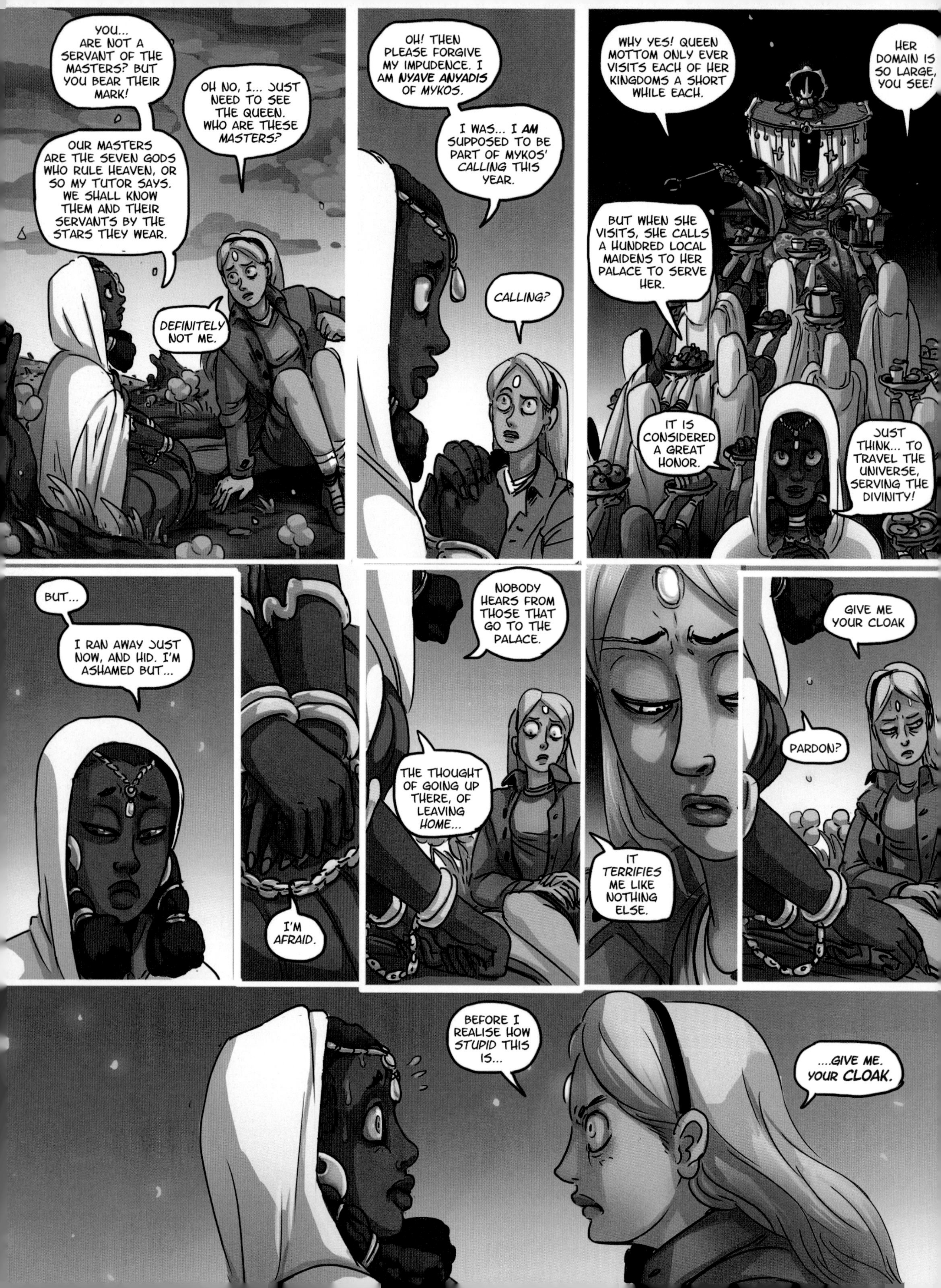
YOU... ARE NOT A SERVANT OF THE MASTERS? BUT YOU BEAR THEIR MARK!
OUR MASTERS ARE THE SEVEN GODS WHO RULE HEAVEN, OR SO MY TUTOR SAYS. WE SHALL KNOW THEM AND THEIR SERVANTS BY THE STARS THEY WEAR.
OH NO, I... JUST NEED TO SEE THE QUEEN. WHO ARE THESE MASTERS?
DEFINITELY NOT ME.
OH! THEN PLEASE FORGIVE MY IMPUDENCE. I AM NYAVE ANYADIS OF MYKOS.
I WAS... I AM SUPPOSED TO BE PART OF MYKOS' CALLING THIS YEAR.
CALLING?
WHY YES! QUEEN MOTTOM ONLY EVER VISITS EACH OF HER KINGDOMS A SHORT WHILE EACH.
HER DOMAIN IS SO LARGE, YOU SEE!
BUT WHEN SHE VISITS, SHE CALLS A HUNDRED LOCAL MAIDENS TO HER PALACE TO SERVE HER.
IT IS CONSIDERED A GREAT HONOR.
JUST THINK... TO TRAVEL THE UNIVERSE, SERVING THE DIVINITY!
BUT...
I RAN AWAY JUST NOW, AND HID. I'M ASHAMED BUT...
I'M AFRAID.
NOBODY HEARS FROM THOSE THAT GO TO THE PALACE.
THE THOUGHT OF GOING UP THERE, OF LEAVING HOME...
IT TERRIFIES ME LIKE NOTHING ELSE.
GIVE ME YOUR CLOAK
PARDON?
BEFORE I REALISE HOW STUPID THIS IS...
....GIVE ME. YOUR CLOAK.

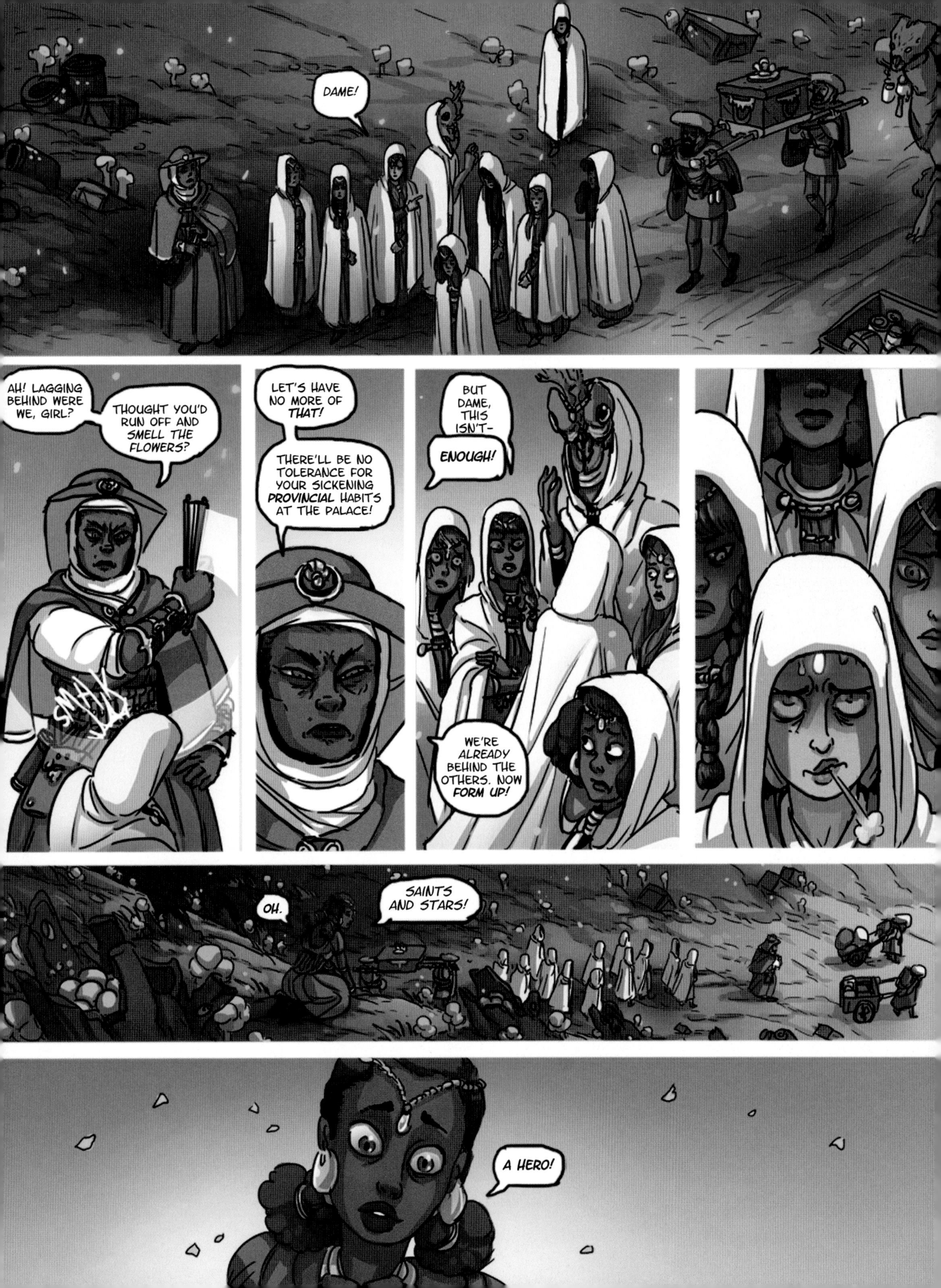
DAME!
AH! LAGGING BEHIND WERE WE, GIRL?
THOUGHT YOU'D RUN OFF AND SMELL THE FLOWERS?
SMACK
LET'S HAVE NO MORE OF *THAT!*
THERE'LL BE NO TOLERANCE FOR YOUR SICKENING *PROVINCIAL* HABITS AT THE PALACE!
BUT DAME, THIS ISN'T-
ENOUGH!
WE'RE *ALREADY* BEHIND THE OTHERS. NOW *FORM UP!*
OH.
SAINTS AND STARS!
A HERO!

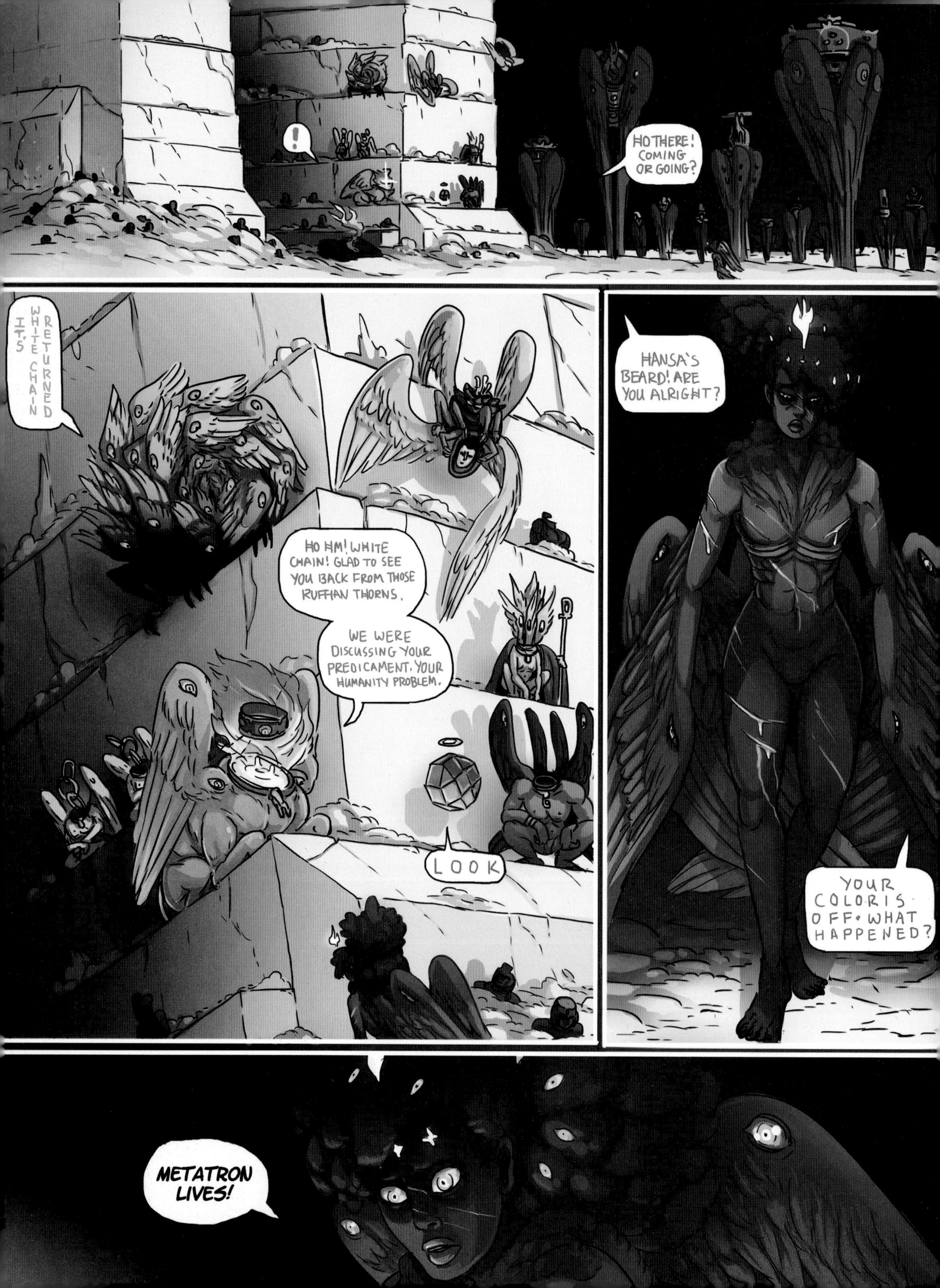
!
HO THERE! COMING OR GOING?
IT'S WHITE CHAIN RETURNED
HO HM! WHITE CHAIN! GLAD TO SEE YOU BACK FROM THOSE RUFFIAN THORNS.
WE WERE DISCUSSING YOUR PREDICAMENT. YOUR HUMANITY PROBLEM.
LOOK
HANSA'S BEARD! ARE YOU ALRIGHT?
YOUR COLOR IS OFF. WHAT HAPPENED?
METATRON LIVES!

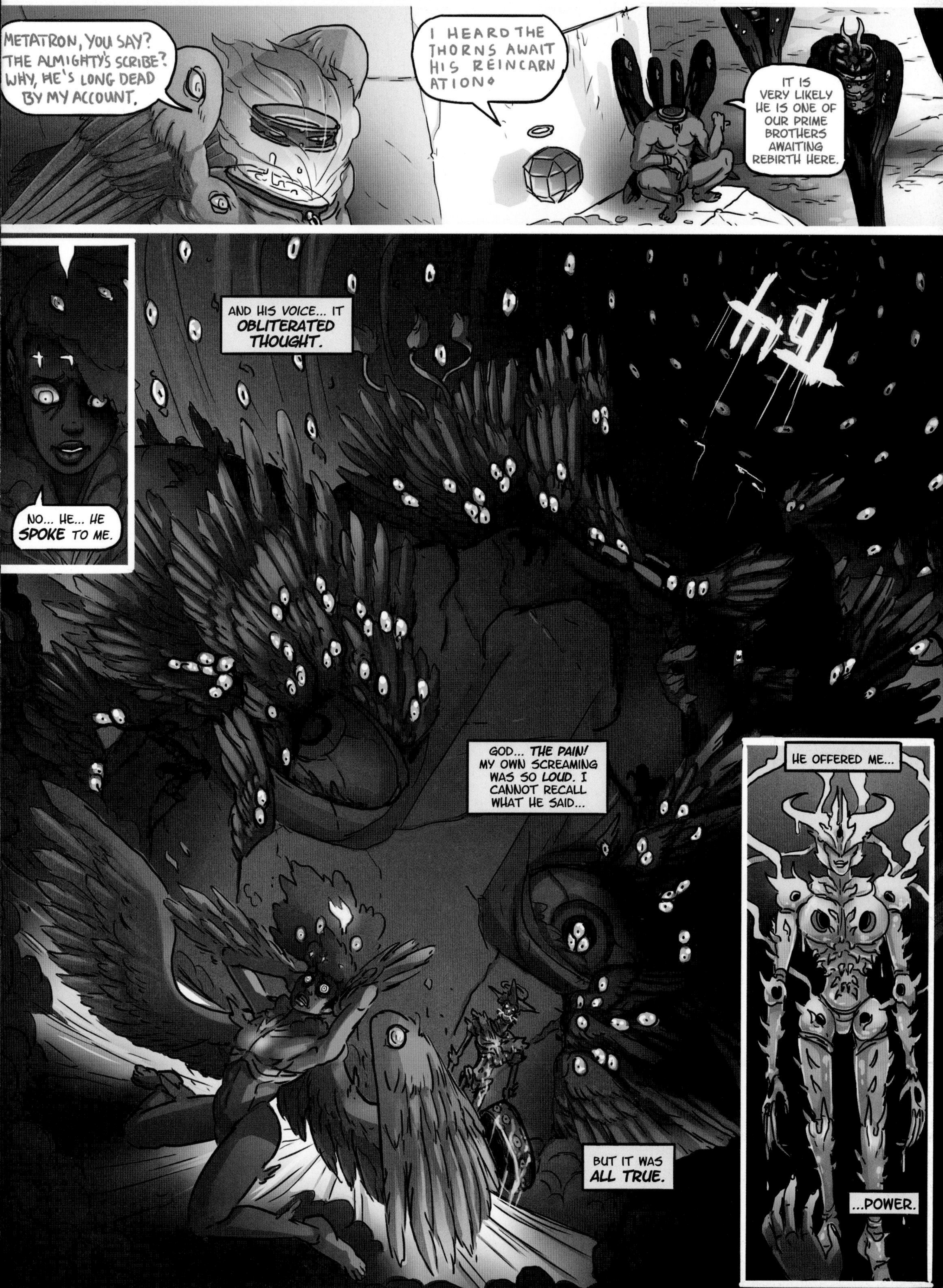
METATRON, YOU SAY? THE ALMIGHTY'S SCRIBE? WHY, HE'S LONG DEAD BY MY ACCOUNT.
I HEARD THE THORNS AWAIT HIS REINCARN ATION.
IT IS VERY LIKELY HE IS ONE OF OUR PRIME BROTHERS AWAITING REBIRTH HERE.
NO... HE... HE SPOKE TO ME.
AND HIS VOICE... IT OBLITERATED THOUGHT.
GOD... THE PAIN! MY OWN SCREAMING WAS SO LOUD. I CANNOT RECALL WHAT HE SAID...
BUT IT WAS ALL TRUE.
HE OFFERED ME...
...POWER.

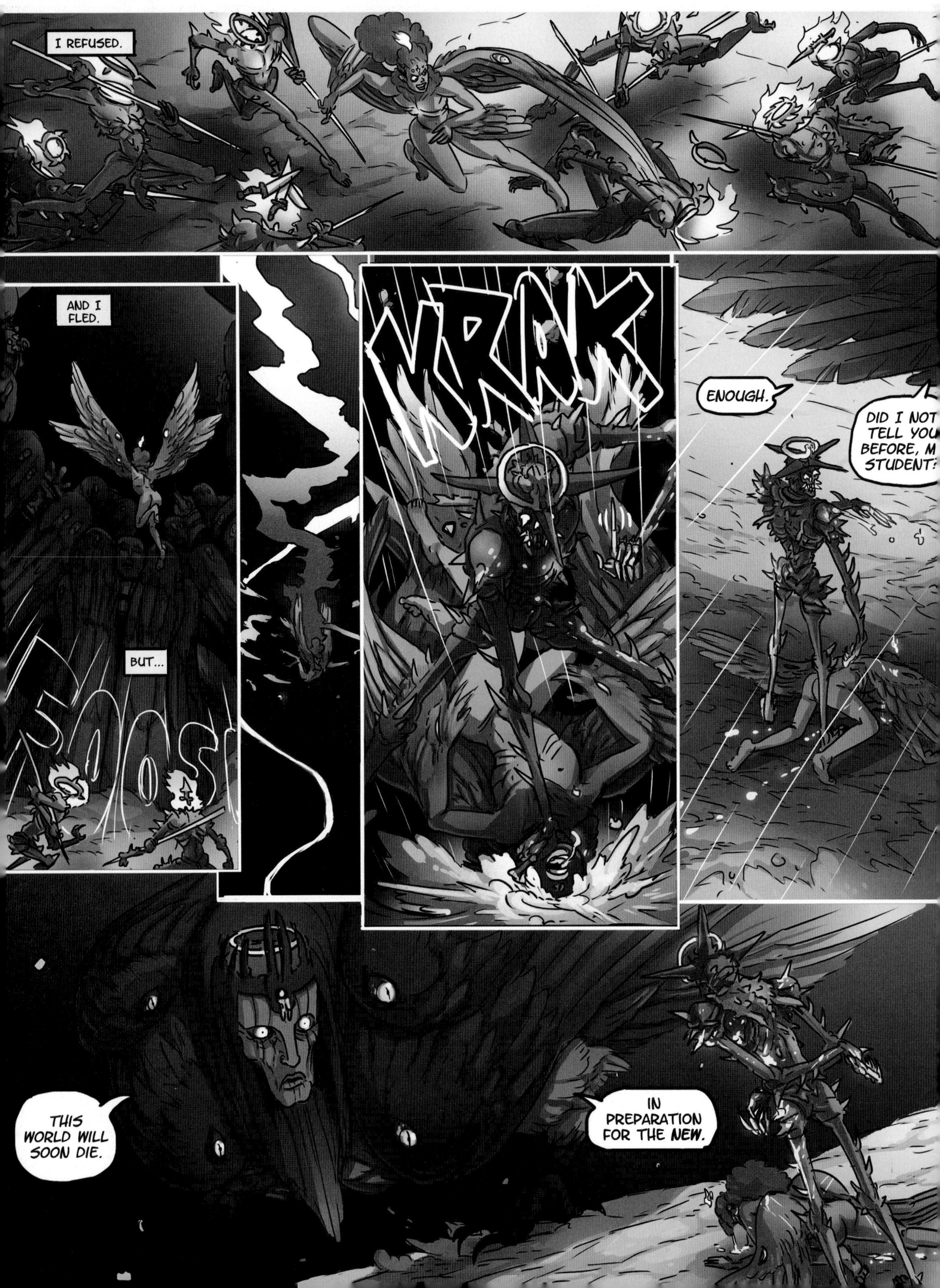
I REFUSED.
AND I FLED.
BUT...
FWOOSH
KRAK
ENOUGH.
DID I NOT TELL YOU BEFORE, MY STUDENT?
THIS WORLD WILL SOON DIE.
IN PREPARATION FOR THE NEW.

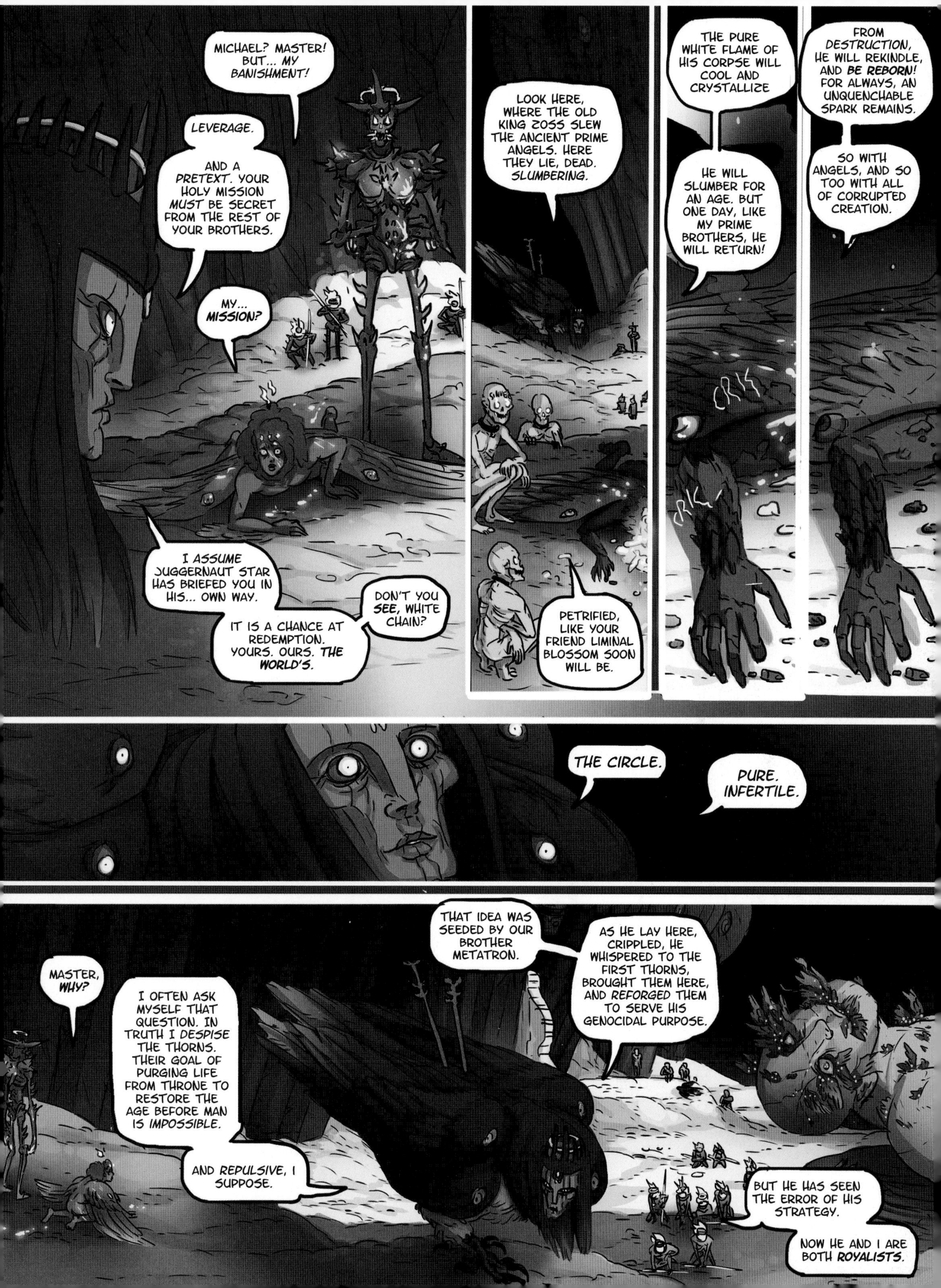
MICHAEL? MASTER! BUT... MY BANISHMENT!
LEVERAGE.
AND A PRETEXT. YOUR HOLY MISSION MUST BE SECRET FROM THE REST OF YOUR BROTHERS.
MY... MISSION?
I ASSUME JUGGERNAUT STAR HAS BRIEFED YOU IN HIS... OWN WAY.
IT IS A CHANCE AT REDEMPTION. YOURS. OURS. THE WORLD'S.
DON'T YOU SEE, WHITE CHAIN?
LOOK HERE, WHERE THE OLD KING ZOSS SLEW THE ANCIENT PRIME ANGELS. HERE THEY LIE, DEAD. SLUMBERING.
PETRIFIED, LIKE YOUR FRIEND LIMINAL BLOSSOM SOON WILL BE.
THE PURE WHITE FLAME OF HIS CORPSE WILL COOL AND CRYSTALLIZE
HE WILL SLUMBER FOR AN AGE. BUT ONE DAY, LIKE MY PRIME BROTHERS, HE WILL RETURN!
CRIS
CRIS
FROM DESTRUCTION, HE WILL REKINDLE, AND BE REBORN! FOR ALWAYS, AN UNQUENCHABLE SPARK REMAINS.
SO WITH ANGELS, AND SO TOO WITH ALL OF CORRUPTED CREATION.
THE CIRCLE.
PURE. INFERTILE.
MASTER, WHY?
I OFTEN ASK MYSELF THAT QUESTION. IN TRUTH I DESPISE THE THORNS. THEIR GOAL OF PURGING LIFE FROM THRONE TO RESTORE THE AGE BEFORE MAN IS IMPOSSIBLE.
AND REPULSIVE, I SUPPOSE.
THAT IDEA WAS SEEDED BY OUR BROTHER METATRON.
AS HE LAY HERE, CRIPPLED, HE WHISPERED TO THE FIRST THORNS, BROUGHT THEM HERE, AND REFORGED THEM TO SERVE HIS GENOCIDAL PURPOSE.
BUT HE HAS SEEN THE ERROR OF HIS STRATEGY.
NOW HE AND I ARE BOTH ROYALISTS.

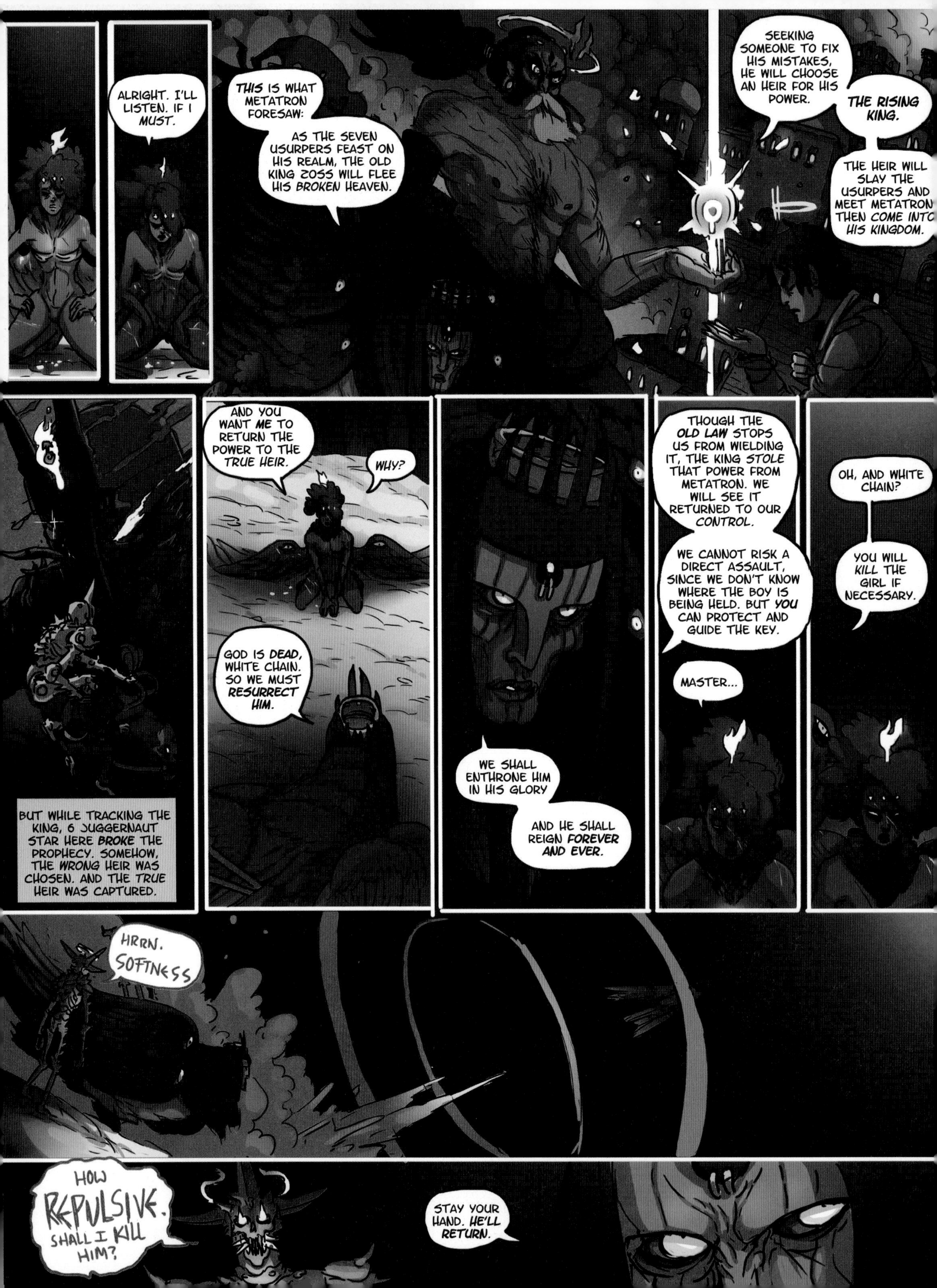
ALRIGHT. I'LL LISTEN. IF I MUST.
THIS IS WHAT METATRON FORESAW:
AS THE SEVEN USURPERS FEAST ON HIS REALM, THE OLD KING ZOSS WILL FLEE HIS BROKEN HEAVEN.
SEEKING SOMEONE TO FIX HIS MISTAKES, HE WILL CHOOSE AN HEIR FOR HIS POWER.
THE RISING KING.
THE HEIR WILL SLAY THE USURPERS AND MEET METATRON THEN COME INTO HIS KINGDOM.
BUT WHILE TRACKING THE KING, 6 JUGGERNAUT STAR HERE BROKE THE PROPHECY. SOMEHOW, THE WRONG HEIR WAS CHOSEN. AND THE TRUE HEIR WAS CAPTURED.
AND YOU WANT ME TO RETURN THE POWER TO THE TRUE HEIR.
WHY?
GOD IS DEAD, WHITE CHAIN. SO WE MUST RESURRECT HIM.
WE SHALL ENTHRONE HIM IN HIS GLORY
AND HE SHALL REIGN FOREVER AND EVER.
THOUGH THE OLD LAW STOPS US FROM WIELDING IT, THE KING STOLE THAT POWER FROM METATRON. WE WILL SEE IT RETURNED TO OUR CONTROL.
WE CANNOT RISK A DIRECT ASSAULT, SINCE WE DON'T KNOW WHERE THE BOY IS BEING HELD. BUT YOU CAN PROTECT AND GUIDE THE KEY.
MASTER...
OH, AND WHITE CHAIN?
YOU WILL KILL THE GIRL IF NECESSARY.
HRRN. SOFTNESS
HOW REPULSIVE. SHALL I KILL HIM?
STAY YOUR HAND. HE'LL RETURN.

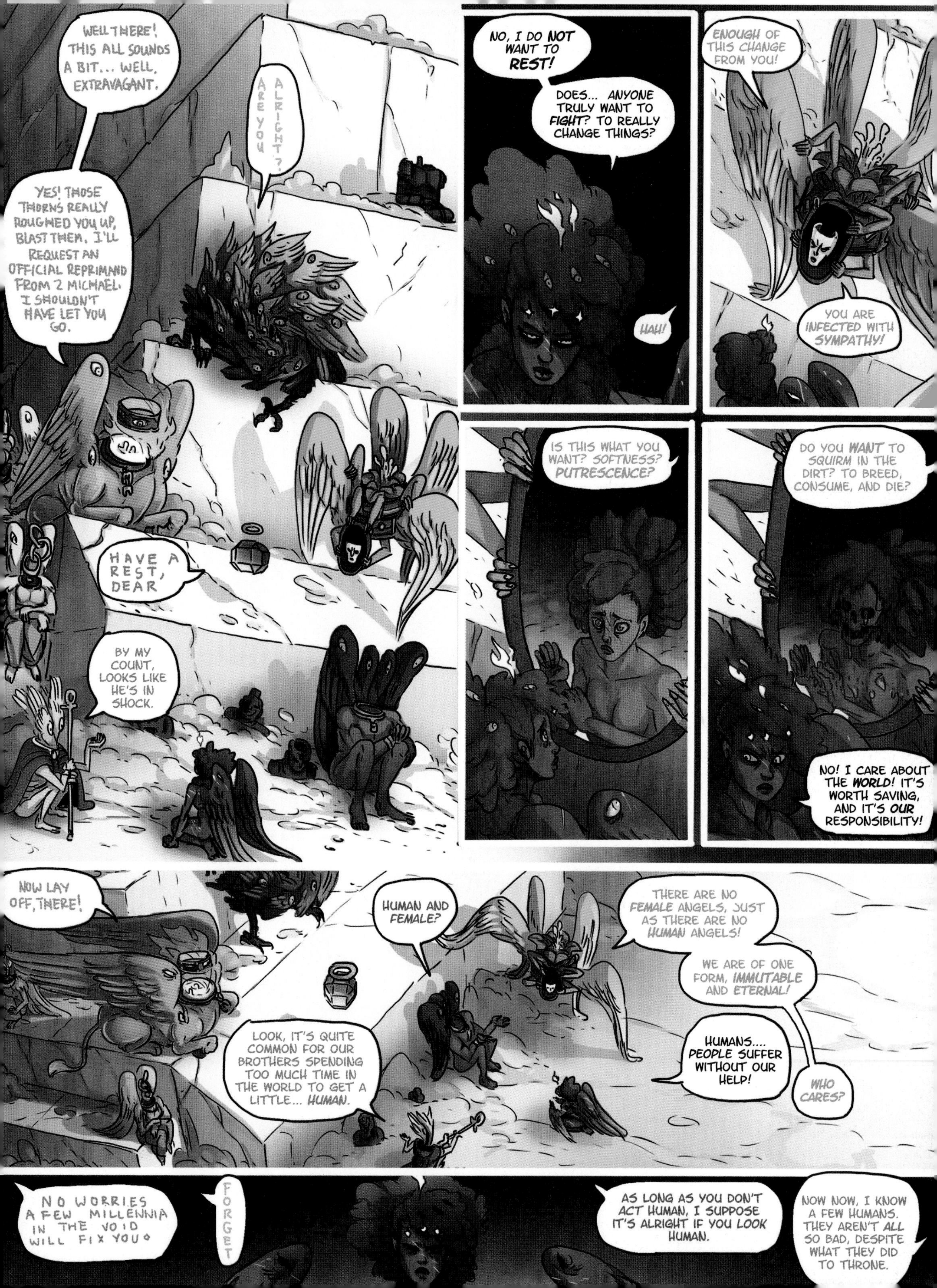
WELL THERE! THIS ALL SOUNDS A BIT... WELL, EXTRAVAGANT.
ARE YOU ALRIGHT?
YES! THOSE THORNS REALLY ROUGHED YOU UP, BLAST THEM. I'LL REQUEST AN OFFICIAL REPRIMAND FROM 2 MICHAEL. I SHOULDN'T HAVE LET YOU GO.
HAVE A REST, DEAR
BY MY COUNT, LOOKS LIKE HE'S IN SHOCK.
NO, I DO NOT WANT TO REST!
DOES... ANYONE TRULY WANT TO FIGHT? TO REALLY CHANGE THINGS?
HAH!
ENOUGH OF THIS CHANGE FROM YOU!
YOU ARE INFECTED WITH SYMPATHY!
IS THIS WHAT YOU WANT? SOFTNESS? PUTRESCENCE?
DO YOU WANT TO SQUIRM IN THE DIRT? TO BREED, CONSUME, AND DIE?
NO! I CARE ABOUT THE WORLD! IT'S WORTH SAVING, AND IT'S OUR RESPONSIBILITY!
NOW LAY OFF, THERE!
HUMAN AND FEMALE?
THERE ARE NO FEMALE ANGELS, JUST AS THERE ARE NO HUMAN ANGELS!
WE ARE OF ONE FORM, IMMUTABLE AND ETERNAL!
LOOK, IT'S QUITE COMMON FOR OUR BROTHERS SPENDING TOO MUCH TIME IN THE WORLD TO GET A LITTLE... HUMAN.
HUMANS.... PEOPLE SUFFER WITHOUT OUR HELP!
WHO CARES?
NO WORRIES A FEW MILLENNIA IN THE VOID WILL FIX YOU
FORGET
AS LONG AS YOU DON'T ACT HUMAN, I SUPPOSE IT'S ALRIGHT IF YOU LOOK HUMAN.
NOW NOW, I KNOW A FEW HUMANS. THEY AREN'T ALL SO BAD, DESPITE WHAT THEY DID TO THRONE.

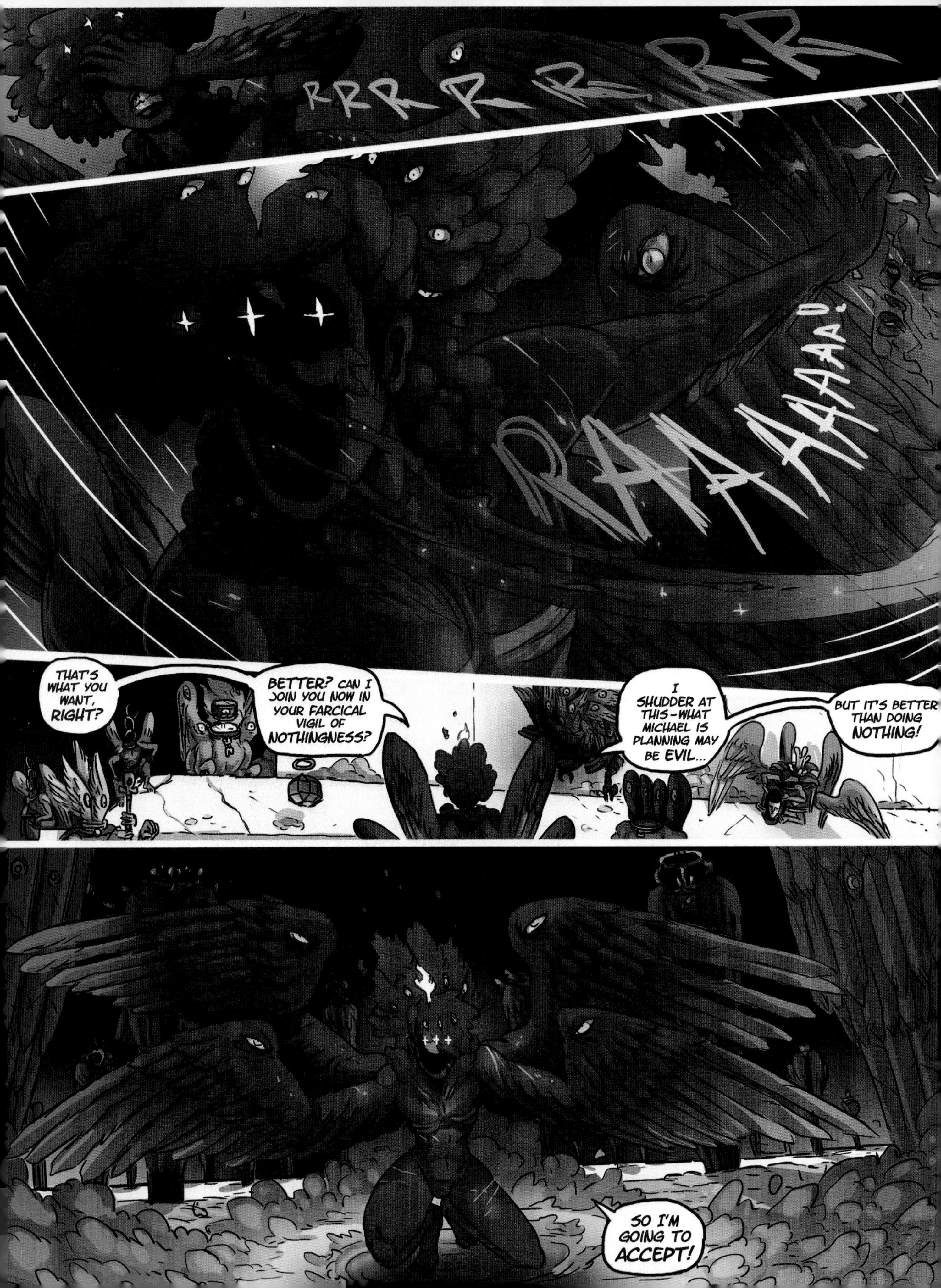
RRRR-R-R-R-R
RAAAAAAAA!
THAT'S WHAT YOU WANT, RIGHT?
BETTER? CAN I JOIN YOU NOW IN YOUR FARCICAL VIGIL OF NOTHINGNESS?
I SHUDDER AT THIS—WHAT MICHAEL IS PLANNING MAY BE EVIL...
BUT IT'S BETTER THAN DOING NOTHING!
SO I'M GOING TO ACCEPT!

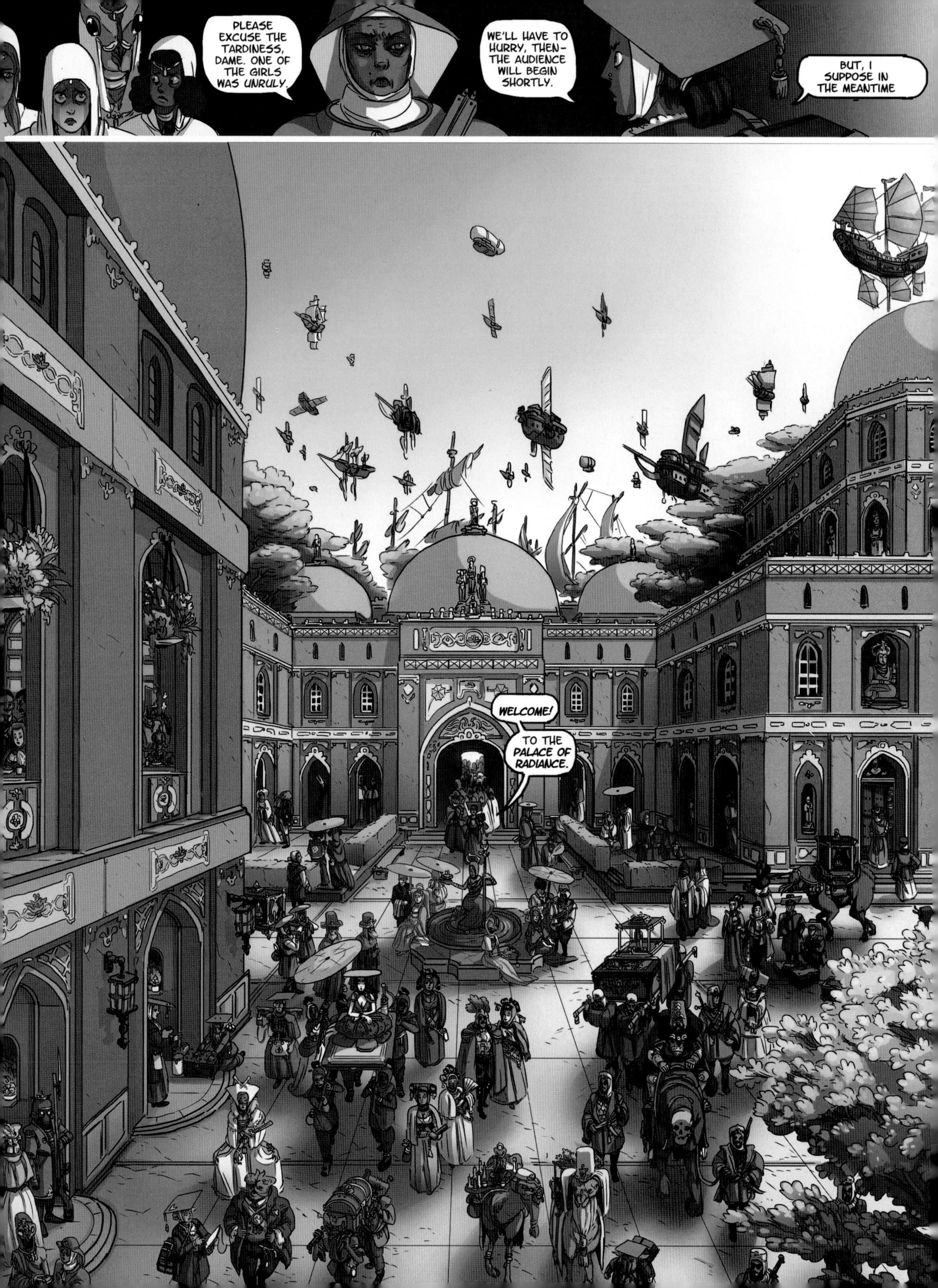
PLEASE EXCUSE THE TARDINESS, DAME. ONE OF THE GIRLS WAS UNRULY.
WE'LL HAVE TO HURRY, THEN-THE AUDIENCE WILL BEGIN SHORTLY.
BUT, I SUPPOSE IN THE MEANTIME
WELCOME!
TO THE PALACE OF RADIANCE.

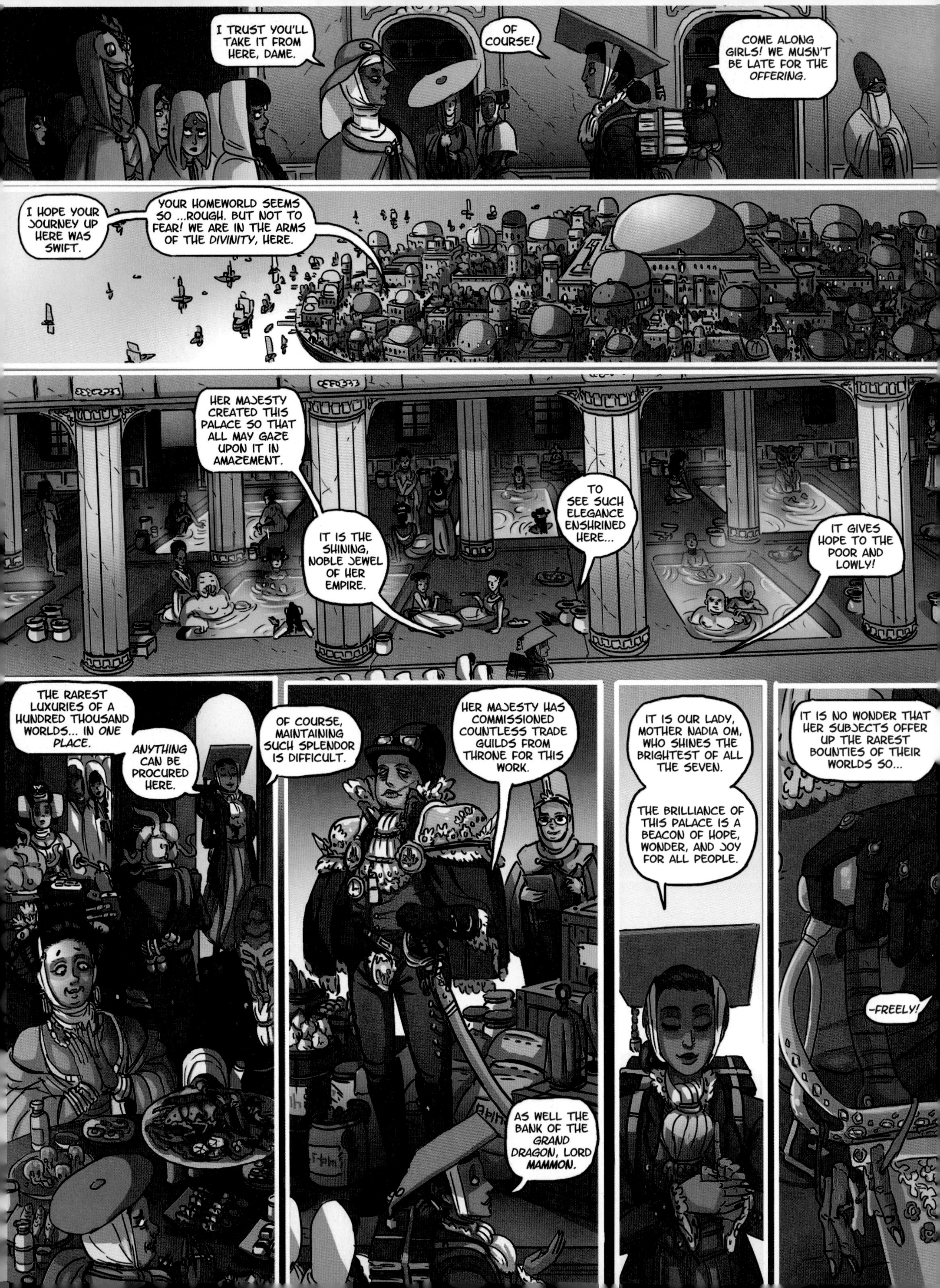
I TRUST YOU'LL TAKE IT FROM HERE, DAME.
OF COURSE!
COME ALONG GIRLS! WE MUSN'T BE LATE FOR THE OFFERING.
I HOPE YOUR JOURNEY UP HERE WAS SWIFT.
YOUR HOMEWORLD SEEMS SO ...ROUGH. BUT NOT TO FEAR! WE ARE IN THE ARMS OF THE DIVINITY, HERE.
HER MAJESTY CREATED THIS PALACE SO THAT ALL MAY GAZE UPON IT IN AMAZEMENT.
IT IS THE SHINING, NOBLE JEWEL OF HER EMPIRE.
TO SEE SUCH ELEGANCE ENSHRINED HERE...
IT GIVES HOPE TO THE POOR AND LOWLY!
THE RAREST LUXURIES OF A HUNDRED THOUSAND WORLDS... IN ONE PLACE.
ANYTHING CAN BE PROCURED HERE.
OF COURSE, MAINTAINING SUCH SPLENDOR IS DIFFICULT.
HER MAJESTY HAS COMMISSIONED COUNTLESS TRADE GUILDS FROM THRONE FOR THIS WORK.
AS WELL THE BANK OF THE GRAND DRAGON, LORD MAMMON.
IT IS OUR LADY, MOTHER NADIA OM, WHO SHINES THE BRIGHTEST OF ALL THE SEVEN.
THE BRILLIANCE OF THIS PALACE IS A BEACON OF HOPE, WONDER, AND JOY FOR ALL PEOPLE.
IT IS NO WONDER THAT HER SUBJECTS OFFER UP THE RAREST BOUNTIES OF THEIR WORLDS SO...
-FREELY!

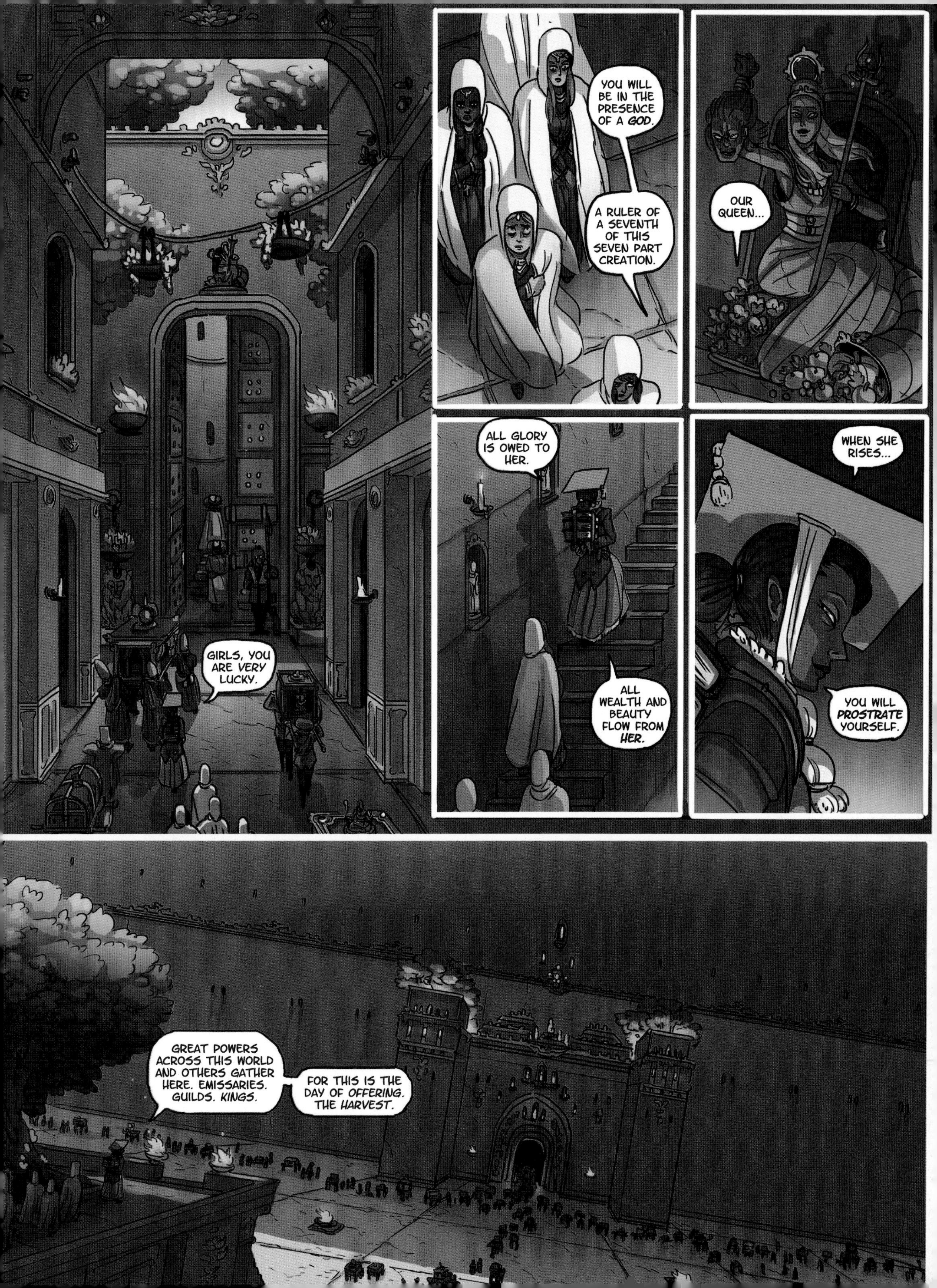
GIRLS, YOU ARE VERY LUCKY.
YOU WILL BE IN THE PRESENCE OF A GOD.
A RULER OF A SEVENTH OF THIS SEVEN PART CREATION.
OUR QUEEN...
ALL GLORY IS OWED TO HER.
ALL WEALTH AND BEAUTY FLOW FROM HER.
WHEN SHE RISES...
YOU WILL PROSTRATE YOURSELF.
GREAT POWERS ACROSS THIS WORLD AND OTHERS GATHER HERE. EMISSARIES. GUILDS. KINGS.
FOR THIS IS THE DAY OF OFFERING. THE HARVEST.

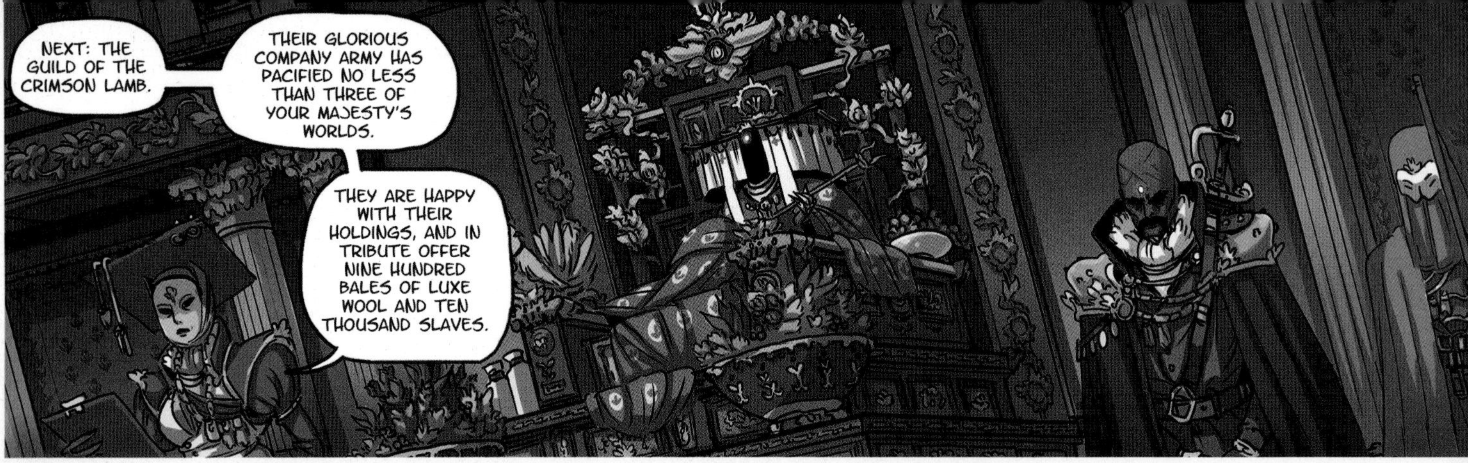
NEXT: THE GUILD OF THE CRIMSON LAMB.
THEIR GLORIOUS COMPANY ARMY HAS PACIFIED NO LESS THAN THREE OF YOUR MAJESTY'S WORLDS.
THEY ARE HAPPY WITH THEIR HOLDINGS, AND IN TRIBUTE OFFER NINE HUNDRED BALES OF LUXE WOOL AND TEN THOUSAND SLAVES.

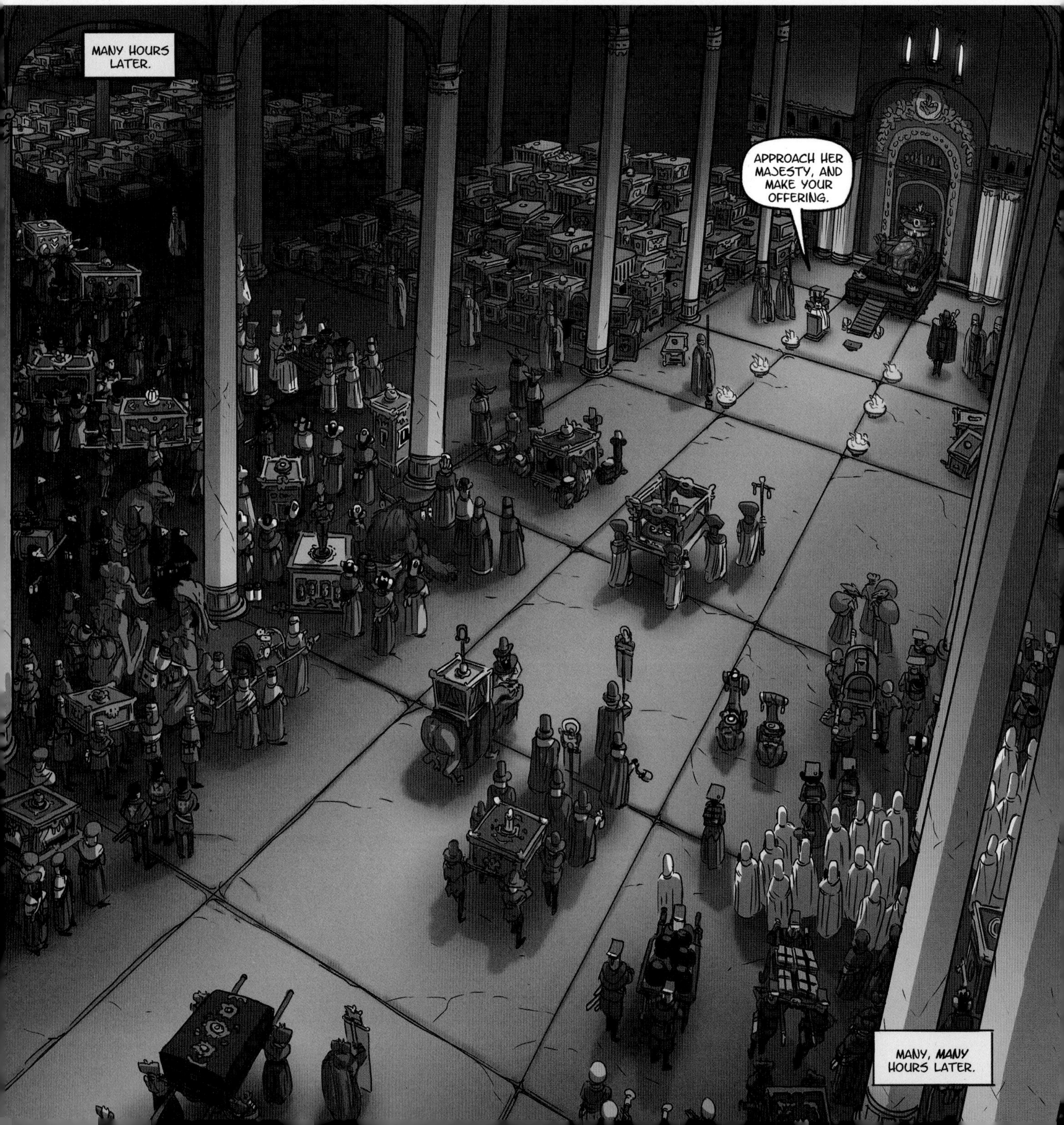
MANY HOURS LATER.
APPROACH HER MAJESTY, AND MAKE YOUR OFFERING.
MANY, MANY HOURS LATER.

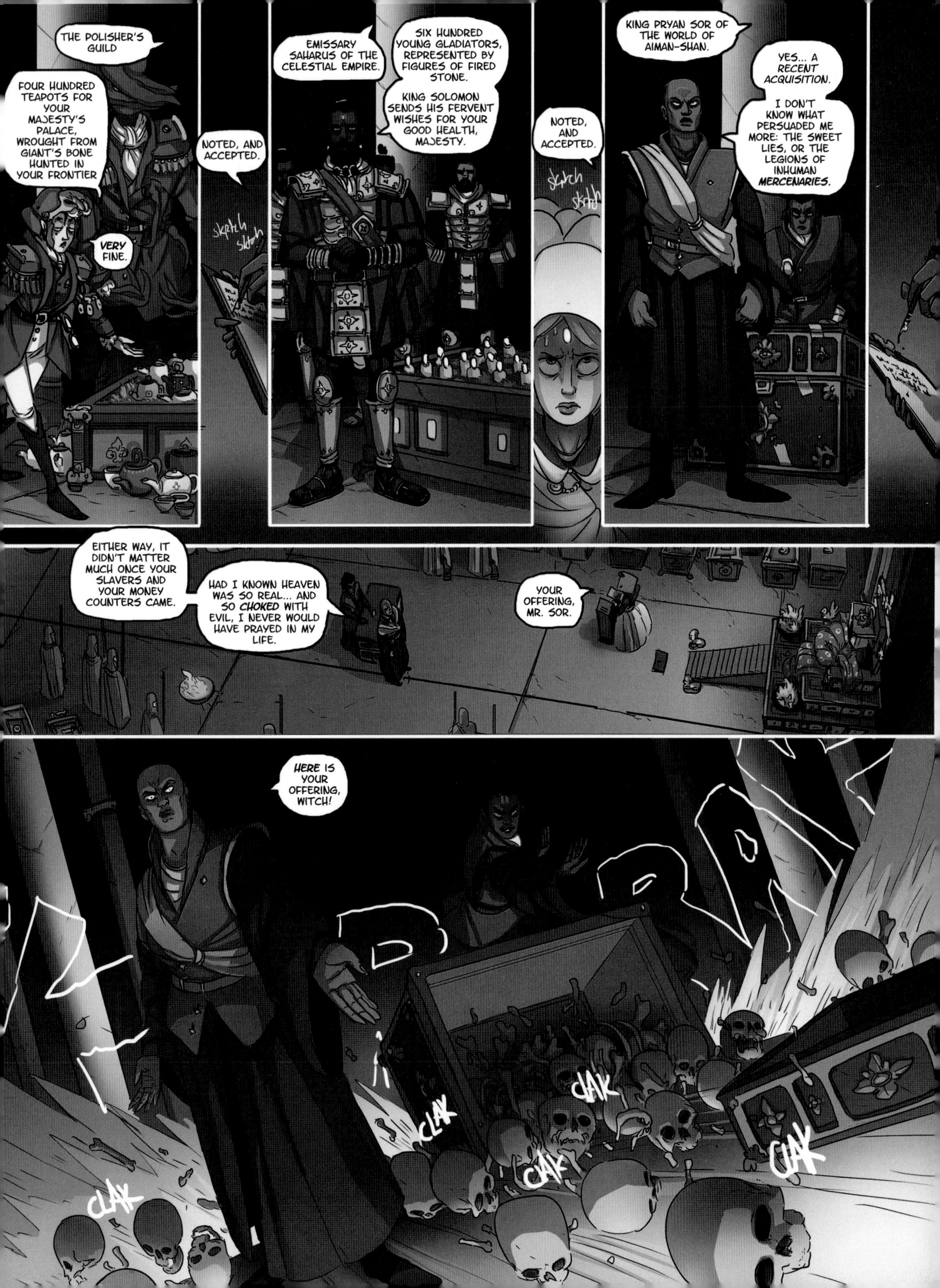
THE POLISHER'S GUILD
FOUR HUNDRED TEAPOTS FOR YOUR MAJESTY'S PALACE, WROUGHT FROM GIANT'S BONE HUNTED IN YOUR FRONTIER
VERY FINE.
NOTED, AND ACCEPTED.
skrtch skrtch
EMISSARY SAHARUS OF THE CELESTIAL EMPIRE.
SIX HUNDRED YOUNG GLADIATORS, REPRESENTED BY FIGURES OF FIRED STONE.
KING SOLOMON SENDS HIS FERVENT WISHES FOR YOUR GOOD HEALTH, MAJESTY.
NOTED, AND ACCEPTED.
skrtch skrtch
KING PRYAN SOR OF THE WORLD OF AIMAN-SHAN.
YES... A RECENT ACQUISITION.
I DON'T KNOW WHAT PERSUADED ME MORE: THE SWEET LIES, OR THE LEGIONS OF INHUMAN MERCENARIES.
EITHER WAY, IT DIDN'T MATTER MUCH ONCE YOUR SLAVERS AND YOUR MONEY COUNTERS CAME.
HAD I KNOWN HEAVEN WAS SO REAL... AND SO CHOKED WITH EVIL, I NEVER WOULD HAVE PRAYED IN MY LIFE.
YOUR OFFERING, MR. SOR.
HERE IS YOUR OFFERING, WITCH!
CLAK
CLAK
CLAK
CLAK
CLAK

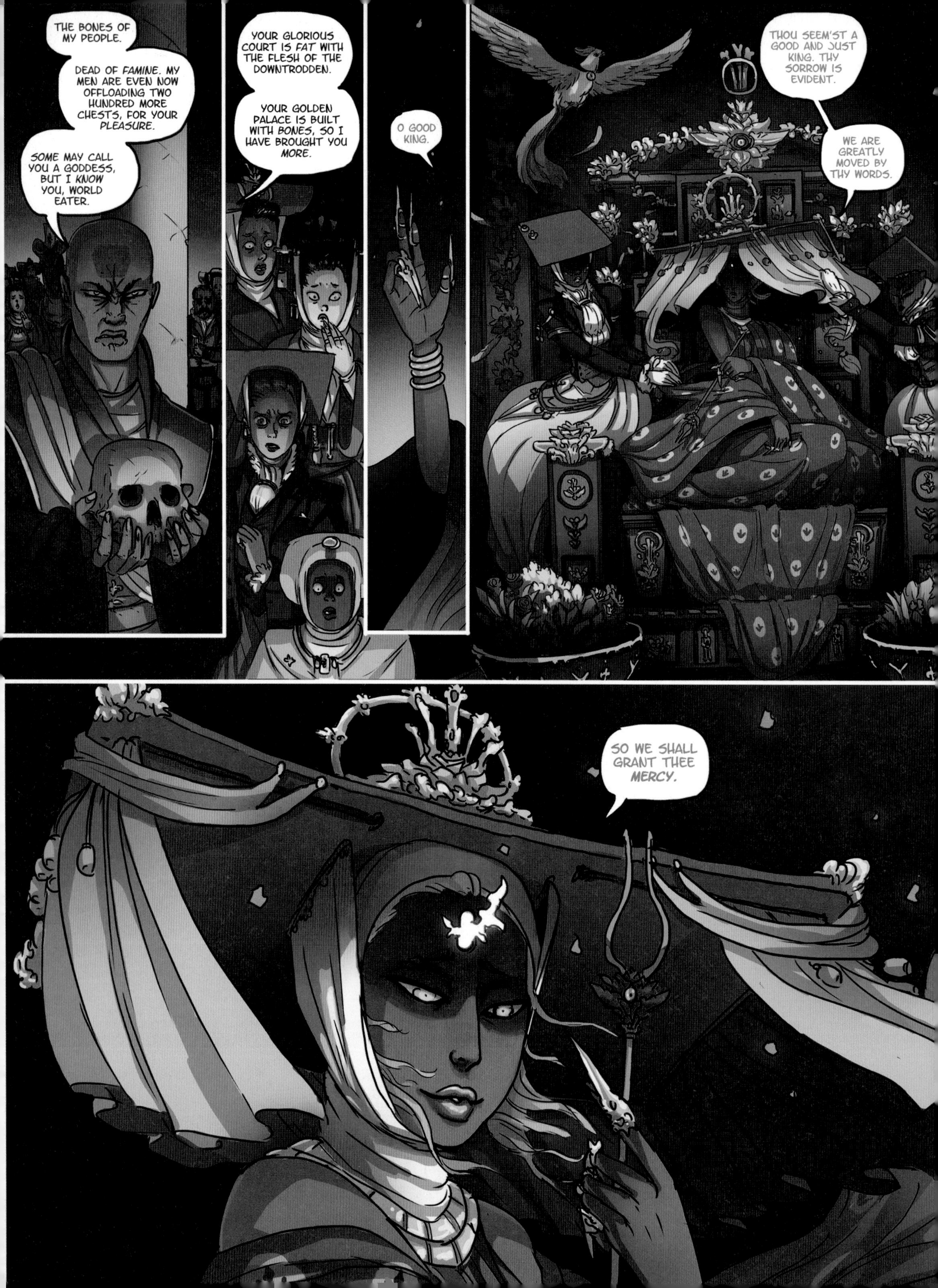
THE BONES OF MY PEOPLE.
DEAD OF FAMINE. MY MEN ARE EVEN NOW OFFLOADING TWO HUNDRED MORE CHESTS, FOR YOUR PLEASURE.
SOME MAY CALL YOU A GODDESS, BUT I KNOW YOU, WORLD EATER.
YOUR GLORIOUS COURT IS FAT WITH THE FLESH OF THE DOWNTRODDEN.
YOUR GOLDEN PALACE IS BUILT WITH BONES, SO I HAVE BROUGHT YOU MORE.
O GOOD KING.
THOU SEEM'ST A GOOD AND JUST KING. THY SORROW IS EVIDENT.
WE ARE GREATLY MOVED BY THY WORDS.
SO WE SHALL GRANT THEE MERCY.

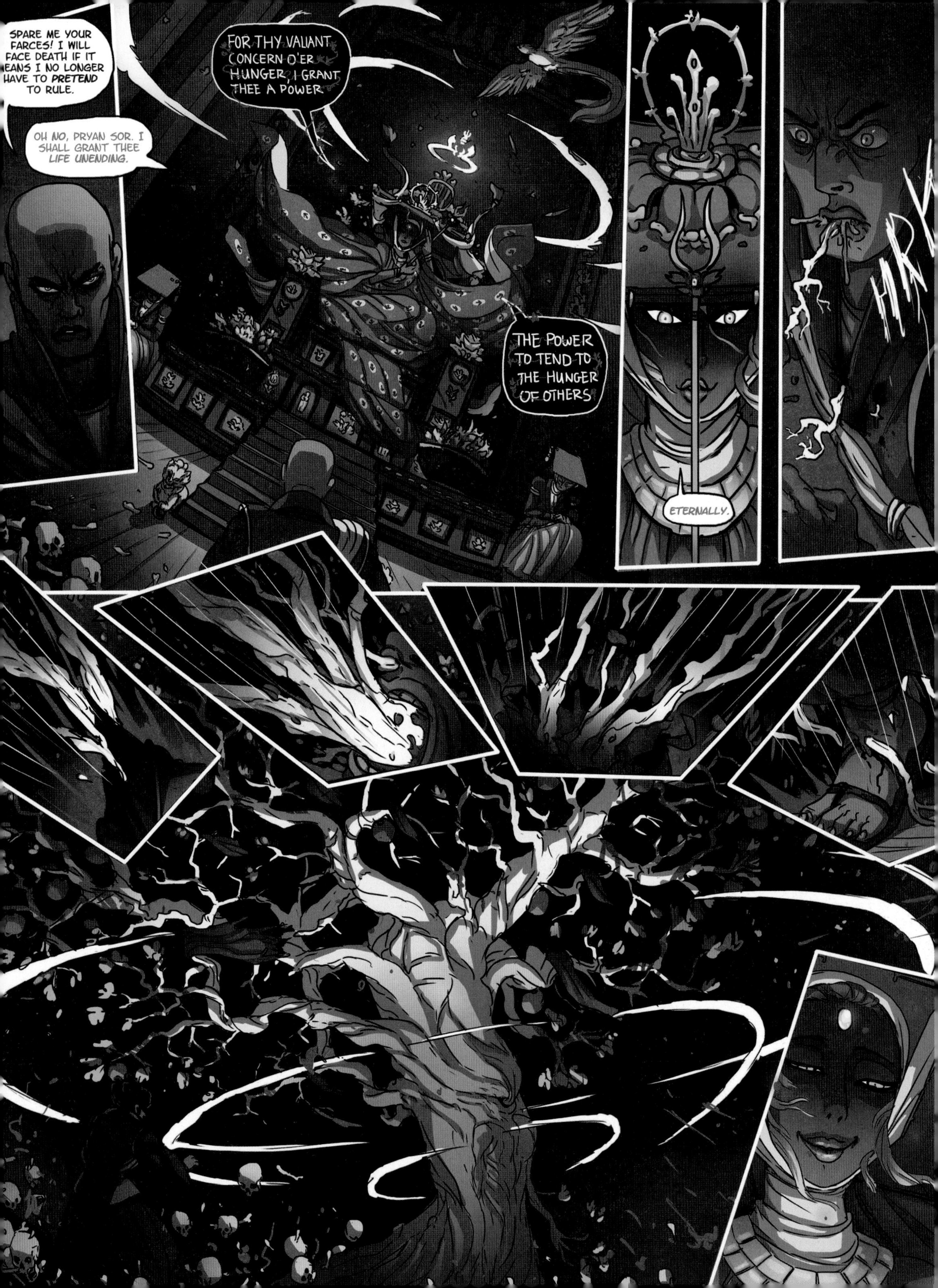
SPARE ME YOUR FARCES! I WILL FACE DEATH IF IT EANS I NO LONGER HAVE TO PRETEND TO RULE.
OH NO, PRYAN SOR. I SHALL GRANT THEE LIFE UNENDING.
FOR THY VALIANT CONCERN O'ER HUNGER, I GRANT THEE A POWER
THE POWER TO TEND TO THE HUNGER OF OTHERS
ETERNALLY.
HRK

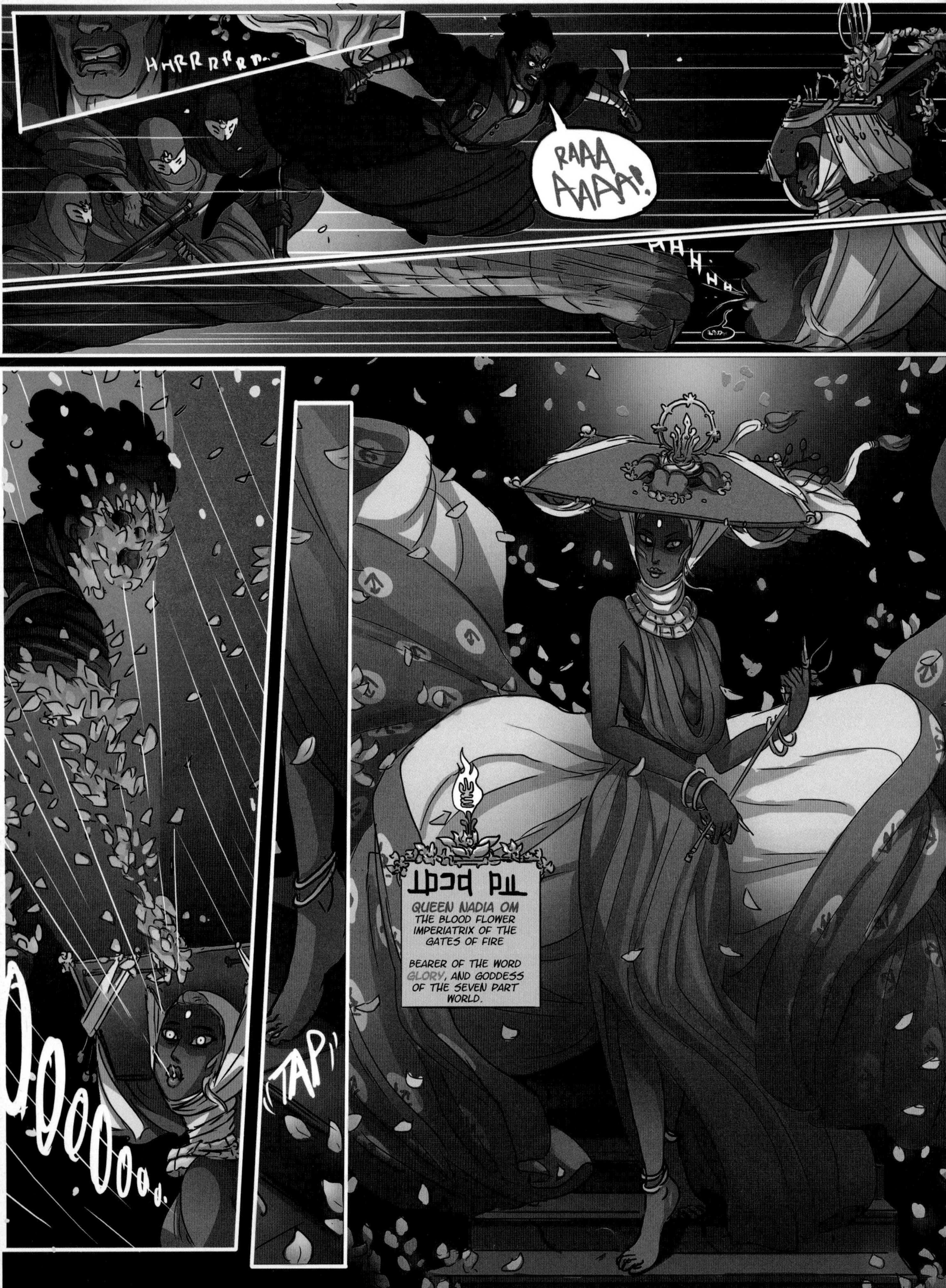
HHRRRRRR...
RAAAAAAA!
HAHHAHA
TAP
OOOOOOoo.
QUEEN NADIA OM
THE BLOOD FLOWER
IMPERIATRIX OF THE
GATES OF FIRE
BEARER OF THE WORD
GLORY, AND GODDESS
OF THE SEVEN PART
WORLD.

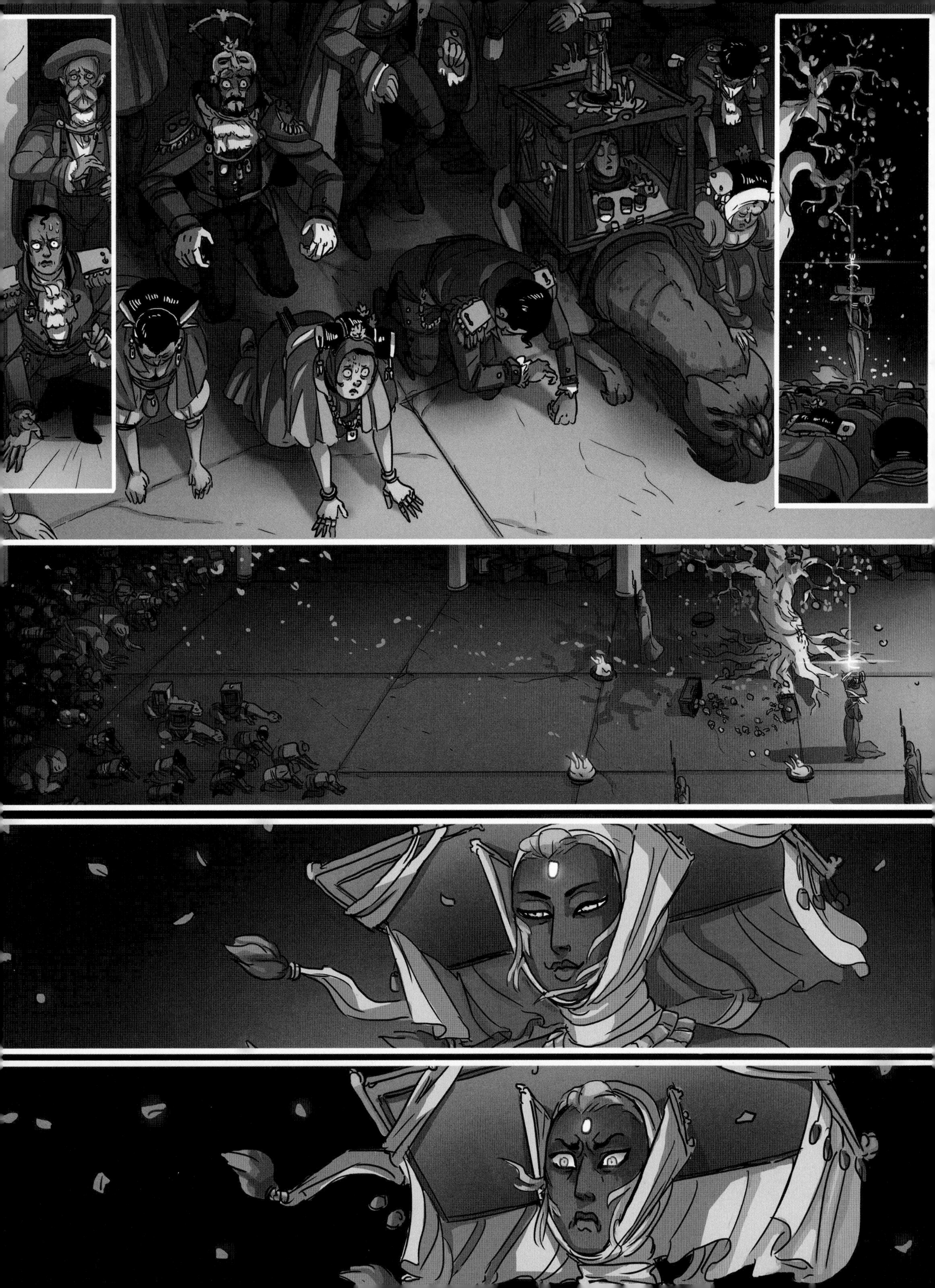

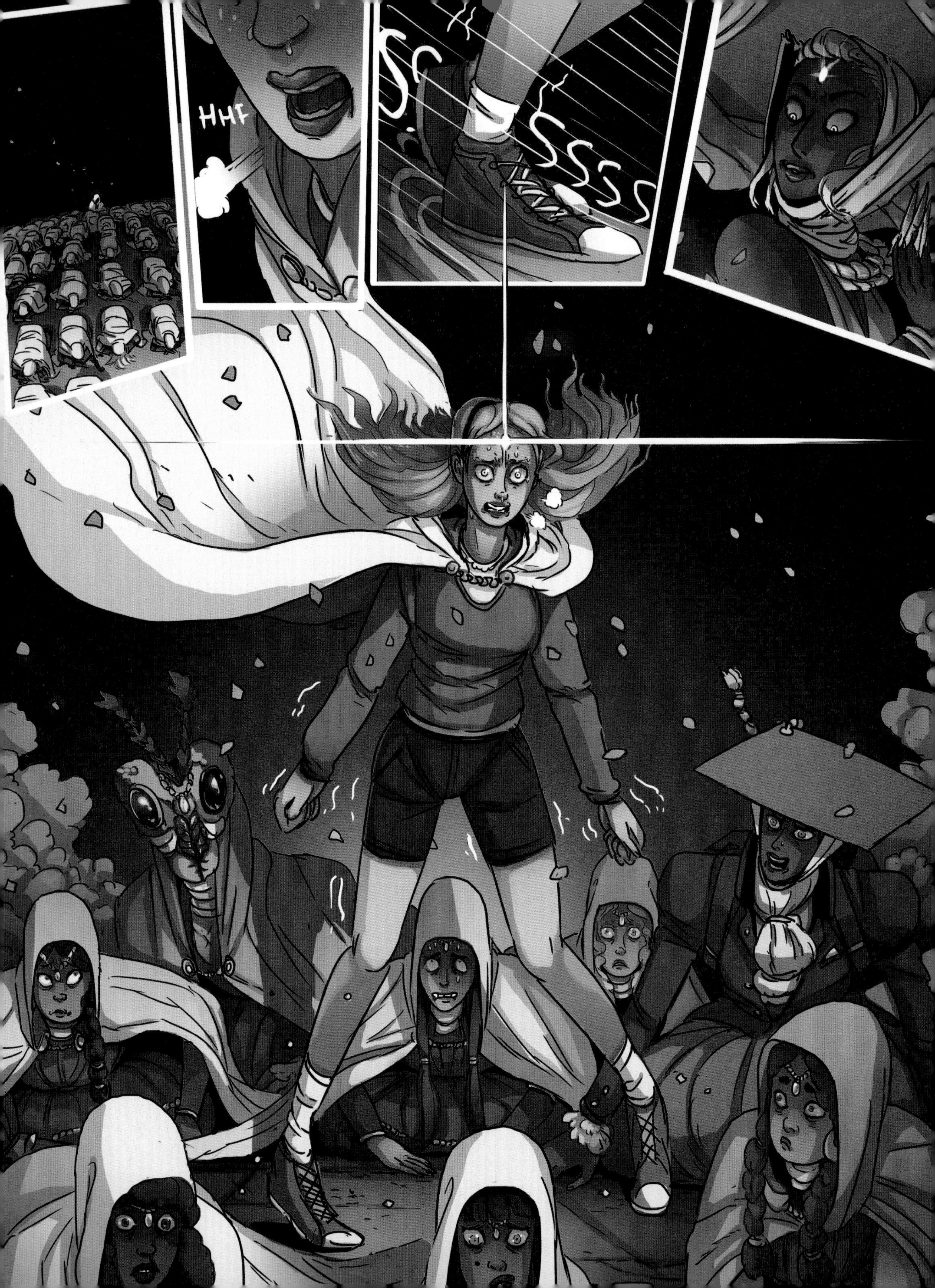
HHF
SSSSSS

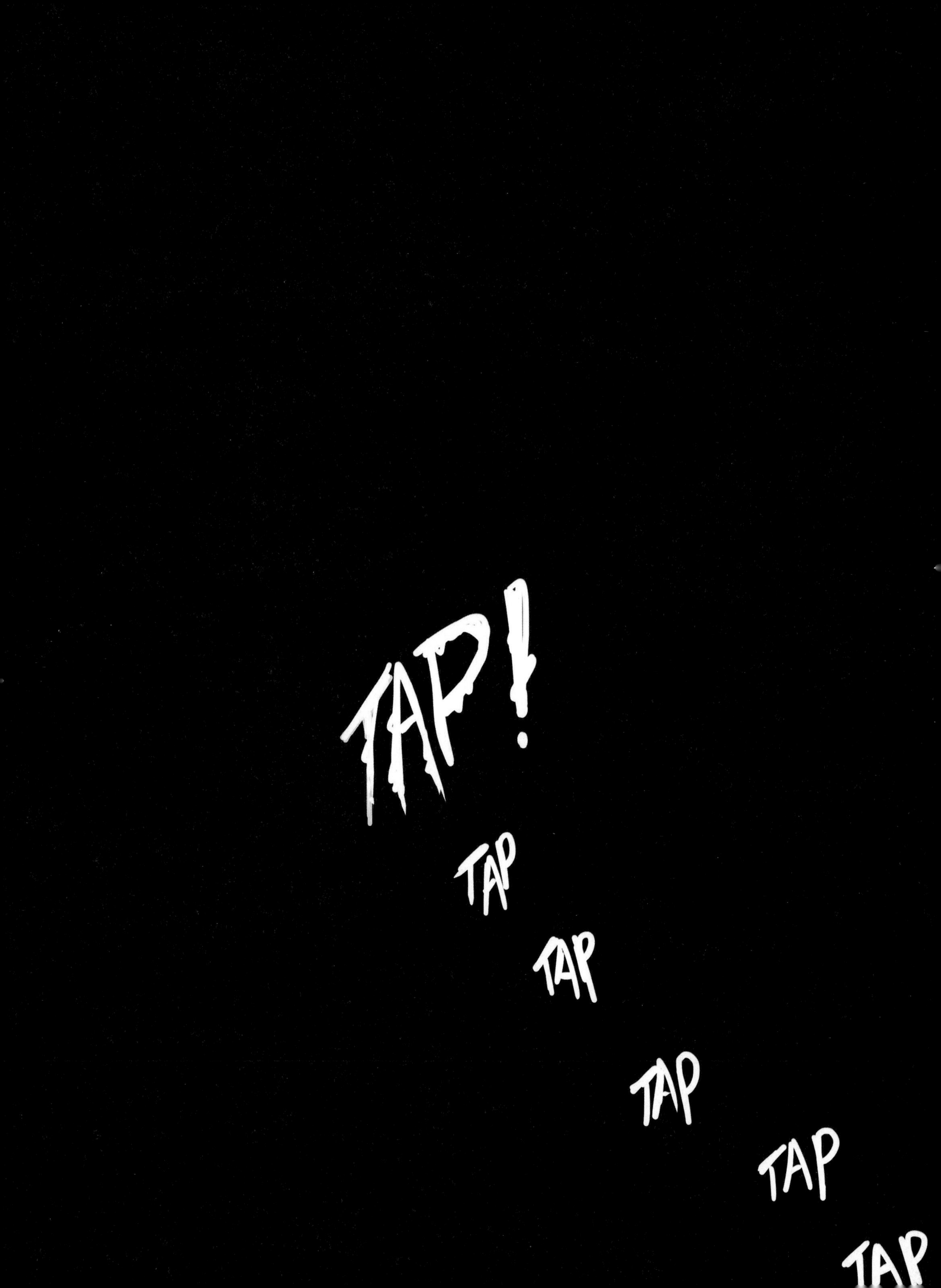
TAP!
TAP
TAP
TAP
TAP
TAP

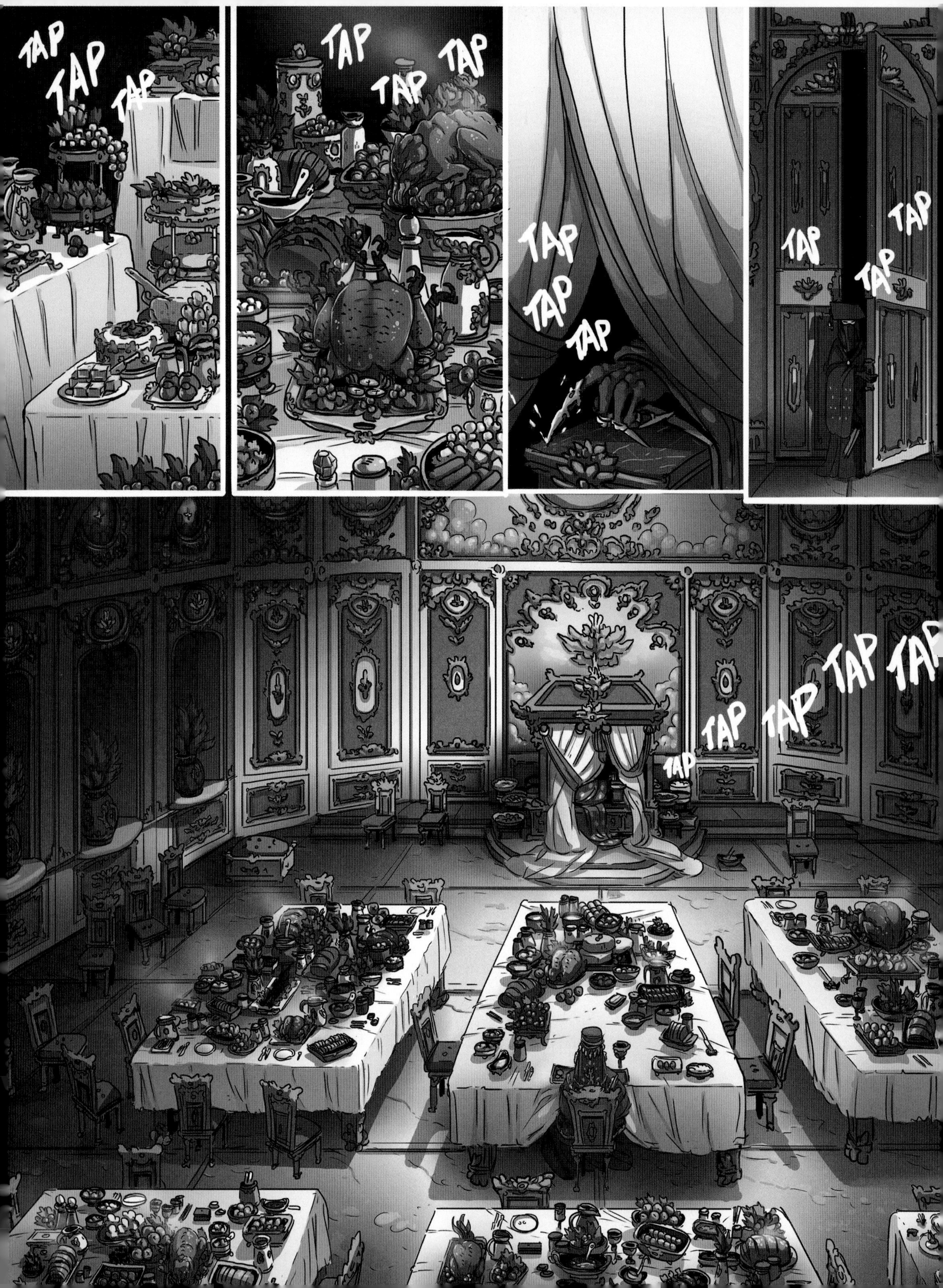
TAP
TAP
TAP
TAP
TAP
TAP
TAP
TAP
TAP
TAP
TAP
TAP
TAP
TAP
TAP
TAP
TAP
TAP

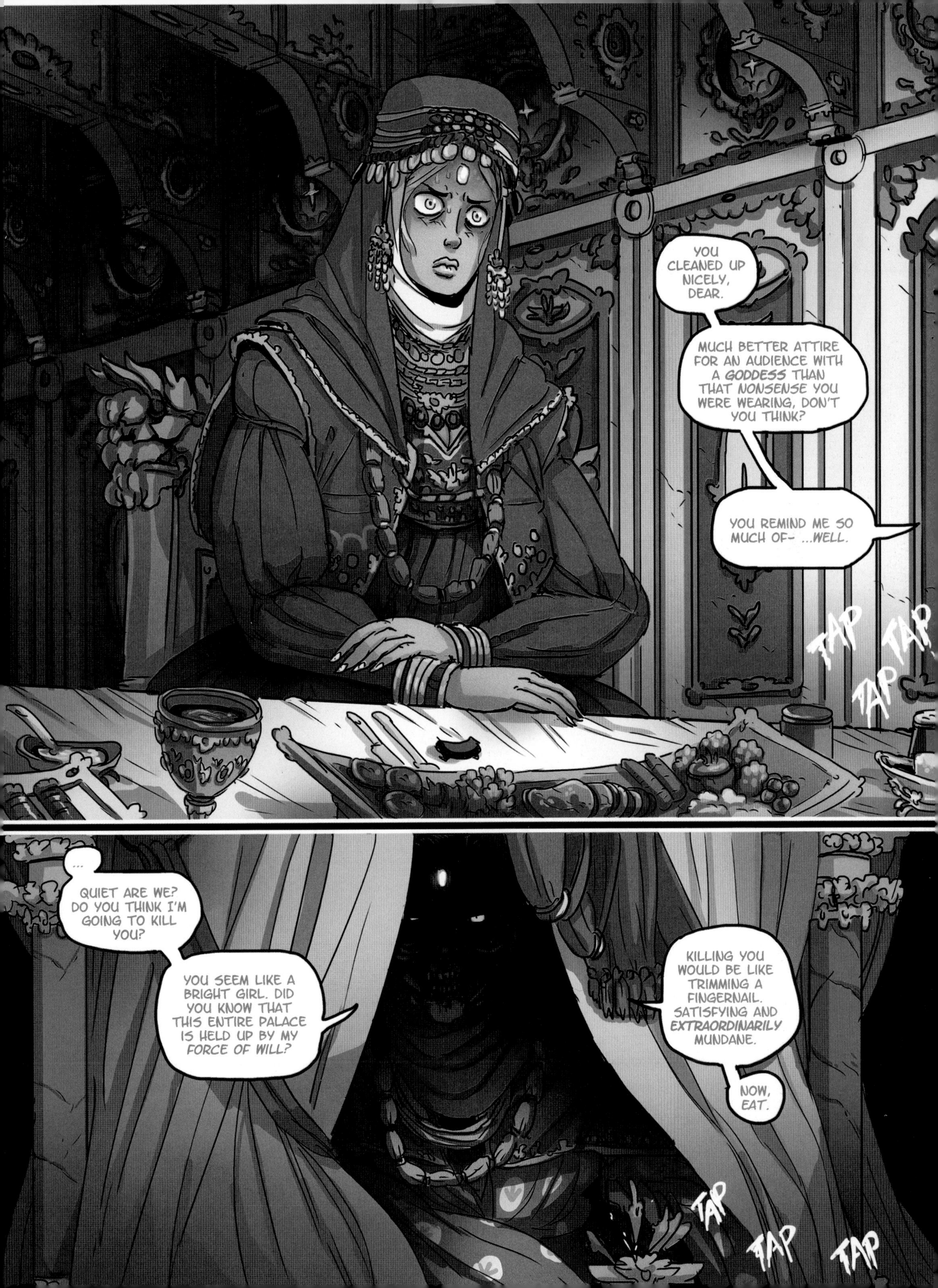

YOU CLEANED UP NICELY, DEAR.
MUCH BETTER ATTIRE FOR AN AUDIENCE WITH A *GODDESS* THAN THAT *NONSENSE* YOU WERE WEARING, DON'T YOU THINK?
YOU REMIND ME SO MUCH OF- ...*WELL.*
TAP TAP TAP TAP
...
QUIET ARE WE? DO YOU THINK I'M GOING TO KILL YOU?
YOU SEEM LIKE A BRIGHT GIRL. DID YOU KNOW THAT THIS ENTIRE PALACE IS HELD UP BY MY *FORCE OF WILL?*
KILLING YOU WOULD BE LIKE TRIMMING A FINGERNAIL. SATISFYING AND ***EXTRAORDINARILY*** MUNDANE.
NOW, EAT.
TAP TAP TAP

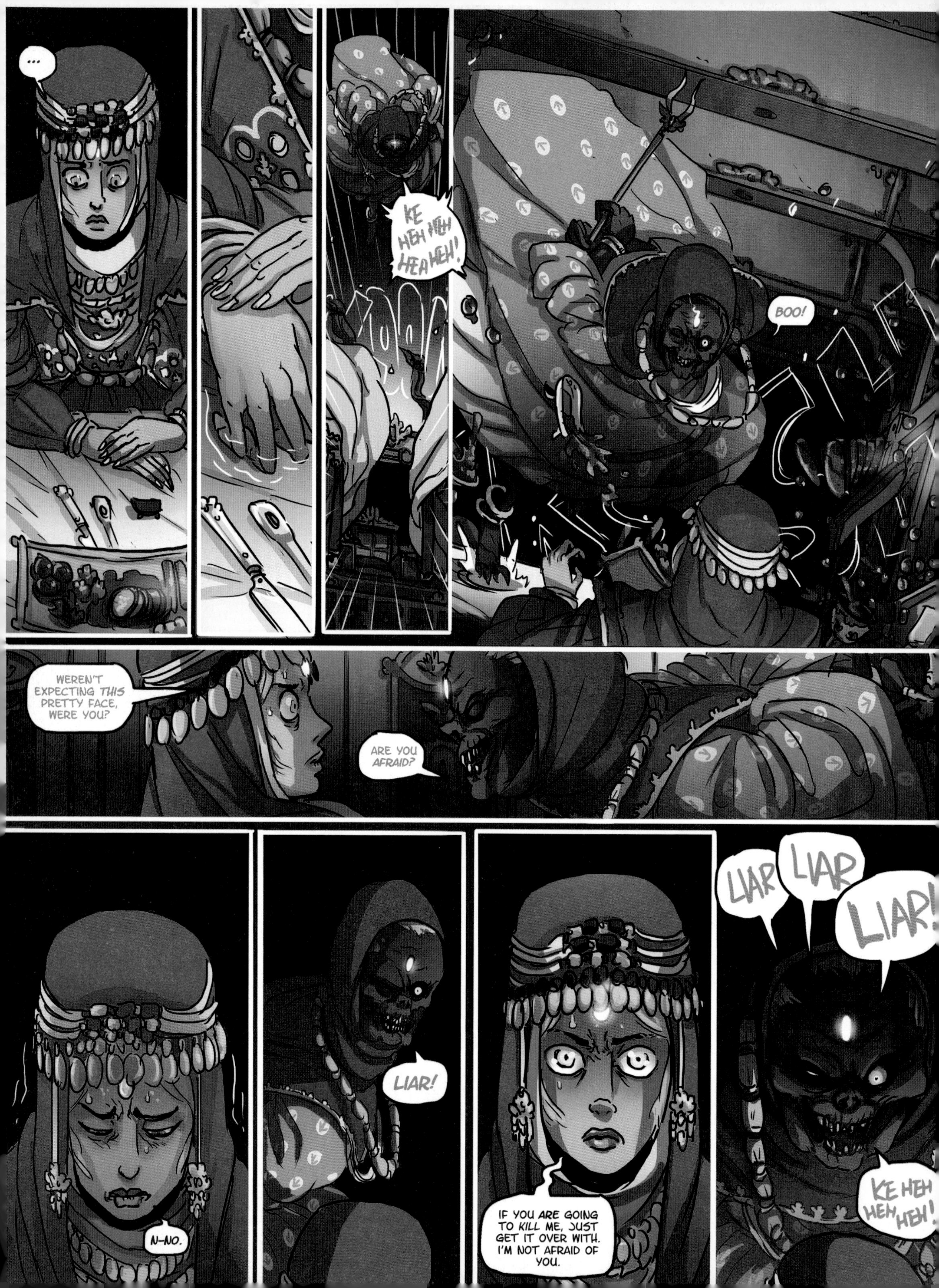
...
KE HEH HEH HEA HEH!
BOO!
WEREN'T EXPECTING THIS PRETTY FACE, WERE YOU?
ARE YOU AFRAID?
N-NO.
LIAR!
IF YOU ARE GOING TO KILL ME, JUST GET IT OVER WITH. I'M NOT AFRAID OF YOU.
LIAR
LIAR
LIAR!
KE HEH HEH HEH!

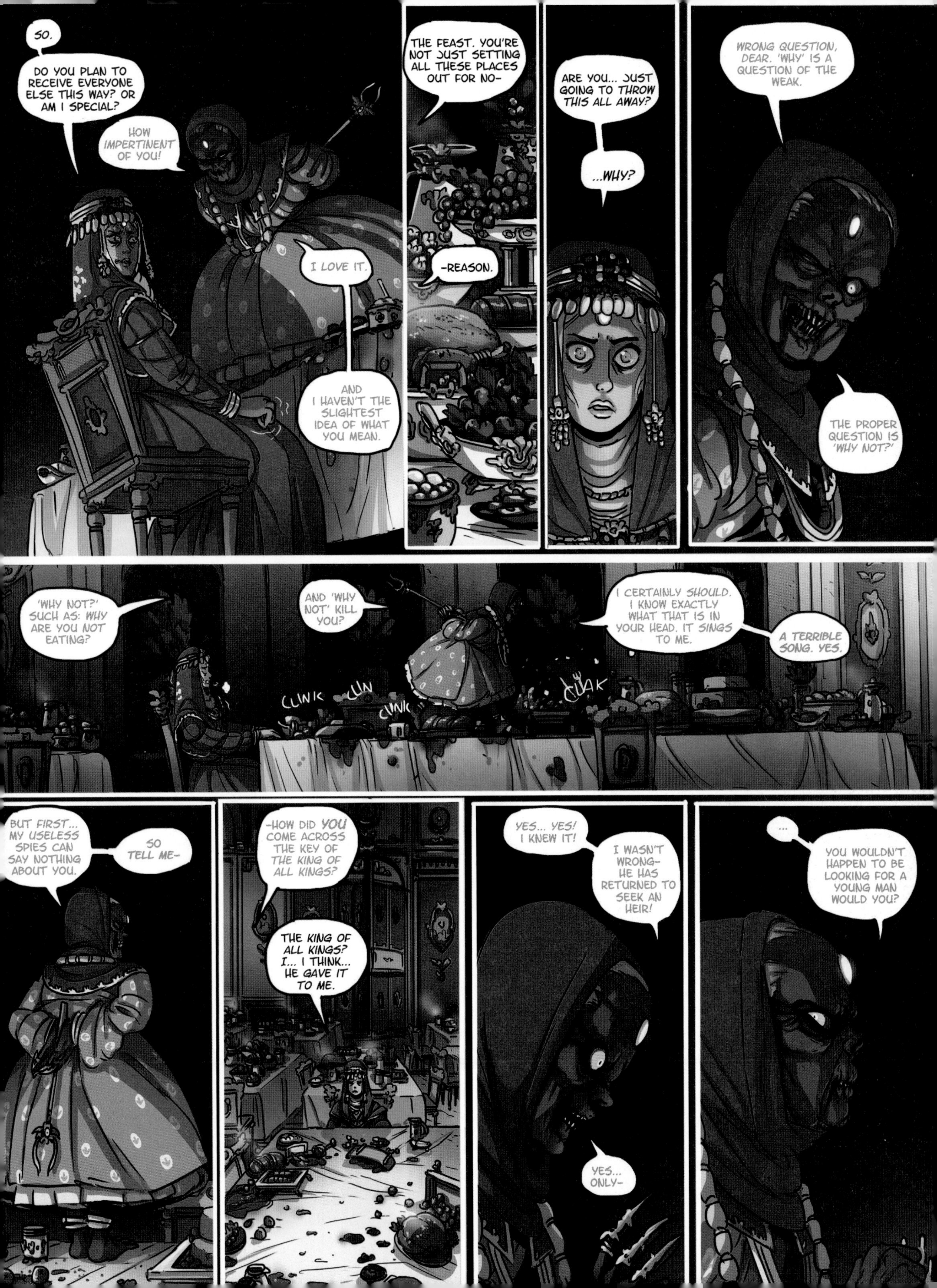
SO.
DO YOU PLAN TO RECEIVE EVERYONE ELSE THIS WAY? OR AM I SPECIAL?
HOW IMPERTINENT OF YOU!
I LOVE IT.
AND I HAVEN'T THE SLIGHTEST IDEA OF WHAT YOU MEAN.
THE FEAST. YOU'RE NOT JUST SETTING ALL THESE PLACES OUT FOR NO-
-REASON.
ARE YOU... JUST GOING TO THROW THIS ALL AWAY?
...WHY?
WRONG QUESTION, DEAR. 'WHY' IS A QUESTION OF THE WEAK.
THE PROPER QUESTION IS 'WHY NOT?'
'WHY NOT?' SUCH AS: WHY ARE YOU NOT EATING?
AND 'WHY NOT' KILL YOU?
I CERTAINLY SHOULD. I KNOW EXACTLY WHAT THAT IS IN YOUR HEAD. IT SINGS TO ME.
A TERRIBLE SONG. YES.
CLINK CLIN CLINK CLAK
BUT FIRST... MY USELESS SPIES CAN SAY NOTHING ABOUT YOU.
SO TELL ME-
-HOW DID YOU COME ACROSS THE KEY OF THE KING OF ALL KINGS?
THE KING OF ALL KINGS? I... I THINK... HE GAVE IT TO ME.
YES... YES! I KNEW IT!
I WASN'T WRONG- HE HAS RETURNED TO SEEK AN HEIR!
YES... ONLY-
...
YOU WOULDN'T HAPPEN TO BE LOOKING FOR A YOUNG MAN WOULD YOU?

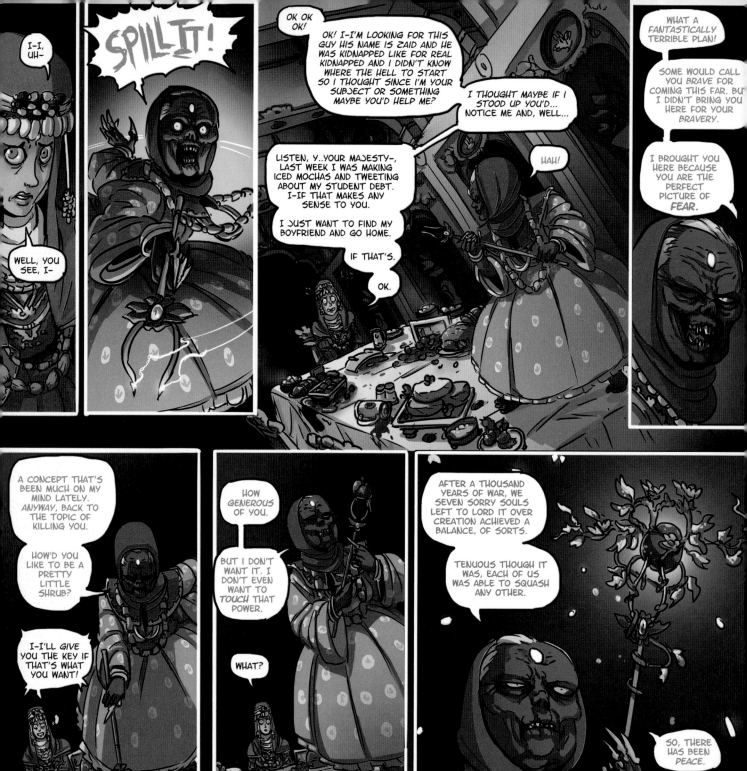

I-I, UH-

SPILL IT!

WELL, YOU SEE, I-

OK OK OK!

OK! I-I'M LOOKING FOR THIS GUY HIS NAME IS ZAID AND HE WAS KIDNAPPED LIKE FOR REAL KIDNAPPED AND I DIDN'T KNOW WHERE THE HELL TO START SO I THOUGHT SINCE I'M YOUR SUBJECT OR SOMETHING MAYBE YOU'D HELP ME?

I THOUGHT MAYBE IF I STOOD UP YOU'D... NOTICE ME AND, WELL...

HAH!

LISTEN, Y..YOUR MAJESTY— LAST WEEK I WAS MAKING ICED MOCHAS AND TWEETING ABOUT MY STUDENT DEBT. I-IF THAT MAKES ANY SENSE TO YOU.

I JUST WANT TO FIND MY BOYFRIEND AND GO HOME.

IF THAT'S.

OK.

WHAT A FANTASTICALLY TERRIBLE PLAN!

SOME WOULD CALL YOU BRAVE FOR COMING THIS FAR. BUT I DIDN'T BRING YOU HERE FOR YOUR BRAVERY.

I BROUGHT YOU HERE BECAUSE YOU ARE THE PERFECT PICTURE OF FEAR.

A CONCEPT THAT'S BEEN MUCH ON MY MIND LATELY. ANYWAY, BACK TO THE TOPIC OF KILLING YOU.

HOW'D YOU LIKE TO BE A PRETTY LITTLE SHRUB?

I-I'LL GIVE YOU THE KEY IF THAT'S WHAT YOU WANT!

HOW GENEROUS OF YOU.

BUT I DON'T WANT IT. I DON'T EVEN WANT TO TOUCH THAT POWER.

WHAT?

AFTER A THOUSAND YEARS OF WAR, WE SEVEN SORRY SOULS LEFT TO LORD IT OVER CREATION ACHIEVED A BALANCE, OF SORTS.

TENUOUS THOUGH IT WAS, EACH OF US WAS ABLE TO SQUASH ANY OTHER.

SO, THERE HAS BEEN PEACE.

BUT NOW... THERE IS JAGGANOTH.

JAGGANOTH...

THE RED GOD. ONE OF THE OTHER SIX IDIOTS WHO RULE THIS BLASTED COSMOS.

HE HAD ALWAYS BEEN RECLUSIVE AND SULLEN. PEACE WAS... NOT FOR HIM.

WE WERE TOO BUSY IN OUR STUPID, PETTY SQUABBLES OVER HOW TO CARVE UP THE RUINED CORPSE OF CREATION.

WE THOUGHT NOTHING WHEN HE SUDDENLY WITHDREW. LATER, HE TOLD US AN ANGEL OF *YISUN* HAD COME TO HIM IN A DREAM AND GIVEN HIM A HOLY MISSION.

THE ANGEL GAVE HIM THIRTY IRON FEATHERS, WHICH HE FORGED INTO NAILS AND DROVE INTO HIS FLESH.

HE BECAME *UNTOUCHABLE*. IT WAS BEYOND BELIEF.

ONLY THE COMBINED MIGHT OF ALL SIX OF US COULD HOPE TO STAND AGAINST HIM NOW.

NOT TO MENTION HIS ARMIES. HE IS PREPARING NON-STOP.

FOR *WHAT*?

WHAT IS THIS HOLY MISSION?

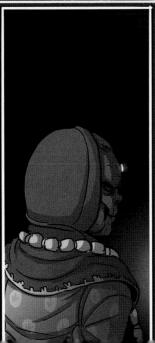

TO ANNIHILATE THE MULTIVERSE.

...HE COULD DO IT, YOU KNOW.

HE REALLY COULD. AND ALL IT TAKES IS ONE LITTLE CRACK BETWEEN THE OTHER SIX OF US.

SO YOU SEE, I, TOO, AM RULED BY FEAR.

Y-YOUR MAJESTY, I APPRECIATE YOU TELLING ME ALL THIS, EVEN IF I DON'T REALLY UNDERSTAND WHY.

THAT'S... KIND OF BEEN NORMAL FOR ME.

BUT IF YOU'RE NOT GOING TO HELP ME, JUST TELL ME ONE THING—

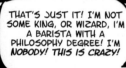

WHERE THE **FUCK** IS MY BOYFRIEND?

MAMMON HAS HIM IMPRISONED IN THE TREASURE FORTRESS OF YRE BY VERY TENUOUS AGREEMENT.

MY, MY—

—YOU ARE A SAUCY ONE.

HOW DID A SCRAWNY LITTLE NOTHING LIKE YOU GET WRAPPED UP IN ALL OF THIS?

THAT'S JUST IT! I'M NOT SOME KING, OR WIZARD, I'M A BARISTA WITH A PHILOSOPHY DEGREE! I'M NOBODY! THIS IS CRAZY!

I'VE BEEN TRYING MY WHOLE BORING, MUNDANE FUCKING LIFE TO ESCAPE BEING A NOBODY. BUT YOU KNOW WHAT?

NOW I WANT IT BACK!

YOU ARE SO LIKE ME WHEN I WAS YOUR AGE. YOUR FATAL ERROR IS THINKING YOU CAN STILL RUN.

THE BOY IS PROPHESIZED TO BECOME THE RISING KING, THE RULER THAT DESTROYS ME AND MY COMPATRIOTS. THE HEIR OF OLD KING ZOSS.

THE PROPHET, I SHOULD MENTION, IS NEVER WRONG, YET...

YET?!

...YET HERE YOU ARE, WIELDING HIS MISSING POWER...

THAT'S THE PROBLEM WITH POWER. THE MOMENT IT TOUCHES YOU, DESTINY SINKS ITS CLAWS INTO YOUR PRETTY LITTLE FLESH.

AND OH, BY THE ROTTING GODS

IT WILL TUG.

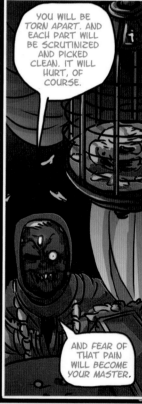
YOU WILL BE TORN APART. AND EACH PART WILL BE SCRUTINIZED AND PICKED CLEAN. IT WILL HURT, OF COURSE.

AND FEAR OF THAT PAIN WILL BECOME YOUR MASTER.

YES, WELL DO I KNOW YOUR FATE, GIRL.

AGAINST YOUR WILL, YOU HAVE BECOME A **SLAVE**, LASHED BY UNSEEN CHAINS TO A STORY YOU CANNOT WRITE

AND WANT NO PART IN.

YOU **WILL** LOSE YOURSELF.

FATE WILL WARP YOU BEYOND RECOGNITION, LITTLE MISS NOBODY.

YOU WILL BECOME MALFORMED. AND YOU WILL HATE EVERY SECOND OF IT. SUCH IS YOUR PATH NOW.

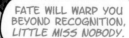

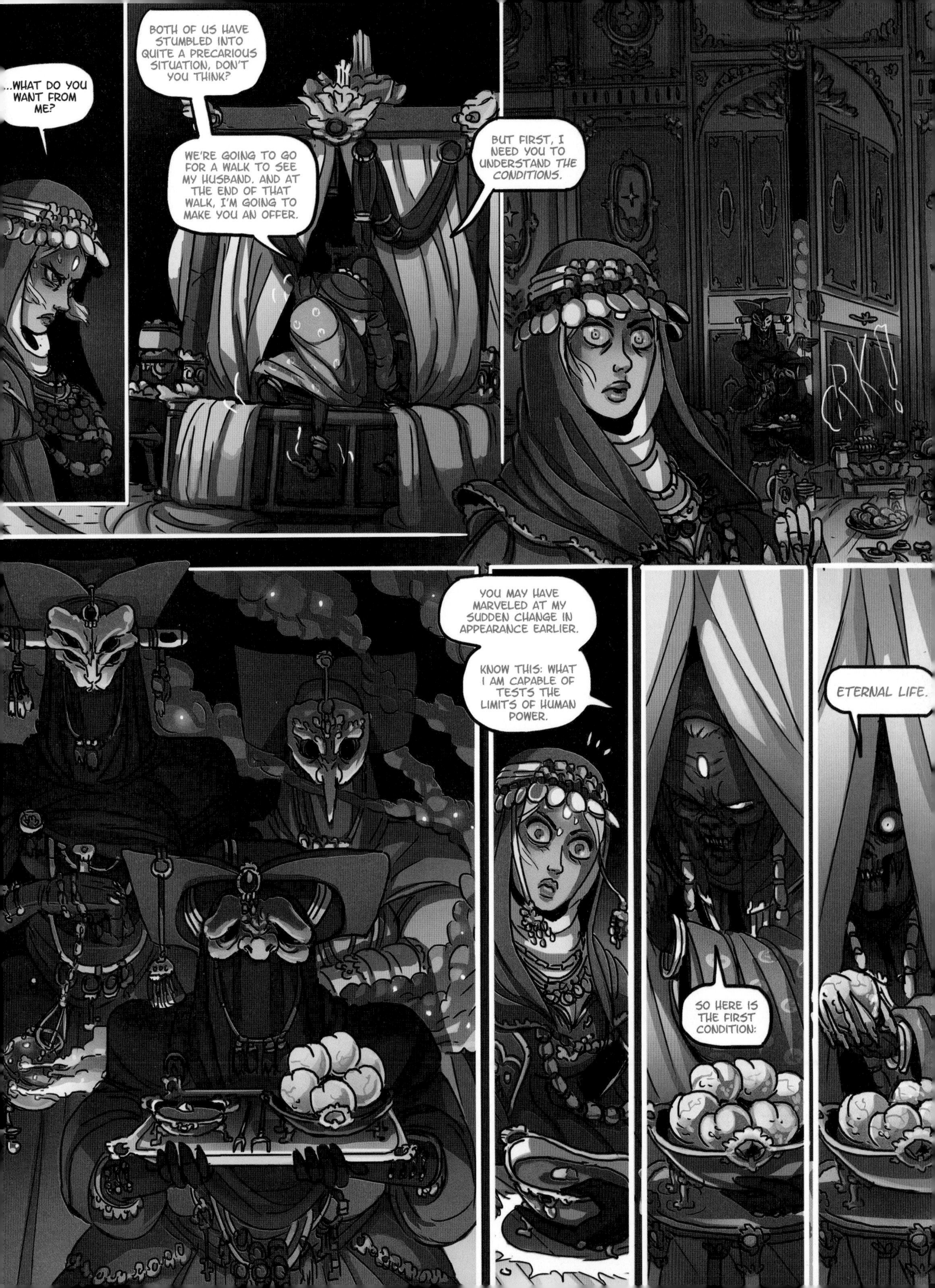
...WHAT DO YOU WANT FROM ME?
BOTH OF US HAVE STUMBLED INTO QUITE A PRECARIOUS SITUATION, DON'T YOU THINK?
WE'RE GOING TO GO FOR A WALK TO SEE MY HUSBAND. AND AT THE END OF THAT WALK, I'M GOING TO MAKE YOU AN OFFER.
BUT FIRST, I NEED YOU TO UNDERSTAND THE CONDITIONS.
YOU MAY HAVE MARVELED AT MY SUDDEN CHANGE IN APPEARANCE EARLIER.
KNOW THIS: WHAT I AM CAPABLE OF TESTS THE LIMITS OF HUMAN POWER.
SO HERE IS THE FIRST CONDITION:
ETERNAL LIFE.

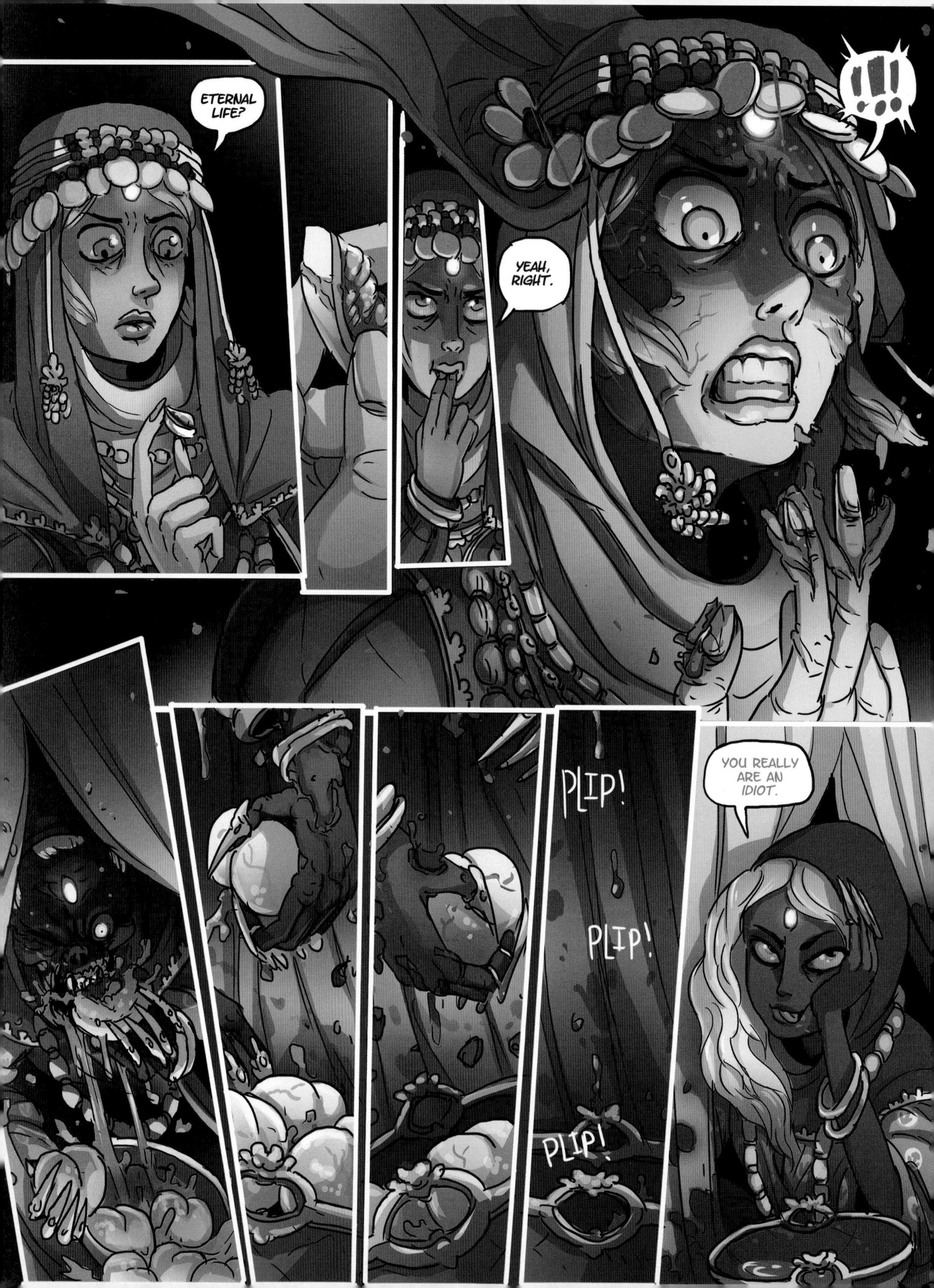
!!!
ETERNAL LIFE?
YEAH, RIGHT.
PLIP!
PLIP!
PLIP!
YOU REALLY ARE AN IDIOT.

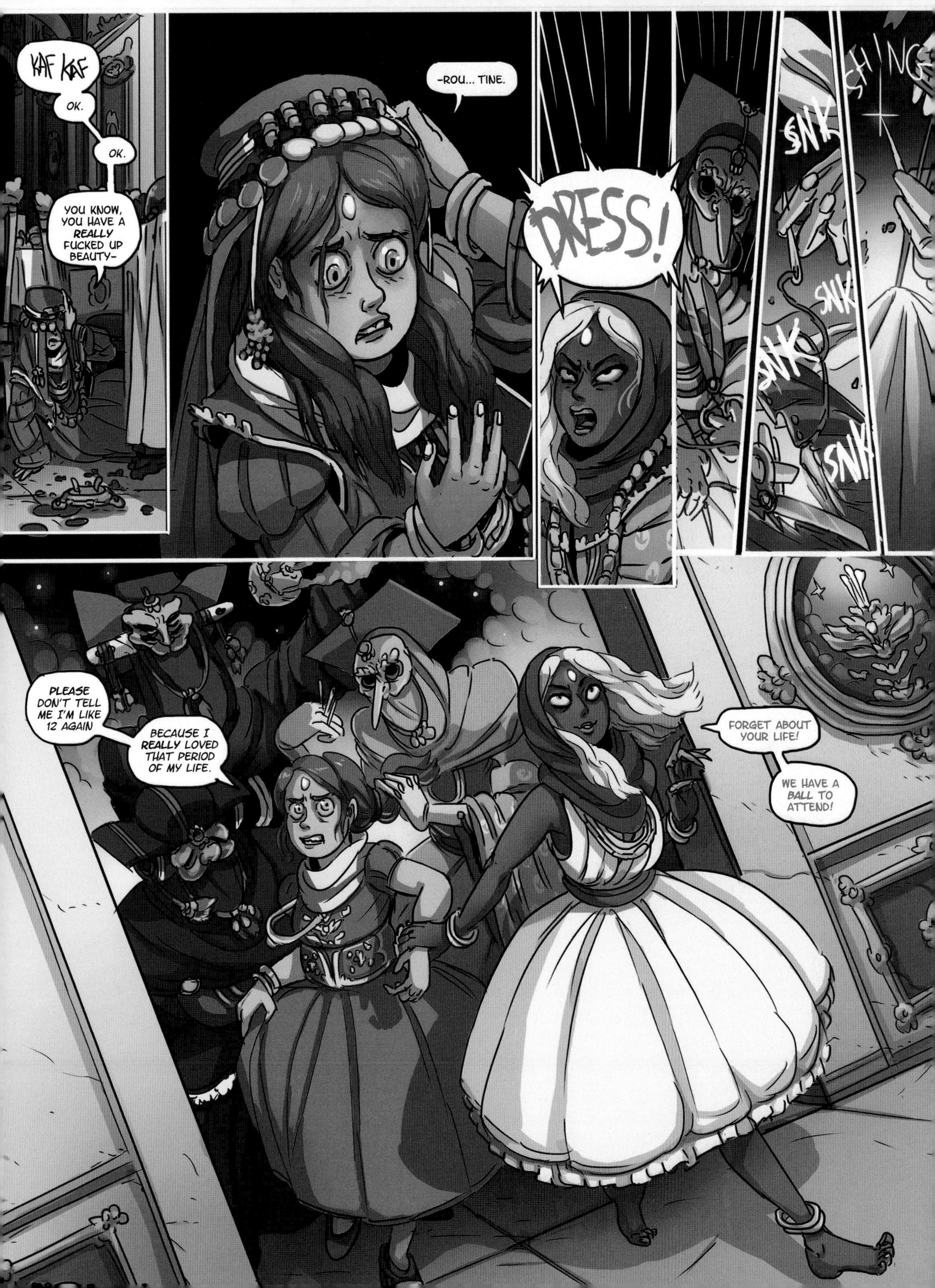
KAF KAF
OK.
OK.
YOU KNOW, YOU HAVE A REALLY FUCKED UP BEAUTY-
-ROU... TINE.
DRESS!
SNK
SHING
SNK
SNK
SNK
SNK
PLEASE DON'T TELL ME I'M LIKE 12 AGAIN
BECAUSE I REALLY LOVED THAT PERIOD OF MY LIFE.
FORGET ABOUT YOUR LIFE!
WE HAVE A BALL TO ATTEND!

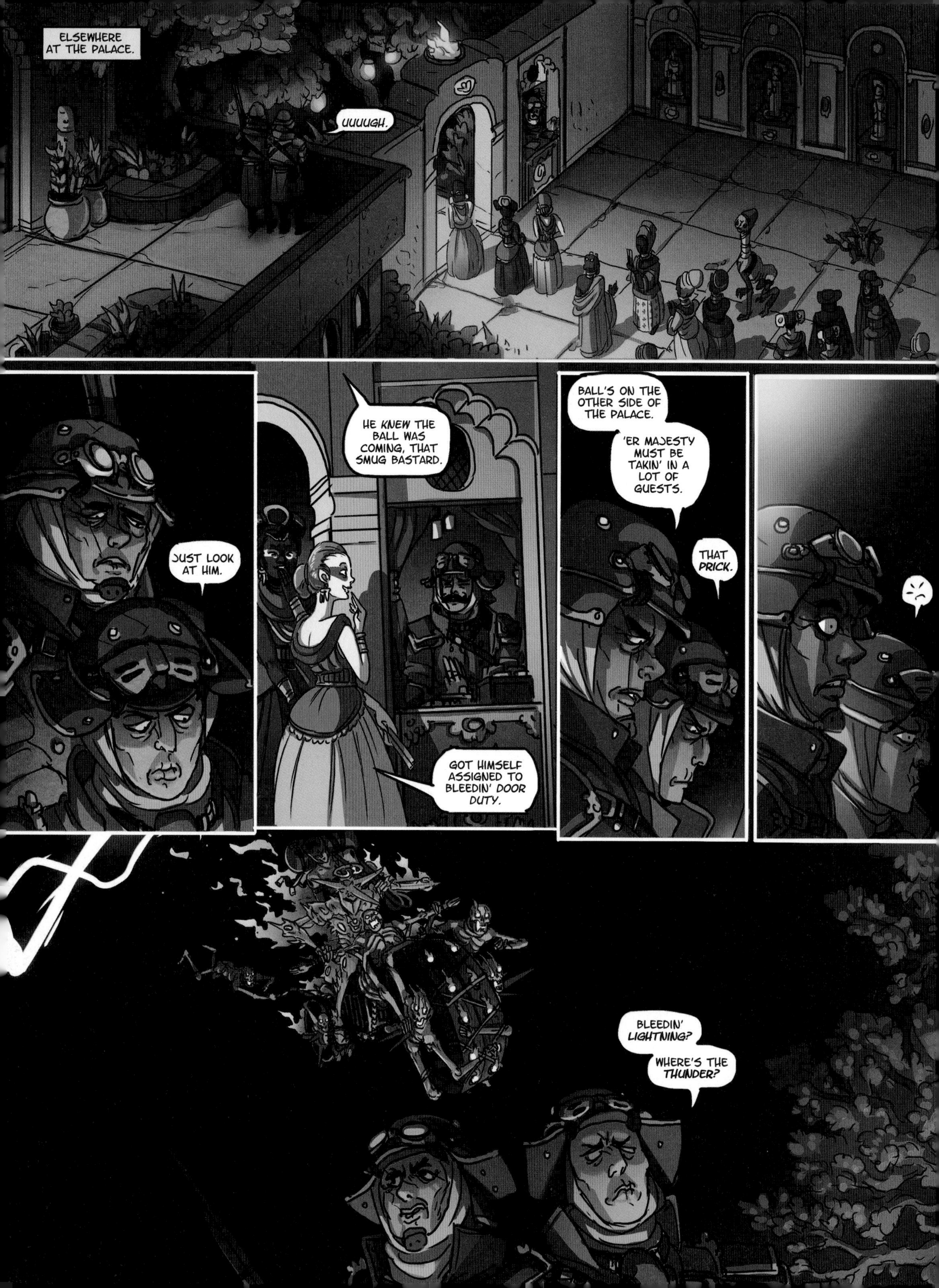

ELSEWHERE AT THE PALACE.
UUUUGH.
JUST LOOK AT HIM.
HE KNEW THE BALL WAS COMING, THAT SMUG BASTARD.
GOT HIMSELF ASSIGNED TO BLEEDIN' DOOR DUTY.
BALL'S ON THE OTHER SIDE OF THE PALACE.
'ER MAJESTY MUST BE TAKIN' IN A LOT OF GUESTS.
THAT PRICK.
BLEEDIN' LIGHTNING?
WHERE'S THE THUNDER?

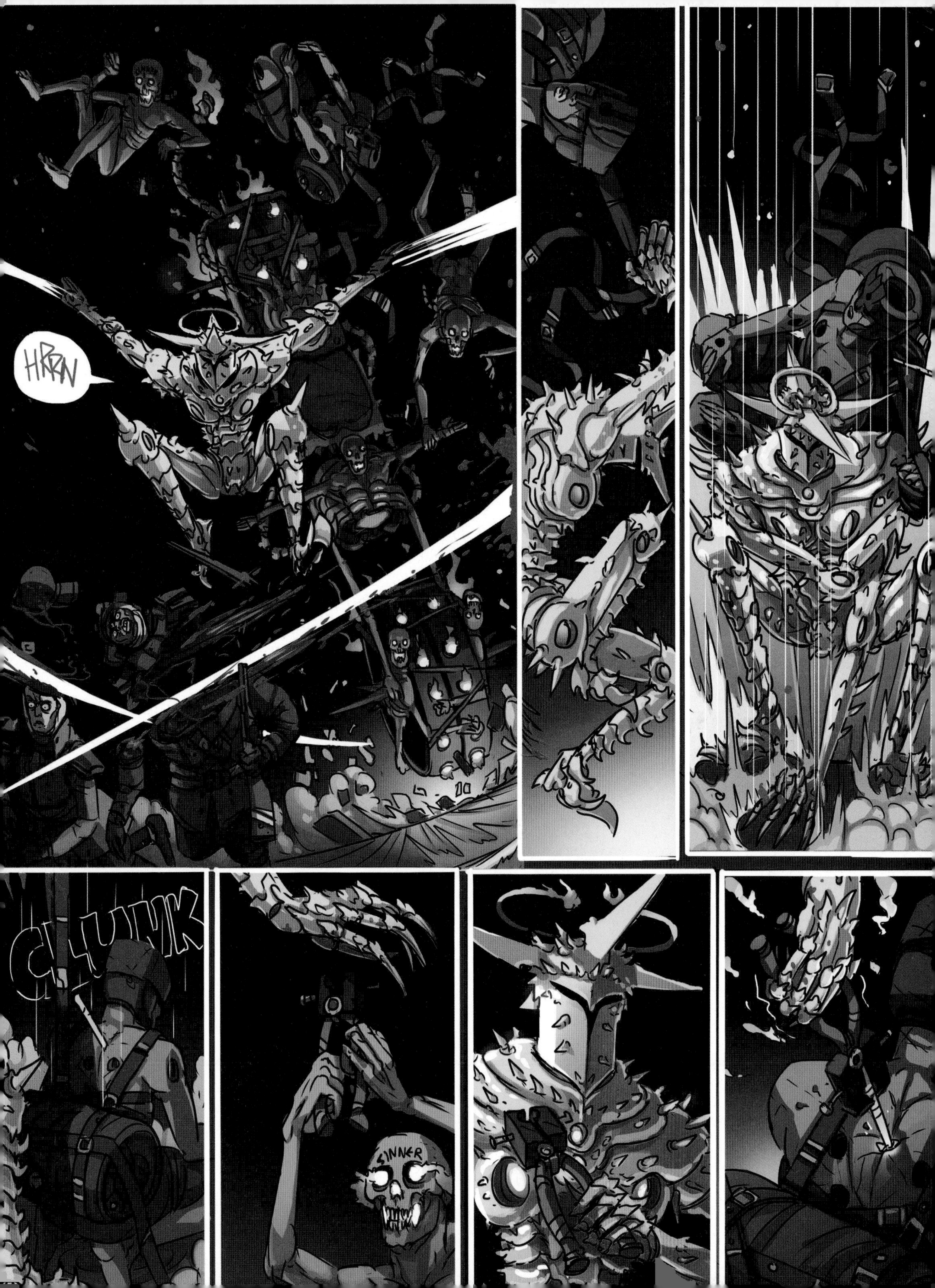
HRRN
CHUNK
SINNER

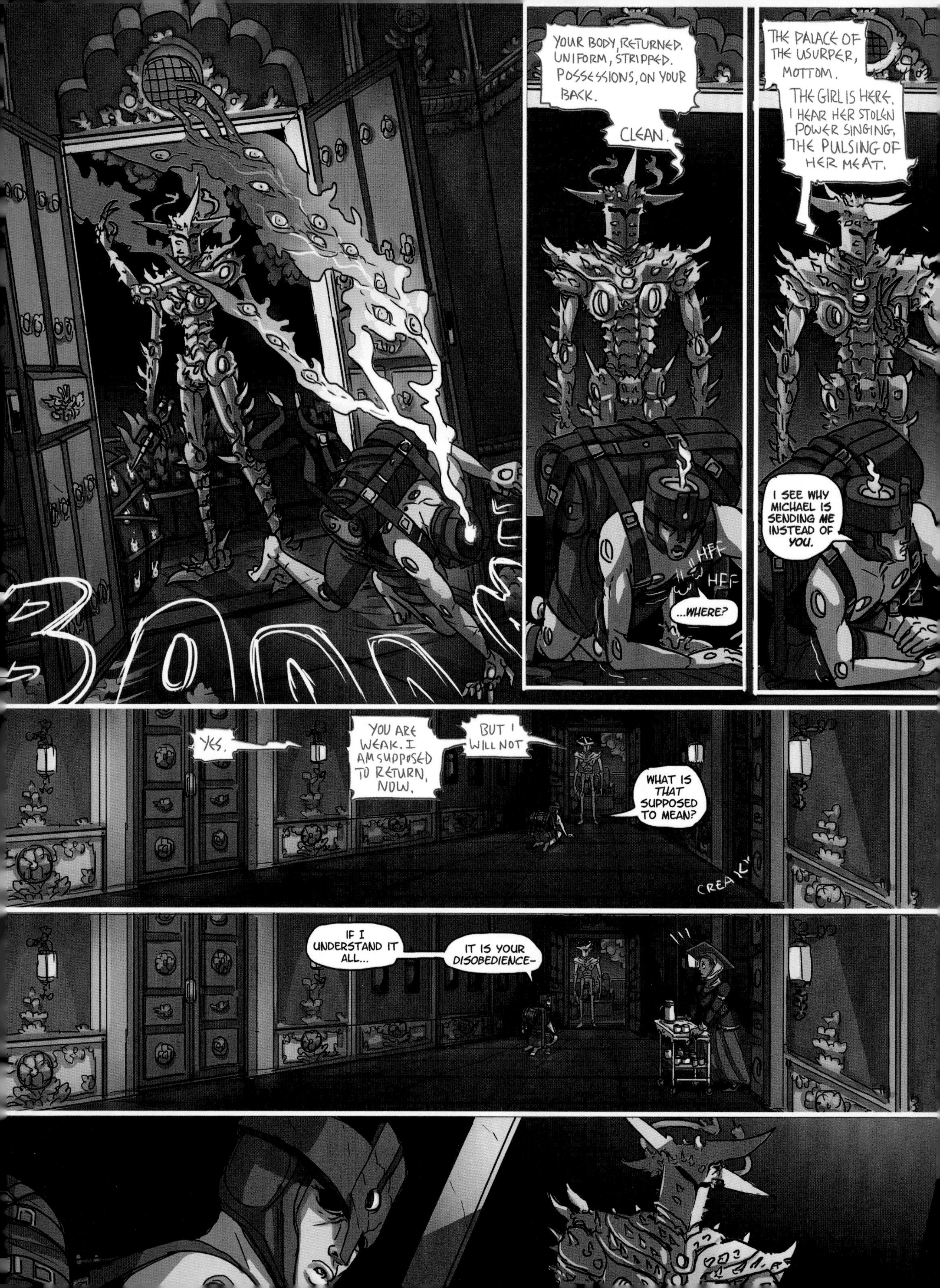
BOOOM
YOUR BODY, RETURNED. UNIFORM, STRIPPED. POSSESSIONS, ON YOUR BACK.
CLEAN.
HFF HFF
...WHERE?
THE PALACE OF THE USURPER, MOTTOM.
THE GIRL IS HERE. I HEAR HER STOLEN POWER SINGING, THE PULSING OF HER MEAT.
I SEE WHY MICHAEL IS SENDING ME INSTEAD OF YOU.
YES.
YOU ARE WEAK. I AM SUPPOSED TO RETURN, NOW.
BUT I WILL NOT
WHAT IS THAT SUPPOSED TO MEAN?
CREAK
IF I UNDERSTAND IT ALL...
IT IS YOUR DISOBEDIENCE-

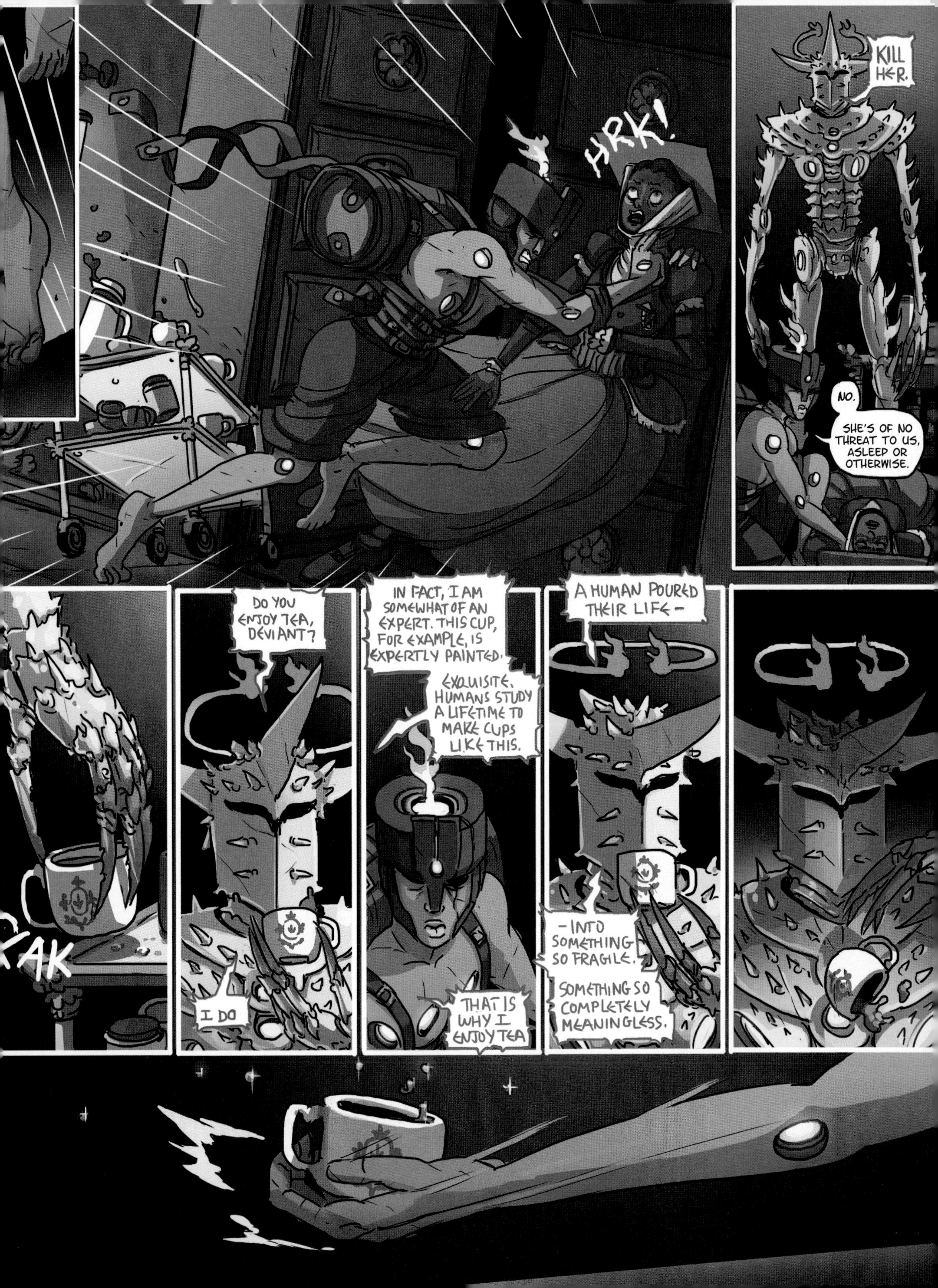
HRK!
KILL HER.
NO.
SHE'S OF NO THREAT TO US, ASLEEP OR OTHERWISE.
AK
DO YOU ENJOY TEA, DEVIANT?
I DO
IN FACT, I AM SOMEWHAT OF AN EXPERT. THIS CUP, FOR EXAMPLE, IS EXPERTLY PAINTED.
EXQUISITE. HUMANS STUDY A LIFETIME TO MAKE CUPS LIKE THIS.
THAT IS WHY I ENJOY TEA
A HUMAN POURED THEIR LIFE—
—INTO SOMETHING SO FRAGILE.
SOMETHING SO COMPLETELY MEANINGLESS.

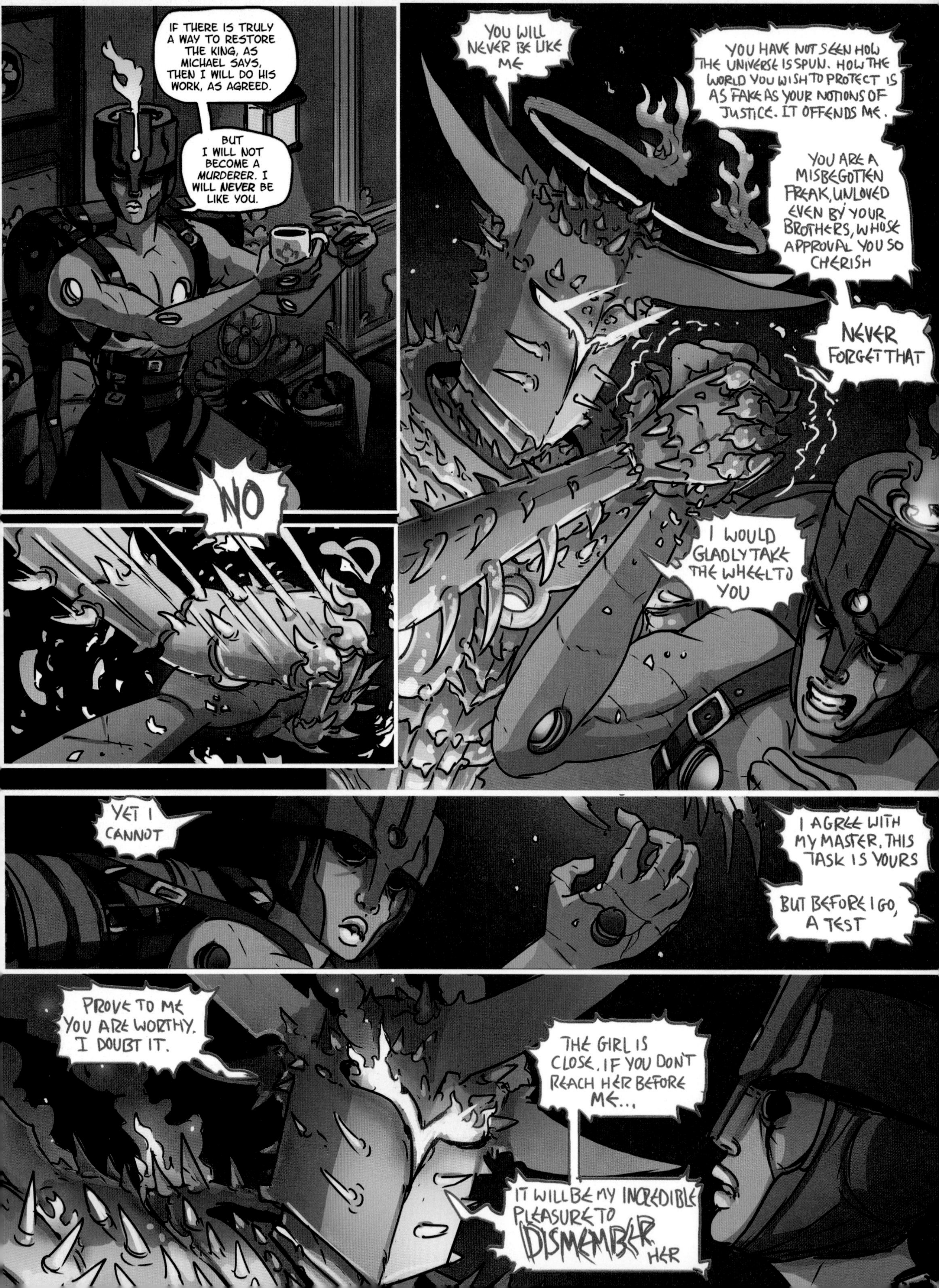
IF THERE IS TRULY A WAY TO RESTORE THE KING, AS MICHAEL SAYS, THEN I WILL DO HIS WORK, AS AGREED.
BUT I WILL NOT BECOME A MURDERER. I WILL NEVER BE LIKE YOU.
NO
YOU WILL NEVER BE LIKE ME
YOU HAVE NOT SEEN HOW THE UNIVERSE IS SPUN. HOW THE WORLD YOU WISH TO PROTECT IS AS FAKE AS YOUR NOTIONS OF JUSTICE. IT OFFENDS ME.
YOU ARE A MISBEGOTTEN FREAK, UNLOVED EVEN BY YOUR BROTHERS, WHOSE APPROVAL YOU SO CHERISH
NEVER FORGET THAT
I WOULD GLADLY TAKE THE WHEEL TO YOU
YET I CANNOT
I AGREE WITH MY MASTER. THIS TASK IS YOURS
BUT BEFORE I GO, A TEST
PROVE TO ME YOU ARE WORTHY. I DOUBT IT.
THE GIRL IS CLOSE. IF YOU DON'T REACH HER BEFORE ME...
IT WILL BE MY INCREDIBLE PLEASURE TO DISMEMBER HER

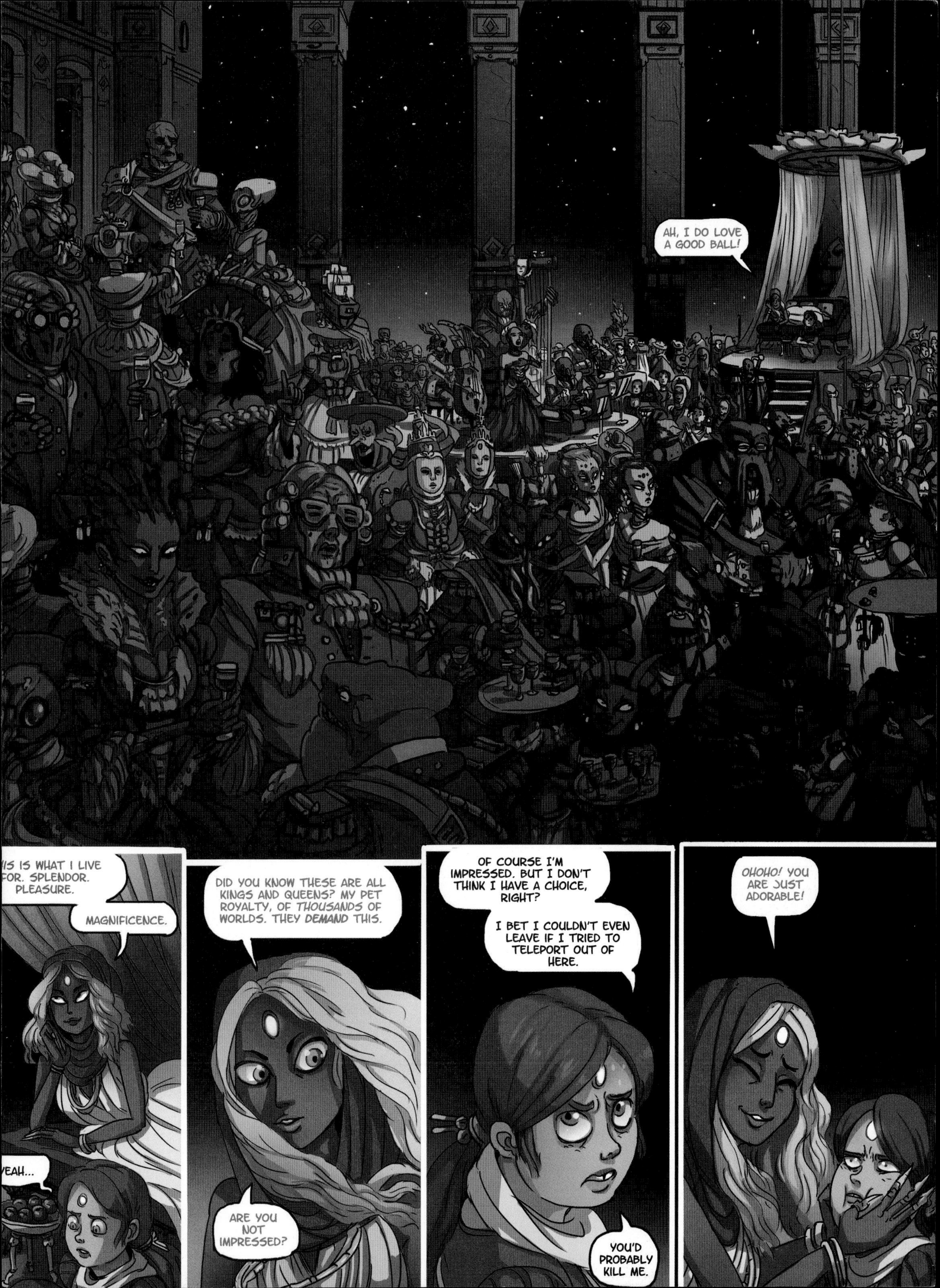
AH, I DO LOVE A GOOD BALL!
HIS IS WHAT I LIVE FOR. SPLENDOR. PLEASURE.
MAGNIFICENCE.
YEAH...
DID YOU KNOW THESE ARE ALL KINGS AND QUEENS? MY PET ROYALTY, OF THOUSANDS OF WORLDS. THEY DEMAND THIS.
ARE YOU NOT IMPRESSED?
OF COURSE I'M IMPRESSED. BUT I DON'T THINK I HAVE A CHOICE, RIGHT?
I BET I COULDN'T EVEN LEAVE IF I TRIED TO TELEPORT OUT OF HERE.
YOU'D PROBABLY KILL ME.
OHOHO! YOU ARE JUST ADORABLE!

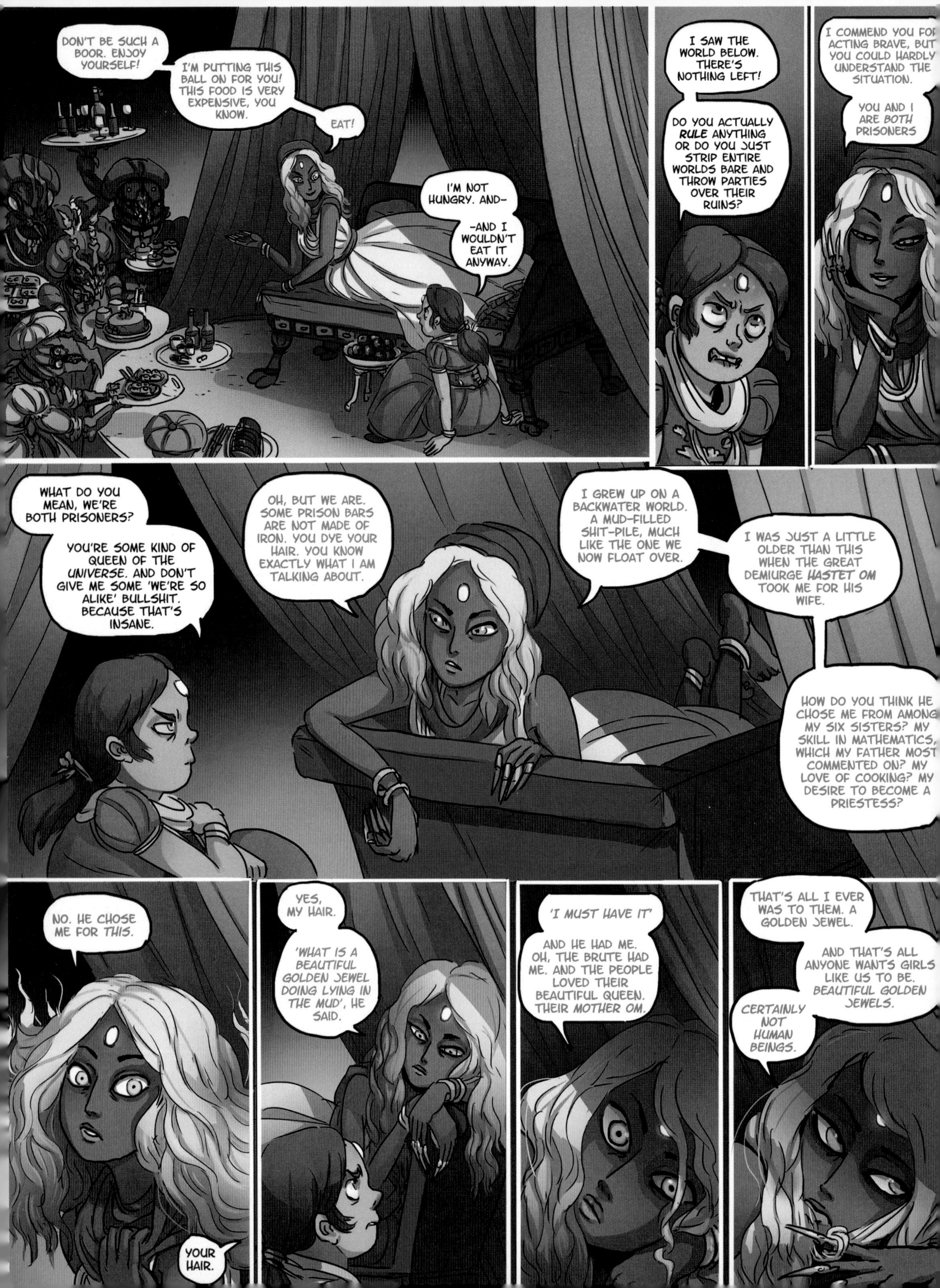
DON'T BE SUCH A BOOR. ENJOY YOURSELF!
I'M PUTTING THIS BALL ON FOR YOU! THIS FOOD IS VERY EXPENSIVE, YOU KNOW.
EAT!
I'M NOT HUNGRY. AND-
-AND I WOULDN'T EAT IT ANYWAY.
I SAW THE WORLD BELOW. THERE'S NOTHING LEFT!
DO YOU ACTUALLY RULE ANYTHING OR DO YOU JUST STRIP ENTIRE WORLDS BARE AND THROW PARTIES OVER THEIR RUINS?
I COMMEND YOU FOR ACTING BRAVE, BUT YOU COULD HARDLY UNDERSTAND THE SITUATION.
YOU AND I ARE BOTH PRISONERS
WHAT DO YOU MEAN, WE'RE BOTH PRISONERS?
YOU'RE SOME KIND OF QUEEN OF THE UNIVERSE. AND DON'T GIVE ME SOME 'WE'RE SO ALIKE' BULLSHIT. BECAUSE THAT'S INSANE.
OH, BUT WE ARE. SOME PRISON BARS ARE NOT MADE OF IRON. YOU DYE YOUR HAIR. YOU KNOW EXACTLY WHAT I AM TALKING ABOUT.
I GREW UP ON A BACKWATER WORLD. A MUD-FILLED SHIT-PILE, MUCH LIKE THE ONE WE NOW FLOAT OVER.
I WAS JUST A LITTLE OLDER THAN THIS WHEN THE GREAT DEMIURGE HASTET OM TOOK ME FOR HIS WIFE.
HOW DO YOU THINK HE CHOSE ME FROM AMONG MY SIX SISTERS? MY SKILL IN MATHEMATICS, WHICH MY FATHER MOST COMMENTED ON? MY LOVE OF COOKING? MY DESIRE TO BECOME A PRIESTESS?
NO. HE CHOSE ME FOR THIS.
YOUR HAIR.
YES, MY HAIR.
'WHAT IS A BEAUTIFUL GOLDEN JEWEL DOING LYING IN THE MUD', HE SAID.
'I MUST HAVE IT'
AND HE HAD ME. OH, THE BRUTE HAD ME. AND THE PEOPLE LOVED THEIR BEAUTIFUL QUEEN. THEIR MOTHER OM.
THAT'S ALL I EVER WAS TO THEM. A GOLDEN JEWEL.
AND THAT'S ALL ANYONE WANTS GIRLS LIKE US TO BE. BEAUTIFUL GOLDEN JEWELS.
CERTAINLY NOT HUMAN BEINGS.

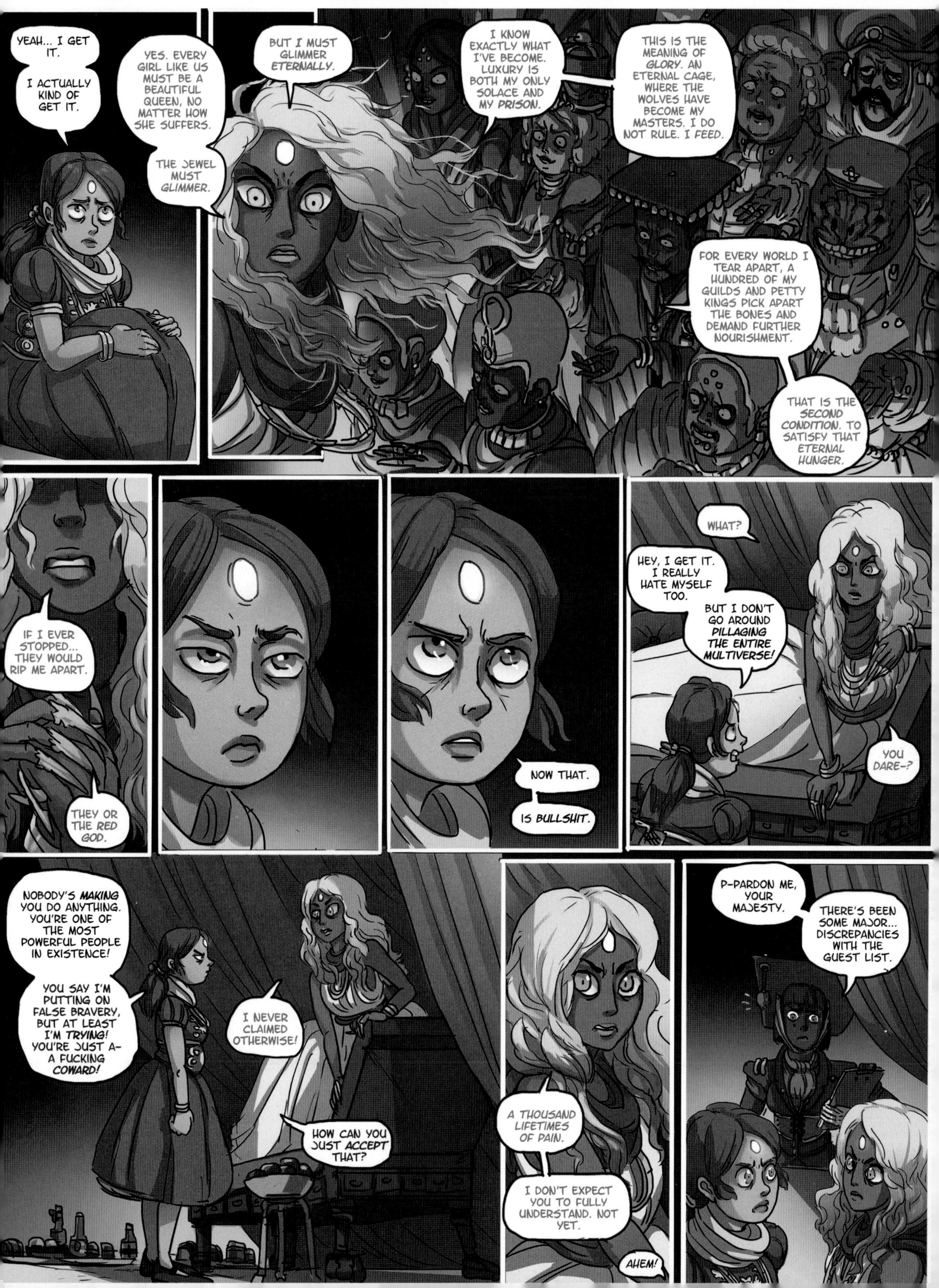

YEAH... I GET IT.
I ACTUALLY KIND OF GET IT.
YES. EVERY GIRL LIKE US MUST BE A BEAUTIFUL QUEEN, NO MATTER HOW SHE SUFFERS.
THE JEWEL MUST GLIMMER.
BUT I MUST GLIMMER ETERNALLY.
I KNOW EXACTLY WHAT I'VE BECOME. LUXURY IS BOTH MY ONLY SOLACE AND MY PRISON.
THIS IS THE MEANING OF GLORY. AN ETERNAL CAGE, WHERE THE WOLVES HAVE BECOME MY MASTERS. I DO NOT RULE. I FEED.
FOR EVERY WORLD I TEAR APART, A HUNDRED OF MY GUILDS AND PETTY KINGS PICK APART THE BONES AND DEMAND FURTHER NOURISHMENT.
THAT IS THE SECOND CONDITION. TO SATISFY THAT ETERNAL HUNGER.
IF I EVER STOPPED... THEY WOULD RIP ME APART.
THEY OR THE RED GOD.
NOW THAT.
IS BULLSHIT.
WHAT?
HEY, I GET IT. I REALLY HATE MYSELF TOO.
BUT I DON'T GO AROUND PILLAGING THE ENTIRE MULTIVERSE!
YOU DARE-?
NOBODY'S MAKING YOU DO ANYTHING. YOU'RE ONE OF THE MOST POWERFUL PEOPLE IN EXISTENCE!
YOU SAY I'M PUTTING ON FALSE BRAVERY, BUT AT LEAST I'M TRYING! YOU'RE JUST A- A FUCKING COWARD!
I NEVER CLAIMED OTHERWISE!
HOW CAN YOU JUST ACCEPT THAT?
A THOUSAND LIFETIMES OF PAIN.
I DON'T EXPECT YOU TO FULLY UNDERSTAND. NOT YET.
AHEM!
P-PARDON ME, YOUR MAJESTY.
THERE'S BEEN SOME MAJOR... DISCREPANCIES WITH THE GUEST LIST.

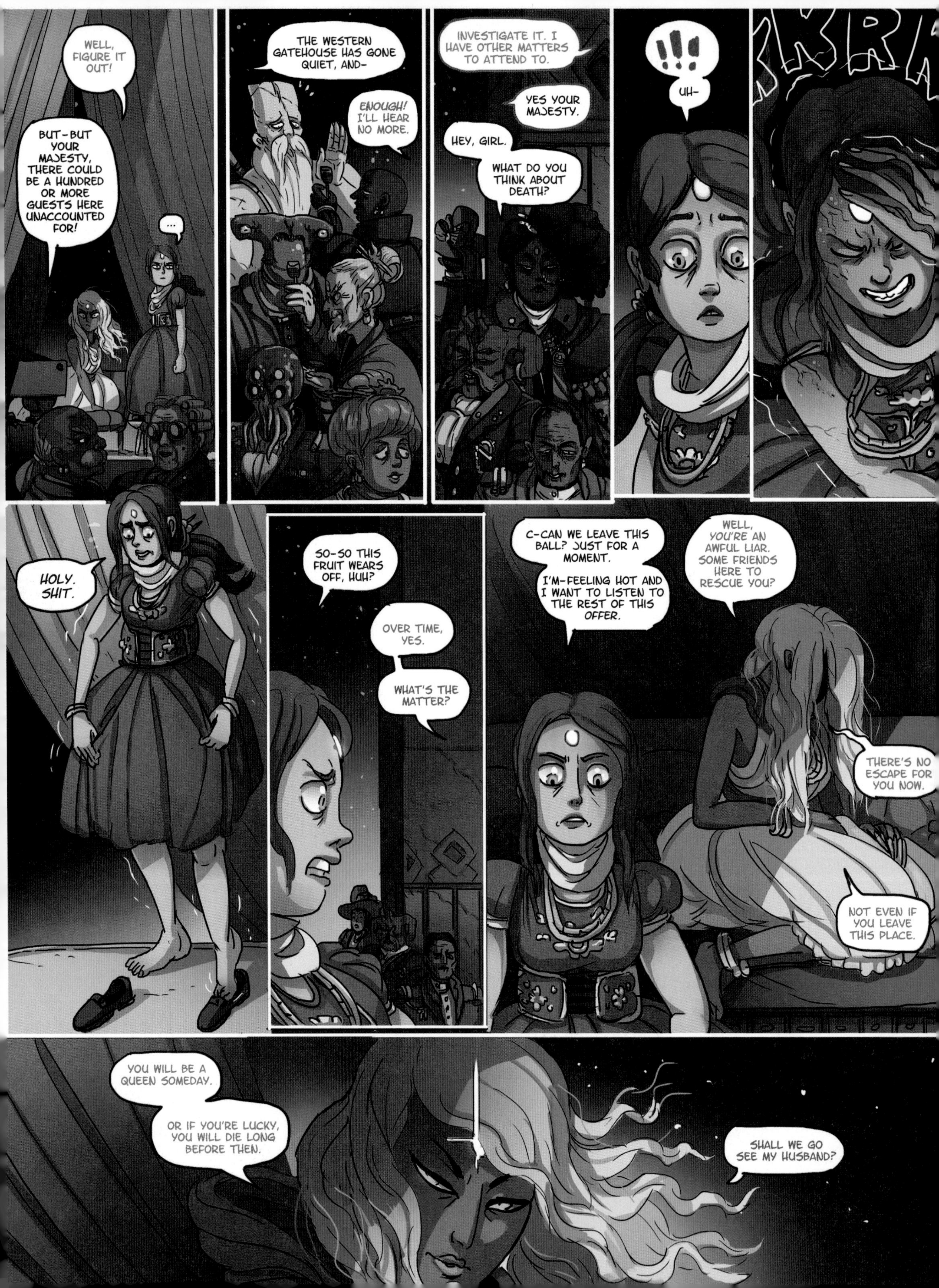
WELL, FIGURE IT OUT!
BUT-BUT YOUR MAJESTY, THERE COULD BE A HUNDRED OR MORE GUESTS HERE UNACCOUNTED FOR!
...
THE WESTERN GATEHOUSE HAS GONE QUIET, AND-
ENOUGH! I'LL HEAR NO MORE.
INVESTIGATE IT. I HAVE OTHER MATTERS TO ATTEND TO.
YES YOUR MAJESTY.
HEY, GIRL.
WHAT DO YOU THINK ABOUT DEATH?
!!!
UH-
KRA
HOLY. SHIT.
SO-SO THIS FRUIT WEARS OFF, HUH?
OVER TIME, YES.
WHAT'S THE MATTER?
C-CAN WE LEAVE THIS BALL? JUST FOR A MOMENT.
I'M-FEELING HOT AND I WANT TO LISTEN TO THE REST OF THIS OFFER.
WELL, YOU'RE AN AWFUL LIAR. SOME FRIENDS HERE TO RESCUE YOU?
THERE'S NO ESCAPE FOR YOU NOW.
NOT EVEN IF YOU LEAVE THIS PLACE.
YOU WILL BE A QUEEN SOMEDAY.
OR IF YOU'RE LUCKY, YOU WILL DIE LONG BEFORE THEN.
SHALL WE GO SEE MY HUSBAND?

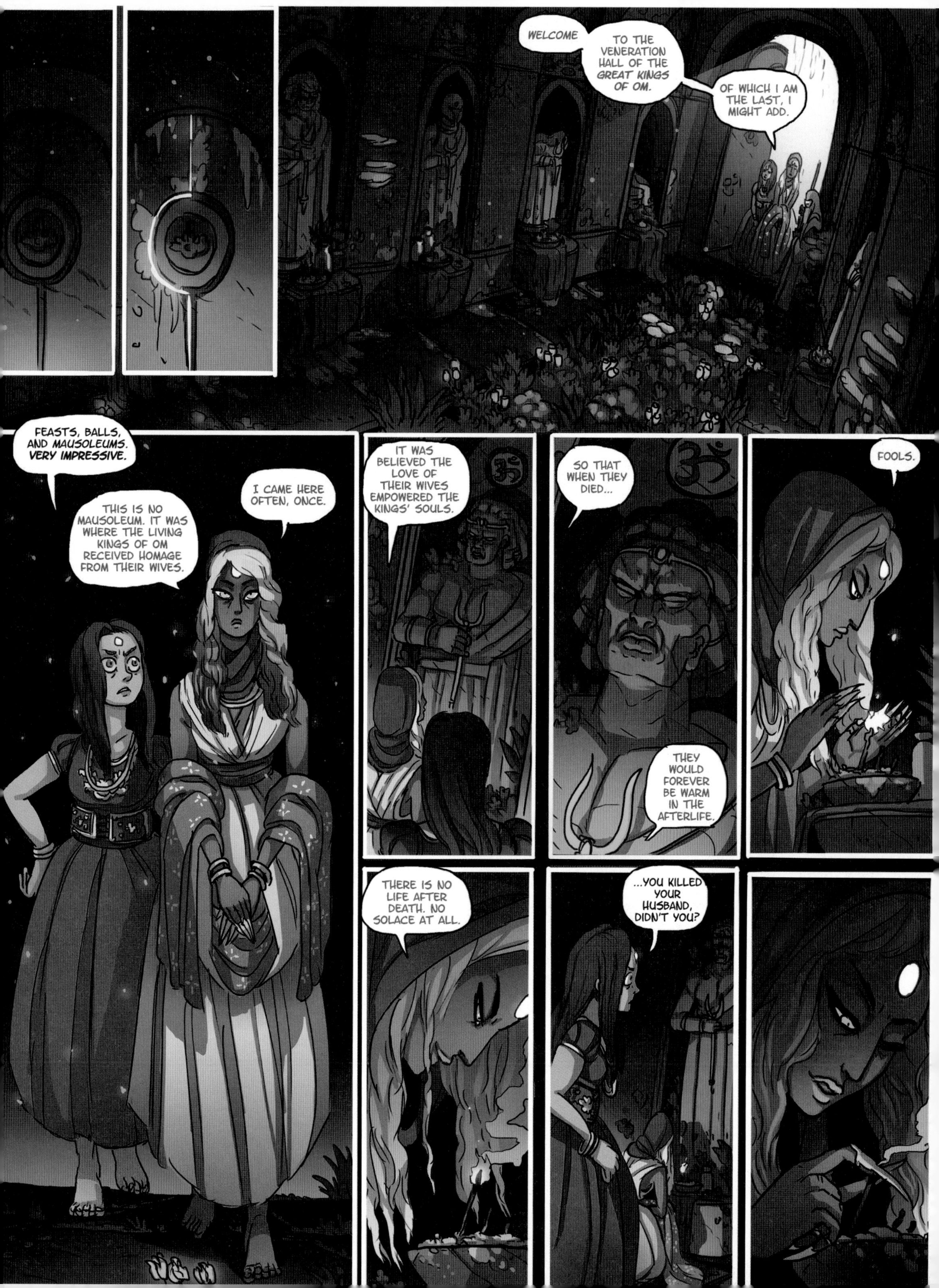
WELCOME
TO THE VENERATION HALL OF THE GREAT KINGS OF OM.
OF WHICH I AM THE LAST, I MIGHT ADD.
FEASTS, BALLS, AND MAUSOLEUMS. VERY IMPRESSIVE.
THIS IS NO MAUSOLEUM. IT WAS WHERE THE LIVING KINGS OF OM RECEIVED HOMAGE FROM THEIR WIVES.
I CAME HERE OFTEN, ONCE.
IT WAS BELIEVED THE LOVE OF THEIR WIVES EMPOWERED THE KINGS' SOULS.
SO THAT WHEN THEY DIED...
THEY WOULD FOREVER BE WARM IN THE AFTERLIFE.
FOOLS.
THERE IS NO LIFE AFTER DEATH. NO SOLACE AT ALL.
...YOU KILLED YOUR HUSBAND, DIDN'T YOU?

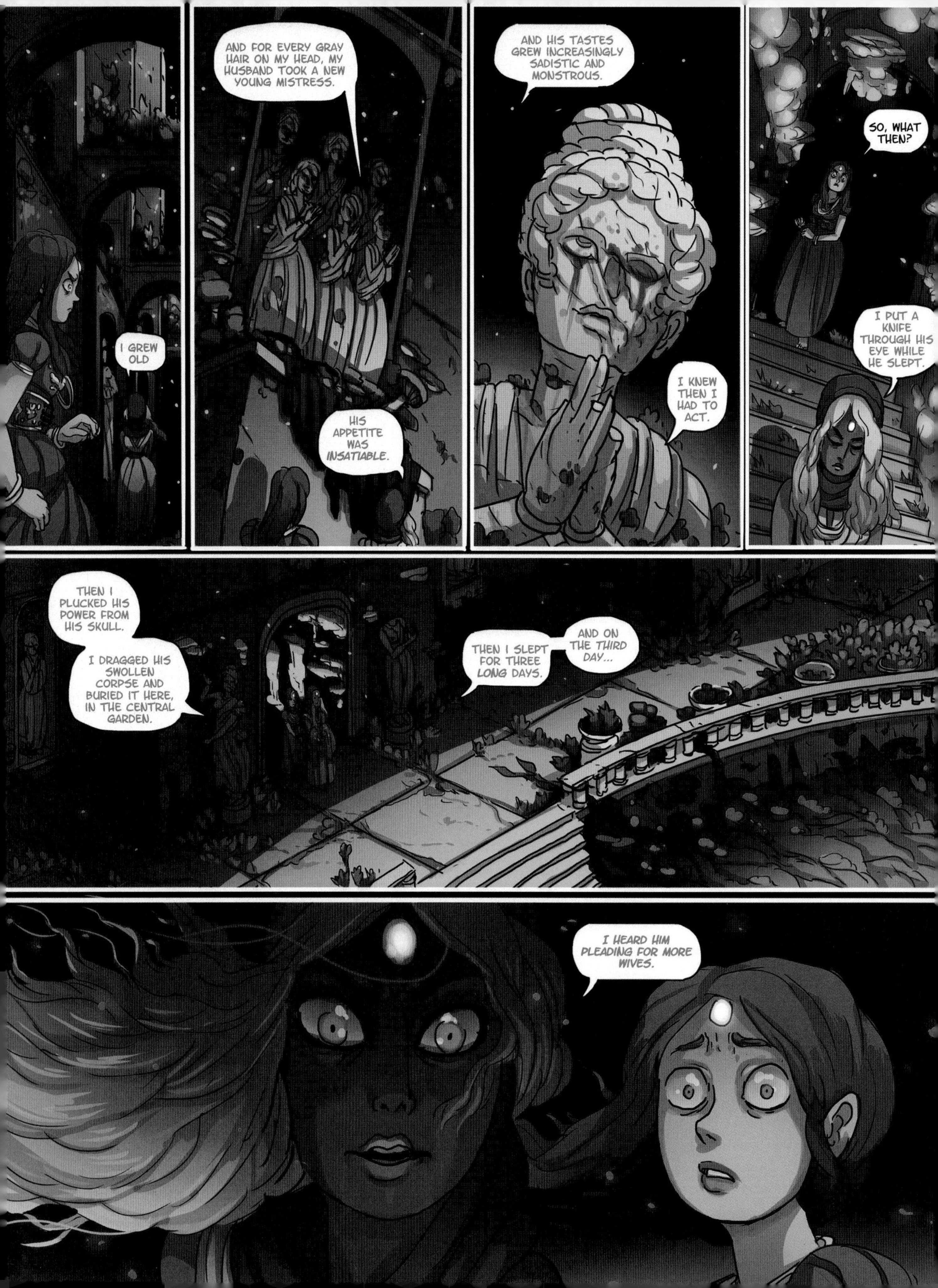
I GREW OLD
AND FOR EVERY GRAY HAIR ON MY HEAD, MY HUSBAND TOOK A NEW YOUNG MISTRESS.
HIS APPETITE WAS INSATIABLE.
AND HIS TASTES GREW INCREASINGLY SADISTIC AND MONSTROUS.
I KNEW THEN I HAD TO ACT.
SO, WHAT THEN?
I PUT A KNIFE THROUGH HIS EYE WHILE HE SLEPT.
THEN I PLUCKED HIS POWER FROM HIS SKULL.
I DRAGGED HIS SWOLLEN CORPSE AND BURIED IT HERE, IN THE CENTRAL GARDEN.
THEN I SLEPT FOR THREE LONG DAYS.
AND ON THE THIRD DAY...
I HEARD HIM PLEADING FOR MORE WIVES.

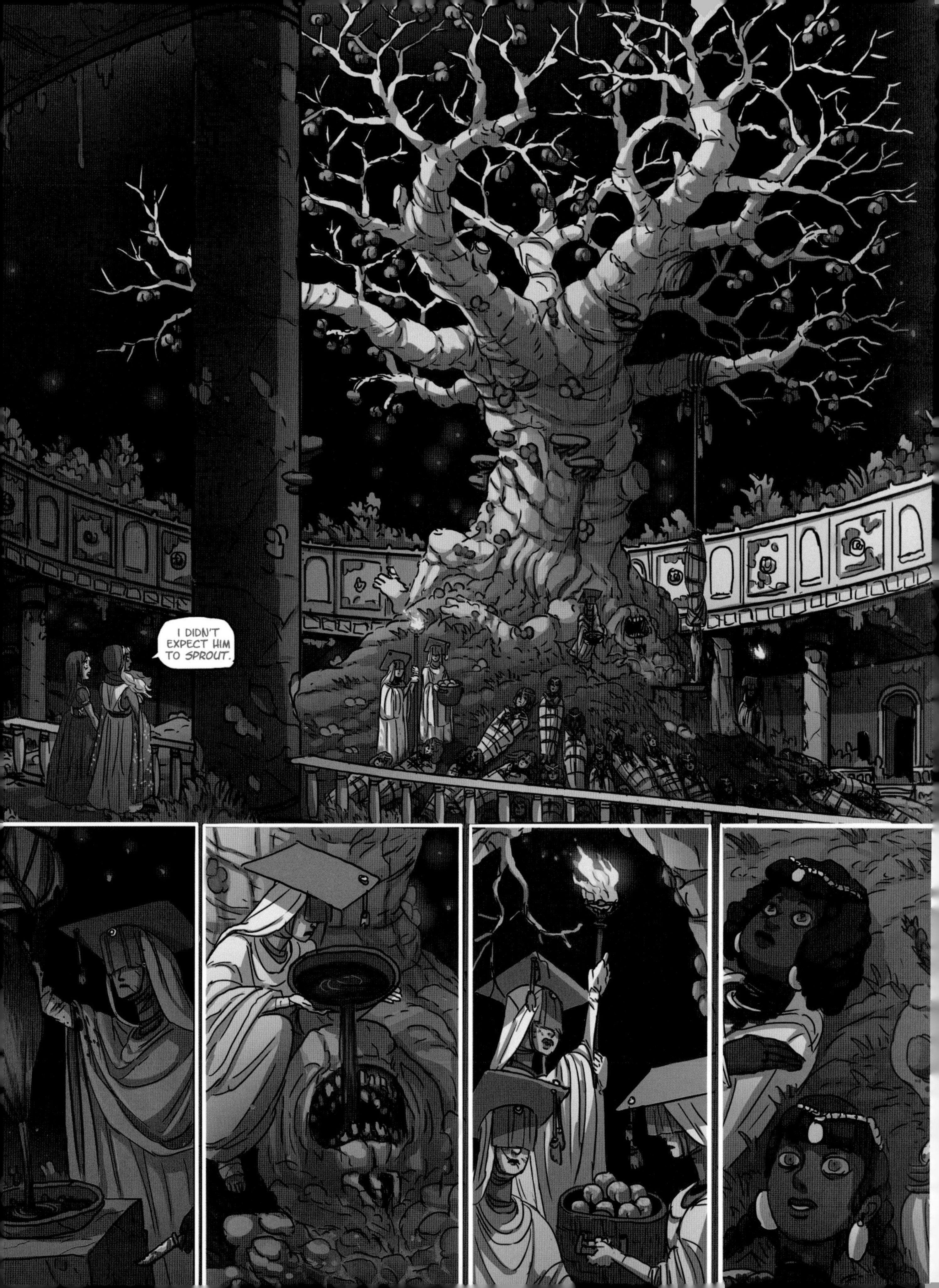
I DIDN'T EXPECT HIM TO SPROUT.

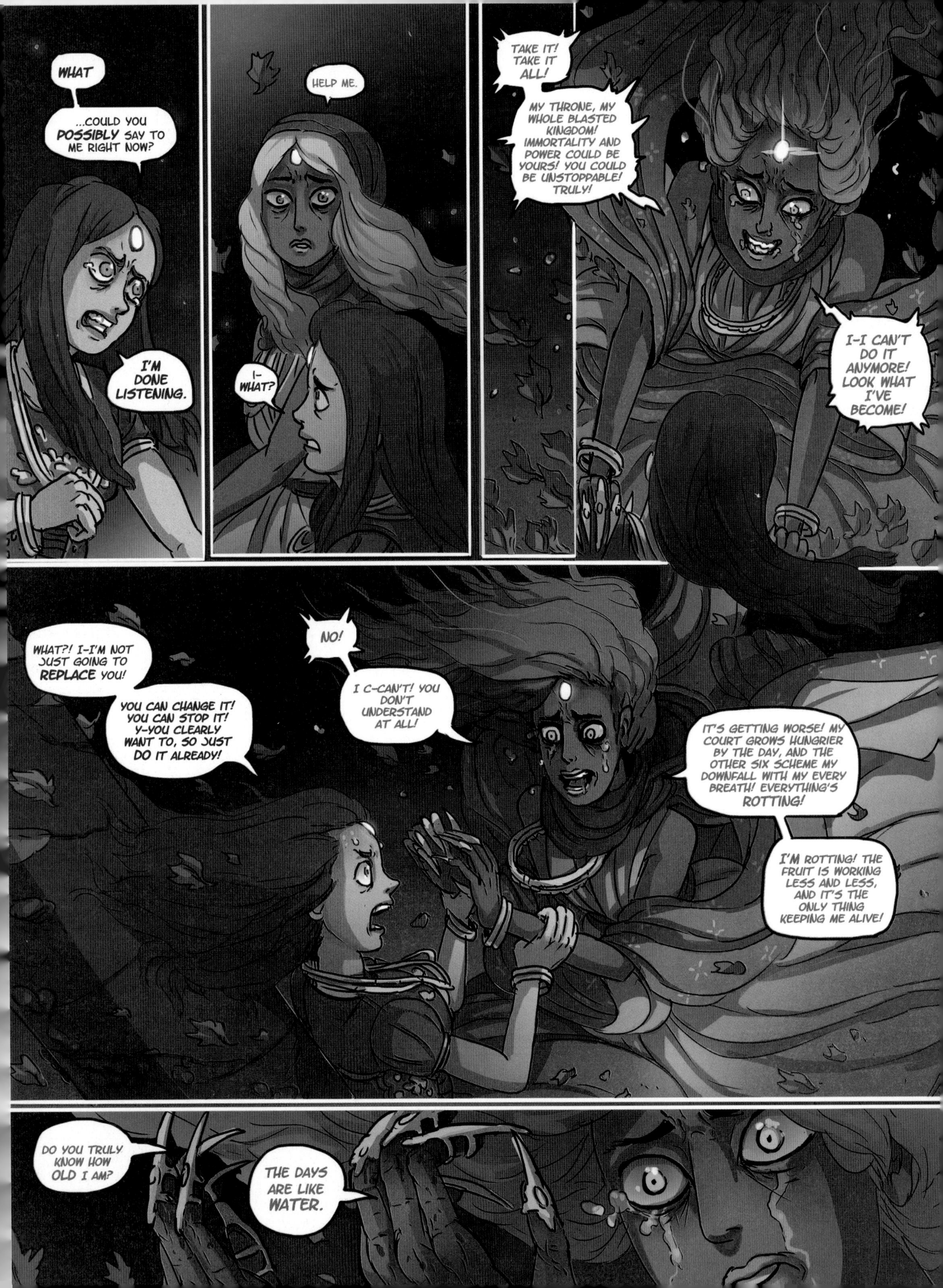

WHAT
...COULD YOU POSSIBLY SAY TO ME RIGHT NOW?
I'M DONE LISTENING.
HELP ME.
I- WHAT?
TAKE IT! TAKE IT ALL!
MY THRONE, MY WHOLE BLASTED KINGDOM! IMMORTALITY AND POWER COULD BE YOURS! YOU COULD BE UNSTOPPABLE! TRULY!
I-I CAN'T DO IT ANYMORE! LOOK WHAT I'VE BECOME!
WHAT?! I-I'M NOT JUST GOING TO REPLACE YOU!
YOU CAN CHANGE IT! YOU CAN STOP IT! Y-YOU CLEARLY WANT TO, SO JUST DO IT ALREADY!
NO!
I C-CAN'T! YOU DON'T UNDERSTAND AT ALL!
IT'S GETTING WORSE! MY COURT GROWS HUNGRIER BY THE DAY, AND THE OTHER SIX SCHEME MY DOWNFALL WITH MY EVERY BREATH! EVERYTHING'S ROTTING!
I'M ROTTING! THE FRUIT IS WORKING LESS AND LESS, AND IT'S THE ONLY THING KEEPING ME ALIVE!
DO YOU TRULY KNOW HOW OLD I AM?
THE DAYS ARE LIKE WATER.

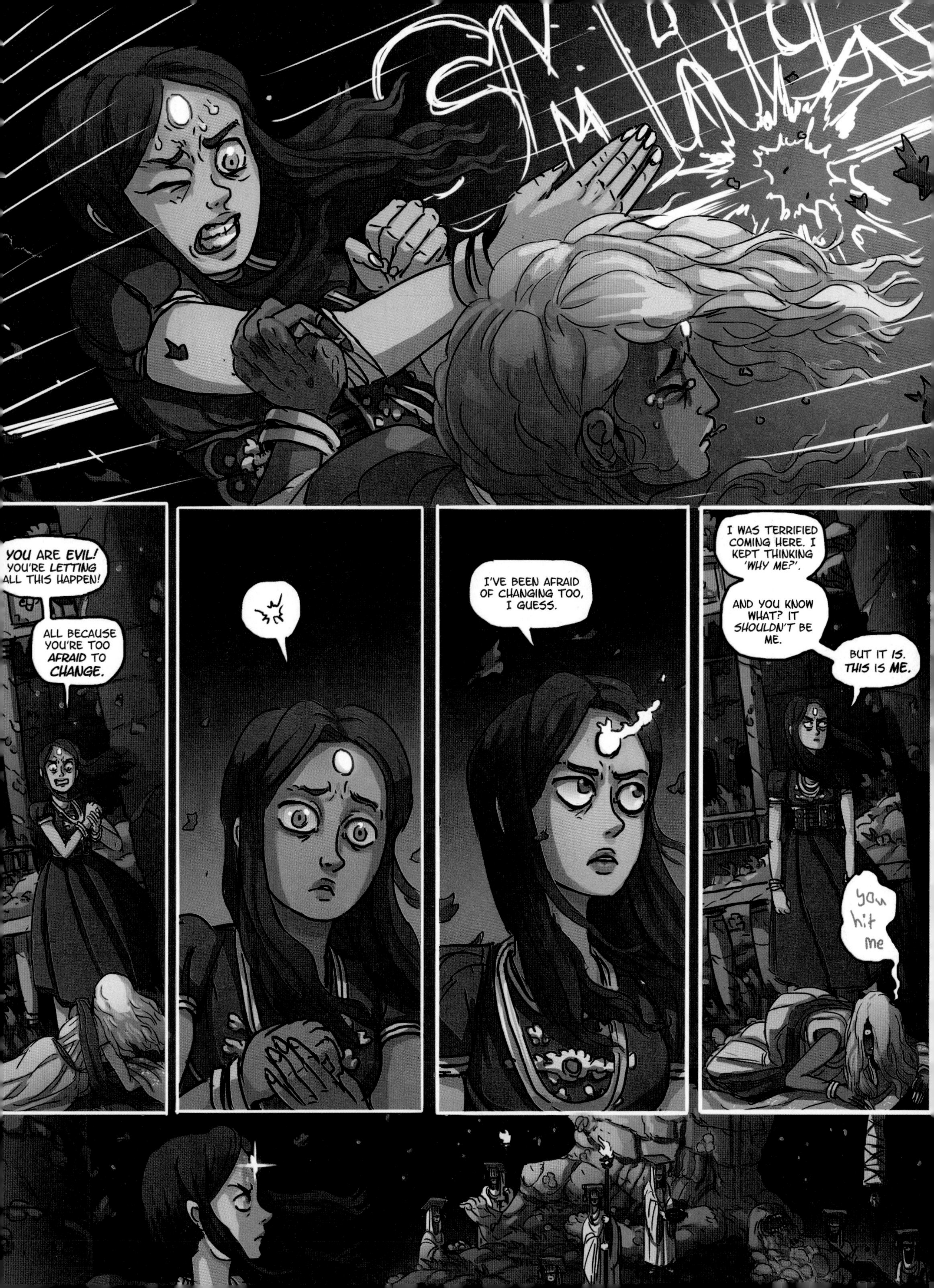
YOU ARE EVIL! YOU'RE LETTING ALL THIS HAPPEN!
ALL BECAUSE YOU'RE TOO AFRAID TO CHANGE.
I'VE BEEN AFRAID OF CHANGING TOO, I GUESS.
I WAS TERRIFIED COMING HERE. I KEPT THINKING 'WHY ME?'.
AND YOU KNOW WHAT? IT SHOULDN'T BE ME.
BUT IT IS. THIS IS ME.
you hit me

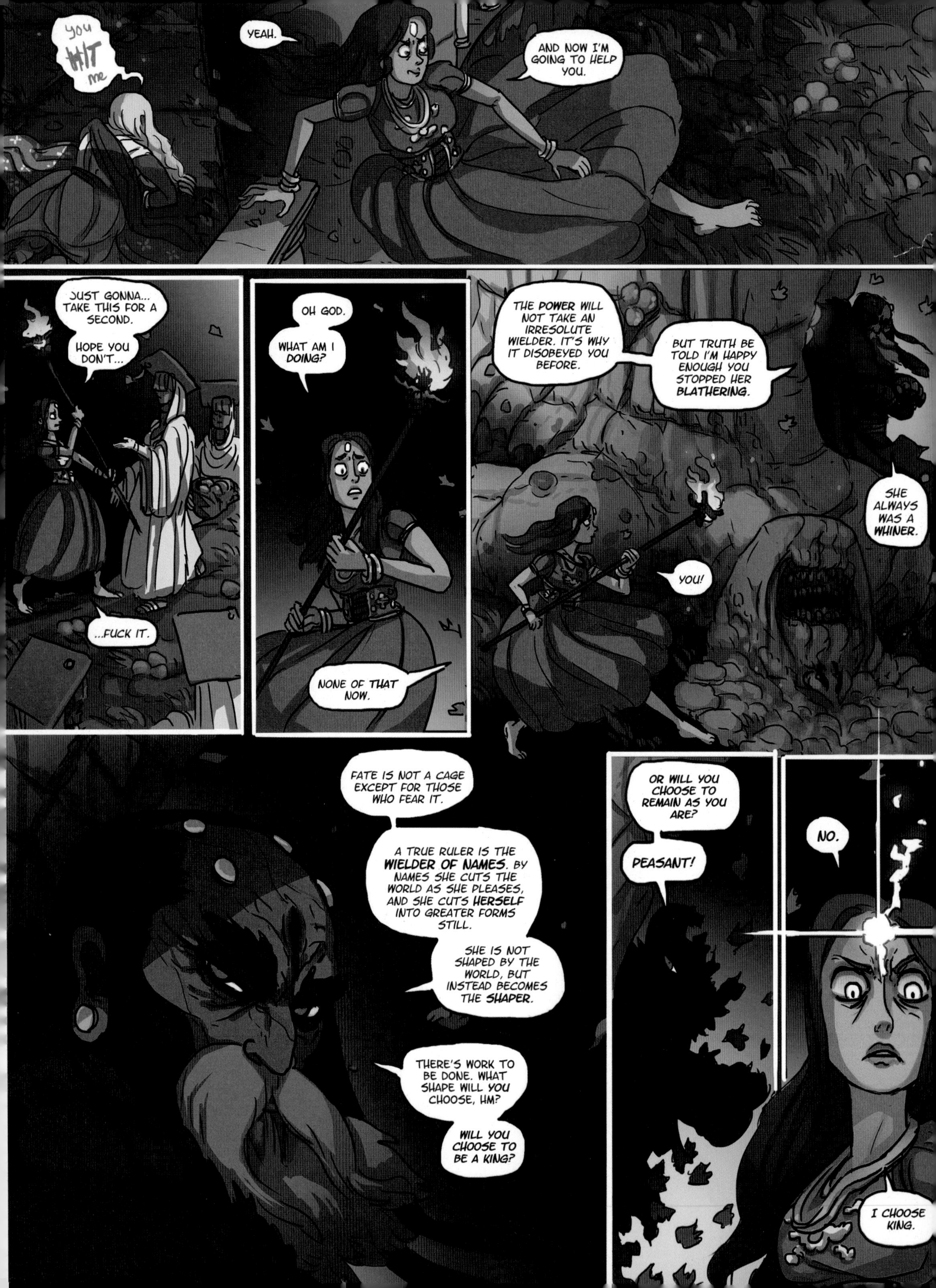

you HIT me
YEAH.
AND NOW I'M GOING TO HELP YOU.
JUST GONNA... TAKE THIS FOR A SECOND.
HOPE YOU DON'T...
...FUCK IT.
OH GOD.
WHAT AM I DOING?
NONE OF THAT NOW.
THE POWER WILL NOT TAKE AN IRRESOLUTE WIELDER. IT'S WHY IT DISOBEYED YOU BEFORE.
BUT TRUTH BE TOLD I'M HAPPY ENOUGH YOU STOPPED HER BLATHERING.
SHE ALWAYS WAS A WHINER.
YOU!
FATE IS NOT A CAGE EXCEPT FOR THOSE WHO FEAR IT.
A TRUE RULER IS THE WIELDER OF NAMES. BY NAMES SHE CUTS THE WORLD AS SHE PLEASES, AND SHE CUTS HERSELF INTO GREATER FORMS STILL.
SHE IS NOT SHAPED BY THE WORLD, BUT INSTEAD BECOMES THE SHAPER.
THERE'S WORK TO BE DONE. WHAT SHAPE WILL YOU CHOOSE, HM?
WILL YOU CHOOSE TO BE A KING?
OR WILL YOU CHOOSE TO REMAIN AS YOU ARE?
PEASANT!
NO.
I CHOOSE KING.

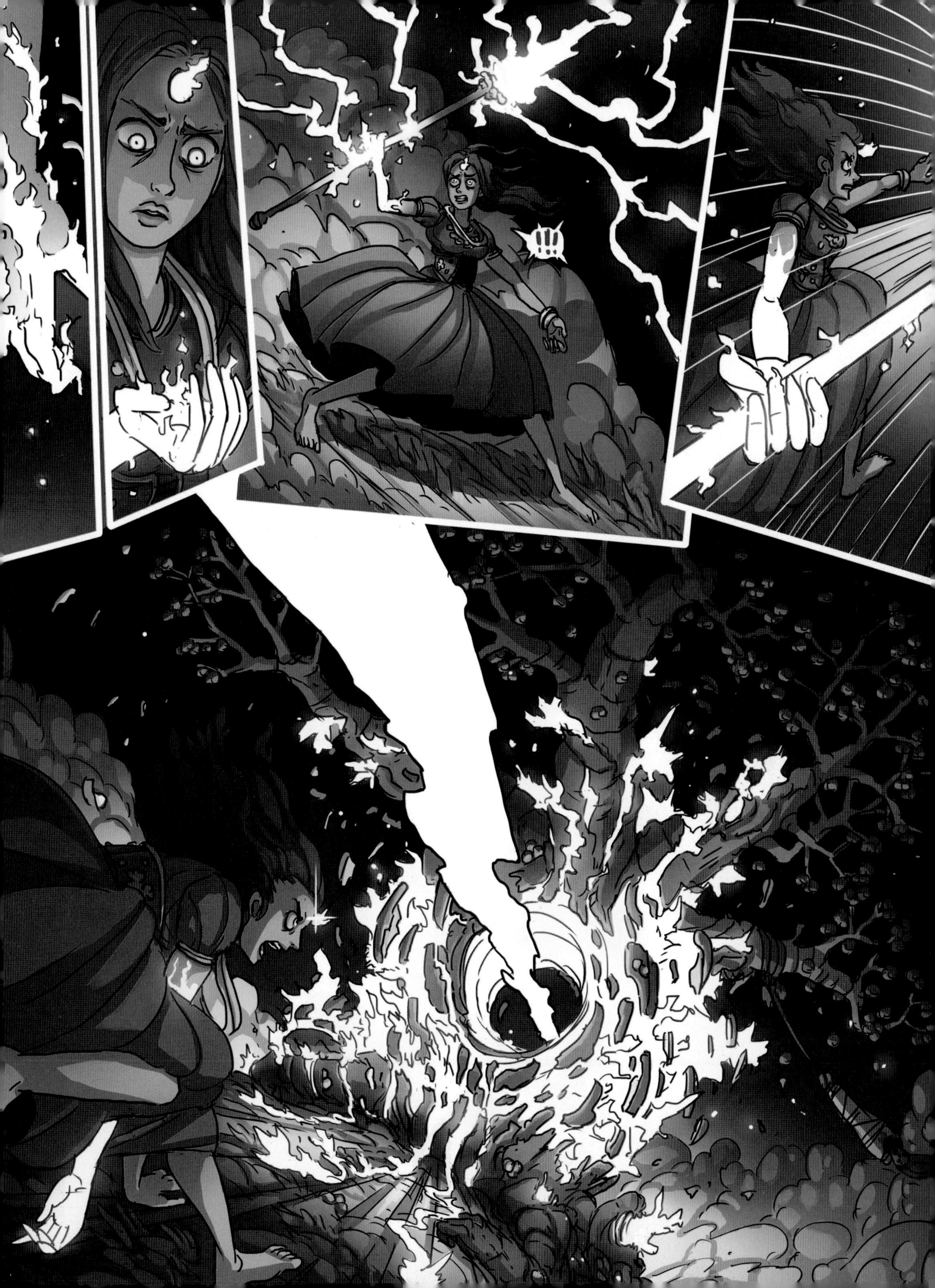
!!!

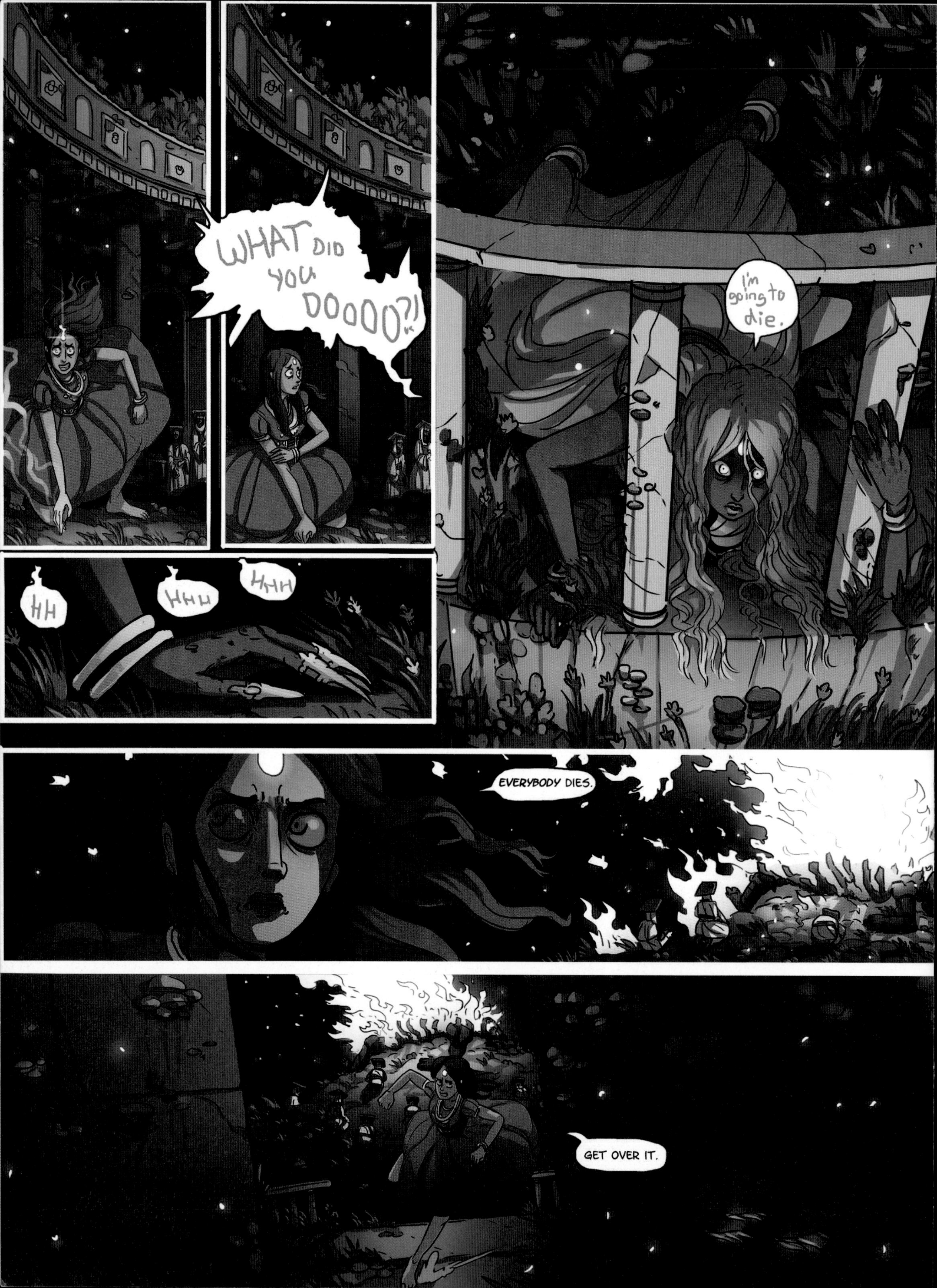
WHAT DID YOU DOOOO?!
I'm going to die.
HH
HHH
HHH
EVERYBODY DIES.
GET OVER IT.

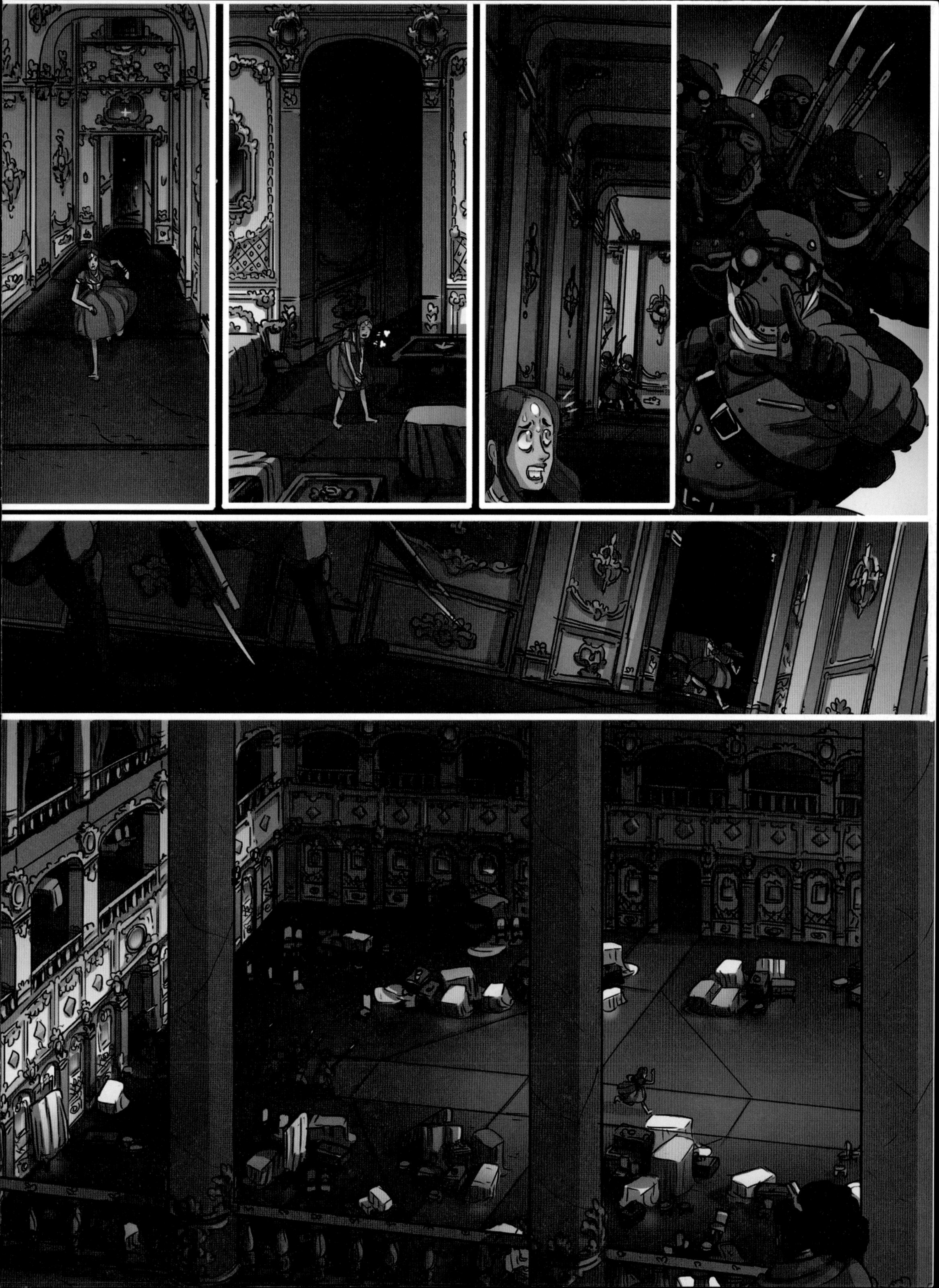

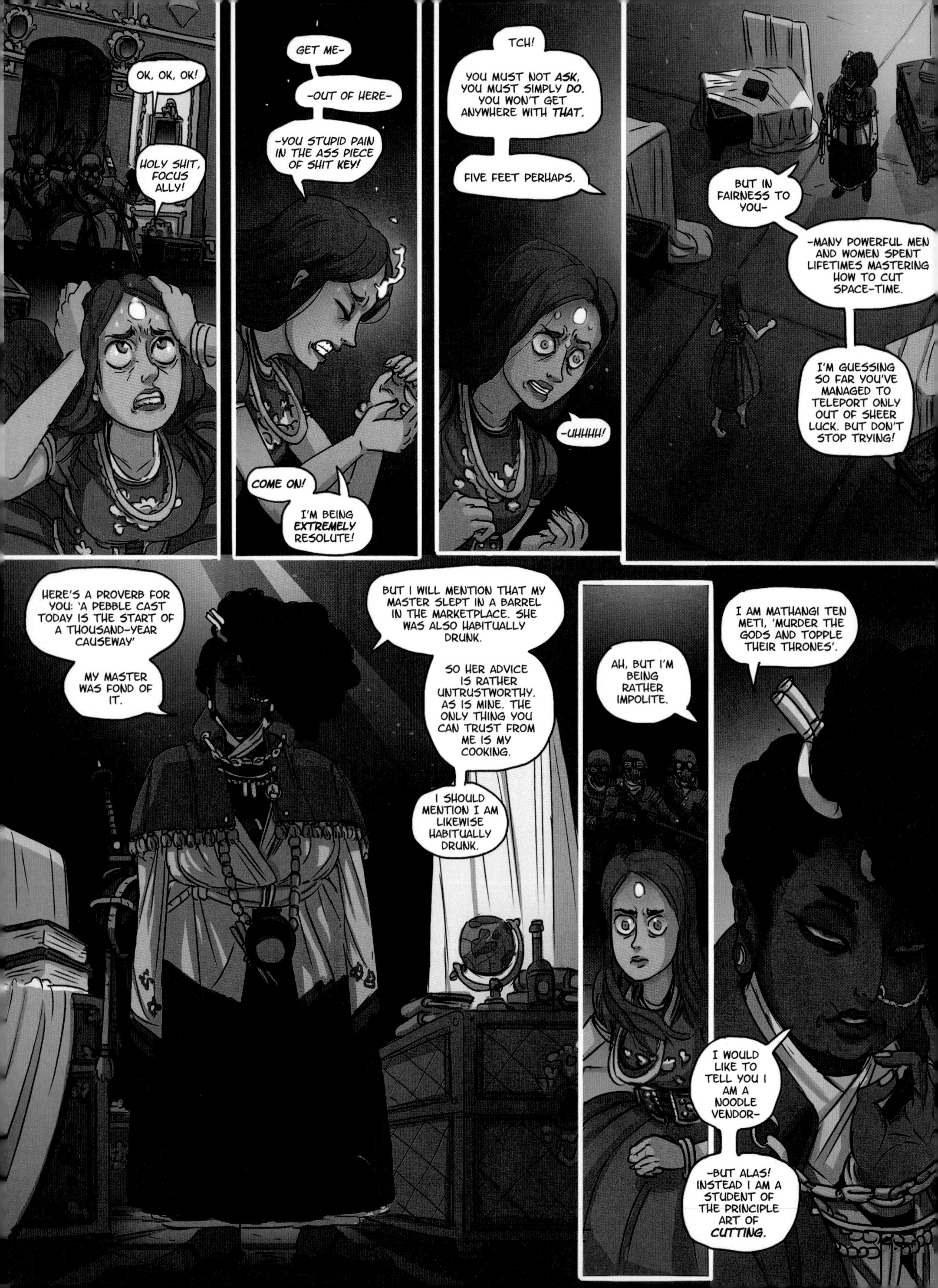
OK, OK, OK!
HOLY SHIT, FOCUS ALLY!
GET ME-
-OUT OF HERE-
-YOU STUPID PAIN IN THE ASS PIECE OF SHIT KEY!
COME ON!
I'M BEING EXTREMELY RESOLUTE!
TCH!
YOU MUST NOT ASK, YOU MUST SIMPLY DO. YOU WON'T GET ANYWHERE WITH THAT.
FIVE FEET PERHAPS.
-UHHHH!
BUT IN FAIRNESS TO YOU-
-MANY POWERFUL MEN AND WOMEN SPENT LIFETIMES MASTERING HOW TO CUT SPACE-TIME.
I'M GUESSING SO FAR YOU'VE MANAGED TO TELEPORT ONLY OUT OF SHEER LUCK. BUT DON'T STOP TRYING!
HERE'S A PROVERB FOR YOU: 'A PEBBLE CAST TODAY IS THE START OF A THOUSAND-YEAR CAUSEWAY'
MY MASTER WAS FOND OF IT.
BUT I WILL MENTION THAT MY MASTER SLEPT IN A BARREL IN THE MARKETPLACE. SHE WAS ALSO HABITUALLY DRUNK.
SO HER ADVICE IS RATHER UNTRUSTWORTHY. AS IS MINE. THE ONLY THING YOU CAN TRUST FROM ME IS MY COOKING.
I SHOULD MENTION I AM LIKEWISE HABITUALLY DRUNK.
AH, BUT I'M BEING RATHER IMPOLITE.
I AM MATHANGI TEN METI, 'MURDER THE GODS AND TOPPLE THEIR THRONES'.
I WOULD LIKE TO TELL YOU I AM A NOODLE VENDOR-
-BUT ALAS! INSTEAD I AM A STUDENT OF THE PRINCIPLE ART OF CUTTING.

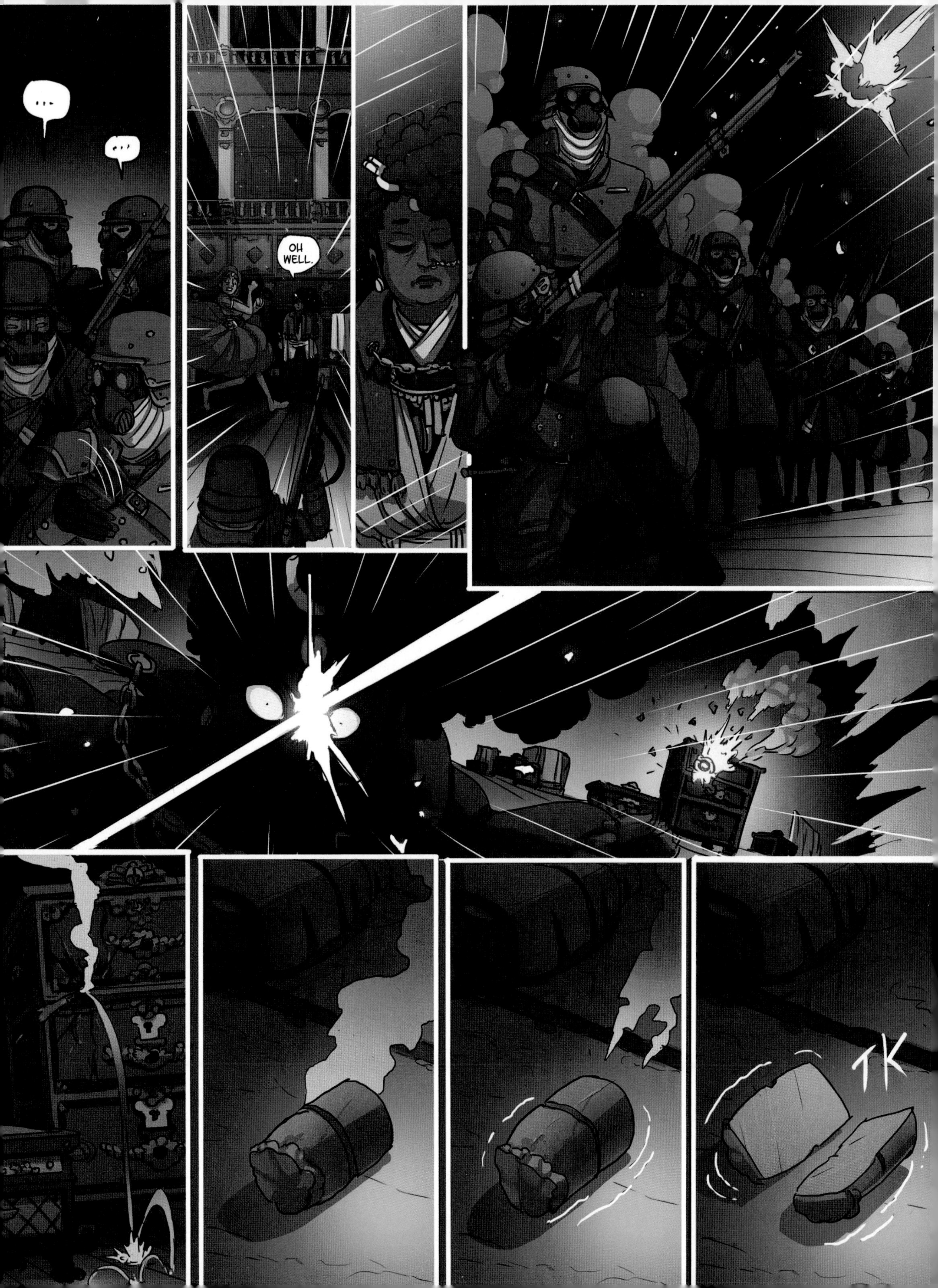
...
...
OH WELL.
TK

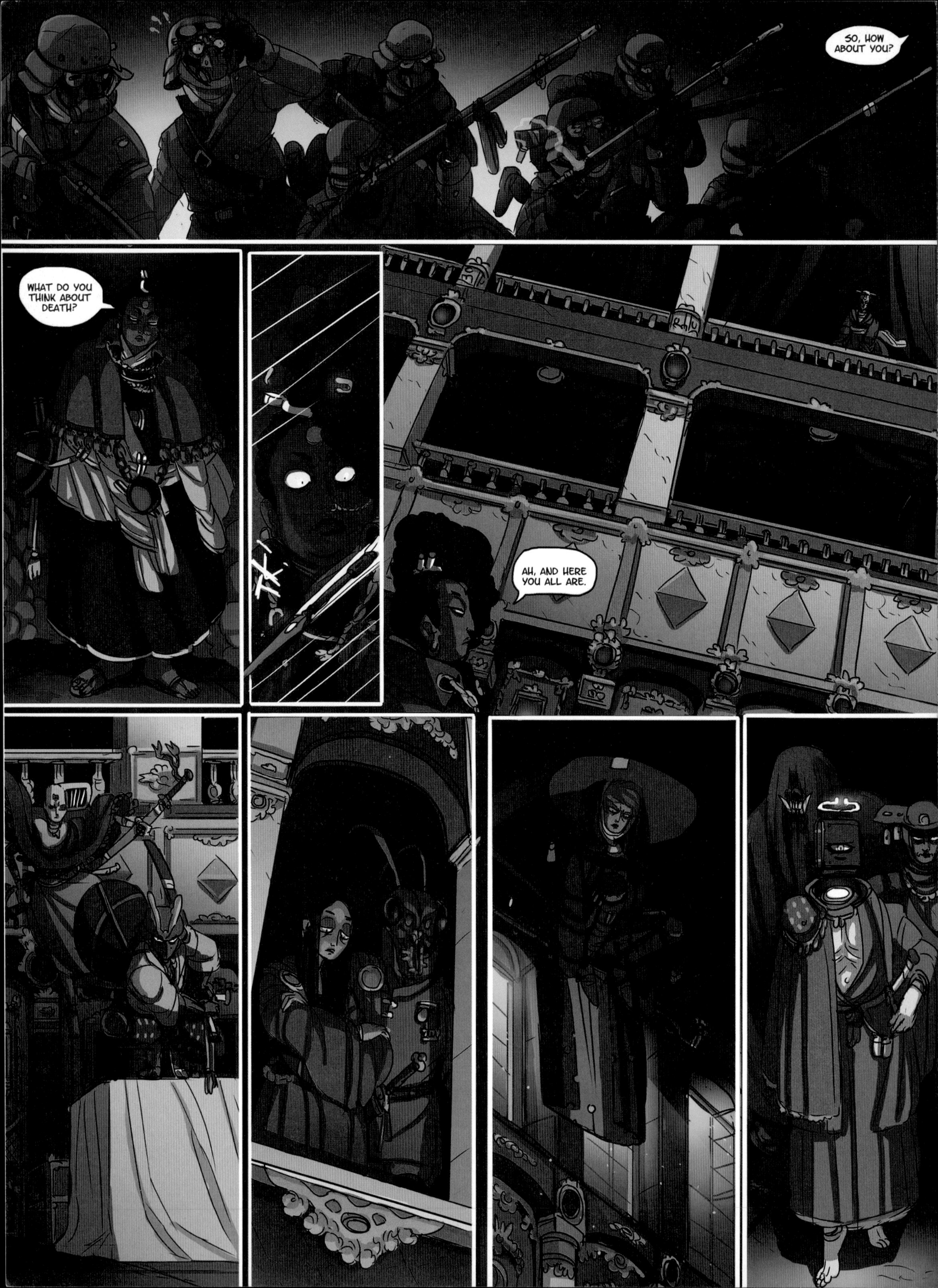
SO, HOW ABOUT YOU?
WHAT DO YOU THINK ABOUT DEATH?
AH, AND HERE YOU ALL ARE.

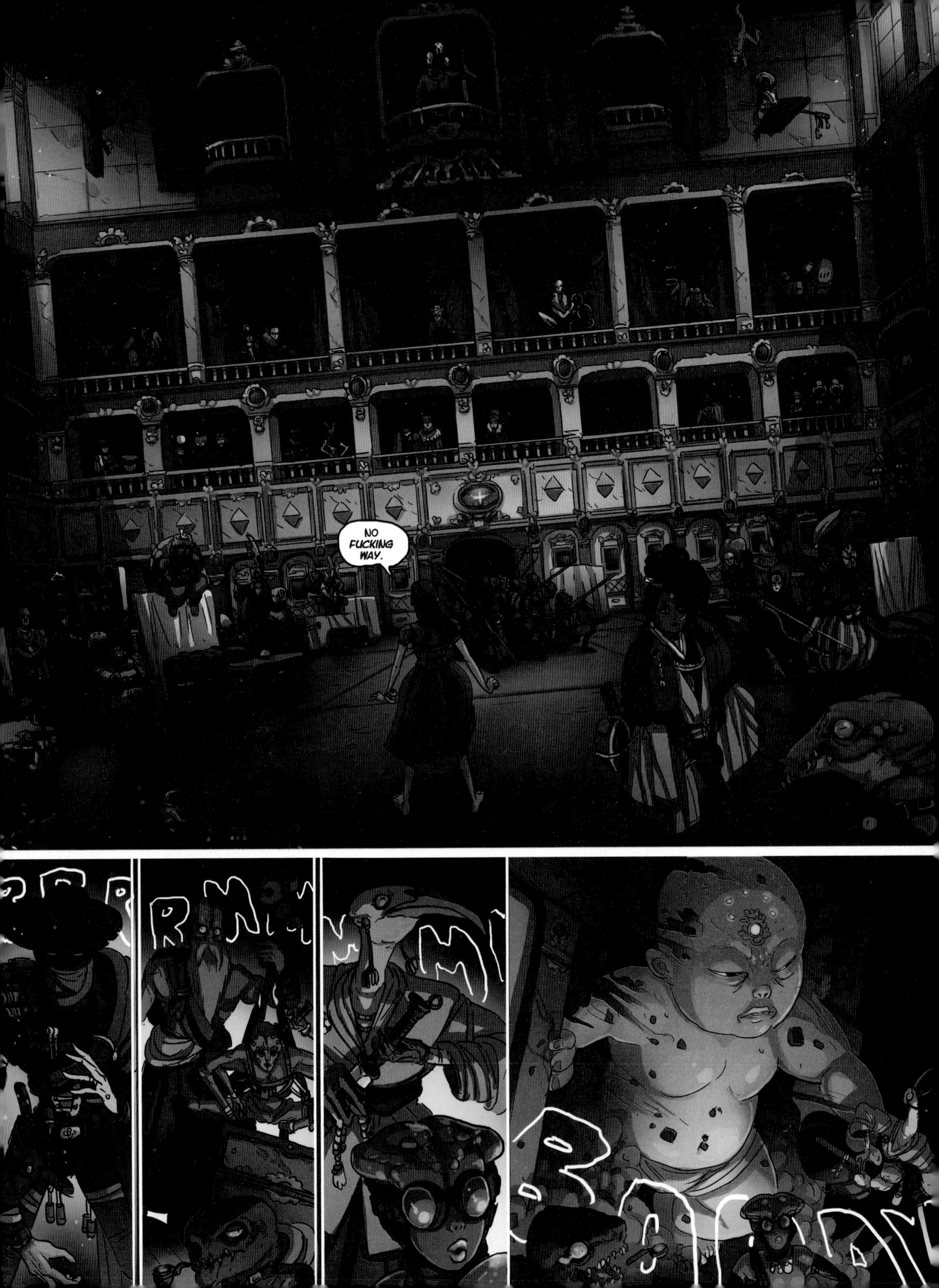
NO FUCKING WAY.

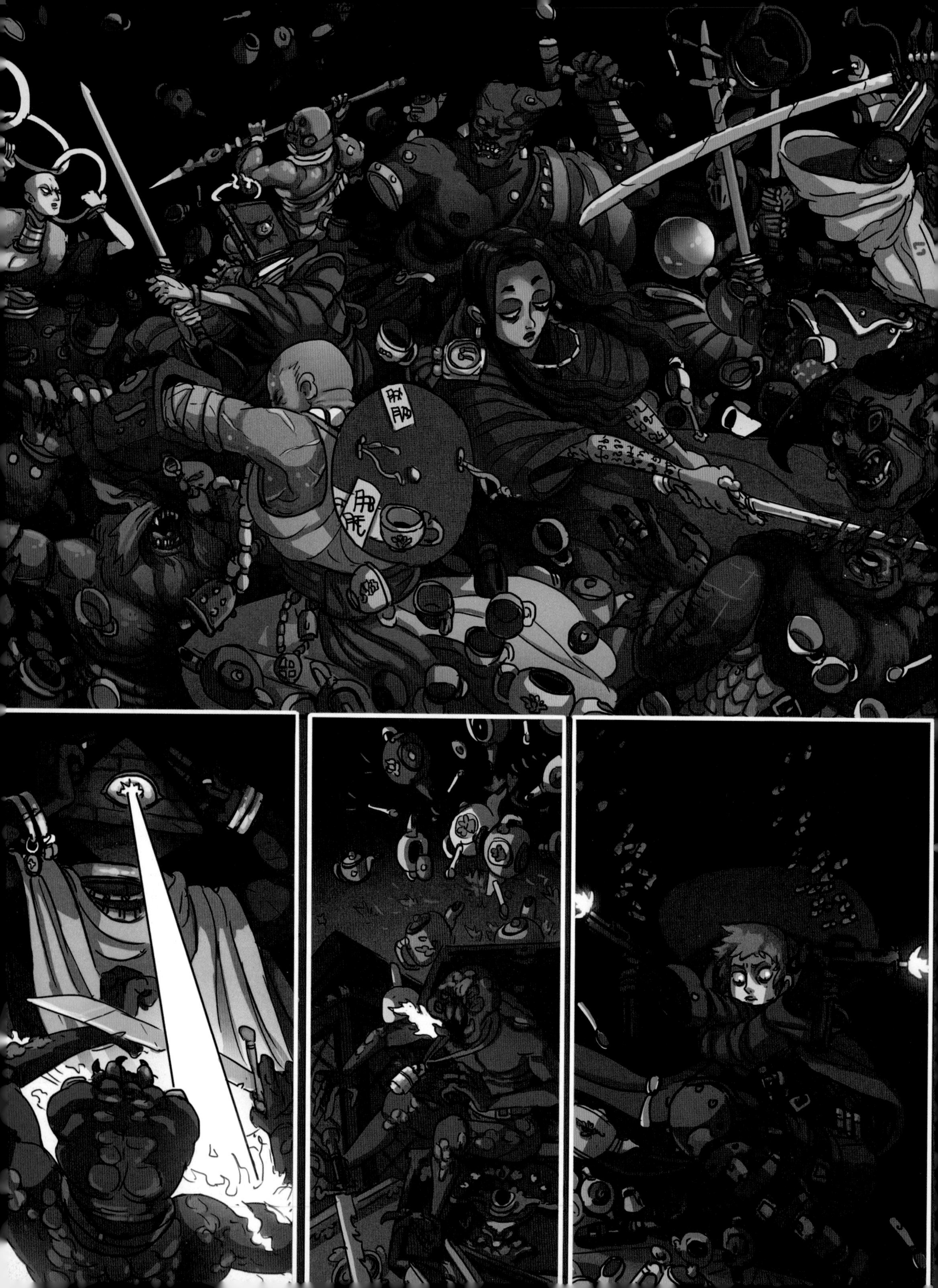

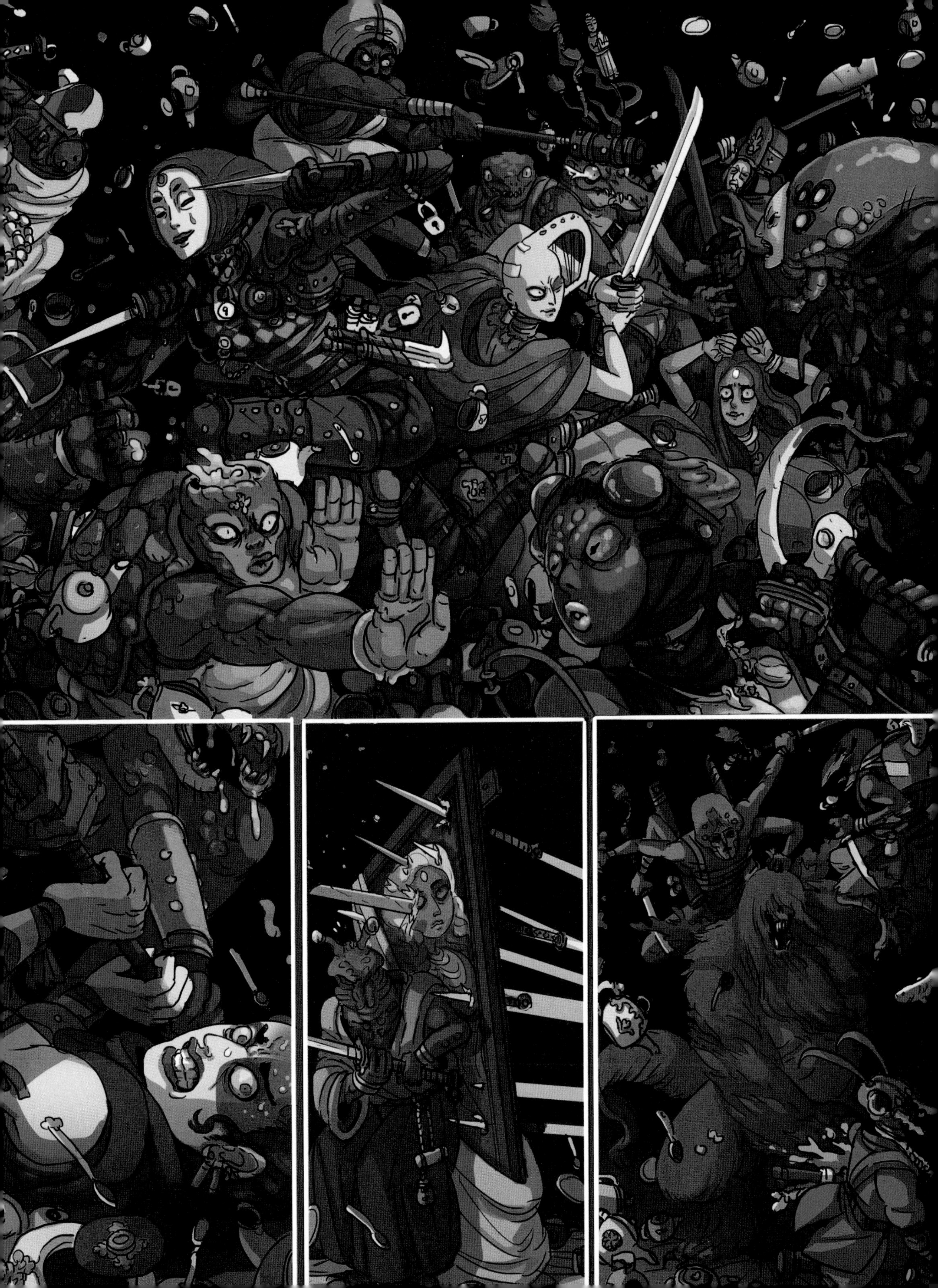

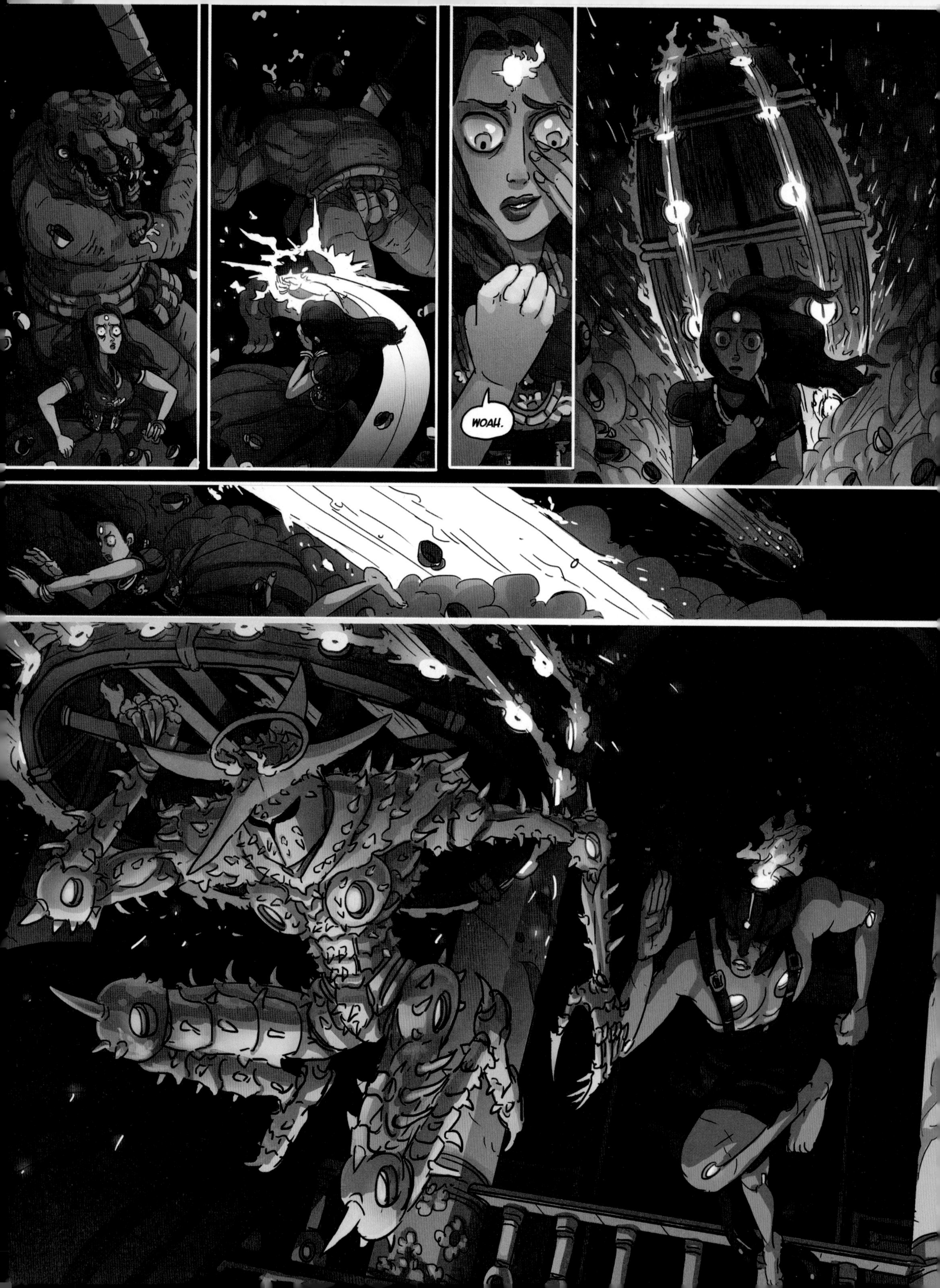
WOAH.

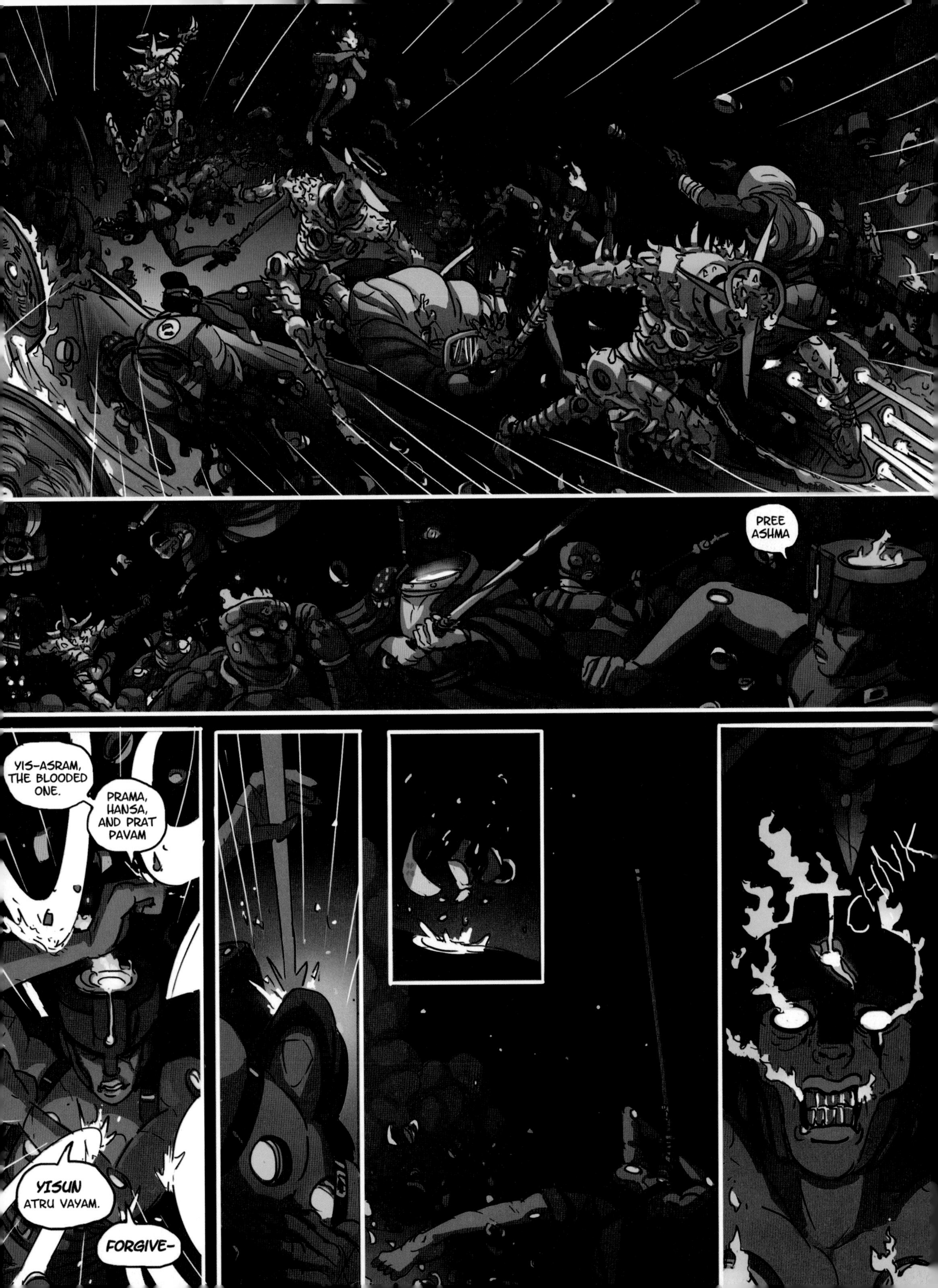
PREE ASHMA
YIS-ASRAM, THE BLOODED ONE.
PRAMA, HANSA, AND PRAT PAVAM
YISUN ATRU VAYAM.
FORGIVE-
CHINK

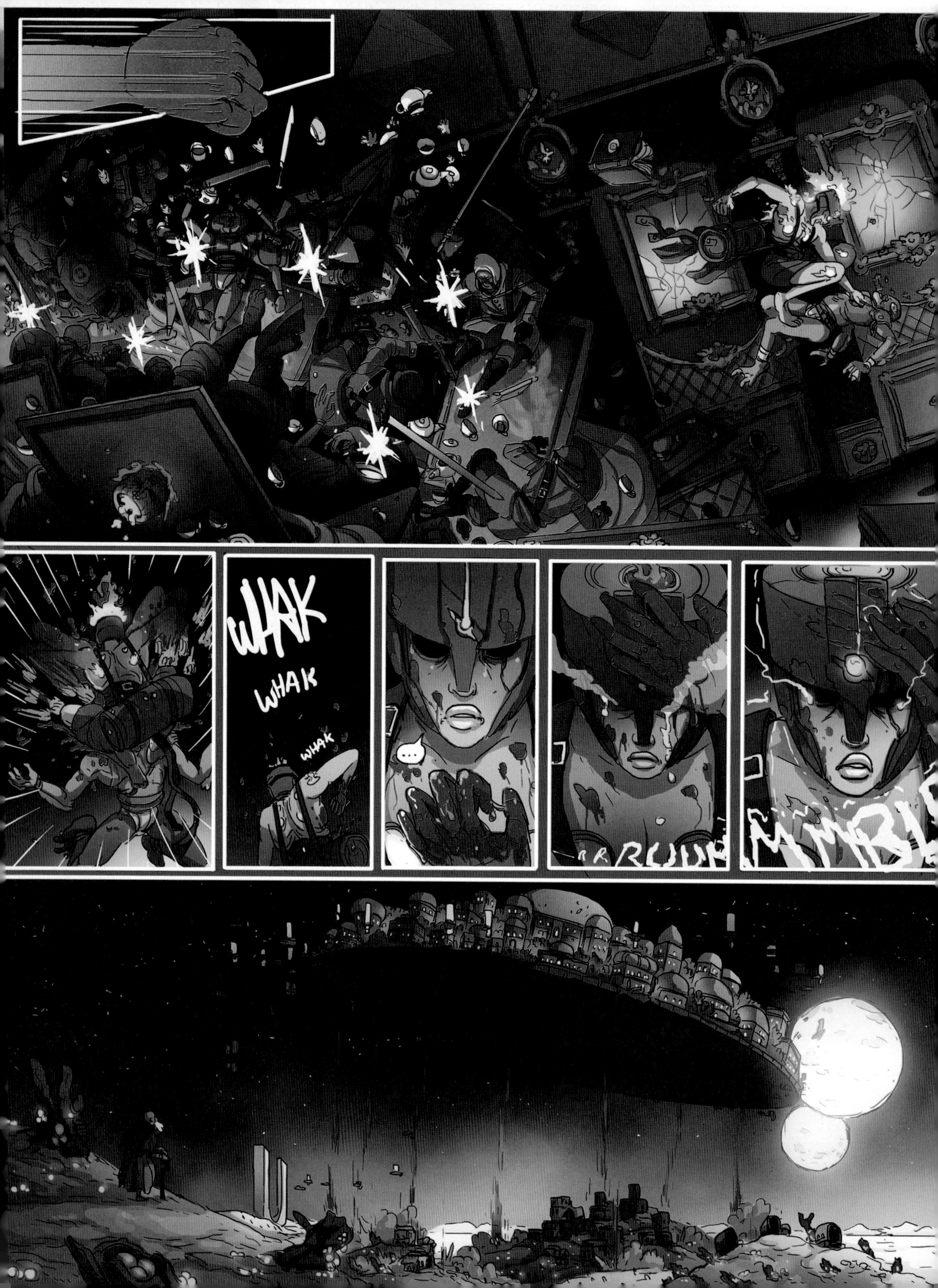
WHAK
WHAK
WHAK
...
RRUUMMBLE

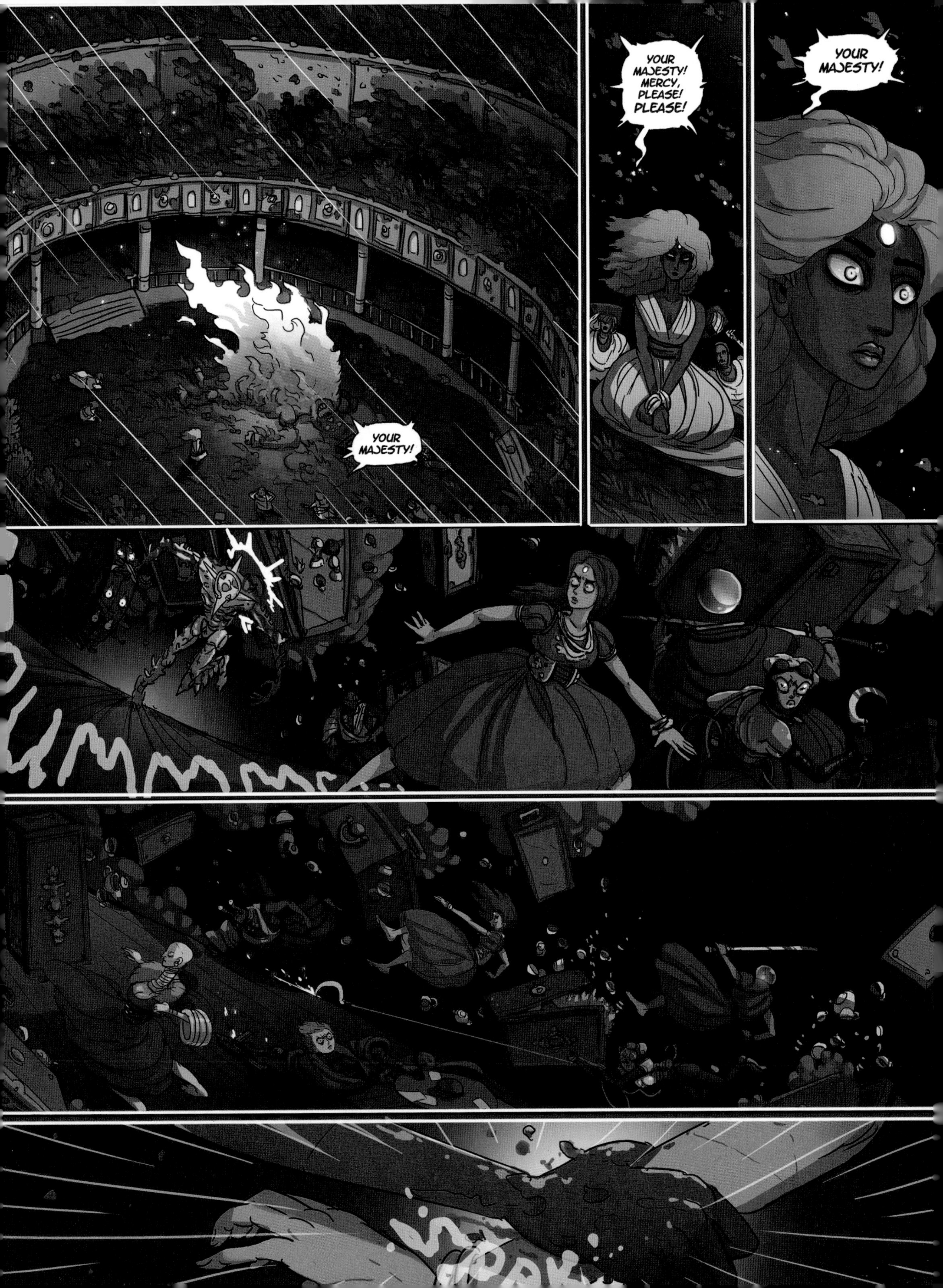
YOUR MAJESTY!
YOUR MAJESTY! MERCY, PLEASE! PLEASE!
YOUR MAJESTY!

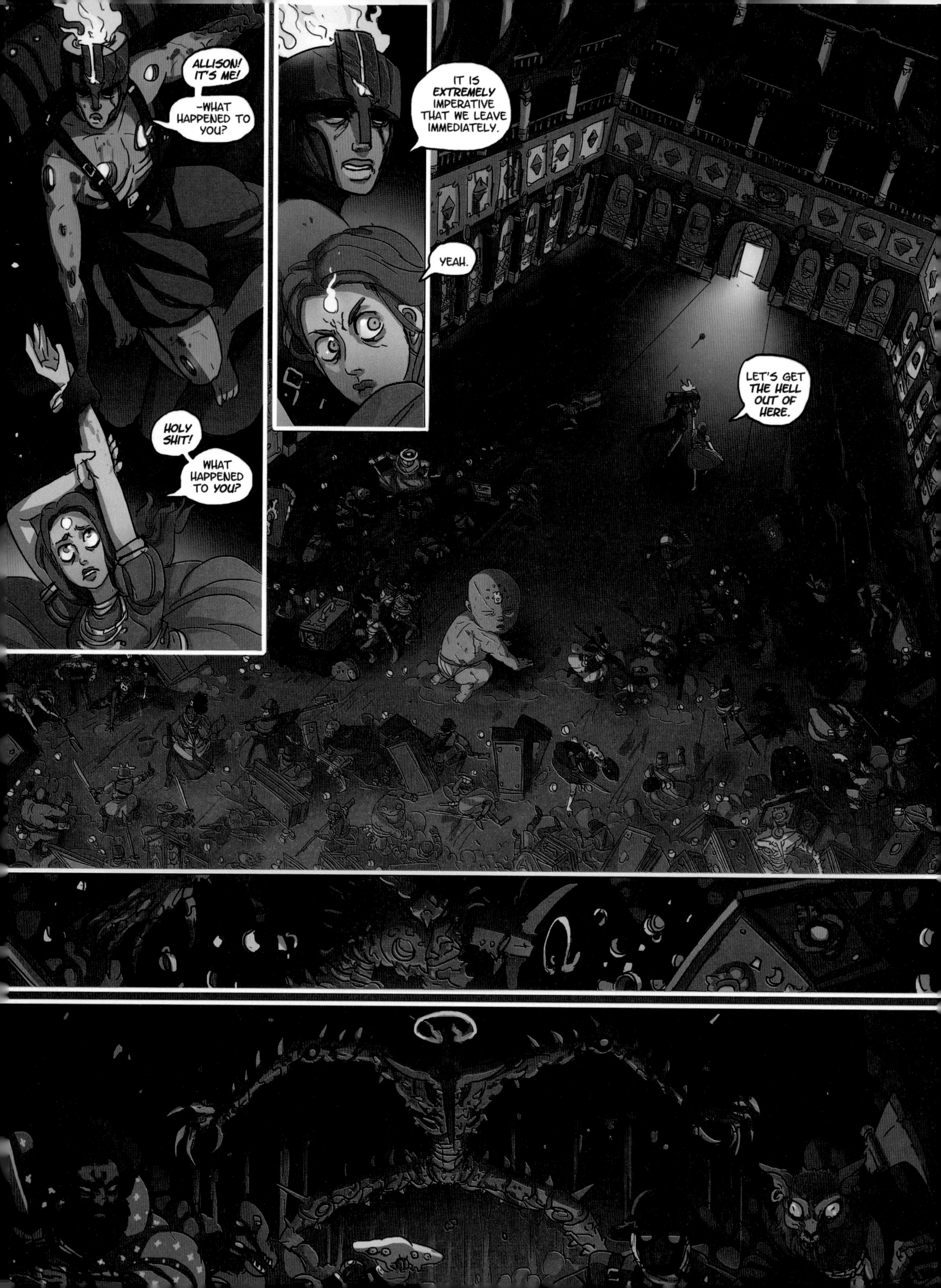
ALLISON! IT'S ME!
-WHAT HAPPENED TO YOU?
HOLY SHIT!
WHAT HAPPENED TO YOU?
IT IS EXTREMELY IMPERATIVE THAT WE LEAVE IMMEDIATELY.
YEAH.
LET'S GET THE HELL OUT OF HERE.

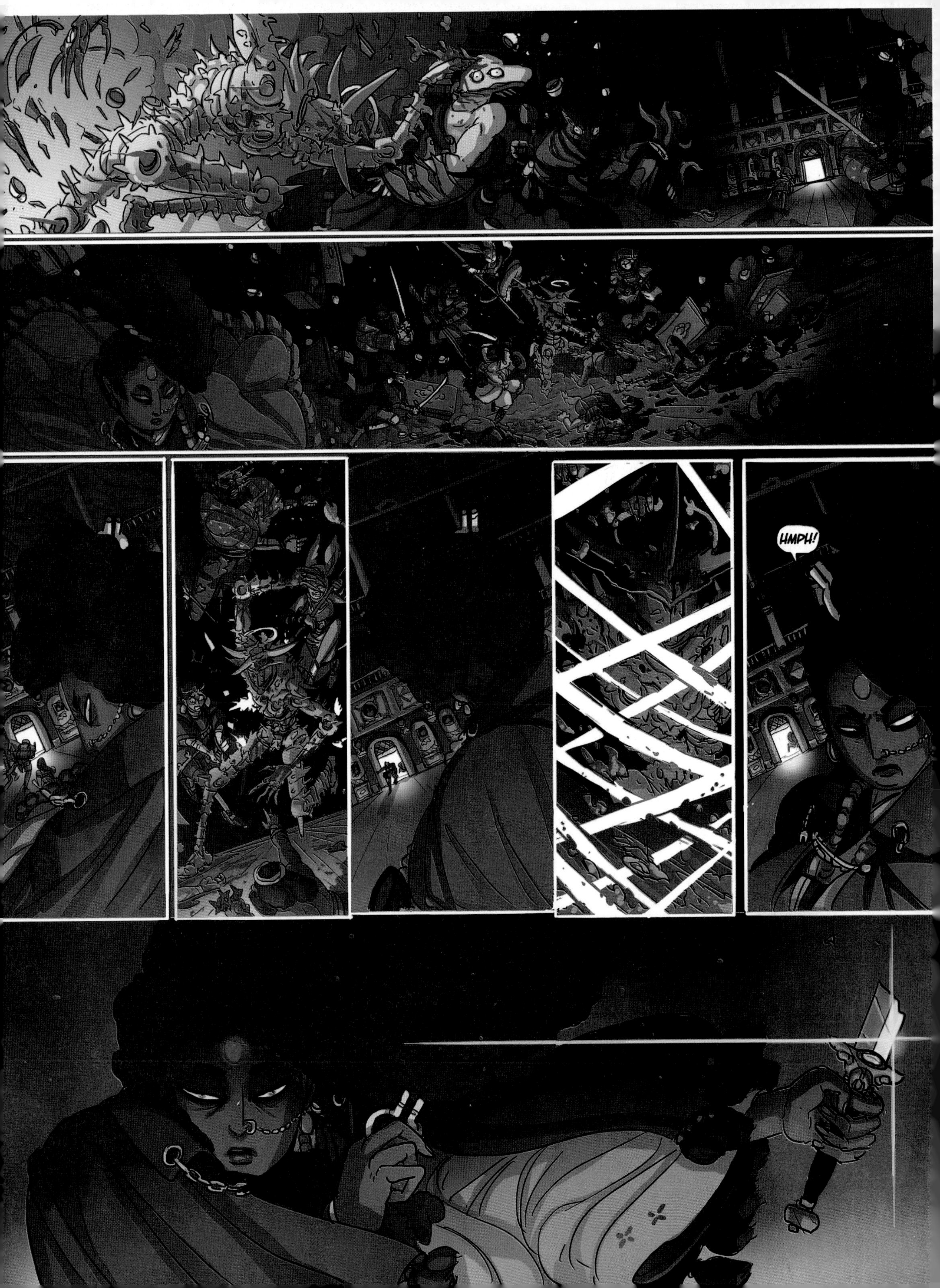
HMPH!

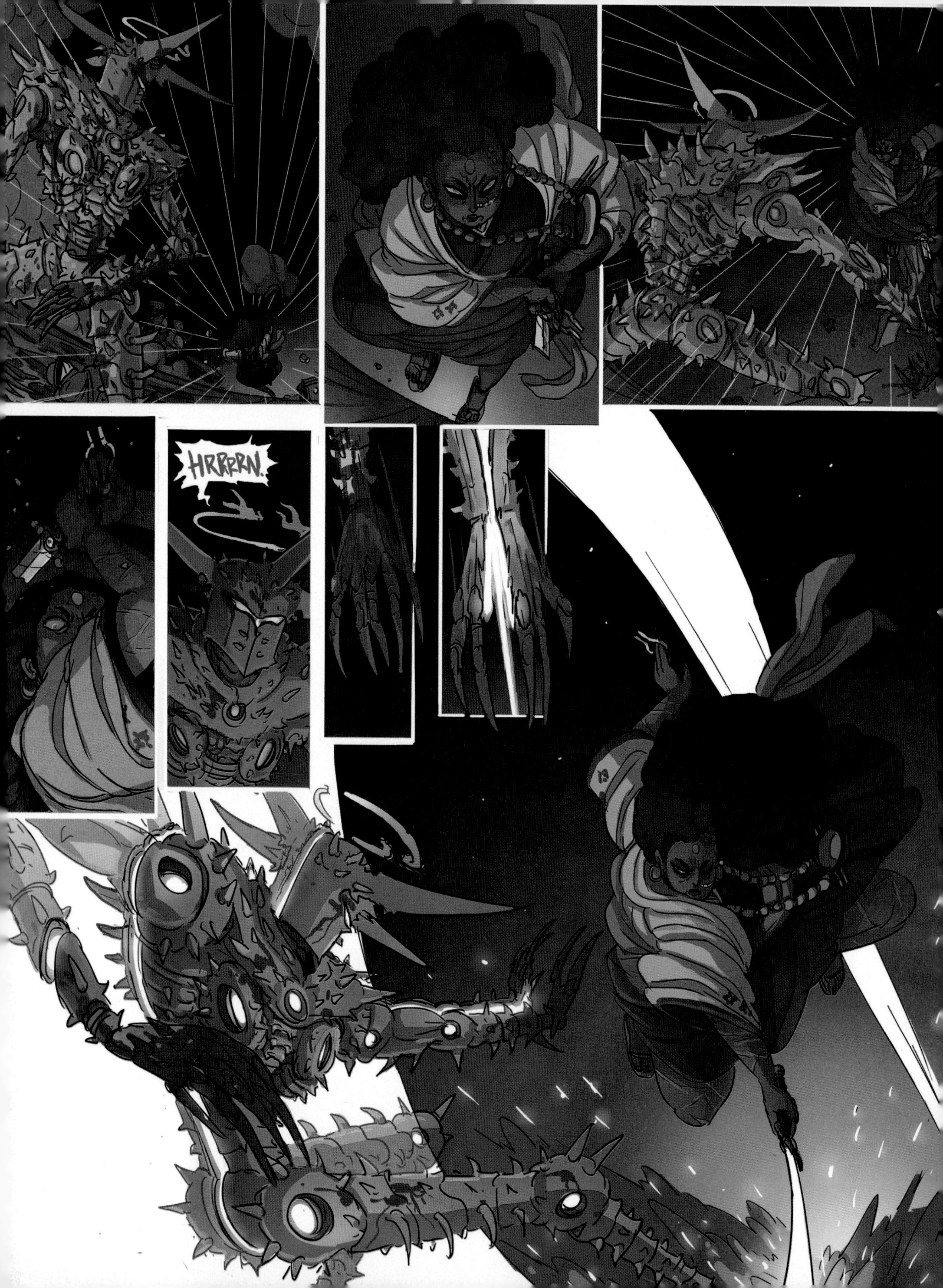
HRRRRN.

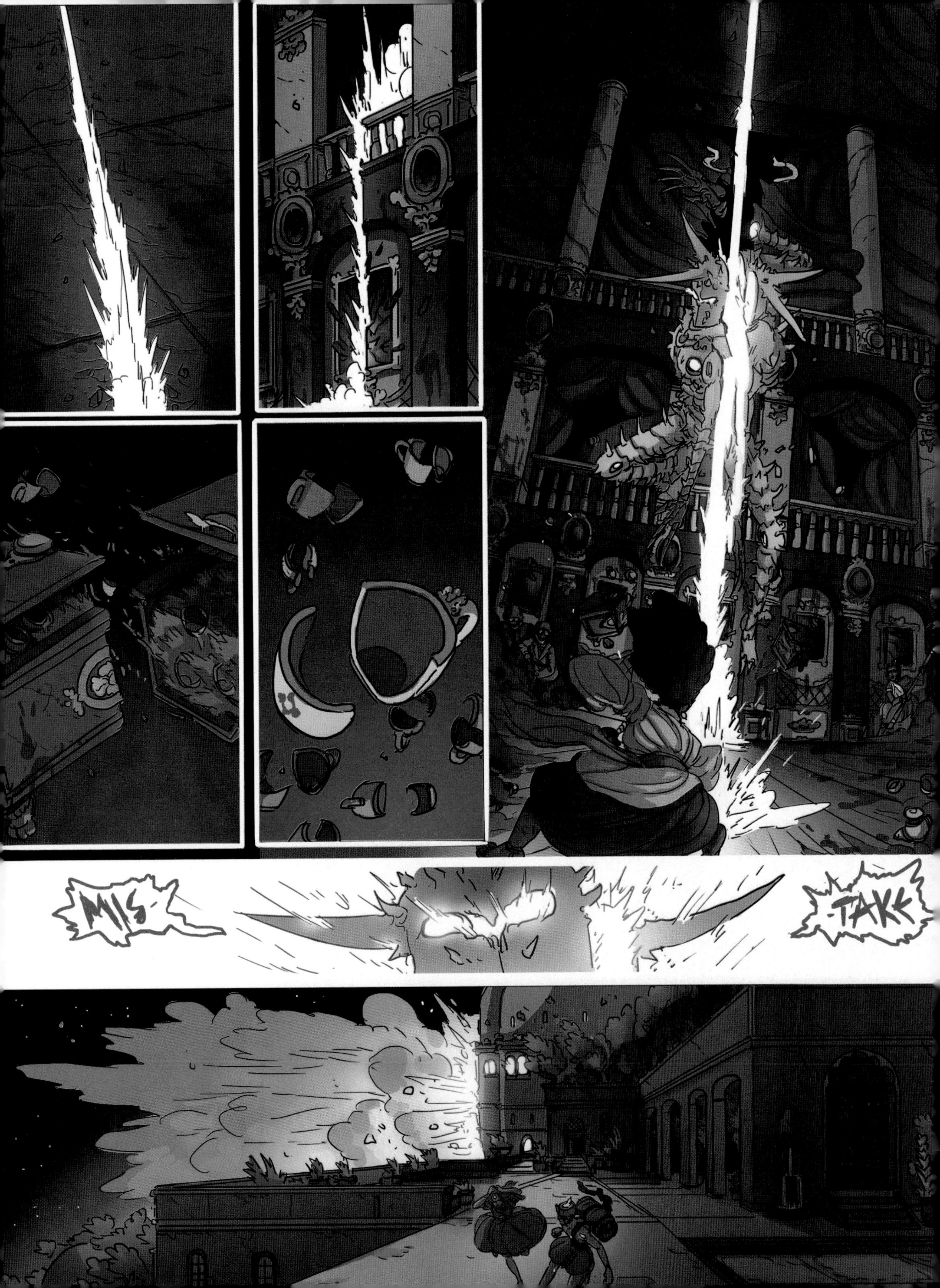
MIS-
-TAKE

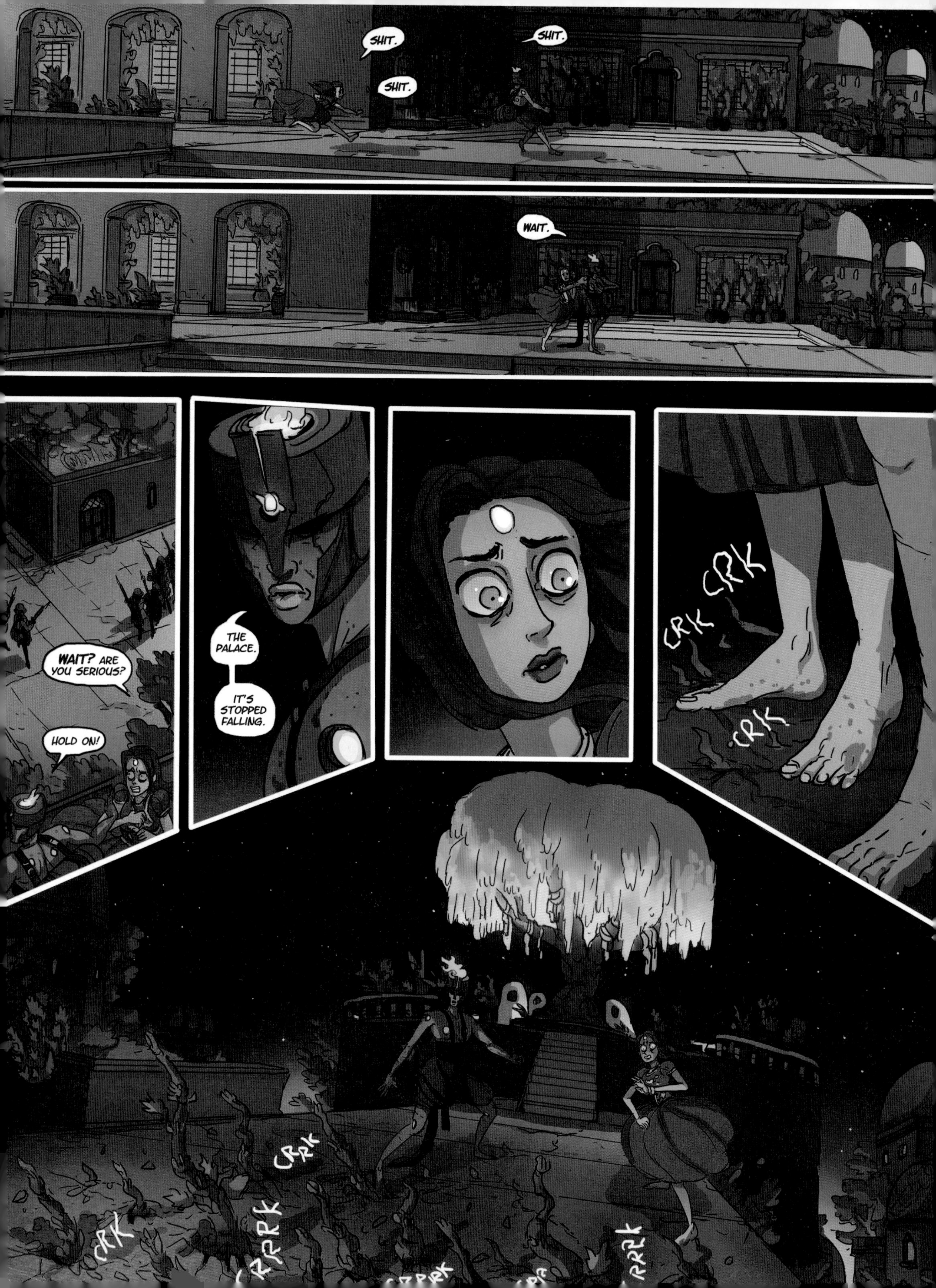
SHIT.
SHIT.
SHIT.
WAIT.
WAIT? ARE YOU SERIOUS?
HOLD ON!
THE PALACE.
IT'S STOPPED FALLING.
CRK
CRK
CRK
CRK
CRK
CRRRK
CRRRK

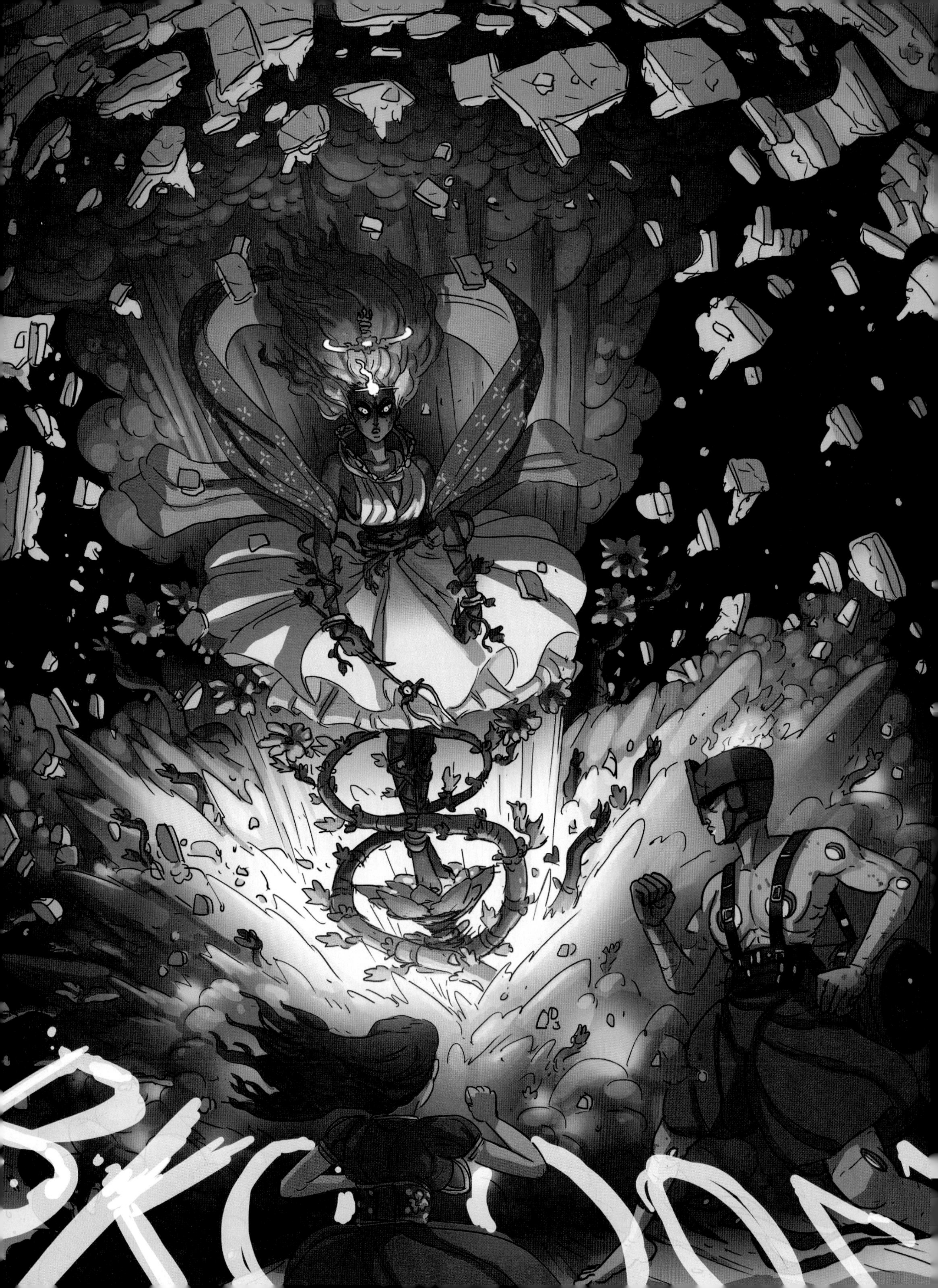
SKOOOM

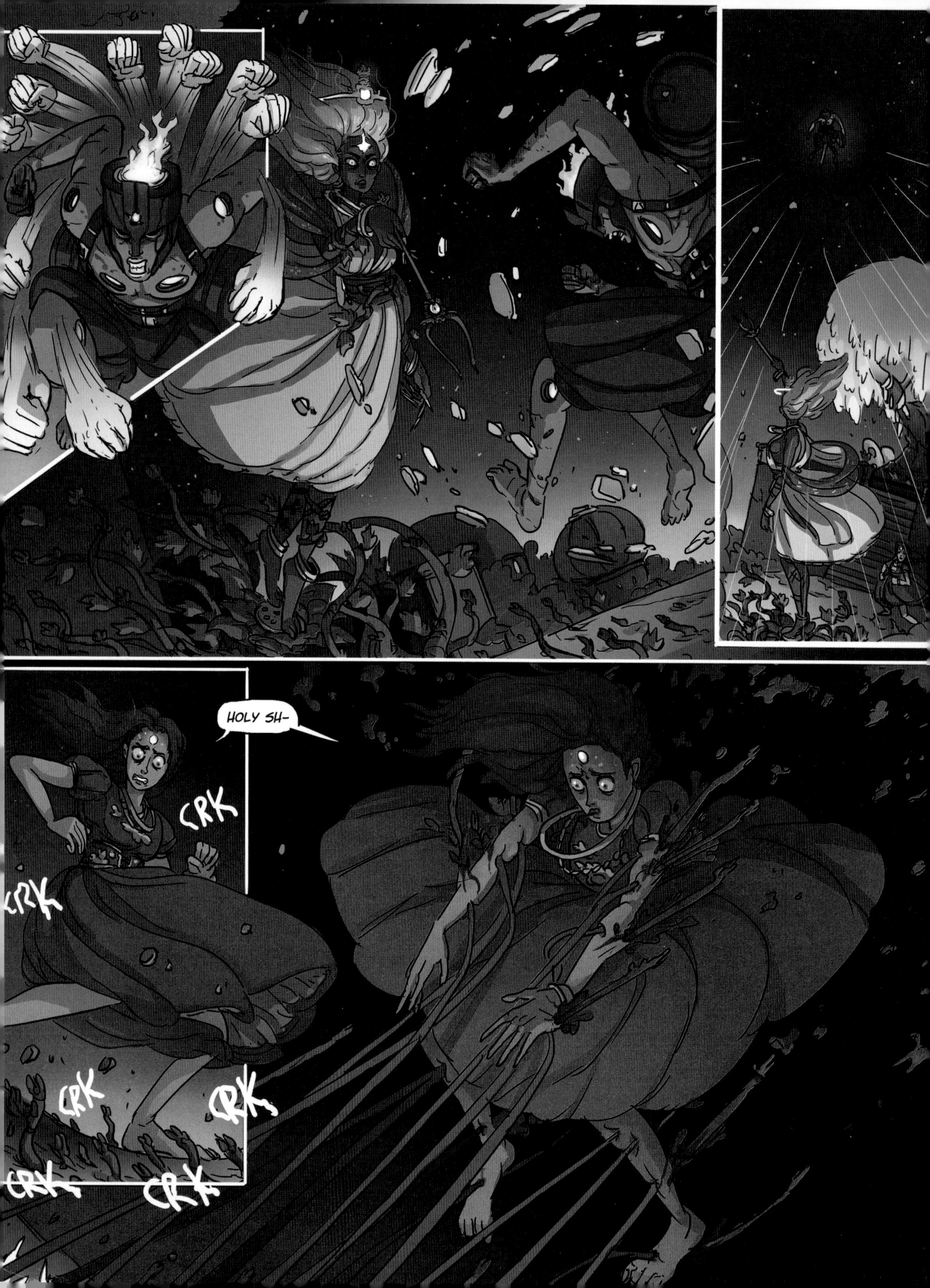
HOLY SH-
CRK
CRK
CRK
CRK
CRK
CRK

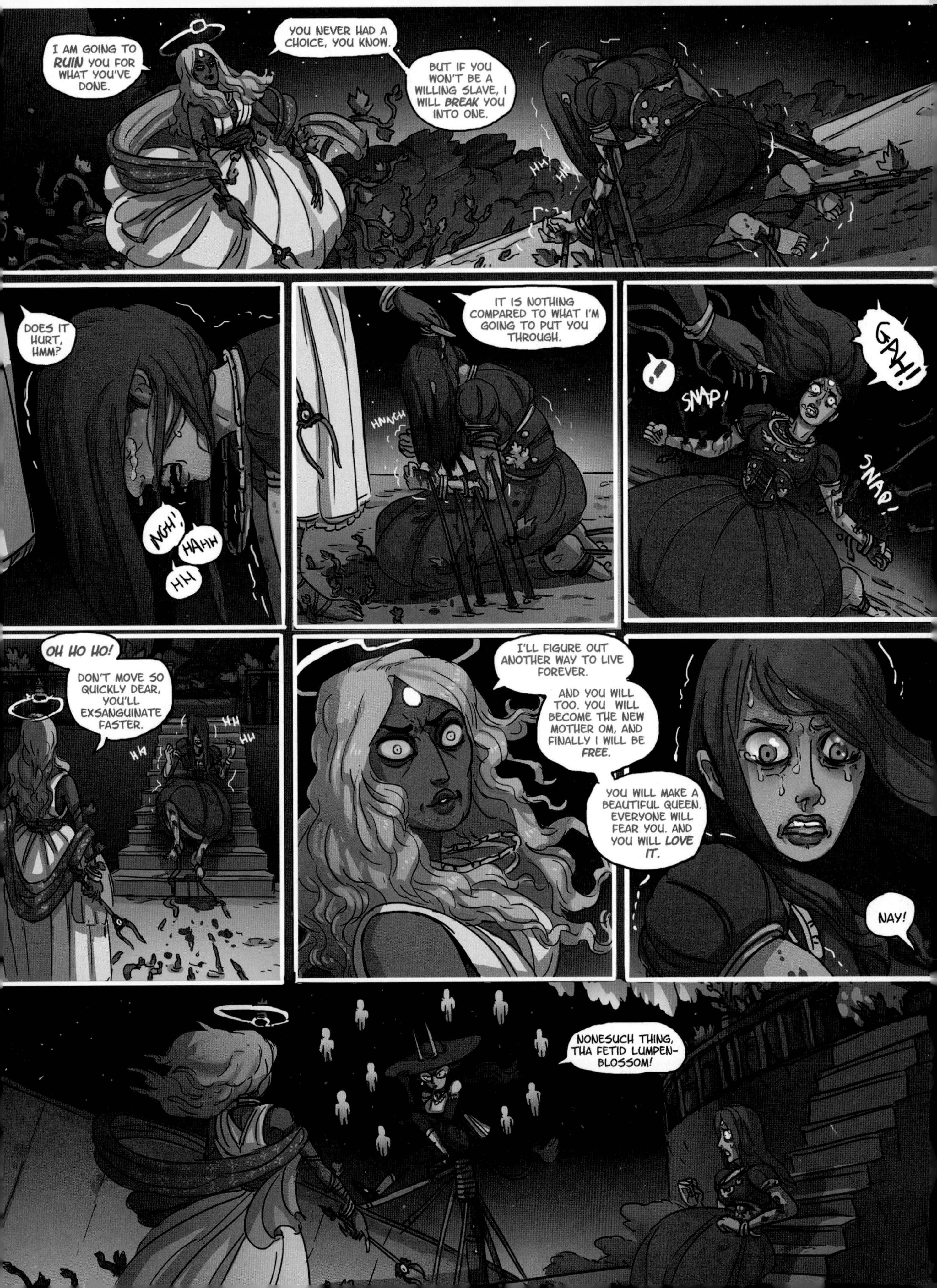

I AM GOING TO RUIN YOU FOR WHAT YOU'VE DONE.
YOU NEVER HAD A CHOICE, YOU KNOW.
BUT IF YOU WON'T BE A WILLING SLAVE, I WILL BREAK YOU INTO ONE.
HH HH
DOES IT HURT, HMM?
NGH! HAHH HH
IT IS NOTHING COMPARED TO WHAT I'M GOING TO PUT YOU THROUGH.
HNNGH
!
SNAP!
GAH!
SNAP!
OH HO HO!
DON'T MOVE SO QUICKLY DEAR, YOU'LL EXSANGUINATE FASTER.
HH HH HH
I'LL FIGURE OUT ANOTHER WAY TO LIVE FOREVER.
AND YOU WILL TOO. YOU WILL BECOME THE NEW MOTHER OM, AND FINALLY I WILL BE FREE.
YOU WILL MAKE A BEAUTIFUL QUEEN. EVERYONE WILL FEAR YOU. AND YOU WILL LOVE IT.
NAY!
NONESUCH THING, THA FETID LUMPEN-BLOSSOM!

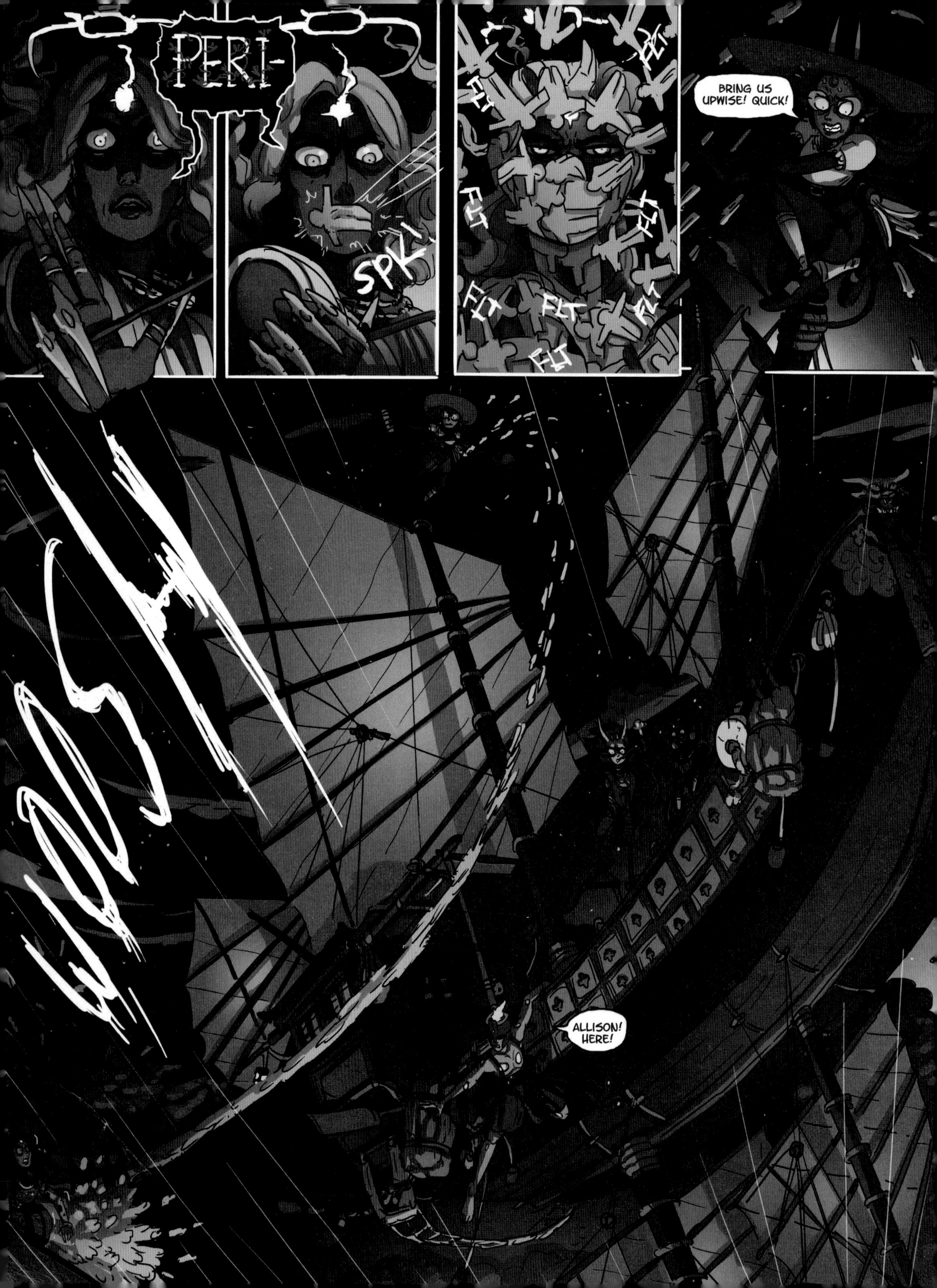
PERI-
SPK!
FLT FLT FLT FLT FLT FLT FLT FLT
BRING US UPWISE! QUICK!
WOOSH
ALLISON! HERE!

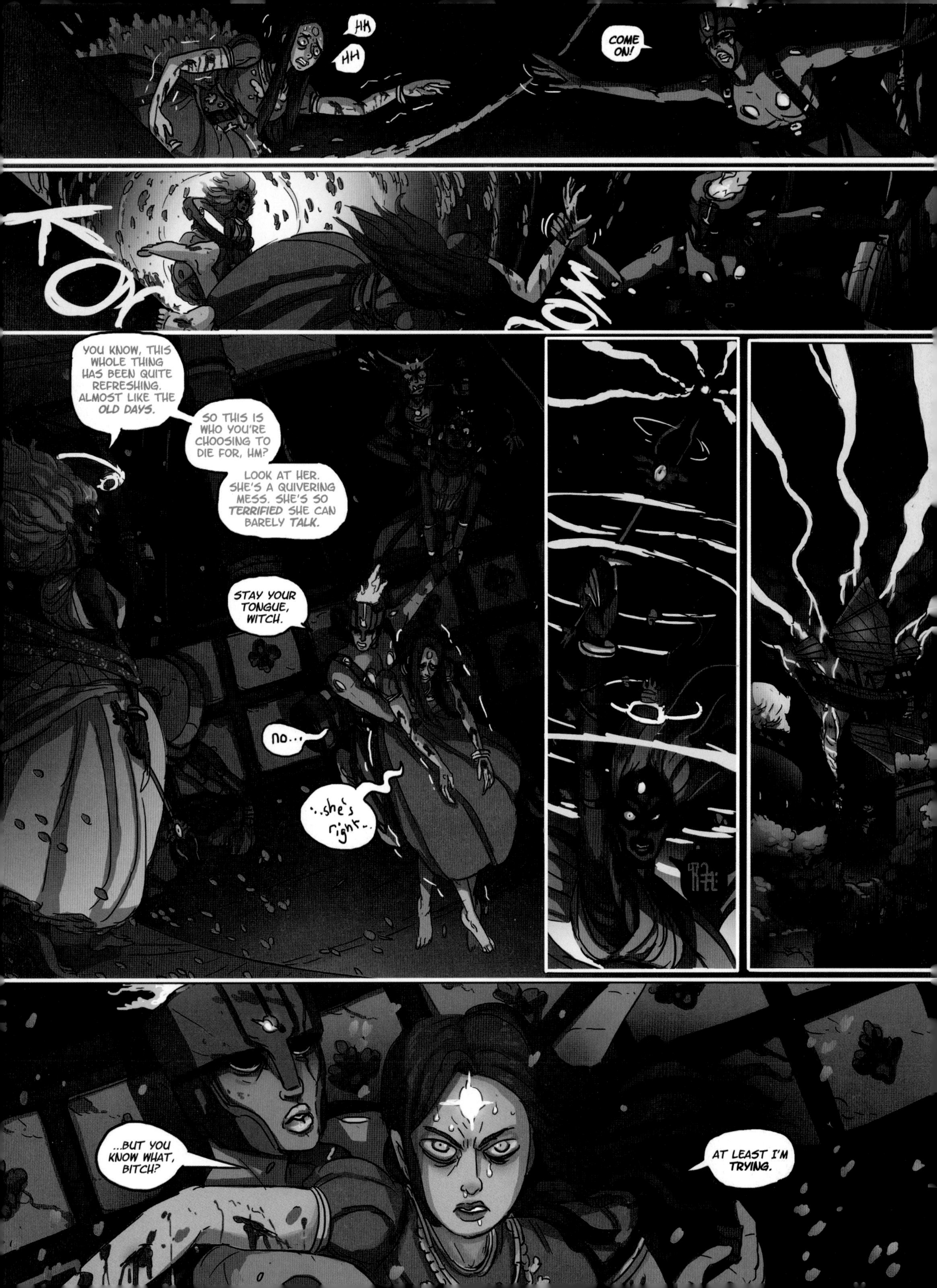
HH
HH
COME ON!
YOU KNOW, THIS WHOLE THING HAS BEEN QUITE REFRESHING. ALMOST LIKE THE OLD DAYS.
SO THIS IS WHO YOU'RE CHOOSING TO DIE FOR, HM?
LOOK AT HER. SHE'S A QUIVERING MESS. SHE'S SO TERRIFIED SHE CAN BARELY TALK.
STAY YOUR TONGUE, WITCH.
no...
...she's right...
...BUT YOU KNOW WHAT, BITCH?
AT LEAST I'M TRYING.

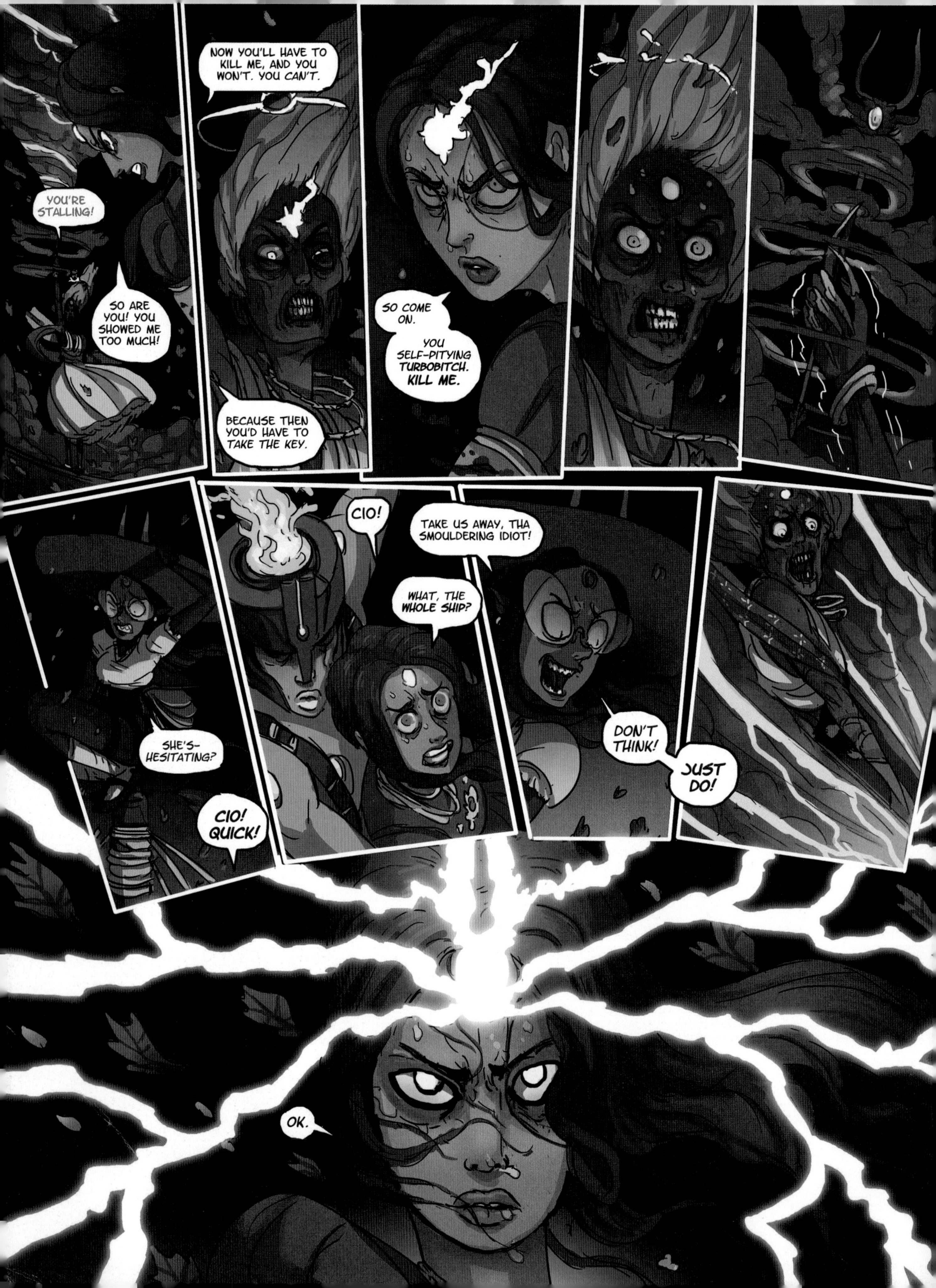

YOU'RE STALLING!
SO ARE YOU! YOU SHOWED ME TOO MUCH!
NOW YOU'LL HAVE TO KILL ME, AND YOU WON'T. YOU CAN'T.
BECAUSE THEN YOU'D HAVE TO TAKE THE KEY.
SO COME ON.
YOU SELF-PITYING TURBOBITCH. KILL ME.
SHE'S- HESITATING?
CIO! QUICK!
CIO!
WHAT, THE WHOLE SHIP?
TAKE US AWAY, THA SMOULDERING IDIOT!
DON'T THINK!
JUST DO!
OK.

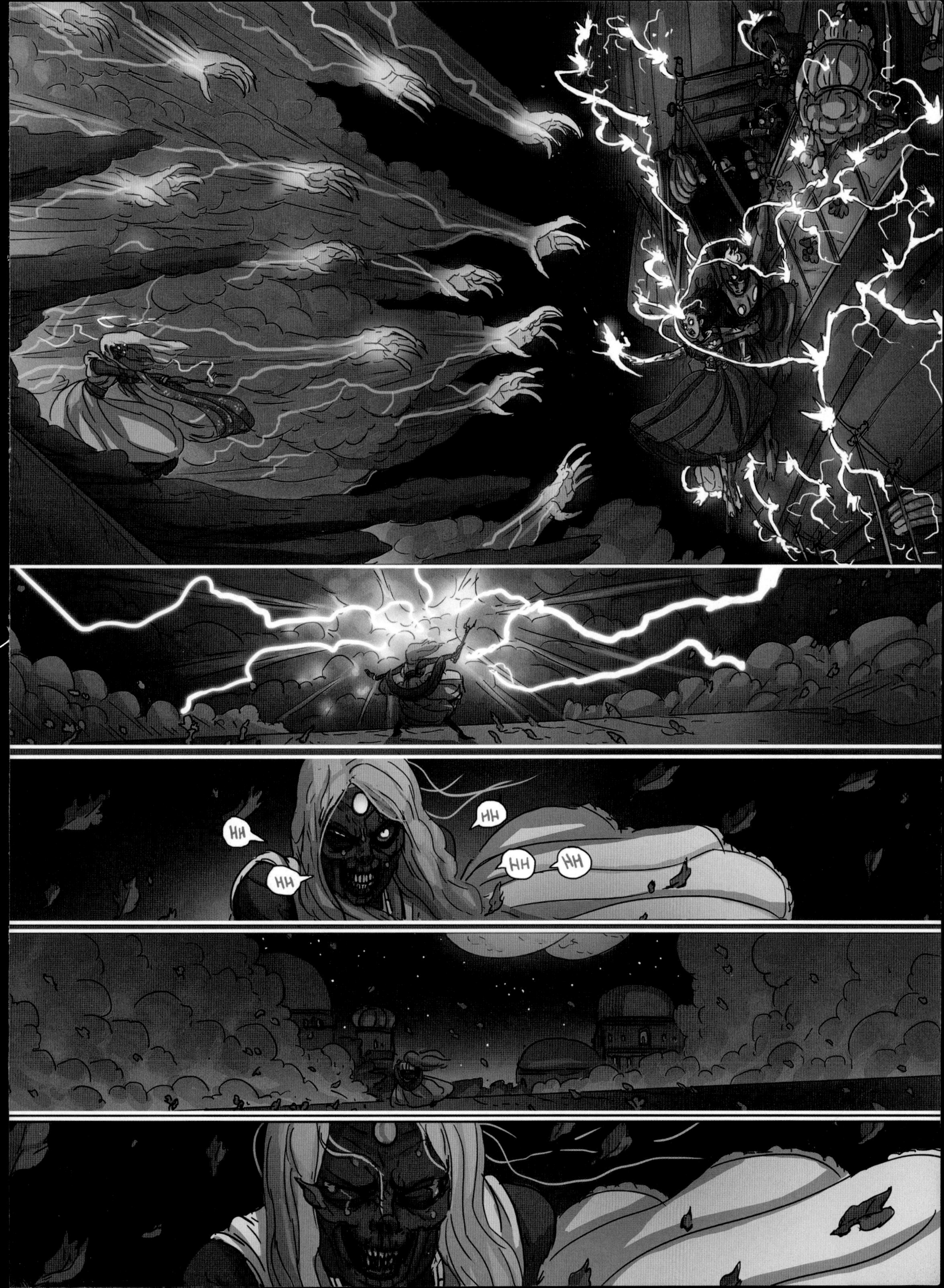
HH
HH
HH
HH
HH

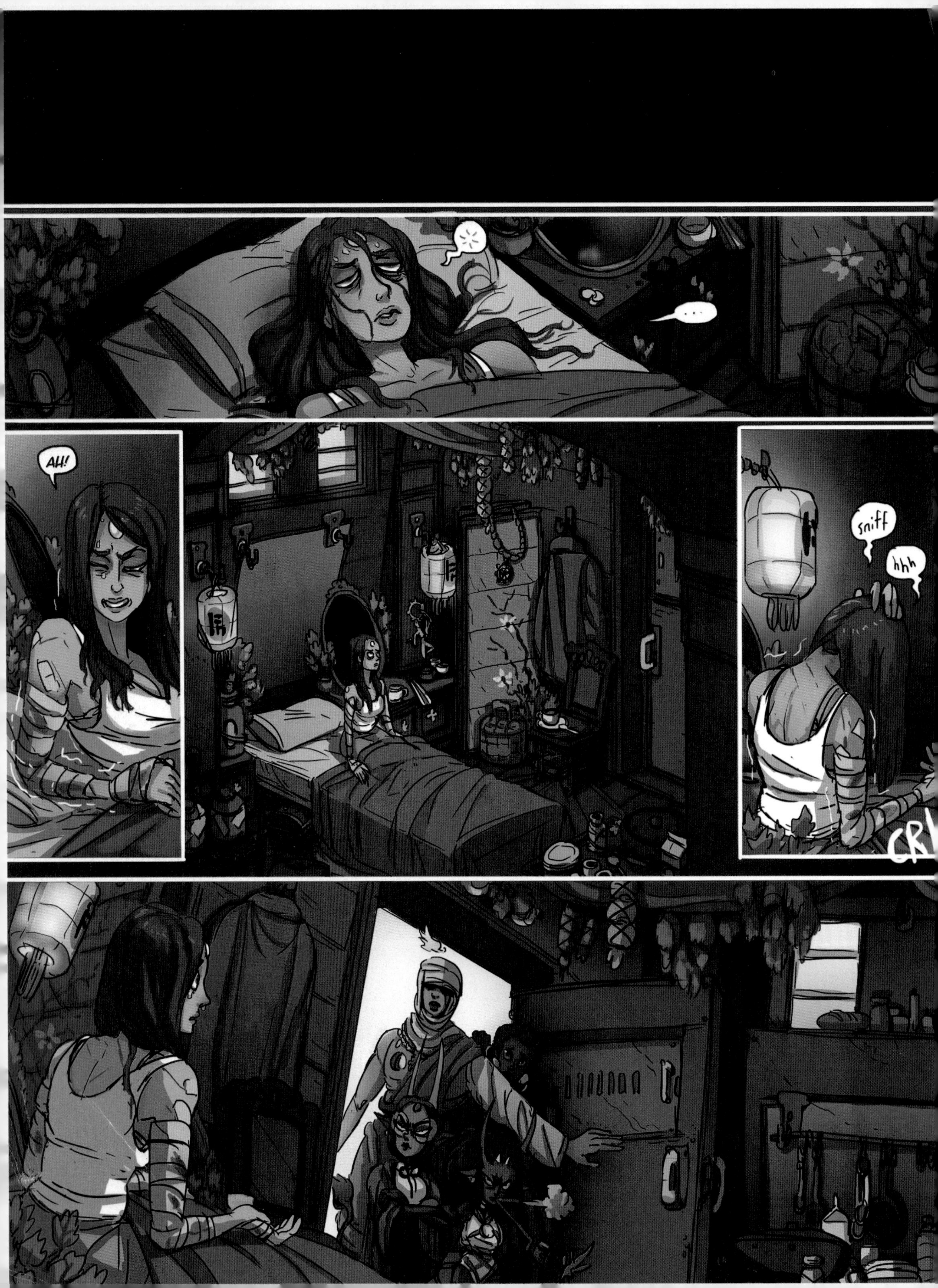

...
AH!
sniff
hhh
CR

THA FLOPSICAL WINNOW BRAINS!

THA SIEVE-HEAD! IDIOT!

CIO, I-

THA-

THA-

OH, FORGET IT.

IN TRUTH...

TWAS' MIGHTY IMPRESSIVE WHAT THA DID THERE.

JUST DON'T DO IT AGAIN

YES OF COURSE, THA HAD THAT WONDERFUL PLAN!

AND WHAT DID IT GET THEE? AERATED!

IDIOT!

NEVER AGAIN?

CAN'T PROMISE THAT.

I HATE TO SAY IT BUT...

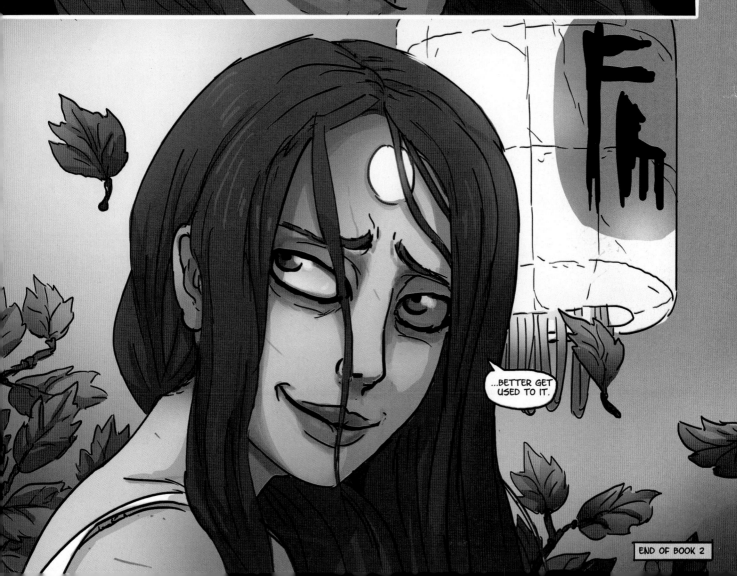

...BETTER GET USED TO IT.

END OF BOOK 2

"Lord Intra," said Intra's sparring partner one day,
"You are called Lord of Swords. Yet you are a man, and men make poor swordsmen."

"It is true," said Intra, for nearly all of the famous sword masters of the day were women and the Ya-at, who were three sexed. This tradition was rather long in the bones, and rumored to have been started by a famous vagrant who rarely cut her hair and lived in a barrel. There was popular theater about it, in those days.

"Men are too preoccupied with their swords," said Lord Intra, "They get distracted."
"You mistake my meaning," said Intra's sparring partner, "What I mean is this: you are a mere man. What can you do to the new gods of the Red City, with their whips of fire and their heavy chariot wheels?"

"I am not concerned with enmity," said Intra, "I am very skilled in Pankrash Circle Fighting"
"It is true you are very fierce," conceded his partner, "But my son's fighting beetle is also very fierce. Could his beetle fell a lion?"
"That depends," said Intra, "How skilled is the beetle in Pankrash Circle Fighting?"
"Beetles cannot learn Pankrash Circle Fighting, Lord Intra," said Intra's attendant, and made a bitter motion.

"Don't tell the beetle that," said Intra, "If you don't tell him he will learn it anyway and cut the lion in half with a single blow."

-The Song of Maybe

THE PINK PANTHER™

Movie Storybook

Based on the Screenplay
by Len Blum and Steve Martin
and the story
by Len Blum and Michael Saltzman
Adapted by Emma Harrison

an imprint of
Hyperion Books for Children
New York

At the time of printing, we worked from the most current script available, but some scenes may have changed in postproduction.

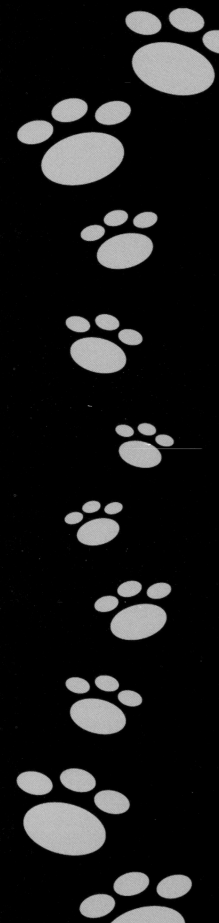

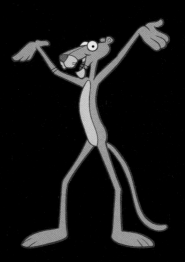

Printed in the United States of America
First Edition
1 3 5 7 9 10 8 6 4 2
ISBN 0-7868-3714-4

This book is set in 14/18 New Baskerville.

www.pinkpantherthemovie.com

It was an exciting day for all of France. The French national soccer team was playing China in the semifinal match of the international championships. It was a huge game. Thousands of people came out to see Yves Gluant, the handsome and famous coach, lead France to victory. The president of France sat in the stands along with Charles Dreyfus, the chief inspector of the national police. Gluant's business partner, Raymond Larocque, was there, as was Xania, Gluant's world-famous pop-star girlfriend.

Before the game, Gluant was greeted by a standing ovation. He raised his fist to the crowd, bejeweled with his famous pink diamond ring. The diamond had a tiny flaw in the center that looked just like a leaping panther. That was how it had gotten its nickname—the Pink Panther. It was the most famous jewel in all of Europe and was, of course, priceless.

The whistle blew, and the game began. It was an exciting battle from start to finish. At the end of the second half, the teams were tied. The game went into sudden-death overtime. Whichever team scored first would win and advance to the final match. At the last minute, Gluant pulled Bizu, one of France's best players, and replaced him with a rookie named Jacquard. Jacquard made a stunning kick that won the game.

The crowd went wild. France was victorious! Everyone crowded around Gluant, their hero. Then, right there in front of thousands of fans, Gluant fell to the ground, dead. There was a tiny dart in his neck, and the Pink Panther was gone. . . .

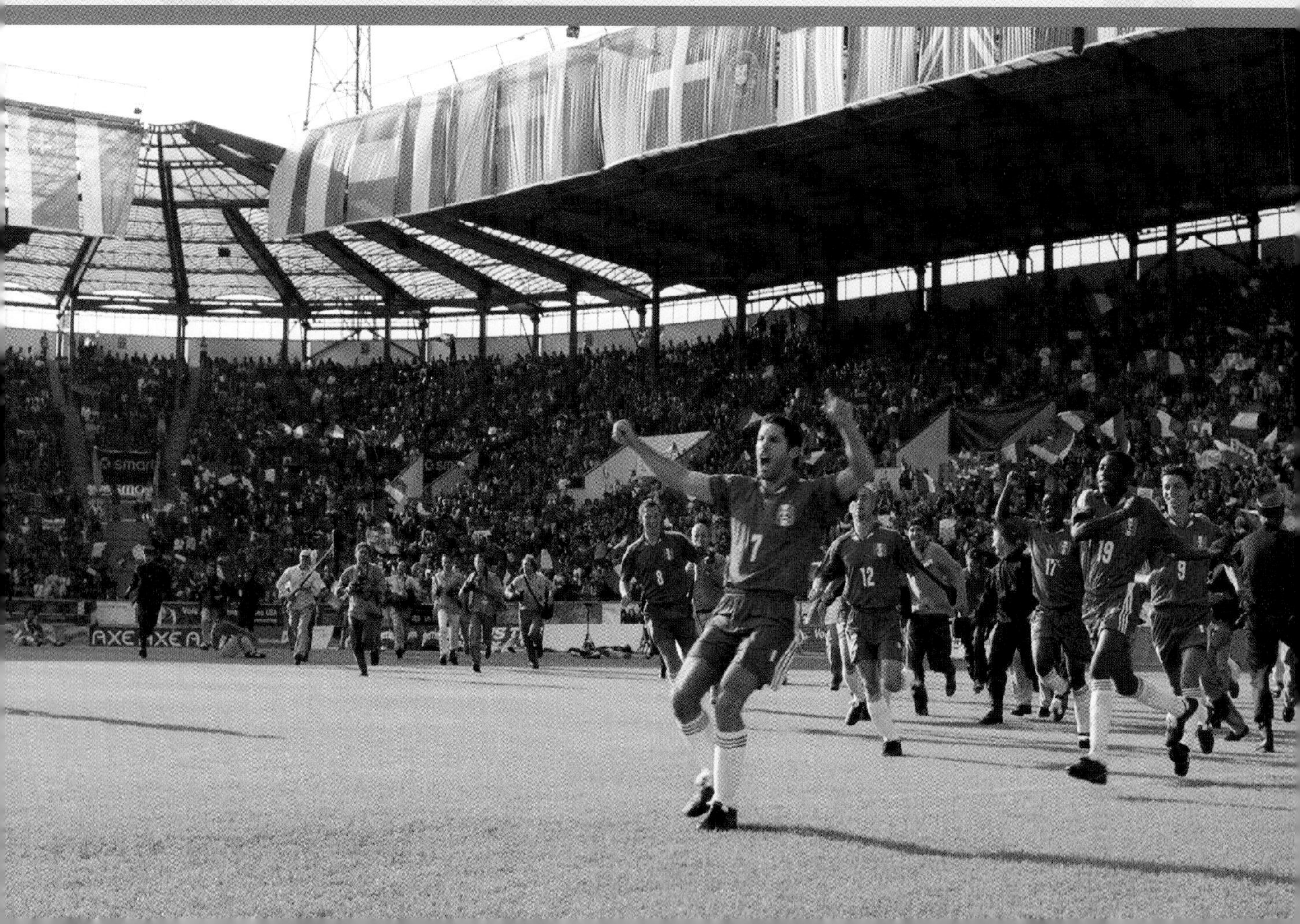

All the newspapers ran headlines about the murder. It was the biggest story to hit France in years. Charles Dreyfus was under a lot of pressure to find the murderer, but he didn't want the press watching his every move. He came up with a plan.

Dreyfus called in Inspector Jacques Clouseau. He wanted to make him the chief investigator in the Gluant case. Clouseau was known for being silly, and very bad at his job. He was not known for his clever investigating skills.

With Clouseau on the case, the press would be watching the bumbling French investigator, and Dreyfus could conduct his own investigation in private. When Dreyfus found the murderer, everyone would be surprised. And he would be a hero.

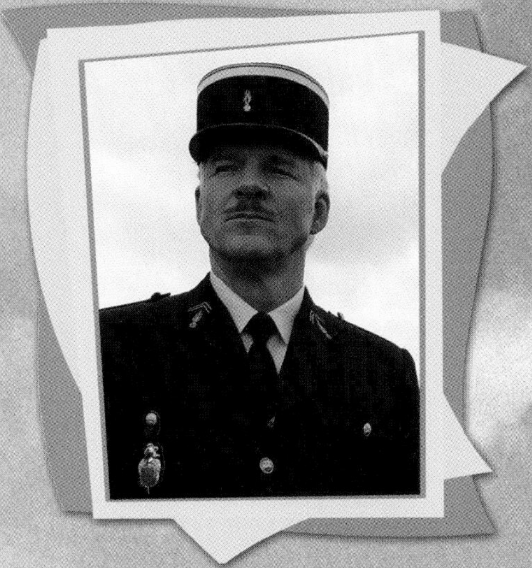

Clouseau drove to Paris in his small red car. All of the people in his village cheered as he drove off.

Finally, he arrived in Paris and went to la Palais de la Justice. He was eager to hear his orders.

Clouseau quickly checked to make sure the place was safe and secure. Wherever Clouseau went, he made sure there were no hidden devices recording his conversations. A good detective always had to be on his toes and check his surroundings.

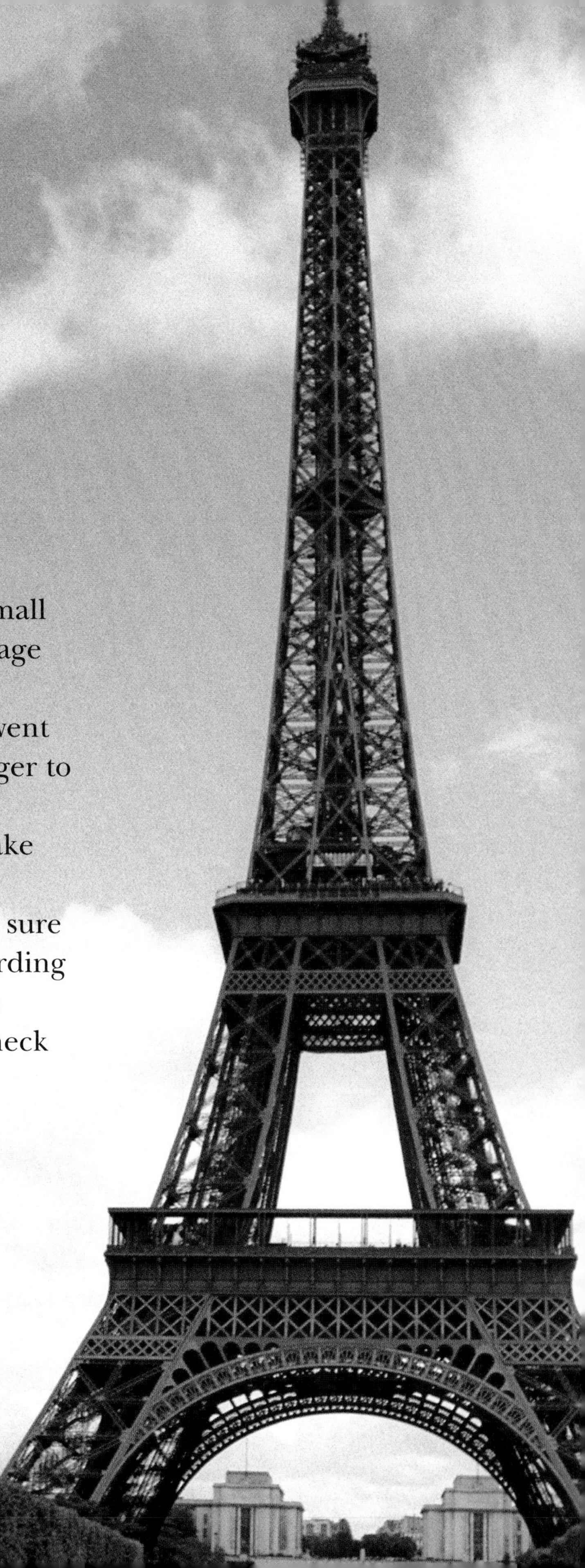

Dreyfus's secretary, Nicole, was very helpful and showed Clouseau where to wait. When Dreyfus told Inspector Clouseau that he had been called to Paris to take on the Gluant case, Clouseau felt honored.

Soon after, a press conference was held announcing that the Inspector was taking on the Gluant case. Chief Inspector Dreyfus introduced Clouseau to all of the reporters.

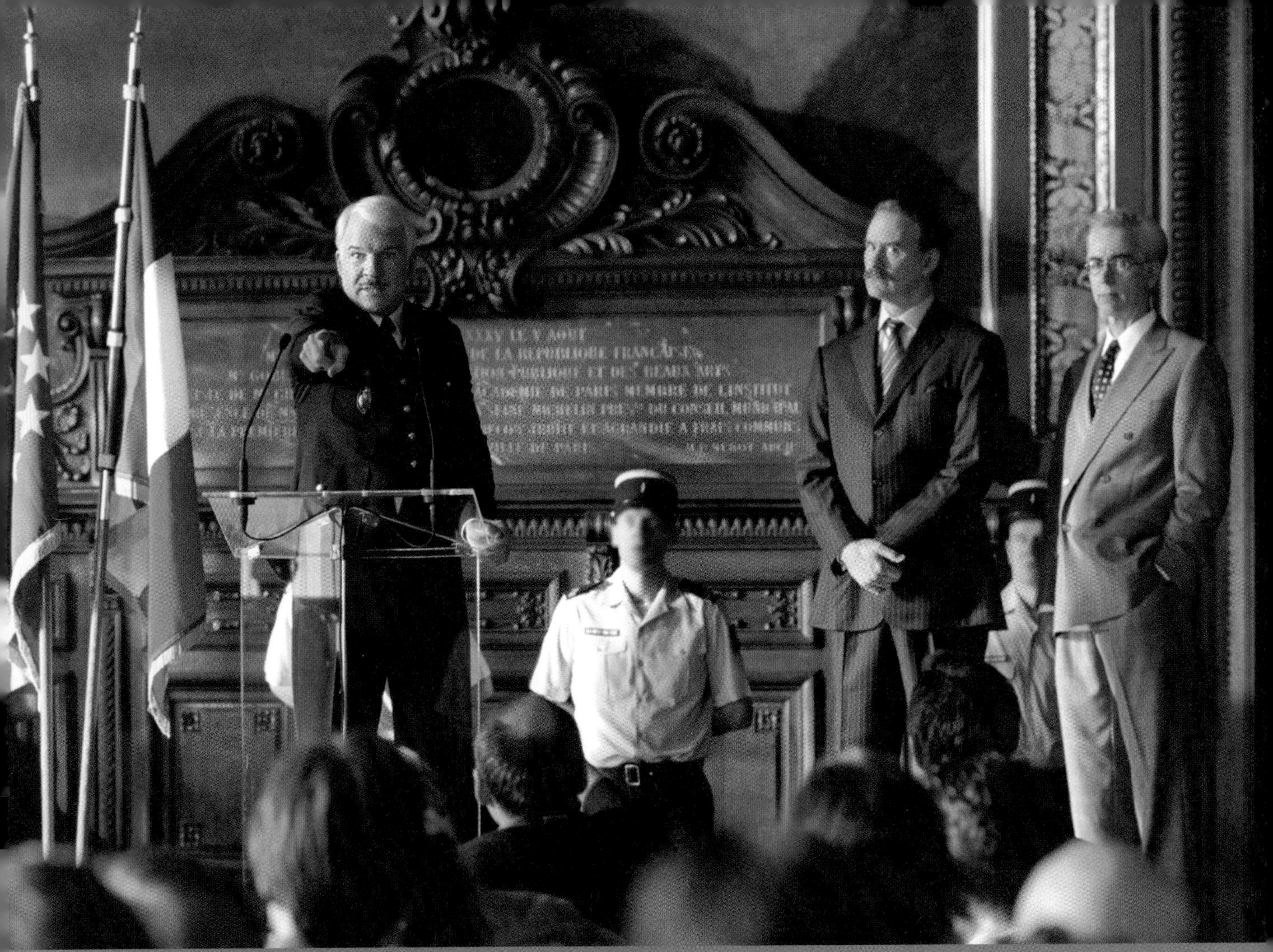

Clouseau looked into the cameras and delivered a message to the murderer.

"There is no place you can hide, no place you cannot be seen. Killer, I will find you! Because I am a servant of our nation, because justice is justice, and because France is France!"

The press loved him. All of France was certain that this confident, strong man would solve the case. Little did they know that he had only been hired in order to mess it up.

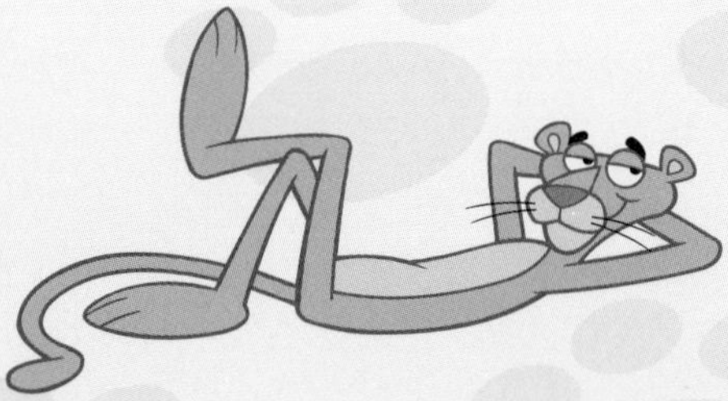

After the press conference, Clouseau met his new partner, Gilbert Ponton, a detective second class. Ponton was a good man, and his whole family (nine generations!) were in the police force. But since Ponton was only a detective second class, Clouseau offered to teach him everything he knew about being a police officer.

"Without warning, I will attack you—whenever and wherever it is least expected. In this way I will keep you alert and ready for the unexpected," Clouseau said. "Agreed?"

"All right," Ponton said.

A moment later, Clouseau tried to strike Ponton, but Ponton saw it coming. He hit Clouseau right in the face.

"Oh!" Clouseau groaned, holding his nose. It looked as though his student were already learning.

Clouseau and Ponton went to see Xania at her recording studio. She had been close to Gluant when he died, so they thought she might know something about the murder.

There was a flashing red light above the recording-studio door and a sign that read: DO NOT OPEN DOOR WHEN RED LIGHT IS FLASHING. So Clouseau waited for a moment in between flashes and then opened the door.

A group of classical musicians was playing inside the studio, and as Clouseau squeezed through them he waved his hands in the air for balance. Some of the musicians stopped following the conductor and instead started following Clouseau's wild gestures.

The music producer got angry. He tried to throw
Clouseau out. But Clouseau was there to interview Xania,
and he didn't want to leave without talking to her. Then,
when he saw her and saw how beautiful she was, he *really*
didn't want to leave. He asked her about a fight she had
had with Gluant the day he was murdered.

"I was angry. I caught him with another woman. This was after he said he loved me and asked me to marry him," Xania said. "He cheated on me, and I hated him, but I didn't kill him."

Clouseau believed Xania immediately. After all, how could someone so beautiful be a murderer? Xania told Clouseau that there was one other person who hated Gluant enough to kill him—Bizu.

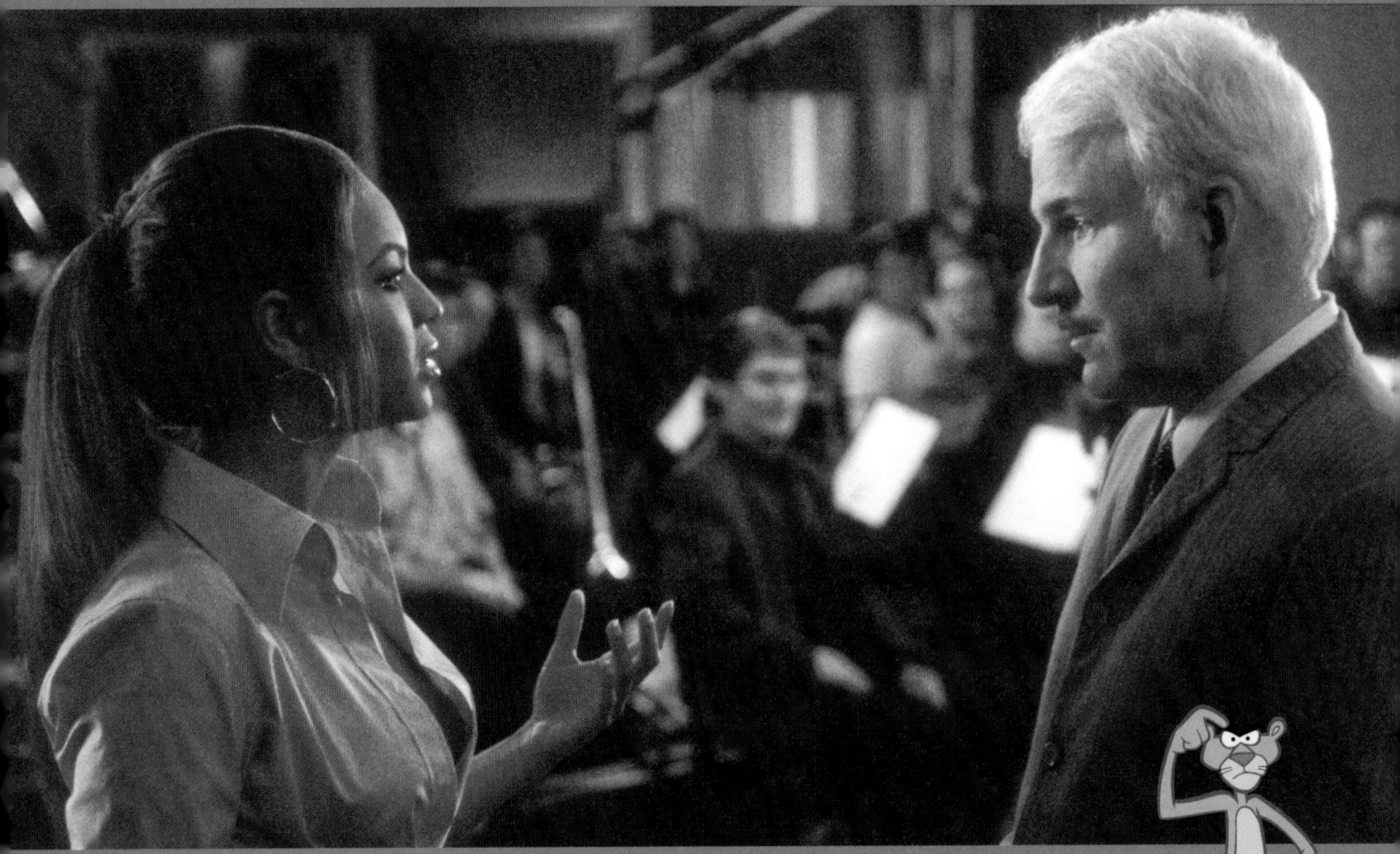

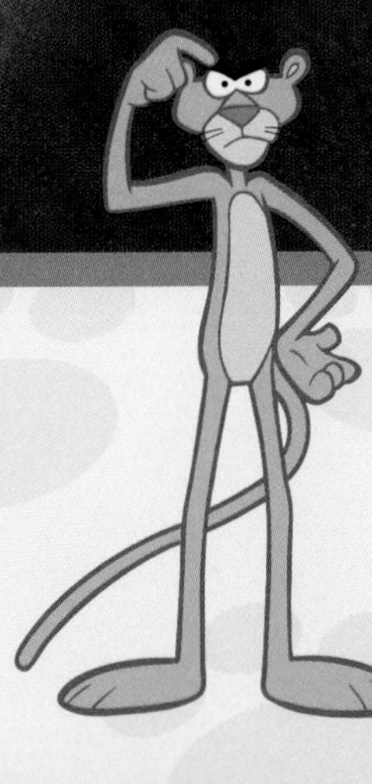

Clouseau and Ponton went to the soccer stadium to meet Gluant's team. They met the team's trainer, Yuri, who didn't say much at all.

The team was on the field practicing, so Clouseau sat on the bleachers and waited to question the star, Bizu. Clouseau fiddled with a bolt next to his leg as he watched the superstar kick the ball around.

"You looking at something?" Bizu called up to Clouseau.

Clouseau stood up. "Yes, my friend," he called down. "I want you to . . ." Just then, the benches snapped and folded up. Clouseau slid all the way down onto the field and landed at Bizu's feet. ". . . Come down to the station," Clouseau said, completing his sentence.

Bizu told Clouseau that he would have loved to get rid of Gluant but that somebody had beaten him to it. Bizu then suggested that Clouseau interview Raymond Larocque, Gluant's business partner. Together Gluant and Larocque owned several restaurants and casinos. Bizu said that Gluant had been taking money from the restaurants and gambling with it. Larocque had every reason to be angry with Gluant.

Ponton thought that Bizu was guilty of the murder. After all, Gluant had pulled Bizu from the semifinal game, embarrassing him in front of the world. Gluant had also stolen Bizu's girlfriend, Xania. Bizu had every reason to want Gluant dead. But Clouseau did not think Bizu was guilty.

That night Clouseau went home very tired. When he got to his apartment, he noticed something strange. The front door was open. He reached up along the frame of the door to check for wires or a recording device. *Slam!* The door suddenly closed on his fingers! He quickly kicked the door in and found Nicole, Dreyfus's kind secretary, standing there. She was apparently dropping off clothes for Clouseau. Of course, she had a spare key for the apartment Clouseau was staying in.

Later that night, Ponton came over to Clouseau's apartment with shocking news. Bizu had been murdered!

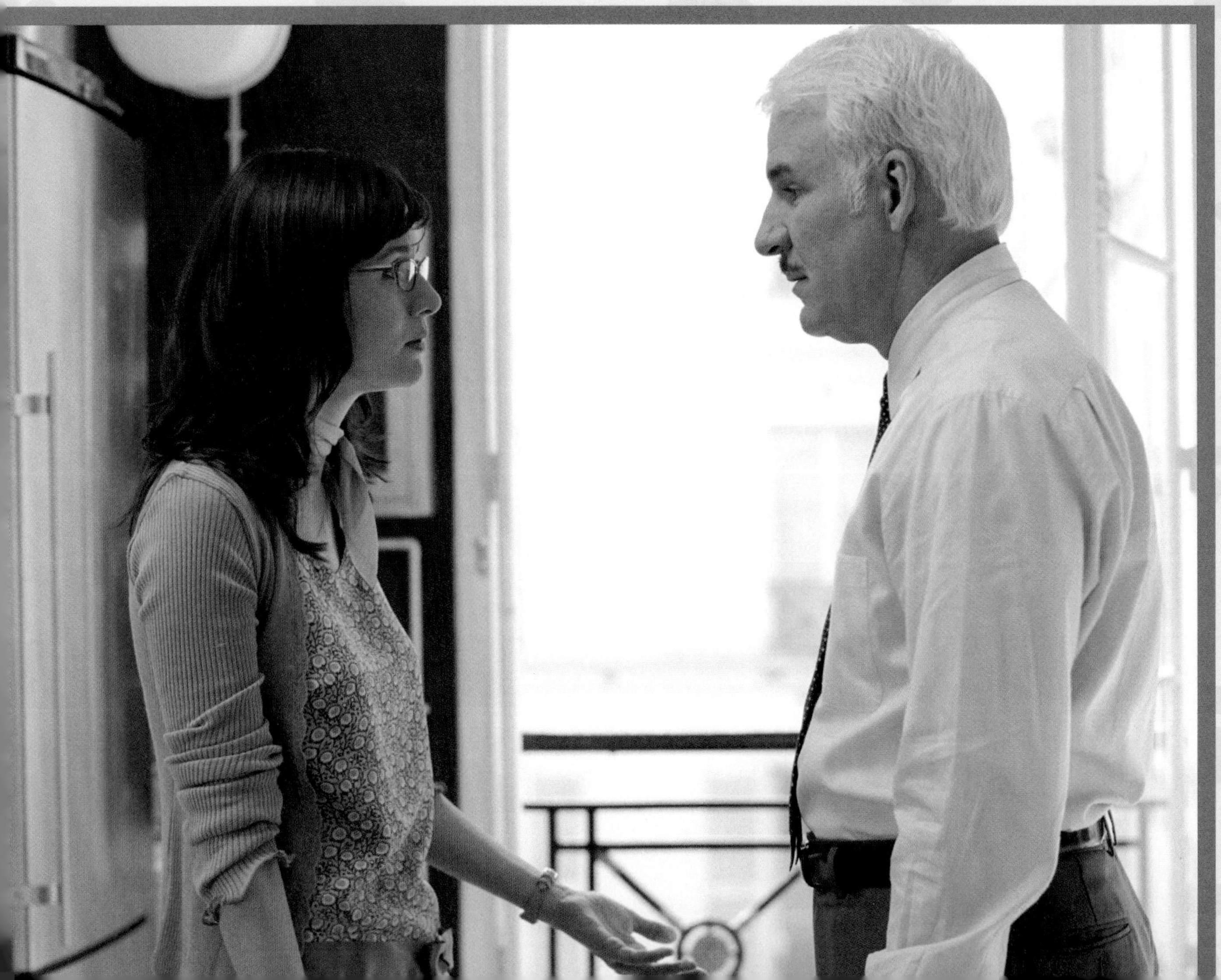

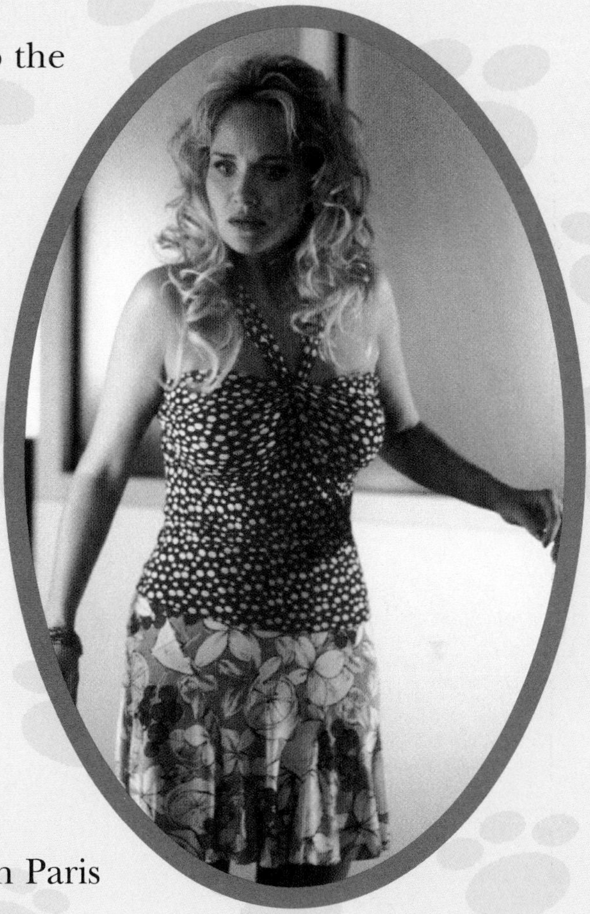

The next day, Clouseau went to the soccer team's locker room, where Bizu had been shot. On the floor was a chalk outline, marking the place where the body had been found. Clouseau interviewed Cherie, the woman who had found Bizu.

"Please, tell me what you saw," he said.

"Well, I didn't see anything," she replied. "I heard movement on the other side of the locker-room door. I heard Bizu say, 'Oh, it's you.' And then there was gunfire."

Clouseau took Ponton aside. "I want to interrogate every person in Paris with the name 'You,'" he said.

Ponton thought that that was a silly idea, but Clouseau was his boss, so he agreed. Clouseau looked at the chalk outline on the floor.

"Ponton, don't you find it a bit of a coincidence that the body fell perfectly within the chalk outline on the floor?" Clouseau asked, thinking he might have found a clue.

Ponton stared at Clouseau. "I think they drew the chalk outline later," he said.

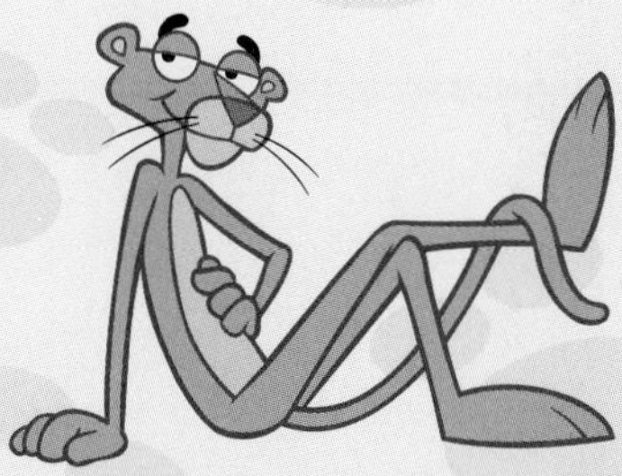

Next, Clouseau and Ponton went to Rome to interview Raymond Larocque at his casino. On the way, Clouseau stopped in at the casino to place a bet. There he met Nigel Boswell, an English detective. Boswell told Clouseau that he was in Rome on a top-secret case, and that Clouseau should tell no one that he had seen Boswell. Clouseau promised to keep the secret. Clouseau gave Boswell his cell phone number and told him to call if he needed any help with his case.

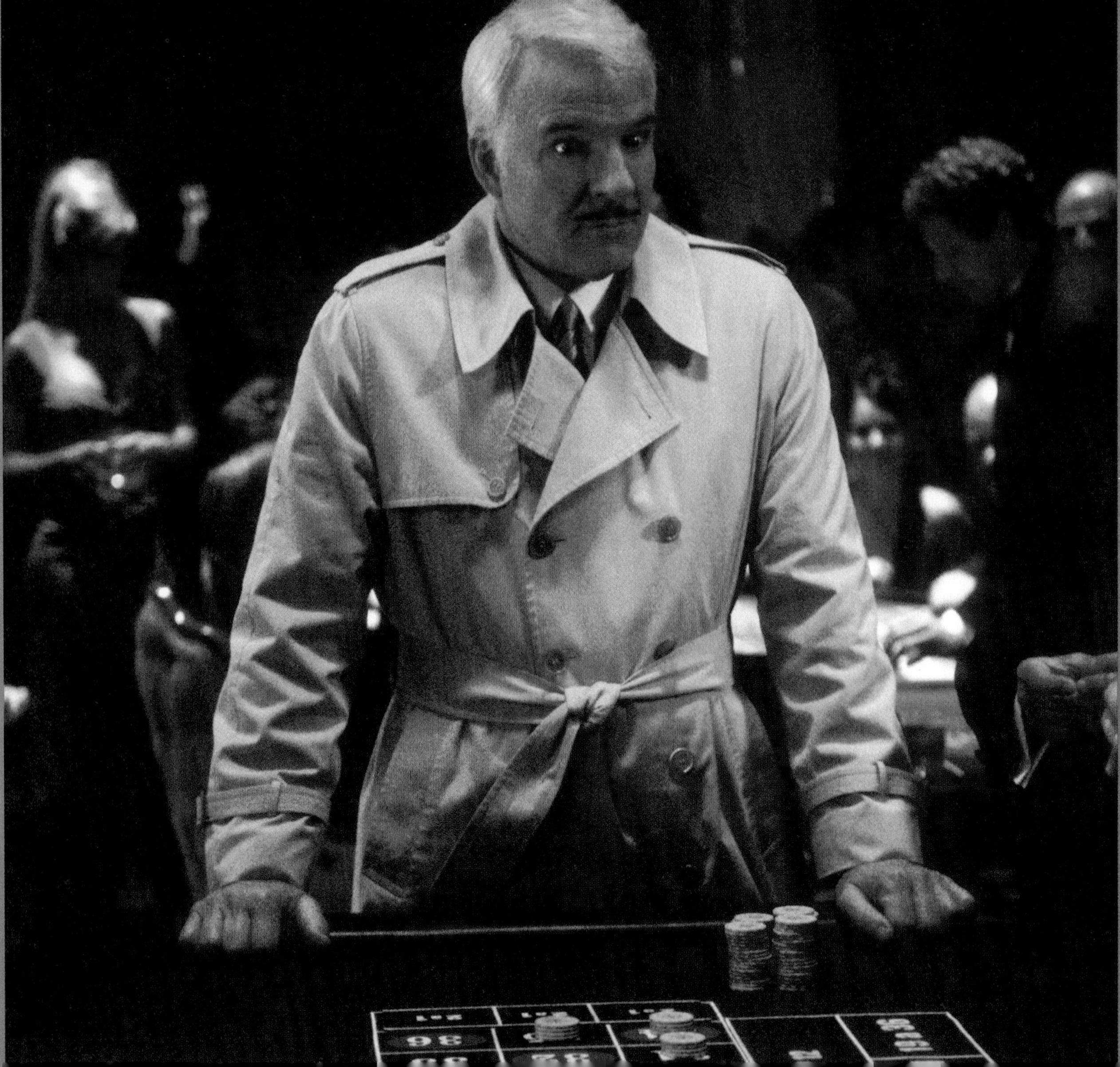

Clouseau and Ponton went to Larocque's office, where they met Larocque and his bodyguard, Huang. The office was filled with beautiful antiques. Clouseau placed his hand inside a vase in order to pick it up and take a closer look.

When he tried to put the vase down again, his hand got stuck. Finding this odd, he placed his other hand in another vase, to see if the same thing would happen. It did. Now Clouseau had a vase stuck on each hand! He tried to look calm and leaned an elbow on the table. But it wasn't a table! It was the edge of a tank that had a piranha, which started chomping on his elbow.

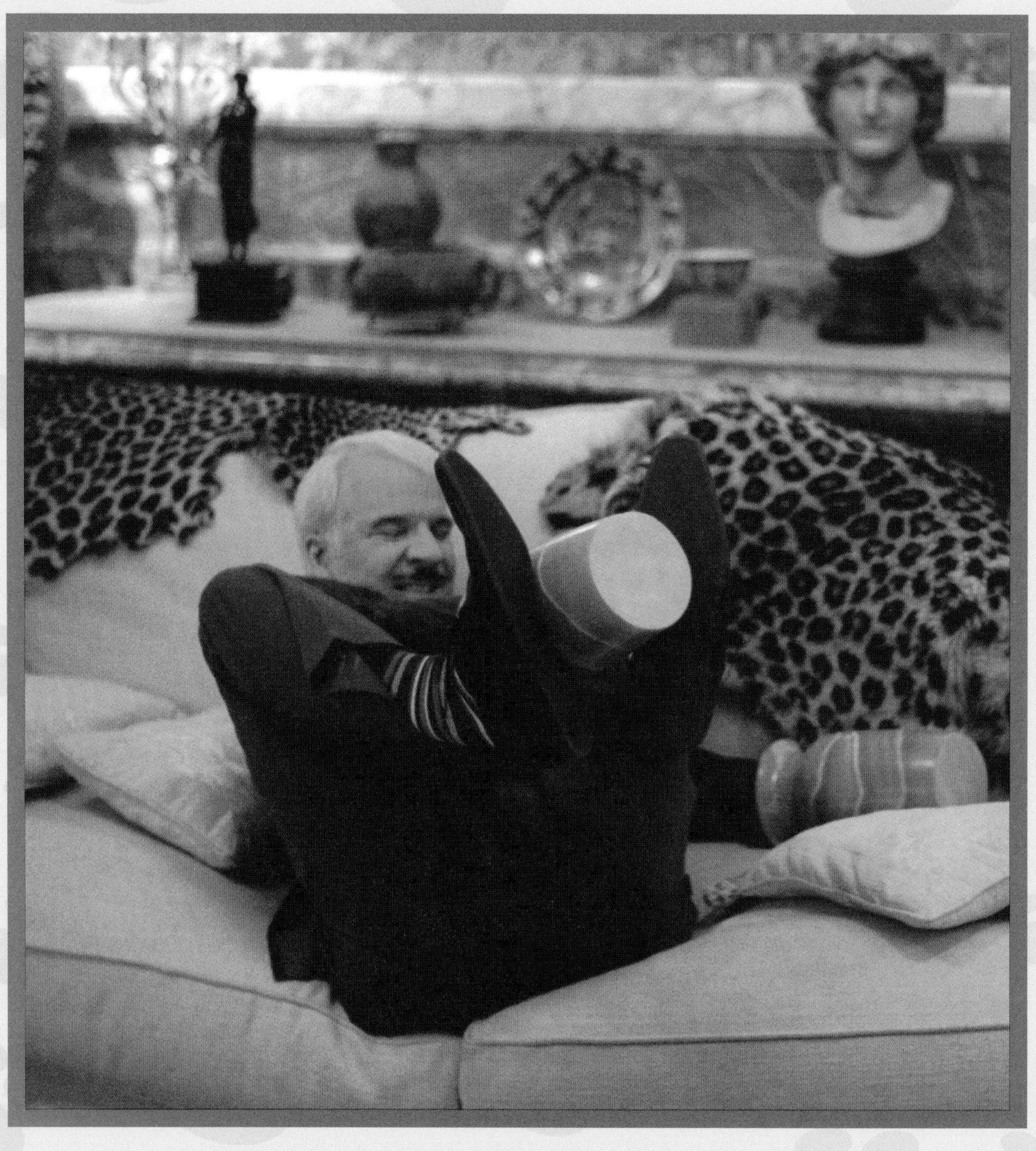

While Clouseau struggled to free his hands, Ponton conducted the interview.

Larocque claimed he had nothing to gain by Gluant's death. He told Ponton that if the Pink Panther were to be found, however, it should be returned to him. Gluant had promised it to Larocque as payment for the many debts he owed him.

This was an interesting fact, but Clouseau was even more interested in getting the vases off his hands.

He whirled, and the first vase flew off. Huang ducked out of the way, and Ponton caught the vase easily. Now Clouseau just had to get rid of the second one.

"Excuse me. Is this vase of great value?" he asked Larocque.

"It's a worthless imitation," Larocque answered.

"Ah, good," Clouseau said.

And with that, he smashed the vase against an end table, freeing his hand. The table shattered into bits. Larocque winced in pain. "But the desk was priceless," he said.

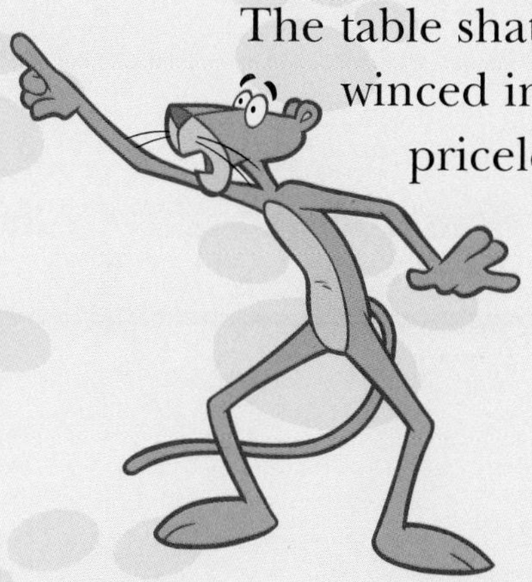

Clouseau's cell phone rang. It was Boswell. He needed help.

Clouseau raced downstairs to the casino and found Boswell. A group of men in gas masks were trying to rob the casino!

Boswell asked for Clouseau's coat. He wanted to stop the robbery, but he needed a disguise, since no one was supposed to know he was in Rome.

Quickly, Clouseau gave Boswell his coat. Boswell rounded up all the bad guys and then, before he left, handed the coat back to Clouseau along with a gas mask. Now everyone thought that it was Clouseau who had saved the day! Clouseau stood there wearing the coat and holding the gas mask. People rushed up to him, congratulating and thanking him. It turned out the Gas-Mask Bandits had been committing crimes all over Europe. Now Clouseau was *really* famous!

Meanwhile, Ponton rounded up everyone in town with the name "You," as Clouseau had asked. Clouseau interrogated his first subject, Mrs. Yu. She shouted at him in Chinese. Clouseau eventually let her go.

"You speak Chinese?" Ponton asked doubtfully.

"Of course I speak Chinese!" Clouseau replied. "Let's all just go home, then, if I don't speak Chinese! That is absurd!"

But Clouseau seemed confused, and Ponton didn't quite believe him.

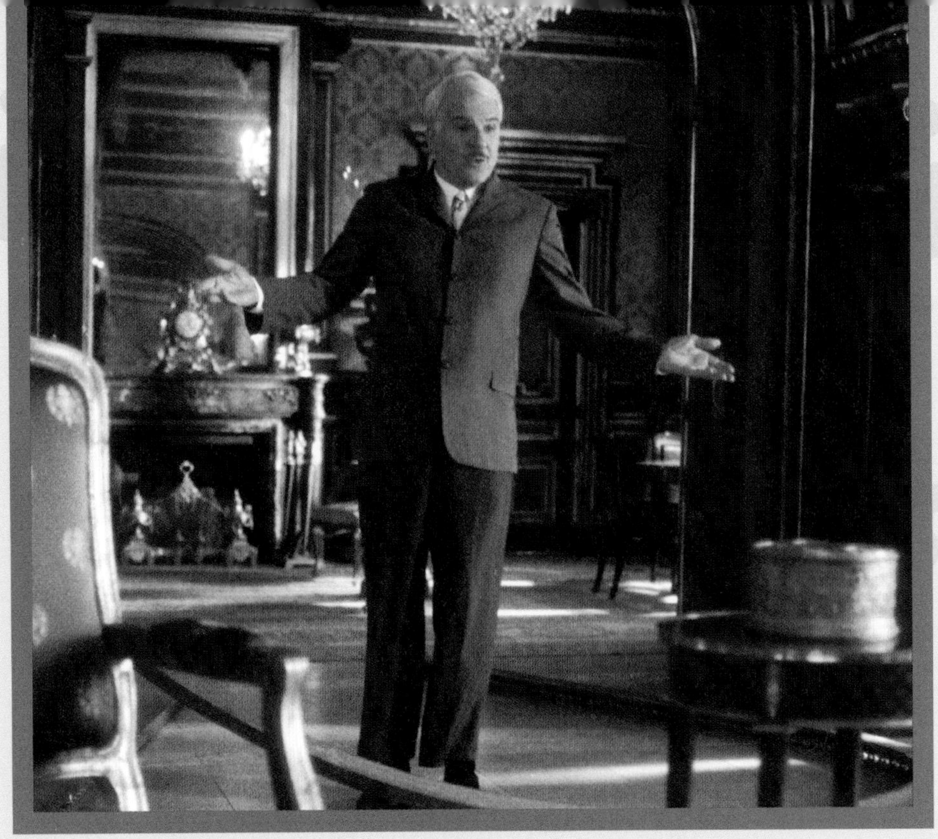

Back in Paris, Chief Inspector Dreyfus checked in with Clouseau to see how he was doing. After watching Clouseau on the news, Dreyfus was worried that Clouseau might actually solve the Pink Panther case before he had a chance to.

"The case is going quite well," Clouseau said. "The crime has three components. The soccer stadium, the people immediately surrounding Gluant, and a small circle of friends. And from that, I have made up a list of suspects."

"How many suspects does that give you?" Dreyfus asked.

"Twenty-seven thousand, six hundred and eighty-three," Clouseau said.

That was a lot of suspects. Dreyfus was no longer worried that Clouseau would solve the case.

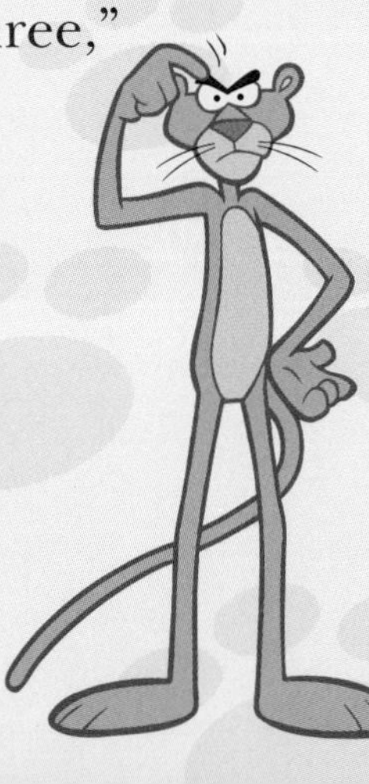

That day the nominations for France's Medal of Honor were announced. The nominees were Charles Dreyfus, Sister Marie-Hugette, and Inspector Jacques Clouseau. If Clouseau caught Yves Gluant's murderer, he would undoubtedly win the Medal of Honor, a prize that Charles Dreyfus wanted more than anything. Dreyfus couldn't believe what was happening. He had to find the murderer before Clouseau did.

Dreyfus snuck into Clouseau's office to see what clues the Inspector had found. But Clouseau came back too soon—Dreyfus realized he might be caught snooping and quickly hid. Unfortunately for him, Clouseau noticed that some things on his desk had been touched, and that a pair of shiny shoes were sticking out from behind the window curtains. *Wham!* Clouseau smashed a chair against the curtain. Dreyfus fell to the floor with a very sore eye.

Ponton thought Xania was the likeliest suspect in the murder case. She was angry with Gluant for cheating on her, and she had been right next to him when he died. Clouseau couldn't believe that this beautiful, amazing woman could have been involved, but he did think that Xania knew more than she had let on. She was in New York, so Clouseau decided to go there to question her again.

Clouseau knew that, to be a good inspector, he had to blend into the surroundings so as to not arouse any suspicion. He decided to take speech classes so he could speak like a real New Yorker while ordering a hamburger.

"A hamburger," the teacher said.

"Ewe ham-bur-ger," Clouseau repeated.

"A hamburger," the teacher said again, very slowly.

"Ewe ham-bearg-air!" the Inspector shouted, thinking that he sounded exactly like a typical New Yorker.

In New York, Clouseau and Ponton waited for Xania outside her hotel. When she came out, they followed her. Xania went to a neighborhood known for crime and visited a sneaky black-market diamond-cutter. It was looking more and more as if Xania were the murderer. After all, a woman with a famous stolen diamond like the Pink Panther would need a diamond-cutter, who could change the diamond so that it wouldn't be recognizable.

Clouseau and Ponton followed Xania into the diamond-cutter's warehouse. First they encountered three men in sleek suits with sunglasses. Clearly, these were the diamond-cutter's thugs. One of the men reached into his coat, and Clouseau, sensing danger, struck him. A massive fight ensued. Ponton threw one of the men and fought the others off until they were all out cold.

Next Clouseau and Ponton were attacked by two sinister Chinese men. With a flurry of karate chops and kicks, Clouseau and Ponton fought them off, too.

Finally they got to the floor where the diamond-cutter, Sykorian, worked. Xania was with Sykorian. He was cutting a diamond. Clouseau stepped off the elevator and yelled, "Stop! You are defenseless. We have already taken care of your thugs!"

The diamond-cutter looked confused. "I don't have any thugs," he said. "The only stores in the building are a sunglasses shop and a Chinese takeout restaurant."

Clouseau gulped and looked at Ponton. "I think we owe someone an apology."

He asked Sykorian more questions as Ponton examined the diamonds.

It turned out that Xania was not having the Pink Panther cut. She had asked the diamond-cutter to make her a diamond-covered purse. Clouseau was relieved. Clearly, Xania did not have the Pink Panther. She was not the murderer.

On their way out of the building, Clouseau and Ponton saw the three men in suits and the two Chinese men being loaded into ambulances. The two detectives walked quickly away.

That evening Clouseau had a date with Xania. He hoped to find out more about the Pink Panther diamond—and about Xania.

Trying to impress his date, the Inspector ordered a flaming drink. He wasn't too cool, though. His hair caught fire!

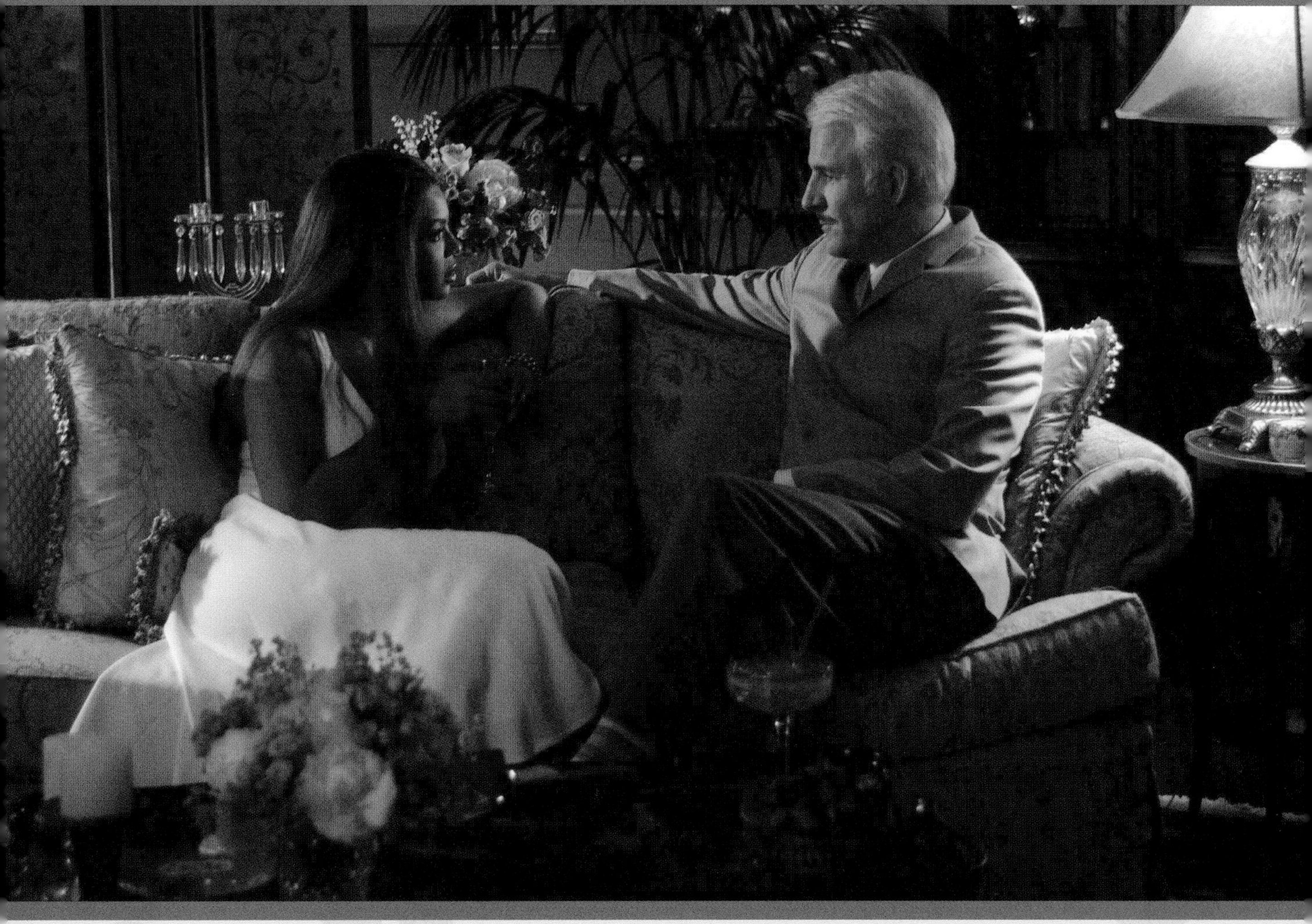

The next day, Clouseau, Ponton, and Xania all went to the airport to take a flight back to Paris. Clouseau was searched by security, while Xania went ahead. Clouseau had to stand in front of hundreds of strangers in nothing but his underwear, while the security guard examined his clothes!

"This is an insult! I will report you!" Clouseau told the man who was searching him. He handed his digital camera to Ponton. "Take a photo of this, so I can show it to the highest person I know in France." Clouseau decided to report his mistreatment the moment he got home.

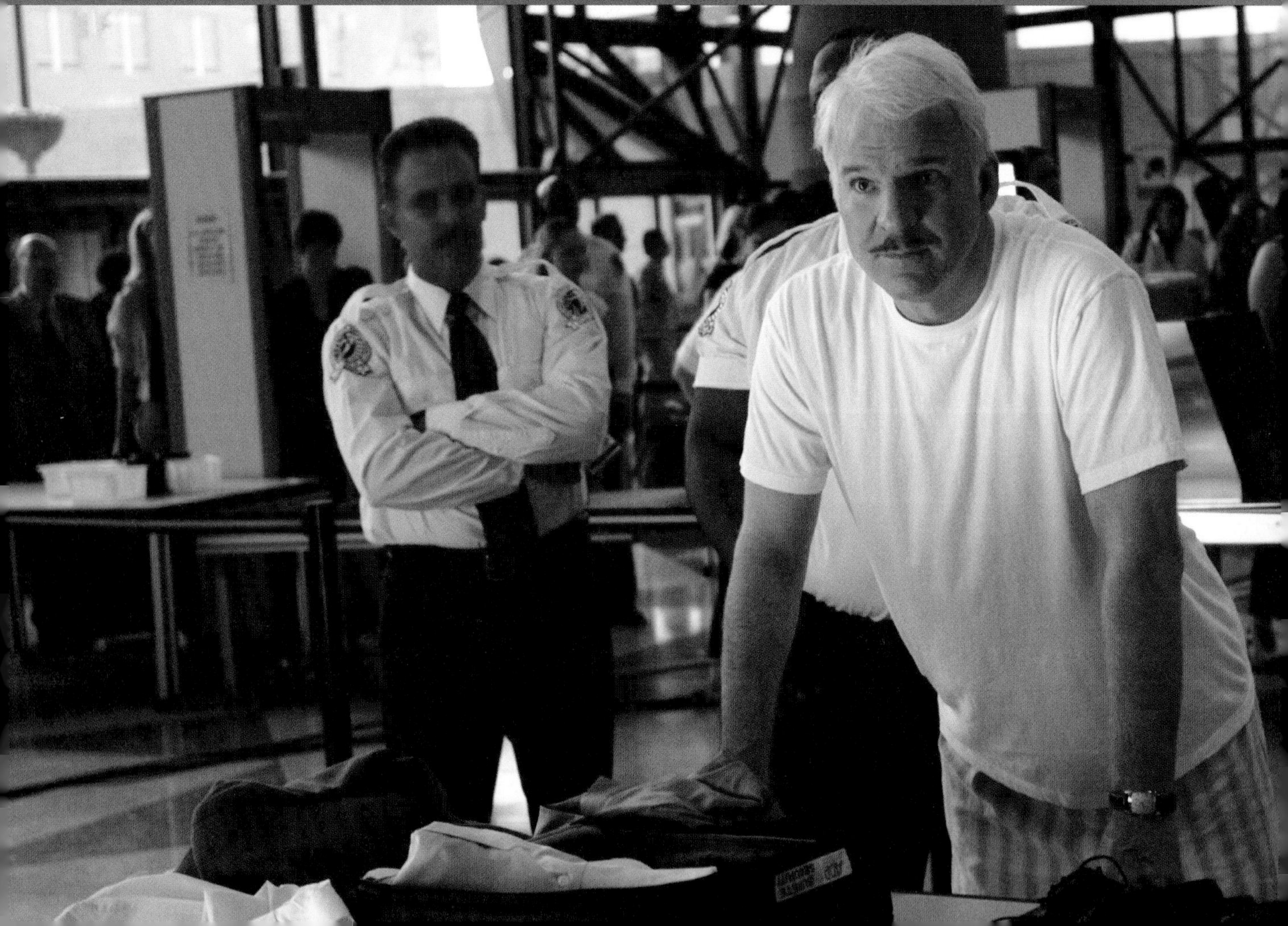

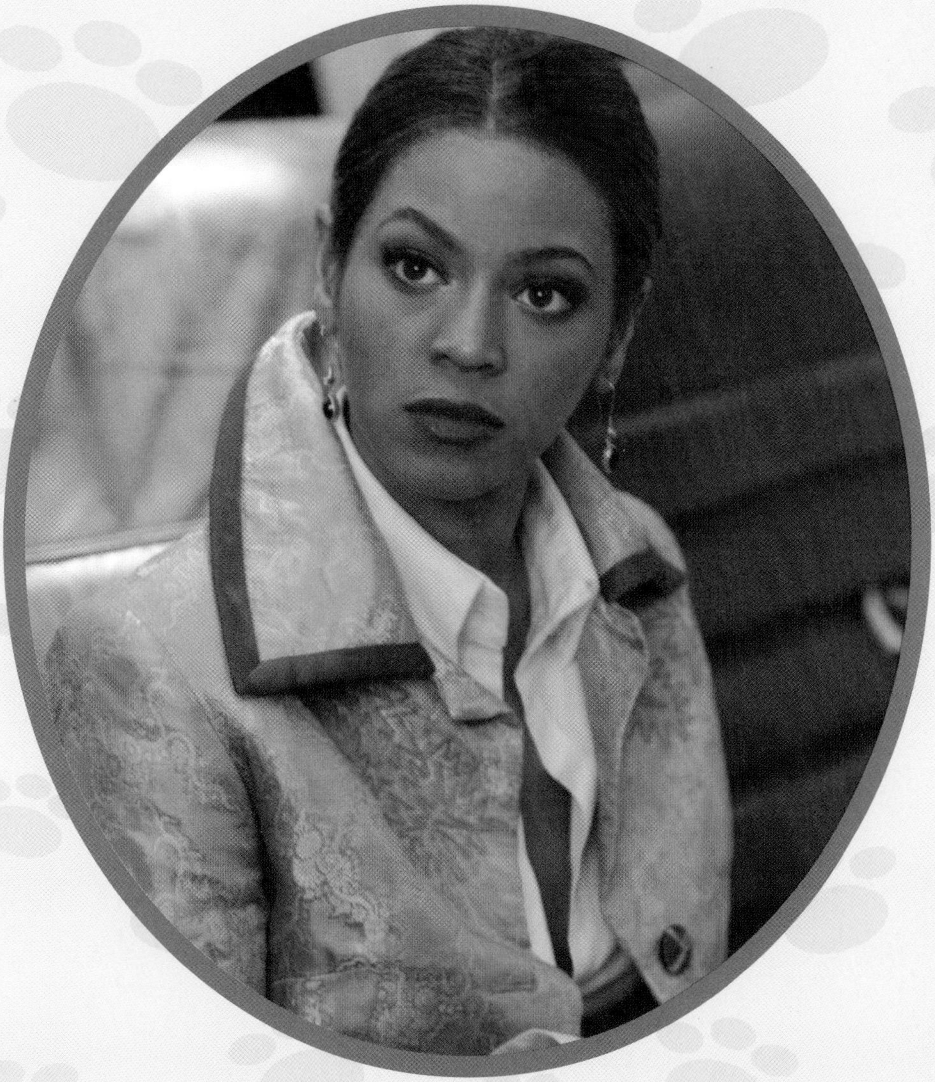

On the flight, Clouseau thought that he would sit next to Xania in first class. But he was quickly informed that he had to move to the back, the *way* back, of the plane.

Xania was surprised as she watched the Inspector being led further and further back toward the very tail of the plane.

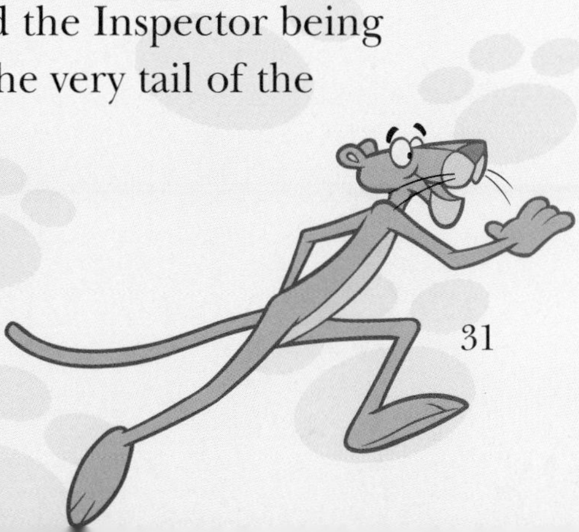

The Inspector's seat was so far back that the sushi he ordered for lunch was rotten by the time Clouseau ate it. He got sick. Very sick. He ran around the plane looking for a bathroom, but they were all either occupied or out of order. Clouseau needed a bathroom fast. He grabbed the nearest door and pulled on the handle.

"Let me in! Let me in or I'm going to explode!" Clouseau yelled.

The next thing he knew, five security men in disguise tackled him. They thought he wanted to blow up the plane!

Clouseau was all over the news again, but this time in a bad way. He was arrested for trying to blow up the airplane and was kicked off the police force. Dreyfus personally fired Clouseau and told him he had just been using him.

"I only made you an inspector because I wanted someone who would quietly get nowhere," Dreyfus ranted, "until I was ready to take over the case myself!"

Clouseau went home in disgrace.

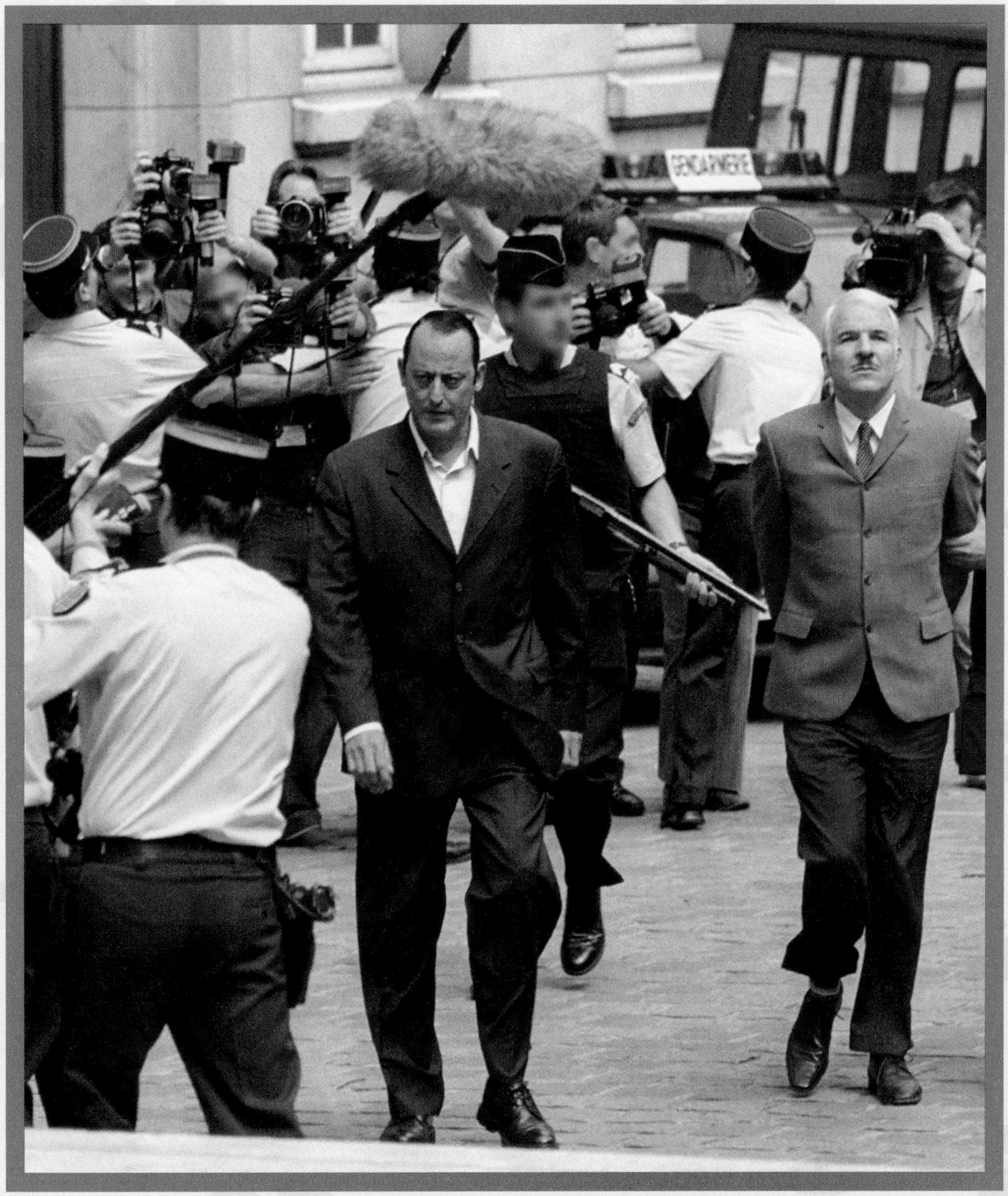
GENDARMERIE

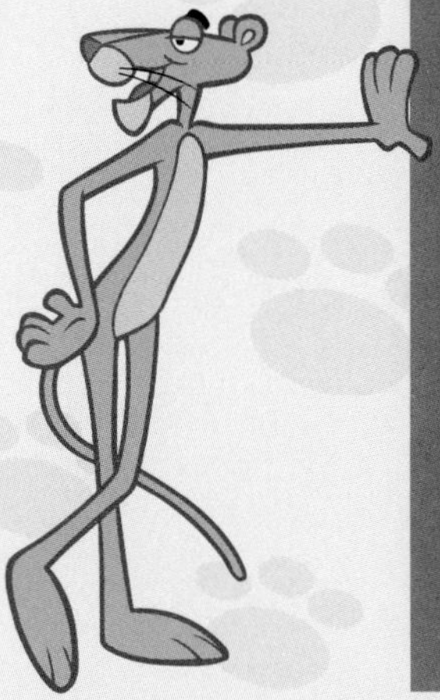

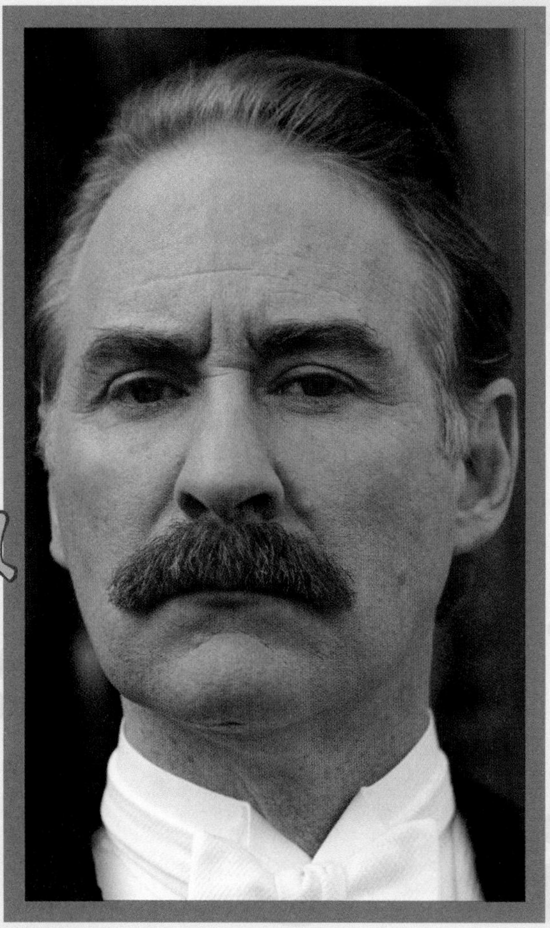

Dreyfus, meanwhile, thought he had found Gluant's murderer. Gluant owed millions of dollars to Dr. Pang, the head of the Chinese sports ministry. He had borrowed the money from Dr. Pang and gambled it away. Dr. Pang had been at the game where Gluant was killed. In addition, the dart that had killed Gluant was filled with a rare Chinese poison. It all seemed to add up.

Dreyfus decided to arrest Dr. Pang that night at the President's Ball, which was being held at France's presidential palace. He would win that Medal of Honor for sure.

Ponton drove Clouseau home. He felt sorry for his partner. "I had no idea you were being used," he said.

That night, Dreyfus went on the news and announced that he was taking over the Pink Panther investigation, including both the Gluant and the Bizu murder cases. He promised to catch the killer. Clouseau watched it all on the small TV in his apartment. Sad and bored, Clouseau decided that he would still report the humiliating incident at the airport. He brought up his digital photos on the computer screen.

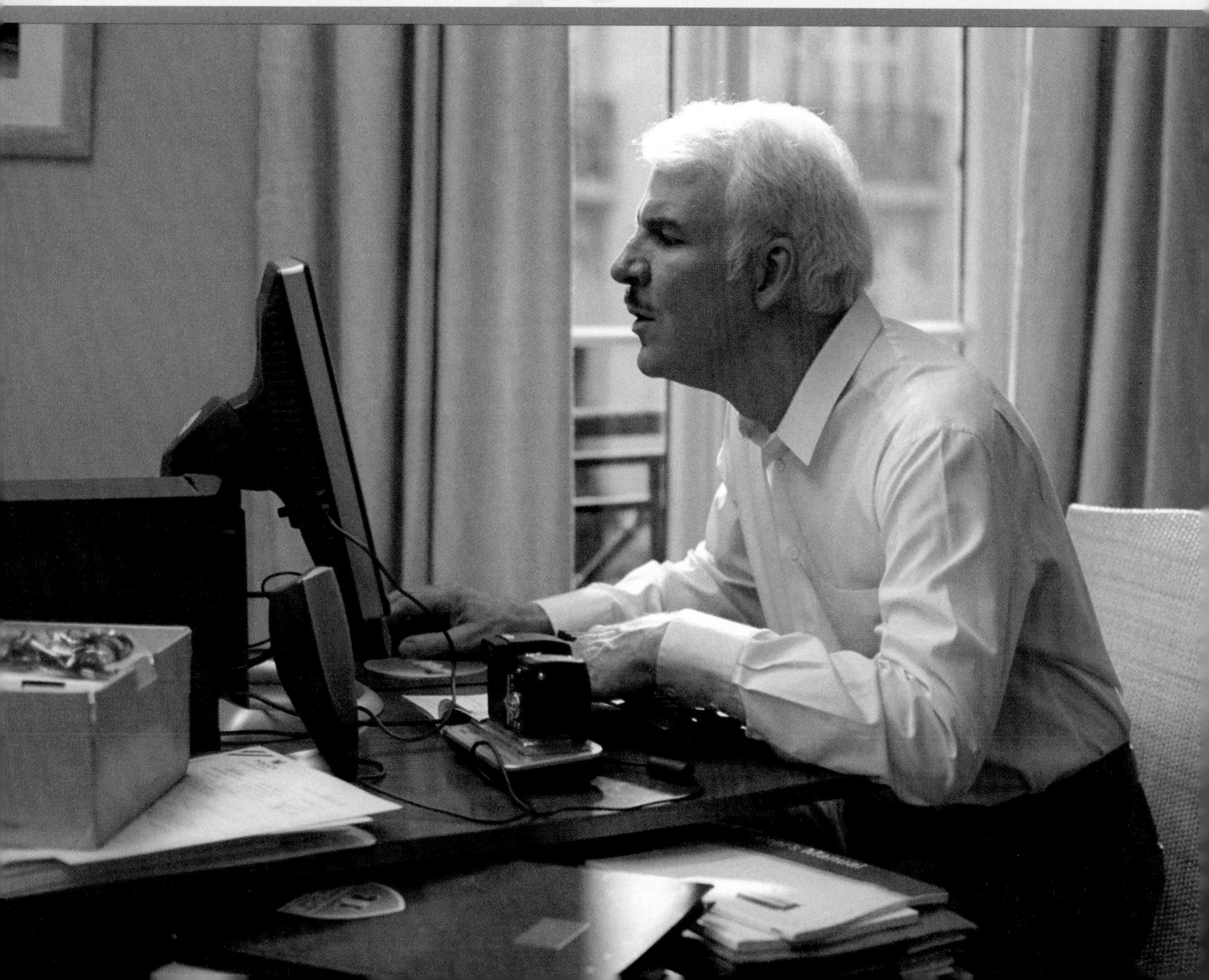

Something in one picture caught his attention. Xania was in the background, and her diamond-covered purse was going through the X-ray machine. Clouseau enlarged the picture and looked closely at the image on the X-ray machine monitor. There was something inside Xania's bag. Something very interesting.

Clouseau's eyes widened. He knew what had happened! He knew who the murderer was . . . and he knew that Xania would be the next victim unless he stepped in!

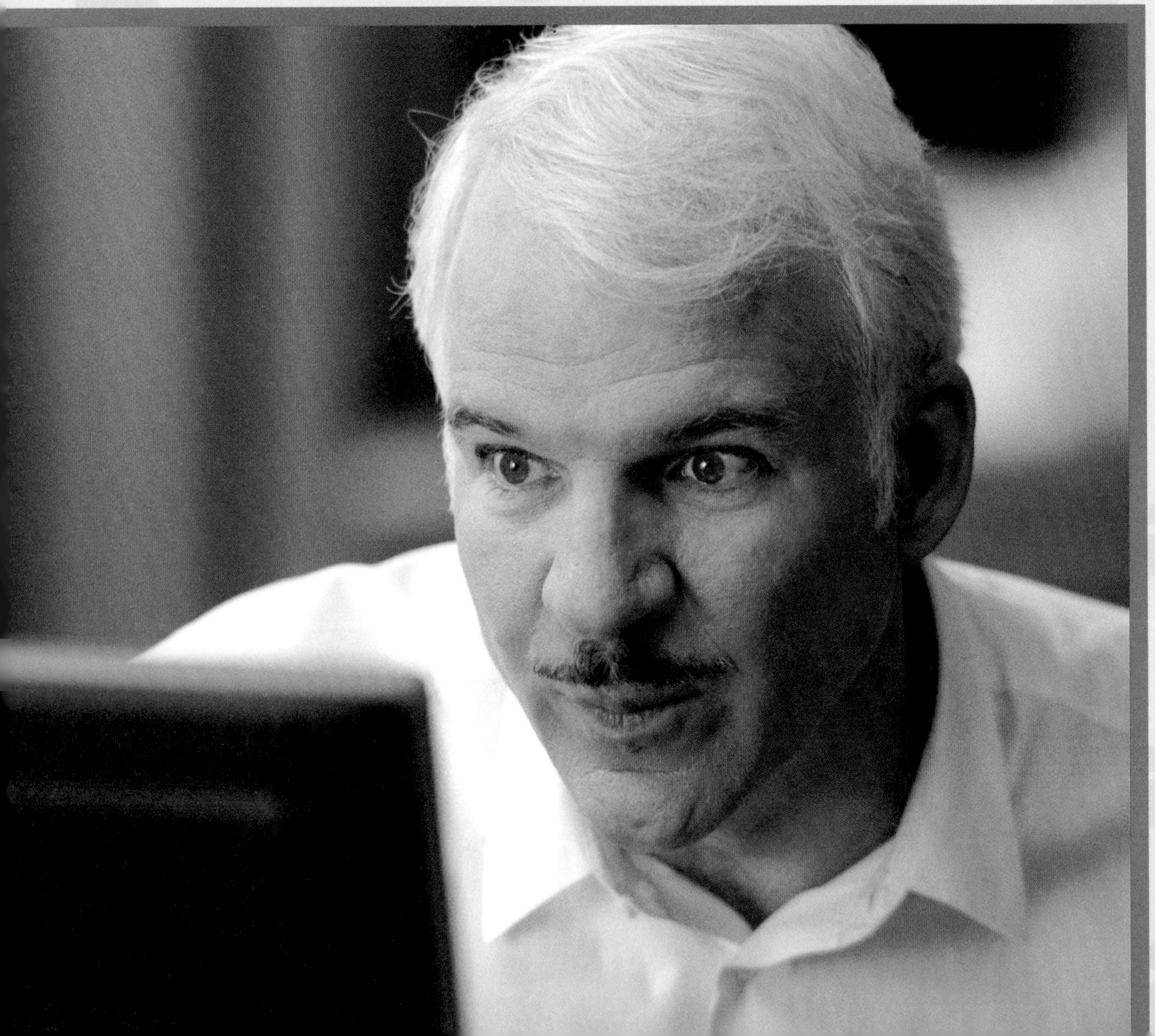

Xania was supposed to perform at the President's
Ball that night. Clouseau called Nicole to instruct her to
get blueprints from his office and his vinyl bag marked
"presidential palace." He asked her to hurry and meet him
at the presidential palace. Next, he called Ponton and
explained his plan. Ponton was glad to help. He didn't
like the way Clouseau had been treated by Dreyfus. He
picked Clouseau up in his car, and together they raced to
the palace.

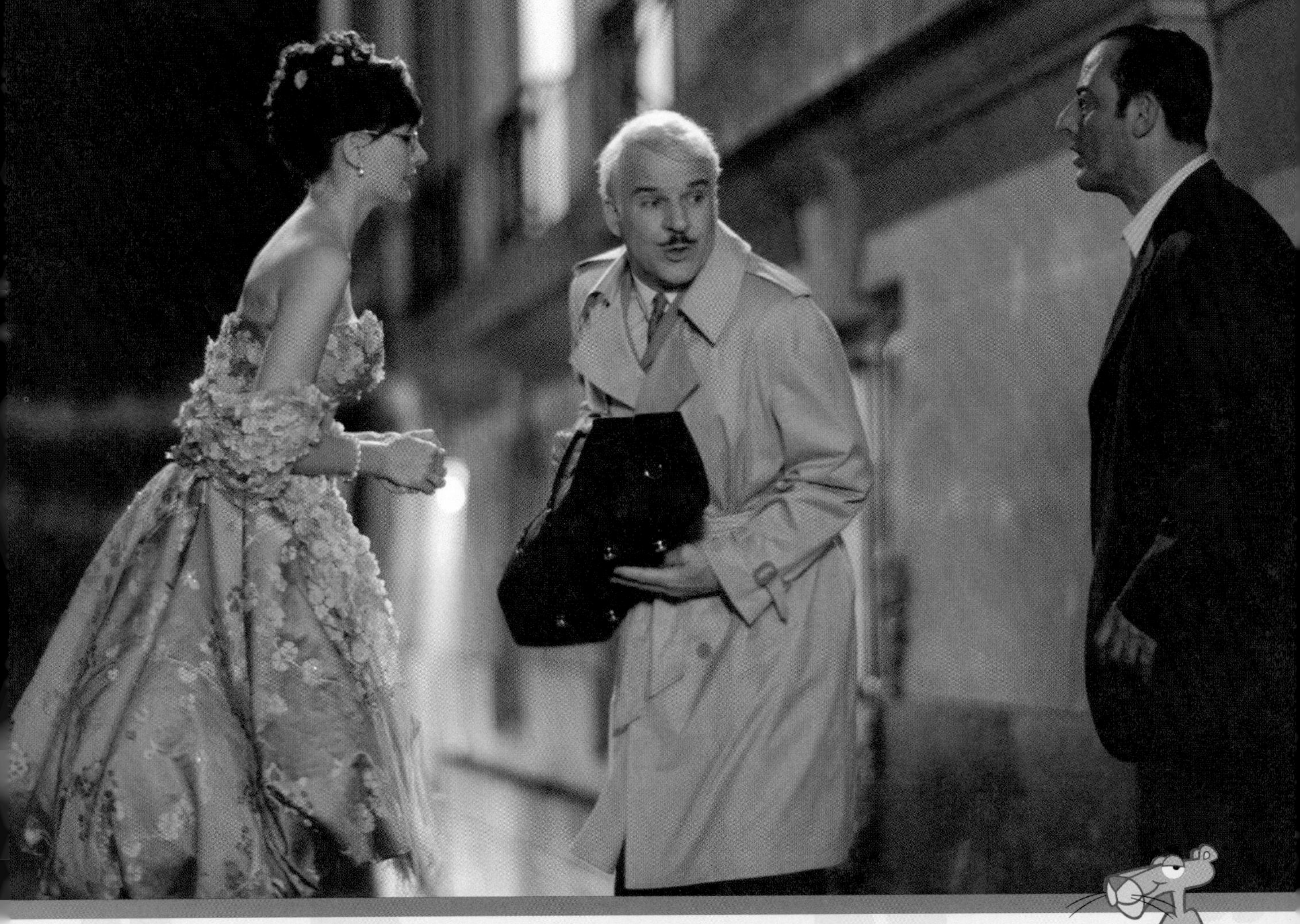

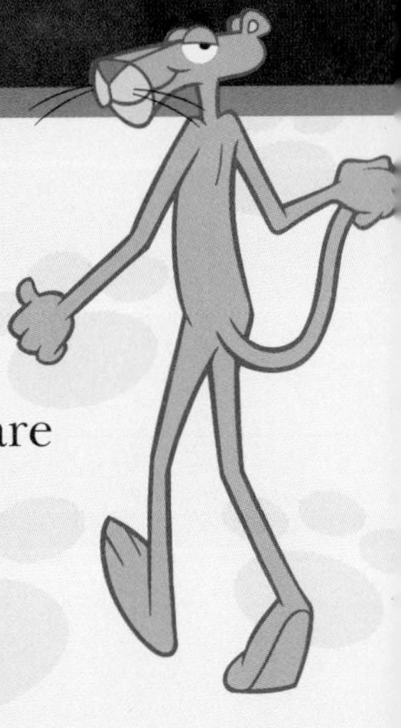

Nicole met them outside with the camouflage suits from Clouseau's office. Clouseau and Ponton put on the suits and snuck into the palace.

Meanwhile, Xania prepared to go out onstage, unaware that she was in danger.

Clouseau's camouflage was made specifically for the palace. When he stepped in front of the drapes, his suit matched them perfectly, and he disappeared. When he stepped in front of the marble wall, he turned around, and the back of his suit matched *that* perfectly. He disappeared again. Slowly, Clouseau and Ponton made their way toward the ballroom, seen by no one.

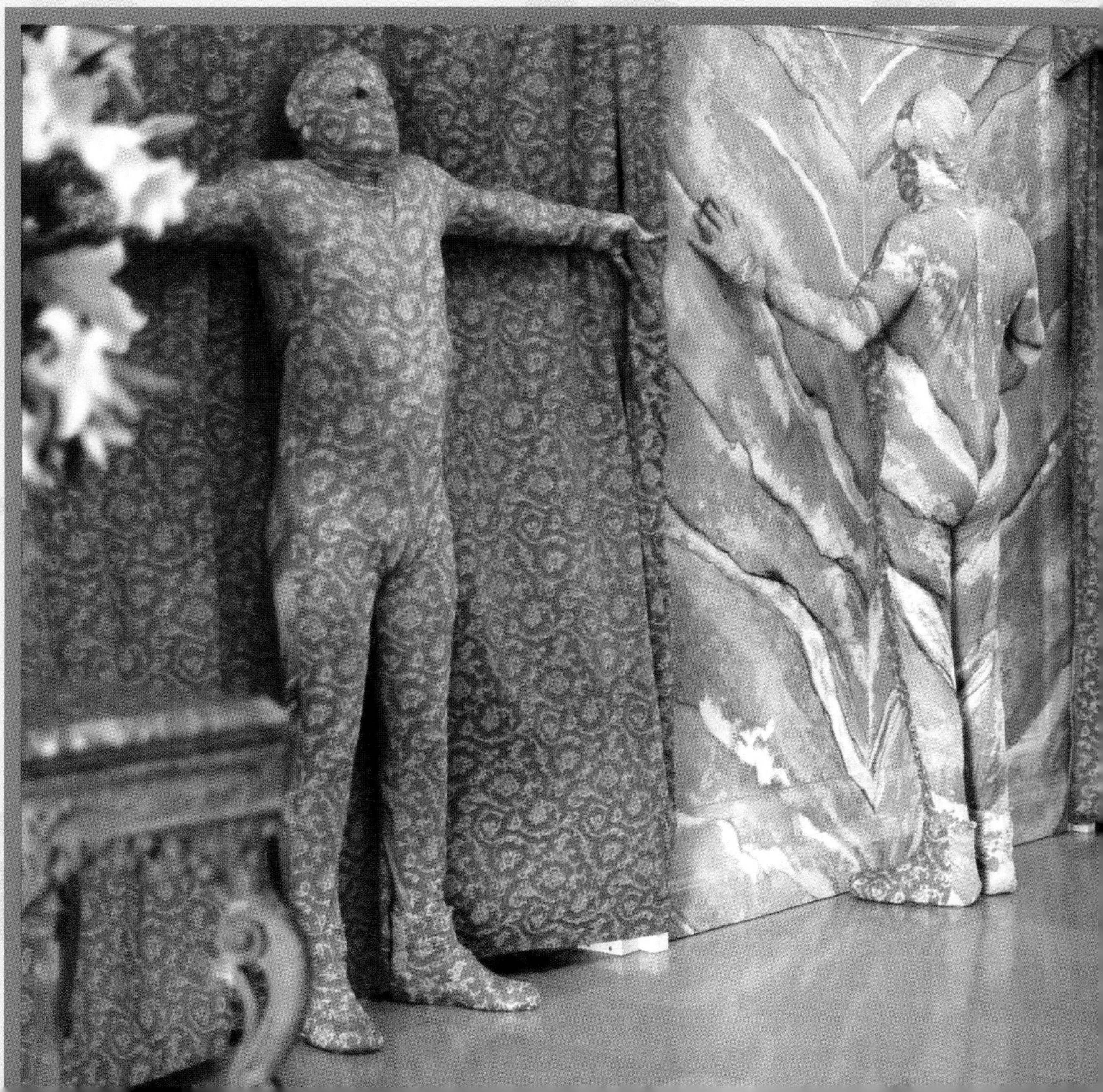

Meanwhile, a mysterious figure in a black catsuit entered the palace, carrying a wrapped weapon. Clouseau and Ponton spotted the person as he made his way upstairs. He seemed to be looking for a spot across from the stage. It had to be the murderer! Clouseau ran to catch up with him. The killer took out a crossbow and pointed it at Xania, but Clouseau got there just in time.

Dreyfus, Nicole, and the other dignitaries looked on.

"The jig is up!" Clouseau said.

The murderer ran, and Clouseau and Ponton chased after him.

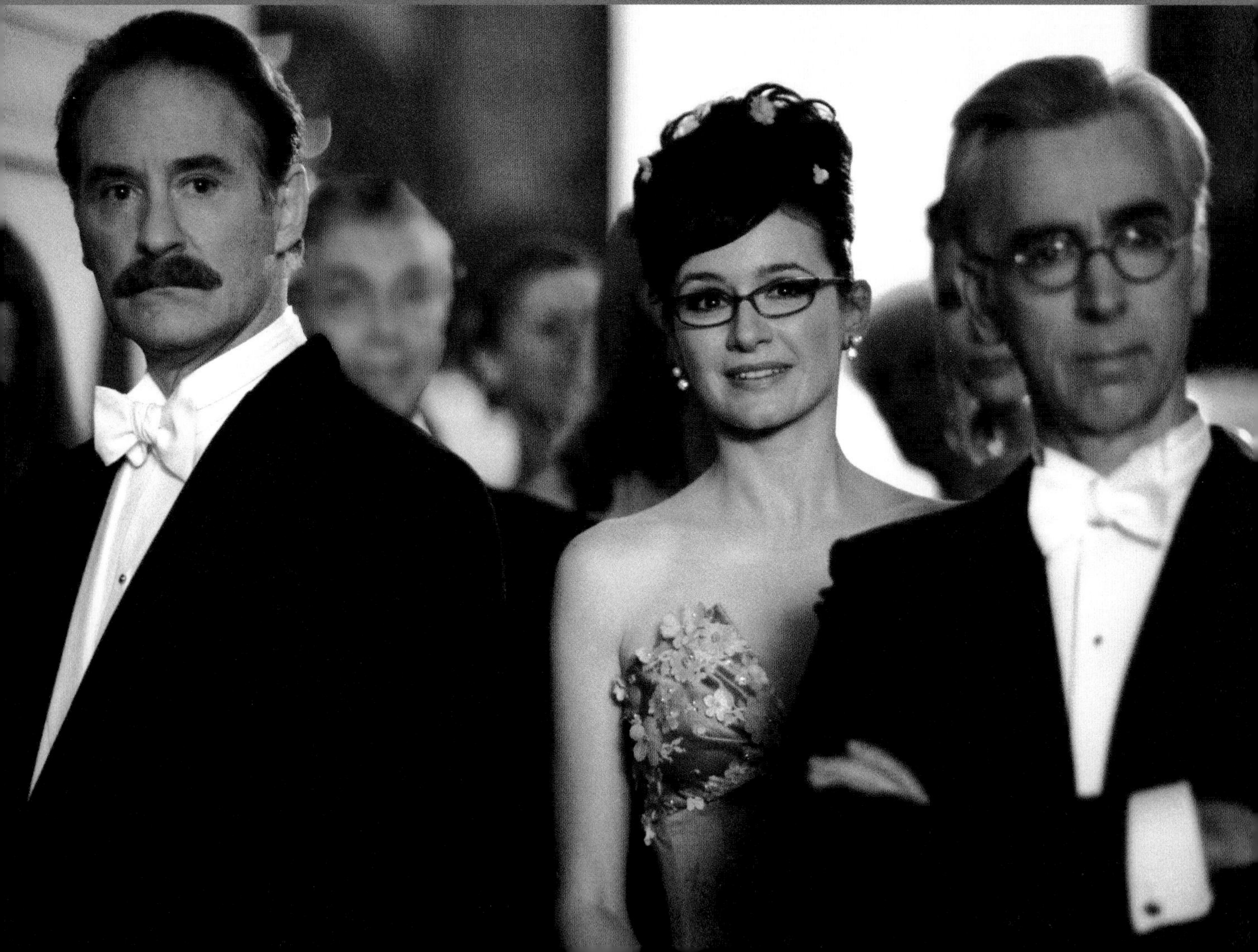

Downstairs in the ballroom, Dreyfus moved in on Dr. Pang; he was going to arrest Pang for the murders. Just as Dreyfus and his men surrounded Dr. Pang, Clouseau and Ponton raced into the room, chasing the true murderer. Clouseau jumped over the banister and landed right on top of the bad guy.

"In the name of the statutes and laws of the great nation of France, I arrest you for the murder of Yves Gluant!" Clouseau shouted.

He ripped the man's mask off and revealed the face of Yuri, the trainer for the national soccer team!

Yuri confessed to the crime. He had despised Gluant, who had always taken all the credit for the team's success.

The crowd in the ballroom was speechless as Clouseau announced the way he had solved the crime. Back when he had interviewed the Chinese woman, Mrs. Yu, she had told him that he should be looking for a soccer trainer. The poison that had killed Gluant was Chinese, and all soccer trainers were required to have a knowledge of Chinese herbs. Yuri was a soccer trainer who had hated Gluant, so it all made sense. Apparently Ponton was wrong to doubt his partner—Clouseau *did* know how to speak Chinese!

Clouseau explained that once Gluant was dead, Yuri had realized he would have to get rid of Bizu as well. Bizu had heard Yuri's many rants against Gluant and would have known that Yuri was guilty.

Finally, Yuri wanted to kill Xania, because, although he had helped her when she had been a struggling singer, once she became a star she had dropped him for Bizu and, later, Gluant. It all made sense. Case closed.

The reporters gathered around Clouseau, amazed at the way he had solved the case.

"But where is the Pink Panther?" they asked.

At that moment, Dreyfus came forward and tried to take credit for the arrest. He demanded that Yuri return the Pink Panther, but Yuri claimed he did not have the diamond.

"Then where is the diamond?" Dreyfus demanded.

"There! In her purse!" Clouseau called out, pointing at Xania and her diamond-covered bag.

Dreyfus grabbed Xania's bag and dumped out its contents. The Pink Panther was not among her things. He looked at Clouseau smugly.

"Sorry, Clouseau. No diamond," he said.

Clouseau walked over to the purse, took out a small knife, and cut the lining of the bag. The beautiful Pink Panther diamond tumbled out into his hand. The whole crowd oohed and aahed. Clouseau had seen the ring in the photograph of the X-ray machine. He had known it was there all along.

Xania told her story to everyone. Just before the semifinal game, Gluant had told her that he loved her. He had promised to stop cheating on her and had given her the Pink Panther as an engagement ring. She hadn't wanted to come forward, because she had thought that if people knew she had the ring, they would think she had killed Gluant.

Dreyfus tried to claim that the ring was the property of France, but Clouseau stepped in and said that by law, a ring given to a woman upon someone's forming an engagement with her was hers to keep. The Pink Panther rightfully belonged to Xania.

The crowd erupted in cheers. "Bravo, Clouseau!" they shouted. "Bravo!"

The following week, Clouseau and Ponton were seated on a stage in the presidential gardens as the president of France himself spoke about their bravery.

"For service to the republic, we award the Star of Valor to Gendarme Detective Gilbert Ponton!" the president announced. "And for exceptional bravery and outstanding service to the people of France, we award the Medal of Honor to a man whose name will forever be linked to this case: the Pink Panther detective, Inspector Jacques Clouseau!"

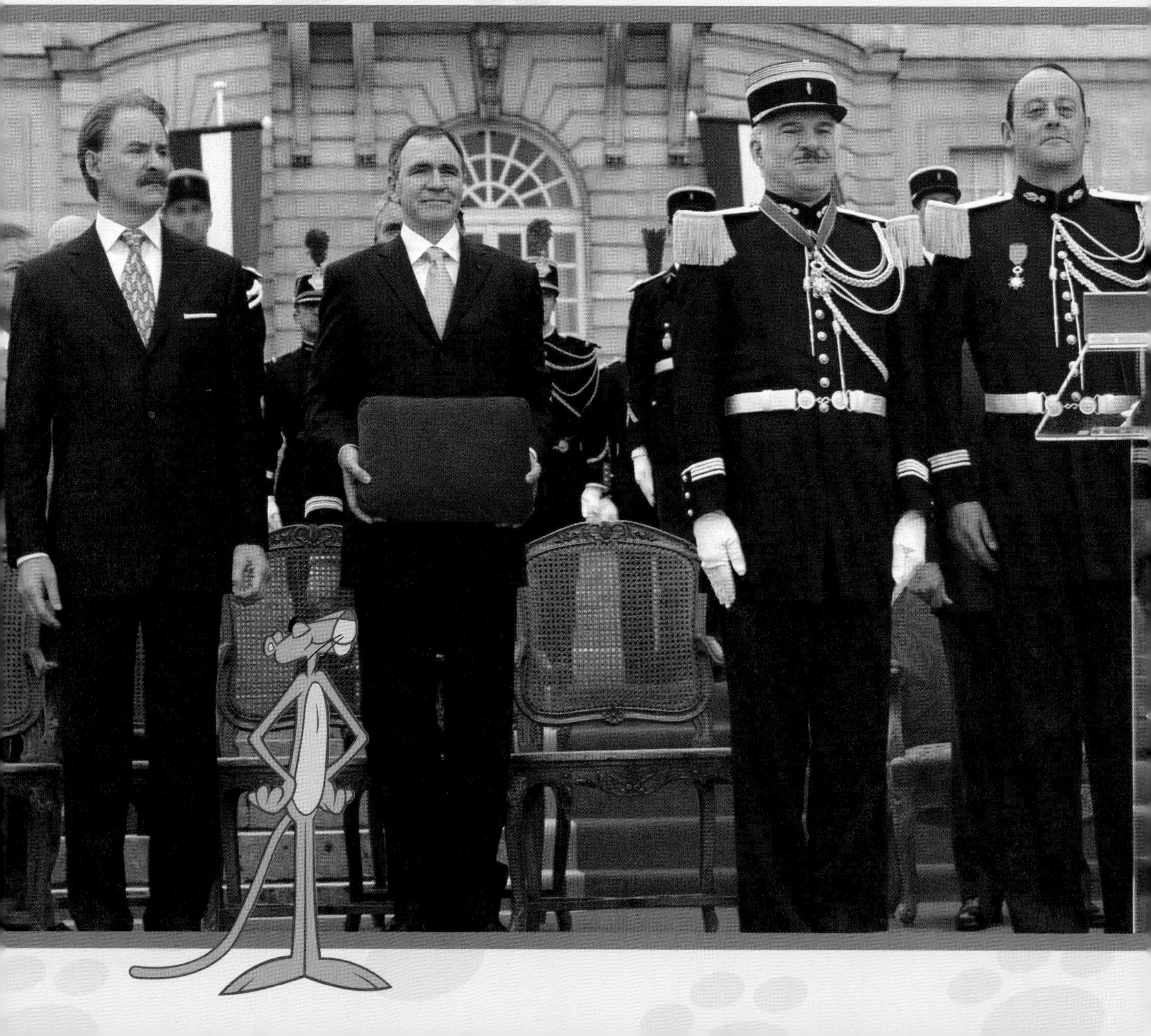